CHEROKEE DAWN

GENELL DELLIN

AVON BOOKS ◆ NEW YORK

CHEROKEE DAWN is an original publication of Avon Books. This work has never before appeared in book form. This work is a novel. Any similarity to actual persons or events is purely coincidental.

AVON BOOKS
A division of
The Hearst Corporation
105 Madison Avenue
New York, New York 10016

For Arlen and Clara,
with love and appreciation

Now! Grandmother Sun!
I rise into the Morning Red.
Like the white lightning you have brought
  my heart to me
Ha! You have given me the dawn.

—Inspired by
  traditional Cherokee
  incantations

Chapter 1

Lacey Longbaugh smiled up into Tom Creek-water's careless brown eyes and tried to decide whether to let him kiss her or not. She knew she shouldn't.

But the dusky evening pulsed all around them, calling to her blood. Thunder rumbled far away, back in the rocky hills that formed the backbone of the Cherokee Nation, and a fresh breeze, born when the sun went down, played on her skin. The day had been hot and still, one more motionless bead on an unbroken string of weeks when the whole world waited for something to happen. Now something would—if she didn't lose her courage.

She dropped her eyes from Tom's and tightened the ribbon bow of her sash. She wouldn't lose her courage. Hadn't she stood in this very spot early that morning and promised herself that before her seventeenth birthday was over she would do *something* to make one of her dreams come true?

"Let's go walking," Tom said, again. "It's such a pretty evening."

She hesitated. In her favorite dream, the dashing young man swept her out of the ballroom and down to a white gate with an arch of honeysuckle growing over it.

"Tom, I think . . ."

He moved closer to her. "Aw, come on, Lacey," he wheedled. "Don't think."

Her dream man wouldn't say "Aw." He was worldly-wise and debonair, from some wonderful, faraway place like Atlanta or Texas or Washington City.

"I don't know whether I should. . . ."

"Your mama ain't paying us no mind."

Her dream man would never worry about Mama. Oh, *why* couldn't he be here right now, instead of Tom?

Overhead, the big oak and locust trees stirred in the new breeze, scraping against the veranda roof of Pleasant Prospect, the big plantation house that had been Lacey's home for the last seven years. The light, dry smells of their leaves mixed with the heavy, sweet ones of the Harison's Yellow roses climbing the post Lacey leaned against.

"Just a *little* walk," Tom whispered. His smile flashed white in the fading light. "Down the stable path and back."

"Did you hear about my birthday present? Papa bought me a new mare and named her Lacey's Lady."

"Well, then, we've got the perfect excuse to walk down to the stables now, don't we?"

He plucked a blossom from behind her and leaned even closer to brush a velvet petal against her cheek. His breath was as soft on her skin as the rose.

She took a deep, shuddery breath. Did she truly dare to do it?

The flower's rich perfume floated between them. Tom waited.

"I don't know, Tom. I really shouldn't leave

my party. Mama would be so upset if she found me gone.''

Mama would have a fit if she even saw them right this minute, Lacey thought. Why, she'd positively go into one of her spells if she knew Lacey had slipped out of her own party with *any* boy, much less the notorious Tom Creekwater!

''Your mama has to know you're a big girl now,'' he said, his voice as smooth as kitten's fur. ''She can't keep you locked up forever, acting like you're too good to have any man around here come courtin'.''

His remark made Lacey straighten to her full five feet three inches. ''Mama doesn't act as if I'm too good . . .''

But she did. Or as if Lacey weren't good enough. Or trustworthy enough. Or . . . something. Mama always said Lacey was too young and her health was too delicate, but she hadn't had a spell of her asthma now for ages. She'd been truly sick only once or twice since Mama had married Judge Melton and he'd brought them out from Virginia to his people in the Cherokee Nation when Lacey was ten years old.

Mama and the Judge had fallen in love like a flash of fire when he had brought his nephews to enroll in the school where Mama taught Deportment. In a week's time they'd been married, and the two of them and Lacey had set out for the faraway Cherokee Nation leaving those poor, homesick boys behind, begging to come, too.

Other Cherokee students had come to Virginia Richland Academy before, and Mama knew that lots of Cherokees were married to white men and women, and were part white themselves. She knew that the Cherokees were civilized and had been for years and years. But, still, Mama had been taking a chance following her heart, hadn't she? So why wouldn't Mama let Lacey take the same chances?

And she wasn't too young for a beau. Why, Mama had married Lacey's real daddy, Colin Longbaugh, when *she* was only sixteen. And times were no different now: most of the girls who'd been in Lacey's class at the Female Seminary had married or begun to teach school when they'd turned sixteen.

But not Lacey! Here she was, turning seventeen tonight, and she'd had to beg and argue to get Mama to have even this birthday social where the older generation was invited, too, so they could keep an eye on the young people.

Whatever her real reason, Mama had never let any young man come courting, not even serious, boring Eli Hawthorne when he had asked to call. Well, tonight things would be different. After all, Lacey was already a whole year behind everybody else. This was her chance to start learning what it was like to be a woman, and she wasn't going to waste it.

Tom wasn't the cultured young man of her dreams, but if she practiced on him she'd be ready when the real one came along. And she was doing all right so far; she'd gotten them out onto the veranda alone.

He looked back over his shoulder toward the parlor; she followed his glance. Talk and laughter spilled out of the wide-open windows and down the long veranda, along with the raspy sounds of Cobby's band tuning up the fiddles. Behind one lace curtain someone was lighting a lamp.

Tom turned back to her, his eyes gleaming. "Nobody's paying a bit of attention to us, and you know it," he drawled. "Besides, how could your mama be mad at you for showing me your birthday present?"

He came so close she could feel the weight of his leg against hers, even through her skirts and petticoats. He smelled of tobacco and hair tonic and . . . well, he smelled like a man. Probably they all smelled like this. He dared to touch one blonde curl that dangled near her shoulder.

Now his breath came hot against her cheek, with a hint of brandy punch on it. Somewhere deep inside her a thrill blossomed. He was so close!

"Now, Tom . . ."

His eyes gazed into hers pleadingly. It made her heart thump hard in her throat, even though she wasn't in love with him at all. She was sure of that much. Why, she hardly even knew him!

Except to know that he had the worst reputation of any boy in the Cherokee Nation.

"How about it?" he whispered.

He also had the handsomest face of any boy in the Cherokee Nation.

But a girl wasn't supposed to give in too soon, was she? She wheeled around and glanced across the spacious, sloping yard. The lightning bugs were just starting to dance. She felt like dancing, too. This was fun, having a boy beg her to go walking with him. On a walk he would surely kiss her and then she would know what it was like. That was one reason she'd chosen Tom; as much as girls chased after him and as much as their mamas whispered warnings about him, he was bound to know how to kiss and do it right.

But she would put him off just one more time, she thought, enjoying the taste of her newfound power. Why, this feeling of omnipotence must be part of being a woman, too! She hadn't even thought of that until just this minute. She was already learning!

"You *could* run on down to the stable and see

my birthday present by yourself,'' she suggested sweetly, just to prolong the game. ''She's the palomino mare in the last stall to your right. Papa Melton says she's the exact same color as my hair.''

Tom's limited patience snapped. His voice cracked harshly back at her. ''Ain't that a rude way to talk to company?''

She whirled to look at him.

His face was tight with anger, suddenly almost ugly in the soft, dusky light. He said, ''Lacey, girl, you've teased me long enough.''

He threw away the rose, grabbed her hand, and yanked her across the veranda to the steps.

Disappointment, then a biting fury flashed through her. Why, she'd never been treated so!

''You let me go, Tom Creekwater!'' she said, tugging to free herself.

He was ruining it—the fantasy of her first kiss! Practice or no practice, she'd not let him kiss her now.

''We'll just walk down to the stables *together*,'' he muttered, pulling her hand through the crook of his arm. ''You can show me your new mare and saddle and I'll show you some things you never . . .''

Fear struck her, as sharp as a needle jab. What was he talking about? Would he actually drag her away from the house against her will? She jerked again, but he held her arm firmly against his side. He was so much stronger than she!

He rushed them down the steps so fast she stumbled.

''What kind of things are you planning to show her, Creekwater?''

She recognized Eli Hawthorne's voice, even though it was strained and unnaturally high-pitched. His tall, thin form separated itself from the snowball bush at the foot of the steps and he stepped directly into Tom's path.

Tom stopped dead. "Mind your own business, Four-Eyes," he snapped. "Go back to your law books."

Eli didn't answer. He just stood still, staring back at Tom.

"What're you doing, anyhow, Hawthorne?" Tom demanded. "You spying on us?"

A long moment passed.

"You're a lily-livered coward," Tom said finally, drawing out each insulting word.

Eli swallowed. "And you're the brave warrior, huh, Creekwater?"

"One of these days when I put you out of your misery, you'll know what I am," Tom shot back. "But right now I'm busy. Get out of my way."

There was an edge to Tom's words that Lacey had never heard before, not in anybody's voice.

A tremor ran through her. Nothing about this situation was fun anymore. She tried again to free her hand. "Eli, no, don't move. . . ."

Eli turned to look at her, his eyeglasses winking faintly in the dim light. He nodded as if to tell her not to worry. Then he looked back at Tom.

Her thoughts raced. If Eli could keep Tom here talking, someone was bound to come out of the house soon. Surely nothing very bad could happen at her own birthday party. Yet Tom had sounded so . . . cruel.

"I'll gladly move out of your way, Creekwater," Eli drawled sarcastically. "And I'll do it now. All you have to do is leave Lacey here with me and you can go anywhere you please." He raised both hands in a placating gesture. "You'll get no argument from me."

Tom tightened his hold on her hand; it hurt. She gasped.

Eli came closer. "I'm not as much a coward as you think, Creekwater, and I'll . . ."

Fast as thought, Tom's free hand went to the pistol on his hip.

"No!" Lacey cried. "Eli hasn't got a gun!"

Her words died into a silence broken only by the boys' rasping breaths. Thank the Lord, Tom's hand and his gun stayed still. She stood motionless, afraid even to breathe for fear of setting him off again.

Inside the house, Cobby's band finished tuning and started playing. The music sounded as if it were miles and miles away.

She willed herself not to try to break free again and said, "Now, you all listen." The words tumbled awkwardly off her dry tongue, but she forced herself to say something, anything. "The music's started. We all need to go back to the party."

Neither of them spoke or moved.

She drew air deep into her lungs and said the first thing that popped into her head. "You two shake hands and say you're sorry or I won't dance with either one of you this entire evening!" The words came out much louder than she had intended.

Slippers clattered on the boards of the veranda. A high voice trilled, "Well, if *she* won't dance with you, *I* surely will!"

Eli's sister, Felicity, came bouncing down the steps, her eyes searching for Tom's face.

"Never mind what Lacey says," she went on breathlessly when she had reached the ground. "Let her go sit with the old ladies if she wants to." She flashed Lacey a look and a little smile as if to say that she was only teasing, but the set of her head said that she wasn't.

Then she turned to Tom and held out both hands. "Let's go in and dance."

He didn't move.

Felicity's eyes flew to Lacey's arm through Tom's and her side pressed against his. Her hands made fists and she slammed them onto her hips.

Lacey sighed. Felicity *would* have to be the one to come out of the house and find them. No telling what she would say or do now; then tomorrow she'd be all tears and apologies.

Sure enough, she burst out, "Lacey, you're a shameless hussy! And an unmannerly hostess to boot!" Her voice broke with the weight of her spite. She recovered it enough to say, "You'd better get right back into that house. Your mama's been looking everywhere for you."

Eli made a shocked, strangled noise. "Fee! Get ahold of yourself! You apologize to Lacey immediately!"

Felicity shot him a withering glance. Then she looked back at Lacey and waited for her to move.

As always, Felicity's bossiness made Lacey's temper rise. "Don't call me names, Fee, and don't tell me what to do," she said haughtily. "I'll go in when I'm good and ready."

What was she saying? A few seconds ago she'd have given anything to go into the house.

Fee's eyes raked over Lacey's face as though she wished she could do the same thing with her fingernails.

Fee just couldn't help it if she was the most jealous girl in the Nation, Lacey thought, and that doubled when it came to Tom Creekwater. Everybody knew Fee had been crazy about him for months, but her folks wouldn't let him court her even if he asked. And, as far as Lacey knew, he had never given any sign of wanting to ask.

"If it's my present company that's bothering

you, Felicity," she said coldly, "you're welcome
to him."

She tried to remove her arm from Tom's, but
he held it in a paralyzing grip.

"Well, I'm so glad we have your permission,"
Felicity mocked. "Aren't you, Tom?"

She took a step toward him.

"Why don't you come on in now and dance?"
she asked in a sugary voice. "Cobby said the first
tune—"

"I ain't ready to come in," he growled.

"Run on back to the house, Fee," Eli said, his
voice more agitated than ever. "We'll be in after
a while."

Felicity's piercing gaze whipped from Tom to
Eli and back again.

"What *is* going on here anyhow?" she asked
sharply.

No one answered.

In that one quiet moment her faultless instinct
for trouble overcame and then meshed with her
interest in Tom. She looked from one of the three
faces to the next, absorbing the situation.

"You all are going to fight, aren't you?" she
asked. "What about?"

Then, as if someone had actually answered, her
eyes swept back to Lacey and held, growing more
venomous by the second.

"You!" she spat. "You always get every single
thing you want. It's not enough to have the prettiest room in the biggest house in the district, and
more dresses than anybody else in the world. It's
not enough to have horses of your own, and riding habits, and servants to wait on you hand and
foot. It's not enough to always be the teacher's
pet because you're so smart, and to order books
from London, England, and Philadelphia, too. It's
not enough for everybody to look up to your step-

father, the judge, and to copy the way your Virginia-lady mama does her house.''

Felicity drew in a deep, ragged breath and finished spitefully, ''No. None of that is enough for you. Now you've got to try to get Tom and have him fighting over you!''

Lacey said, ''I don't want Tom. . . .''

''Fee, get out of here,'' Tom ordered. ''This is none of your affair.''

''It is so!'' she cried. She paused, then said softly, ''I couldn't stand to see you get shot, Tom.''

Lacey laughed shakily. ''That's not very likely,'' she said. ''Tom's the only one with a gun. You'd better be worrying about your brother, Fee.''

''It's not funny,'' Felicity said righteously, keeping her eyes on Tom's face. ''Oh, Tom, I . . .''

She reached toward him; to take his arm, Lacey thought. But she snatched his gun instead, lifting it from the holster into both her hands in one swift motion.

He grabbed for it.

Lacey shook free of his grip.

Felicity scooted just out of his reach. ''I never did know how one of these pistols works,'' she said coquettishly. ''Why don't you come here and show me, Tom?'' She brandished the gun awkwardly.

''Give that back to me, you little fool.'' Tom advanced on her.

Lacey stood rooted to the spot, unable to run or call out. Eli didn't move, either.

They both knew how completely unpredictable Felicity could be when she was angry, and right now she was furious, no matter how sweet she'd sounded talking to Tom. She was liable to shoot them all.

Tom snatched at the pistol.

Felicity danced backward, her square, even teeth showing white in her dark face. "You want it? Come and get it."

Tom reached for the gun again, but his fingers only grazed the barrel before Felicity thrust it behind her.

"Goddammit!"

"Tom!" Felicity reproved him archly. "Watch your language, please."

Oh, why couldn't she flirt with him in some other way? Lacey thought desperately. Felicity with a gun in her hands was as dangerous as Papa's stallion running free. The girl had no control when she was in one of her fits of jealous rage—one time at school she'd thrown her Latin book at the stove and set the room on fire.

Lacey tried to think. If she could reach the gun . . . but if Tom couldn't get it, she certainly couldn't. She glanced toward the open parlor door, a peaceful rectangle of golden light at the top of the stairs. No one in there knew they were alive out here.

Fee moved another slow step backward, her arms weighed down behind her, her small breasts pointing up through her thin, yellow, lawn gown. Tom gave them a perfunctory glance, then glared into her face again.

He lunged at her.

She darted away.

He pounced once more and she whipped the gun around and held it in both her hands.

"I said you had to come and get it, Tom Creekwater," she said with a little pout. "Do it nice and don't be acting so ugly."

She waved the pistol in front of her.

Sure enough, she was going to fool around and shoot somebody, Lacey thought. She looked at

Eli, but he was staring at his sister in a haze of disgust and embarrassment, obviously completely unsure as to the best way to approach her.

He was better at standing up to Tom than to his own sister, Lacey thought impatiently. He always had let her boss him around, even if she was younger than he.

She turned back to Felicity. "Felicity, you don't know how to handle that gun," she called loudly. "Give it to me."

She took a step toward the other girl. Felicity turned to face her squarely, pointing, the gun an extension of her arms. She aimed it straight at Lacey.

"You stay out of this, Miss Perfection," Fee said, her voice dripping with venom. "This is between me and Tom, no one else."

Lacey took another step. "That's fine with me, Fee, but—"

The flashfire of the gun glared yellow against the dusky sky with a brightness that filled up the world, the bullet whizzed by like an angry hornet and she thought she was going to die. Her ears roared. She squeezed her eyes shut with every ounce of strength she had.

The instinct to flee took full possession of her, even after she knew that it was too late. She willed herself to run, but her legs wouldn't work; she could not move one muscle in her body. She was helpless even to cry out.

Both boys shouted into the deafening echo of the shot, but the roaring in her ears drowned out their words. Felicity screamed and started to cry.

Still Lacey stood frozen. Was she hurt? The bullet had come so close. . . .

Trembling, she lifted her left hand and touched her right elbow, then ran her hand up and down the length of her arm, barely aware of the difference in feel between her skin and the fabric of her sleeve. All of it felt like wood; she was completely numb.

"Hold it right there!"

The shout carried an authority that silenced the confusion of noises.

Lacey opened her eyes.

A mounted man rose out of the gun's smoke. Its blue-and-gray wisps floated in front of him; behind him the last, low strips of red streaked the sky. He loomed bigger than life over all of them, the white of his shirt the only distinct, discernible detail.

She could see, though, that he sat the horse with an imperious confidence, his silhouette hard and solid against the evanescent sky. Her eyes widened, straining into the gloom. Who was he?

"Are you hurt, miss?"

His deep voice rang in the silence.

She shook her head, then managed a faint, "No." She twisted her fingers into the ragged hole the bullet had torn in her sleeve.

Suddenly the porch floor squeaked and yellow lamplight came closer, pouring down on them. It livened the shine of the man's boot, traced his long, muscled leg in its sheath of black broadcloth, illumined the strength of his fingers, bronzed and sure around the reins. But she still couldn't see his face.

A soft voice came from the veranda. "Wuz that a shot? Anybody hurt?" asked Linch, the houseboy.

Thank goodness. The music must be so loud that no one else had heard. Mama would *die* if she knew.

Nobody answered the question. The music still played, fast and sweet, but for Lacey it was more remote than ever. The party and everybody in it had disappeared for her. There was only this imposing stranger towering over her, as big and dark as the night to come.

The sunset flared brilliant in one last burst of crimson. From far off, down by the river, a whippoorwill called.

The man swung down from his horse.

He came full into the spill of light, reins in one hand, the other held out for the gun. Felicity thrust it at him in one stiff, hurried movement, as if to deny that she'd ever had it.

His face was as Indian as any Lacey had seen; strong-boned and hard, with high cheekbones and a nose just slightly hooked. Midnight hair showed from beneath his flat-crowned planter's hat; he had a full, sensuous mouth marked at the sides by weathered creases.

He took the gun and turned to Lacey, sweeping off his hat. His eyes were as dark as his hair.

"Did the bullet graze your arm?" His voice made goose bumps rise on her flesh.

He reached her in one long stride and his hand closed over hers. Her knees went weak as a newborn foal's. He moved her hand away to look for himself and she managed to straighten out the flimsy fabric to show him the ragged hole the bullet had cut.

He nodded. "Good. Luck was with you."

Her hand quivered in his; its calluses were sensitizing every inch of her skin.

His eyes held hers for one long look, as intimate as a whisper.

Then he turned away. "Whose pistol is this?" he asked harshly.

Tom stepped forward, his hand out to take it back. "It's mine."

In one smooth motion the stranger tucked the pistol into the tight waistband of his pants. "If you don't have any more sense than to wear a gun on a social occasion, then you don't need one," he snapped.

Tom stood, frozen, still holding out his hand.

Abruptly, more light shone on them; footsteps and voices clattered on the veranda. The man ignored them, but Tom glanced quickly over his shoulder.

The stranger's commanding tones made Tom turn around again. "You've just come very near to a tragedy right here," he said. "This child could be lying dead at your feet, and for no other reason but your own vanity!"

Feelings she couldn't name welled up in Lacey. He was protecting her! This magnificent, mysterious man was defending her! What if he, and not Eli, had been the one to see Tom dragging her off the veranda?

But he'd called her a child!

Voices were buzzing louder on the porch, and people began coming down the steps. Neither the man nor Tom moved a muscle. Then Tom advanced a step.

"You gimme that, mister," he growled. "It's mine." He reached for the gun.

"It's yours when you grow up enough to handle it," the man said. He looked at Tom with pure disgust. "Let me know when that happens, *son.*"

He turned on his heel and strode back to his horse.

Just then Papa Melton burst into their tense circle with Lacey's mother, Babe, close behind him. Babe rushed to throw her arms around Lacey, but Lacey was only aware of the incredible man who'd just put Tom in his place. She watched him untying a black coat from behind his saddle.

Papa Melton didn't notice him. "Creekwater!"

he bellowed. "Are you behind all this commotion? Get your horse and ride out right now!"

"Don't think you can give me orders just because you're the great high-and-mighty judge," Tom shouted back. He was standing exactly where the stranger had left him, his face flushed and twisted in the yellow light.

"What's the matter, Tommy boy, lost your toy?" a young masculine voice taunted from the dark edges of the porch. "Somebody take it away from you?"

"He'll pay for that!" Tom yelled, each word vibrating with a rage of its own.

"Which army you gonna get to help you?" the anonymous voice retorted. "Union or Confederate?"

Laughter welled up all over the place.

"By God," Tom roared, "the bastard'll wish he'd never seen me!" He swung around to shake his fist at the formidable man who'd taken his gun.

"Watch your language!" Papa Melton roared. "There are ladies present, you foul-mouthed young stripling! I'll not have them insulted in my house."

"You'll wish *you'd* never seen me, either!" Tom shouted back. "The both of you will know I ain't no stripling before this is all over."

"Boy, you're drunk," Papa Melton told him loudly. "And you're not fit for decent company. I asked you to get your horse and I mean for you to do just that. Right now."

Tom snorted in wordless fury, pushed through the crowd, and stamped away into the night.

Then Papa Melton saw the stranger. "Why, Ridge Chekote!" he said, his tone changing to one of respectful hospitality. "Good to see you! What in the world brings you all this way? Come in, come in this house.''

Ridge Chekote. The name sang its way into Lacey's veins.

Ridge turned to shake Papa's outstretched hand. The light wind picked at the full-gathered sleeves of Ridge's shirt; its deep V neck and wide collar glowed pale as frost against the copper-colored warmth of his skin. The sight caused an unfamiliar tightness deep inside Lacey.

He shrugged into the coat. The way his shoulders moved made her hands tremble.

Then Felicity and Eli ran to her and everything was chaos. Felicity was hugging her and Mama, too, begging forgiveness. Eli was apologizing for Fee and worrying over Lacey. And Mama was threatening one of her swoons, now that she knew Lacey was safe. Half the party gathered around them asking questions, rejoicing in the fact that no one was hurt, calling for drinks to celebrate.

Papa began escorting Ridge to the steps. The stranger moved with a natural, raw power, like Papa's big Thoroughbred. Watching him made the ache inside her twist and turn.

They reached the door. Ridge's shoulders, broad and thick above the narrowness of his waist and hips, blocked out the light for a minute, then he disappeared into the house. Lacey felt suddenly empty.

The trees surrounding the house rustled louder. The breeze was picking up, but she couldn't feel it for the crush of people around her. She shivered anyway.

What *were* these strange feelings taking hold of her? Ridge couldn't be the man in her dream; he'd hardly noticed her at all, and certainly not as a woman. Why, he thought she was a child!

But she knew, as if the words had been written in lightning on the black sky over her head, that, true to her wish, something had happened, something had begun. That something felt completely different and amazingly more powerful than any dream she had ever imagined.

The breeze became a wind, lifting her hair and caressing her face, filling her with a sense of dangerous distances and far-off longings.

The whippoorwill called again. This time, from somewhere deep within the grasses of the summer-smelling meadows, another one answered.

Chapter 2

Ridge let his head rest against the stiff back of the tall wing chair and closed his eyes. He hoped no one would notice. George Thompson's voice droned on. The old man had been holding forth when Judge Melton ushered Ridge into the book-lined study and hadn't paused long enough to draw a breath in the quarter hour since then.

If he'd known George would be here, he wouldn't have ridden quite so hard, Ridge thought cynically. At this rate it'd be morning before he could deliver the message. He'd come eighty long, hot miles from his plantation, in the middle of hay harvest, just to sit and listen to a pack of senile ramblings.

He shifted his legs, his muscles tired from having spent even more hours in the saddle than usual, and crossed one ankle over the other knee. The gun in his belt poked painfully into his stomach. He took it out and laid it gently on the polished mahogany table beside his chair. Young fool, he thought, remembering the boy's fury. Cocky, shortsighted kid. The girl could've been shot dead at his feet.

He frowned, remembering how frightened she'd looked, her eyes so huge and dark in her white face. She'd reminded him of a porcelain doll, with that mass of pale hair tumbling to her shoulders. Her hand had been real enough in his, though; her fingers had trembled like a caught butterfly

Well, she'd be more frightened than that before it was all over, he thought. The judge should send her and her mother away; they had no business being here with the Nation standing on the brink of a ravaging war. It would be a horror, the Trail of Tears all over again; he knew it in his bones.

George Thompson's quavering tenor contradicted his thought. "We have nothing to fear from the white man's civil war," the old man said. "This conflict is not the concern of the Principal People. We need to stop all talk about which side to make treaty with and think instead about our own affairs."

Their own affairs were in the worst condition Ridge could remember. All the Nation, it seemed, was choosing sides between John Ross, who was trying to keep the Cherokees neutral in the white man's war, and Stand Watie, who favored an alliance with the Confederacy. Many said that Watie was maneuvering to take Ross's place as Principal Chief. Tribal organizations supported both men, further dividing the Nation.

In every territory of the Cherokee Nation, from Ridge's own Canadian District on the Canadian River, far south of the capital of Tahlequah, to the Cooweescoowee District along the Kansas Border, brother opposed brother.

Ridge shot a look at his host, then glanced at John Ross. Both faces were impassive; both men were watching the elderly statesman and listening to his voluble ramblings as if he were the soul of reason. No one would interrupt him. His advanced age and his past leadership commanded too much respect for that.

Unable to sit still a minute longer, Ridge straightened and cleared his throat. He spoke before the old man could start another sentence.

"Grandfather," he said respectfully, "I wish to do as you say and speak of Cherokee affairs. There is trouble coming for our people that we must act upon tonight. I have ridden from the far Canadian District to bring word."

George Thompson's rheumy black eyes turned to him, as did all the others in the room.

Ridge looked straight at John Ross. The short, white-haired chief would ultimately decide what to do about the warning he brought, although the opinions of the others in the room would be important, too. All of them were leaders in the tribe's major faction.

He stood up. Even before he began to speak, relief at sharing the bad news came over him. He'd feel even more relieved when the whole meeting was done with and he was on his way back home. All he wanted was to seclude himself on his own land once more and ignore the insanity of the war until it actually intruded on him.

Unobtrusively, a grizzled black man stepped to the table beside Ridge. He took away Tom's gun and refilled Ridge's wineglass.

"I will not say who told me because it would mean that person's life," Ridge began, looking slowly from one prominent Cherokee to another, "but this is my news. There will be an attempt by our pro-Southern Cherokee brothers to take over the government of the tribe. They will try to raise the Confederate flag over the Council House at noon tomorrow.."

Exclamations of surprise burst like scattered shot across the room; several men leaped to their feet.

"What?" the diminutive chief demanded. "You're sure about this?"

"It's true," Ridge replied sharply. "I give my word."

"Stand Watie again!" boomed Judge Melton. "Well, we'll just see about him!"

"Watie may not be behind this," Ridge said, "but he probably is. He wouldn't be sorry if his Knights of the Golden Circle were able to push us into an alliance with the South."

"Of course not!" the judge snorted. "Then he, no doubt, would be named Principal Chief."

"What's their plan?" Chief Ross demanded.

"They'll gather all morning, in and just outside of Tahlequah. At high noon a mounted contingent will ride straight to the square and raise the flag while the others spread out through town talking up the Confederacy and persuading people to let the flag fly. If that succeeds, they'll occupy the Council House, oust you as chief, and write a treaty to ally us with the Confederacy."

Chief Ross struck his fist into his palm. "And here I am raising heaven and earth so that we can remain neutral," he cried. "Can't they see that that's our best hope for survival?"

"What they see is that your Pin Indians, sir, in your Kee-too-wah Society, have been attacking the homes of slave-holding Cherokees and freeing or killing the slaves," Ridge said.

"And the Knights of the Golden Circle have been burning houses and barns and killing pro-Federal Cherokee!"

"Cherokee are killing Cherokee on both sides," Ridge said wearily. He ran a hand through his hair. "We're determined to destroy ourselves again, just as we were in that first year after the Removal."

"We survived the Trail of Tears," George

Thompson said, lifting one feeble arm into the air for emphasis.

"So that now we can fight and kill amongst ourselves!" Judge Melton shouted sarcastically back at him. The judge looked around the room, urgency written all over his face. "We must unify this tribe now or the Principal People will be no more."

"Well, we can't unify under the Confederate flag," Ridge said. "I, for one, will never fight on the same side with the murdering thieves who stole our homes in Georgia."

"There're thousands of other Cherokee who feel the same way you do, Chekote," William Adair drawled, "but we obviously can't side with the Federals since they've pulled out and left us with the Confederates pressing in."

"I know," Ridge said shortly. "We'll have to take care of ourselves, all of us together. Our only hope is to squelch this coup tomorrow."

The schottische ended with one last high note of the fiddles. Eli finished the pattern with an awkward flourish, swirling Lacey into a circle that brought her back into his arms.

He leaned down and whispered, "How about the next dance, too, Lacey? Or would you like a glass of punch?"

"Punch," she said quickly, thrilled with the opportunity to be rid of him for a moment. "I'd love some punch, please, Eli."

Ever since they'd come inside he had hovered over her until she thought she'd lose her mind.

As soon as he hurried away she whirled to look at Papa's study doors again. They were still closed. The gleaming polished wood winked at her in the glow from the dozens of lamps, but the doors did not open one inch.

Ridge Chekote *must* be in there with Papa and the chief and all the other older men. No doubt they were talking, as usual, about what side the Cherokee should take in the war. That was all people ever talked about when they got together anymore, ever since this past New Year's Day party when 1861 began.

A voice at her elbow made her jump.

"What're you staring at? I don't see anything but some blank doors."

She turned to look into Felicity's sharp, dark eyes.

"Lace, are you looking for somebody?" Fee persisted.

"No," Lacey said. "I . . . I'm waiting for Eli to bring me some punch."

"It'll take forever," Fee said. "Half the people here are crowded around that table." She narrowed her eyes the way she always did when she was being nosy. "I'm surprised to see you back at the party so soon, Lacey. Your mama said she told you to rest until time for refreshments."

"She did."

"Then how come you didn't?"

"I didn't want to miss my own party."

Both girls glanced across the room at the knot of women gathered around Babe. She was talking constantly, fluttering her silk fan and periodically touching a handkerchief to her eyes. Even some of the men who had been dancing had stopped to listen to her story, and as the girls watched, one of the men fetched Babe's smelling salts for her.

Felicity laughed. "I think it's your mama's party," she said. "She's having more fun than anyone else, telling how scared she was when I nearly shot you."

"Every party is Mama's party," Lacey said. "She's always the belle of the ball."

"Not always. Mostly everybody flocks around her, but Tom doesn't like her at all. I can tell by the way he looks at her."

"Well, Tom is different. . . ."

"I don't care if he is, your papa didn't have to run him off." Fee pouted. "*I* did the shooting, not Tom. If this keeps up, I'll never even see him again unless I ask Drowning Bear to say a charm for me."

Lacey gasped. "You'd do that? Fee, that's dabbling in magic. You'd better be careful."

"A medicine man does more than dabble, Lacey," Fee said loftily. "I'm going to ask him to help me get Tom; I don't even care if my parents find out."

"Felicity, I don't think you know Tom very well or you wouldn't want him. Deep down, beneath that smile, he's mean."

A low noise thumped beneath the high-pitched laughter and talk. Lacey glanced at the study doors again. Had they slid open? No. They were still mockingly closed and blank.

"He is *not* mean!" Felicity contradicted. "You just don't understand him, that's all."

"Fee, you don't know what he did. . . ."

"He didn't do anything! I did! And that haughty old Ridge Chekote that you keep watching for didn't have to embarrass him like that, either. *That's* what made him yell and cuss and get thrown out of the party."

Lacey felt her cheeks flame with embarrassment. She forced her tone to be cool. "What do you mean? I'm not watching for Ridge Chekote."

His name sounded wonderfully new on her tongue.

"You are so! You can't see a thing in this room

but those doors. But even when they do open it won't do you any good.''

Lacey turned on her heels so that her back was firmly to the doors in question. ''Felicity, nothing you say makes one bit of sense.''

''I saw the way you looked at him outside even if I was bawling my eyes out.''

''I didn't look at him any certain way.''

''You did so. And he didn't even notice you.''

That echo of her own thoughts cut to the bone. ''Why should he? It's not like he could be my beau or anything.''

''Maybe he could, but he won't. He won't court anybody since his wife got killed.''

''His *wife*?'' The very idea made Lacey suck in her breath.

''Yes. Some outlaws in the Osage country killed her and their baby four or five years back. He's still in love with her and he's vowed never to love anybody else.''

''How do you know?''

''He told my cousin Tahnee. My Aunt Sarah's plantation joins his and Tahnee was in love with him all last year, but he never would court her.''

Felicity crossed her arms and smiled as if this bit of news paid Lacey back for causing all her and Tom's troubles. ''Tahnee is the prettiest girl in the Canadian,'' she finished triumphantly, ''so you don't have a chance in the world, Lacey Longbaugh.''

''Well, thank you very much, Felicity Hawthorne. You are a friend indeed.''

''I am. I'm just trying to help you not to fall in love with him.''

''Don't trouble yourself,'' Lacey snapped. ''That could never happen. He's nothing at all like the man of my dreams.''

Felicity didn't answer. Her face changed, and

Lacey knew before she turned to follow Fee's eyes that the doors had opened.

Ridge stood out from the colorful attire of the milling guests in black-and-white relief. He stood in front of the mantel in the study, one booted foot up on a dogiron, talking with Chief Ross. He gestured widely, his coat moving like black wings against the white of his shirt. Tom's gun was gone from his belt.

He frowned, completely absorbed in what he was saying; his eyes seemed to pierce right through the little white-haired chief without really seeing him. Then he stopped talking and listened, his face so darkly brooding that it scared Lacey.

The music started up again, very softly. Cobby's raspy voice crooned over the beginnings of the waltz. "Ladies' choice. This 'ere dance is ladies' choice."

The sounds of all the strings mingled softly at first, then they welled up behind her, as full of ragged restlessness as her heart.

"Ask him to dance," Felicity said suddenly. "See if I'm not telling you right. He wouldn't even take Tahnee to a single dance."

Lacey didn't move; she couldn't shift her eyes away from him.

"Go on," Fee urged. "And get this out of your system. Your mama won't be any madder about that than she will be about you coming downstairs too soon."

Lacey heard Felicity too distinctly, as if she were in a dream. She was aware of everything—laughter and giggles rippling over the room as the girls took the unaccustomed initiative, the mauve batiste of somebody's dress, the lilting strains of the song, the brushing of feet against the polished floor. Everything was so clear and bright it hurt.

Yet the only person she could see was Ridge.

She started walking toward him. Dimly she knew that she couldn't go in there. Girls didn't go into a male sanctum like Papa's study when it was filled with important men.

And she hardly knew how to dance. She'd never asked a man to dance before; she couldn't possibly do so now.

But her feet kept on taking one step after another, each one carrying her closer to Ridge. She couldn't have turned and gone the other way if Mama herself had stood directly in her path, forbidding her with tears and threats. Some unknown force was compelling her.

She crossed the threshold into Papa Melton's office. Conversation stopped. Vaguely she heard Papa's questioning, "Lacey?"

By the time she reached Ridge he was alone, staring down at the intricate brick pattern of the hearth. He was close enough to touch.

Oh, dear Lord, why had she come in here? How could she possibly speak to him?

The wine in his glass had a sharp, sweet fragrance that drifted up to her and closed her throat. She could hear his breathing in the sudden quiet of the room.

He looked up.

She could not say a word, but she could not look away.

Gradually his eyes lost their faraway look.

"Yes?" he said.

She had to say something; he was waiting.

"It . . . it's ladies' choice," she stammered, very low. "Would you like to dance?"

"Thank you, but I never dance."

Painful heat flooded her face. Oh, why had she done this? She wasn't attractive enough or grown-

up enough to be trying to act like a woman; Mama
and Felicity had both been right.

She wanted to turn and go; she wanted to hide
her hot face in her hands; she wanted at the very
least to drop her eyes and stare at the floor instead of into his eyes. But his look was growing
more intense every second.

He wanted to bite his tongue for refusing her;
the child was dying of embarrassment before his
very eyes. When she realized that everyone in the
room was staring at them, she'd probably faint.

She took a step backward, as if she would leave,
but she didn't.

The music from the next room was the only
sound.

"Uh . . . is it too late for me to change my
mind?" he said quickly. "I believe I might enjoy
a dance, after all." He offered her his arm.

At first he thought she wouldn't take it, but she
did so mechanically, and they crossed the oak
plank floor to the parlor. Every man in the room
watched them leave.

In the doorway, Ridge put his arm around her.
Her head didn't quite reach his chin.

He took one of her hands in his and pulled her
closer, then paused before they moved out into
the swirl of dancing couples. He placed her other
hand on his shoulder.

"Now," he murmured. "We're ready."

But still she didn't relax, not even when they'd
begun swaying in time with the waltz.

The political problems still roiled in his mind,
but he couldn't think about them with the girl so
small and unbelievably fragile in his arms. What
was her name? The judge hadn't spoken it; he'd
simply thanked him for rescuing his stepdaughter. The other girl, though, had screamed a name

when she rushed to see what damage she had caused.

"Lucy?"

She looked up so fast it startled him. Her blush came flooding back.

"Lacey," she said. "My name is Lacey."

She forced her voice not to tremble. He didn't even know her name! The young man in her dream would have found out her name. And that young man would have asked *her* to dance. Oh, what was she doing in this miserable situation? She must get out of his arms as soon as she could.

But they encircled her warmly, and when he said, "Lacey," to correct his error, she trembled inside.

He danced her to one side of another couple, pulled her closer to him, and turned them slowly around. Her feet moved more smoothly than she could have believed. The sweet, lilting strains of the song rose and fell, carrying them over the floor.

"So, Lacey, you're none the worse for being shot at? I'd expect you to be in a swoon over your narrow escape."

She lifted her chin. "I don't swoon. I'm not that kind."

His eyes glinted. He seemed about to smile, but he didn't. Was he laughing at her?

"Then what kind are you?"

She lifted her chin and used her most dignified tone. "I'm the kind who likes adventure. And now that I'm grown up, I intend to have some."

Her eyes were exactly the blue of the sky in October. He looked into them and shook his head. What an innocent! She had no idea what adventures she might find. Or what adventures might find her.

"What sort of adventure?"

"Something of my own, that I decide for myself. Maybe travel to Europe. Maybe the university. Or . . ."

She couldn't mention her dream about the dashing young man.

Her face, heart-shaped as a redbud's leaf, glowed delicately pale. The masses of blond hair, sparkling in the lamplight like spun honey, curled onto her shoulders and halfway down her back. He shifted his hand upward to touch it.

Soft as goose down, the swaying curls brushed his skin, then floated away, only to come back in a moment. The caress, unintentional as it was, stirred him. He wanted to run both hands into that hair; he wanted to use them to press her body against him. Her back was pliant now beneath his palm. How long had it been since he had held a woman?

But this was a girl, a mere child just beginning to look for adventures she couldn't name. This was a white girl, far from her home in a rough country that would soon erupt into war.

Suddenly the old yearning rushed through him again, the wish for the power to stop all the chaos and the killings, and the worse that was to come, but this time it wasn't for his people that he wanted to hold back destruction. It was for this sweet child/woman, so that she could stay innocent and eager for life.

The band shifted smoothly from the sweet melody of "The Last Rose" into the haunting "Come Where My Love Lies Dreaming." He dropped his arms to his sides and stopped still in the middle of the floor.

How foolish could he be? He hadn't been able to save even his own wife; what was he doing wishing to take care of this girl? When Martha had died, he'd vowed, "Never again," and he had meant exactly that.

He took Lacey's arm and led her through the slow-moving dancers to the side of the room lined by open windows. Candled wall sconces burned between the lace panels; in their shadows her eyes looked enormous. He wanted to cup her face in his hands.

But he turned her arm loose and forced himself to say, "I have to go now. Good night, Miss Lacey."

He didn't look back as he left her.

The predawn chirpings of the birds in the black locust tree outside her window woke Lacey from her one fitful nap of the night. She pulled the pillow over her head and tried to slide back into oblivion, but it was too late; her thoughts had already started to race.

They had worn ruts into her mind last night, running back again and again over every minute she'd spent with Ridge Chekote; this in spite of the fact that he bore no similarity at all to the young man of her dreams. He certainly had not swept her off her feet; he had not taken her for a walk in the moonlight. The real truth was that he hadn't even noticed her or bothered to find out her name. So *why* couldn't she stop thinking about him?

Determined to do just that at long last, she flipped over onto her stomach and tried to call up her second favorite fantasy. Every night she put herself to sleep with a detailed reviewing of one or the other of her three dreams. She thought them through so carefully because soon she'd make one of them come true, now that she was a grown woman of seventeen.

In this one she set off to travel the world all by

herself except for Dorcas, her maid. They took
Linch, the houseboy, with them, too, to manage
all the wardrobes and trunks on and off the
coaches and boats and to protect them should anyone bother them. But only Lacey made decisions;
she went to see horse races all over the South
(plus Mama's relatives, the Laceys and the St.
Clairs, too, of course), then she visited the Tower
in London and the Coliseum in Rome, Stratford-
on-Avon and the Champs-Elysées. Oh, it would
be wonderful to go everywhere and do exactly
whatever she pleased!

Usually she began this fantasy by imagining
every single article that she had Dorcas pack in
the trunks, which they then strapped onto a carriage. They told everyone good-bye. Mama protested, of course, but Lacey was firmly in control,
and soon they were off, trotting briskly down
Federal Road to Fort Smith.

Now, however, she couldn't even pick out one
dress to take with her. The only clothing she could
see with her eyes closed was Ridge Chekote's
white shirt, its collar looking as if it'd been
washed in moonlight, up against his earthy skin.

And she could still feel his hand, warm as a
smile on her back. Her waist had fit perfectly into
the crook of his arm.

Why had he left so abruptly? Had he been so
embarrassed that *she* had asked *him* to dance that
he'd rushed away the minute that one song was
over?

Was it because he truly thought she was nothing but a child? Had he thought "ladies' choice"
a childish game?

Impatiently, she snuggled down into the feather
bed and tried to blot out these questions that had
tortured her for hours. She reached for her other
favorite fantasy.

She would become a famous professor. She'd leave the Nation, go back east to a university, and do spectacular work. All the seminaries and normal schools would clamor for her to come and teach their students poetry and stories. She would choose the most exciting one—or maybe she'd come back to the Cherokee Female Seminary, from which she had graduated.

Wherever she was, she would wear hand-tucked white batiste shirtwaists with the tiniest rows of tatting around their stand-up collars and beautifully cut broadcloth skirts from France. She'd make every one of her students swoon over Mr. Shakespeare's poetry and plays, and they'd all talk about what a wonderfully enchanting teacher she was.

But she couldn't imagine a single student's face or remember one line of Shakespeare. The only face she could see was Ridge Chekote's and the only line she could hear in her head was his half-amused question, *Then what kind are you?*

What kind was she? The kind who always dreamed and never did anything? The kind who let an anxious mama and an indulgent papa keep her a child forever? The kind mean, hateful boys jerked around like a toy? The kind a man would never see as a grown woman?

Abruptly she sat up and pushed the covers away. She didn't want to think about all this anymore and she obviously wasn't going to drop off to sleep.

She swung her feet to the floor. Just as they touched the cool boards she heard the men and the horses.

First a low voice or two sounded through the wild chatterings of the birds, then she heard saddles creak and bridles jingle. She crept to her window.

Shivering in the early morning coolness, she stood just behind the curtain to listen. From here the voices were clear, floating up from the side yard two stories below her. Papa Melton was giving the orders.

"You, Charly," he said, "keep your men out of sight in Miss Alice's 'til straight-up noon."

"Why not come out a few minutes before?" was Charly's drawling answer. "Be ready for 'em."

"No, we don't want to start anybody arguing or firing. Wait for the very time they've set and then we'll show our force." He paused. "Ridge Chekote?" he said as if he were calling a roll.

"I go by the Council House and then to the Locust Grove junction to meet Drowning Bear."

Every word spoken in that low voice brought a separate goose bump to Lacey's arms. It felt as if his hand had touched her skin.

"Thank you," Papa said. "You'll need to be at the junction by nine o'clock at the latest. Drowning Bear says he won't wait longer than it takes the sun to pass Cowskin Peak."

"I'll be there."

"Lucas Spaulding?"

"I take my men to wait behind Honey Ridge."

"Right," said Papa. "Until exactly high noon. But first we meet the others at Rose Cottage."

She couldn't even see shapes in the predawn blackness, but she strained her eyes anyway, wishing to catch just one glimpse of Ridge.

"All right, men!" Papa Melton cried. "Let's ride!"

The saddles creaked as they mounted, and then the sounds of hoofbeats drowned out everything else. She leaned as far as she dared into the blackness, but she could see nothing. Feeling cheated, she turned back into the room.

She rubbed her arms to take away the chill,

then wrapped them around herself; finally she went to the bed and pulled the light quilt loose to throw around her shoulders. She paced to the window again, leaning out once more as if through sheer force of will she could see him. Or follow him!

The thought struck her with the force of a blow. Instantly the idea took hold and grew. This could be just what she'd been waiting for: an adventure all her own!

Not only would she see Ridge again but she'd be in on all the excitement. She'd heard the news from the house servants just before she came up to bed about the runners being sent secretly to spread the word to all Ross Indians. There would be a confrontation today in front of the Council House, and Chief Ross, Papa Melton, Ridge, and the other council members would have to take charge. It should be very exciting, but Mama would never let her go.

Far away she could hear the hoofbeats fading down the road to Rose Cottage. That meeting would take a while. Then . . . what had Ridge said? "I go by the Council House and then to the Locust Grove junction."

She could see him at the Council House. She would go out for her usual early morning ride, but go into town instead of across the plantation. No one would know.

Throwing off the quilt, she ran to her wardrobe and searched through her clothes for her riding habit, her mind working at top speed. He had said "I." He was going in to Tahlequah alone. Perfect! Papa would probably stay at Rose Cottage and come in with Chief Ross when it was closer to noon.

She lit her lamp and began to dress, choosing her lightest blouse because the day was sure to be hot. And, she admitted, smiling into the tilted mirror, because everyone said that its periwinkle blue was the perfect match for her eyes.

She took special pains with her hair, arranging the curls all to one side so that they'd spill out from under her hat. She brushed her habit, even though Dorcas had done so before hanging it up, and then she looked for her newest gloves. He would see that she was a woman.

She tiptoed out of the house and, holding her habit up from the wet grass, she crossed the yard. Every breath she took made her feel light enough to fly up into the early morning air and mingle with the smells of honeysuckle and roses. Each drop of dew sparkled in the brand-new sun and made her feel as rich as if they were diamonds. The day of her first adventure was so perfect it almost made her cry.

Chapter 3

Tahlequah was teeming with people. Lacey had ridden in from the Park Hill road and across to the Council House square before she noticed that the great majority of them were men. They were stony-faced full-bloods mostly, sitting in the Council House square or on the dusty corners of the streets.

It was then, too, that she noticed the ominous air hanging over them all. There was too little talking for so many people, and the voices she did hear were too subdued.

Her exuberance faded a little. Last night when Dorcas had told Lacey the news Old Jasper had overheard in Papa's study, she'd kept up a running lament. Over and over she'd said, "Oh, Lord, I hope there ain't no killings. Some innercent peoples is liable to die right there in the square. There'll be brother killing brother, you mark what I say."

Now those dire mutterings came back, fueled by the portentous feeling that filled the town. Lacey searched the crowd for a familiar face.

She straightened in the saddle and took a firmer grip on the reins, although Lady was moving quietly in a sedate trot. Nothing bad would happen. There were always incidents between Ross Indians and Watie Indians, but there'd never be a public battle between them right here in the square.

Two women, obviously mother and daughter, came out of Martin's Mercantile with baskets over their arms. That proved everything was normal. This was just another summer day in Tahlequah—except that Ridge Chekote was here!

But where, in all this crowd?

She slowed Lady to a walk. Lacey's eyes darted everywhere, scanning men and horses alike. Ridge had had time to get to the Council House by now.

Her stomach tightened at the thought of his being close by. When she found him, what would she do? She certainly wouldn't initiate a conversation as she had done last night, not after he'd left her so abruptly. Perhaps he'd done so because she'd naively interrupted the man talk to approach a stranger. No wonder he'd called her a child!

No, she wouldn't talk with him today. She would simply let him see her, a grown woman expertly riding a spirited horse. Perhaps she would raise one gloved hand to him in a dignified greeting.

Her eyes glued themselves to the Council House, a two-story red-brick building nestled among tall sycamores and elms. What office was he visiting? What was he doing in there?

A woman sitting on the bench by the door caught her gaze, and for a long moment her heart leaped up in her throat. No. The woman only looked like Mama.

She smiled to herself in relief. The whole idea was ridiculous. Mama never got up this early, especially not after a social.

Lady carried Lacey the entire length of the

square's north side. She really ought to dismount, Lacey decided. If she kept parading around on the eye-catching mare, somebody was sure to notice them and mention the fact to Mama. She rode into an empty place on the hitching rail beside a big black horse that, with a quick jolt, she recognized as Ridge's.

Her legs trembled as she dismounted, and when she saw someone bent over on the off side of the black, she stood very still against Lady's warm bulk. Was it Ridge?

She looked again. Tom! That obnoxious oaf! Whatever was he doing?

Her fingers clutched at the reins. She had trouble swallowing. Watching him surreptitiously, she walked to the railing and tied the mare.

At that moment he straightened up and turned around as if he'd felt her eyes on his back. The dark, brooding expression she'd seen last night flicked over his features, then he erased it with his old, charming smile.

"Lacey!" He hurried toward her. "You're out early this morning." He was acting as if last evening had never happened.

She turned her back to him, her head held high.

He was at her elbow just as she moved onto the crowded boardwalk. She tried not to look at him. Oh, *why* did she have to see him instead of Ridge when she was alone?

"I hope you ain't still put out with me, Lacey," he said pleasantly. His mouth was too close to her ear. "You or the judge neither. I was a mite drunk last night and I'm sorry."

She whirled to face him, astonished. How could he have changed so much in only a few hours?

He smiled that charmer's smile down into her eyes. "Forgive me?"

"No! You were too mean!"

She turned and began forcing her way through the crowd away from him.

He was beside her in a second. "That dumb Felicity's the one who shot at you. I didn't."

She kept going. "You started it all. You jerked me around."

"Aw, pretty Lacey, don't hold that against me. I just wanted to take you walkin', that's all."

He stepped around her, directly into her path. "You've gotta know that I'm crazy about you," he said, the words coming rapidly, his tone very low. "And I'm gonna court you no matter what your mama or the judge has to say about it. You remember that, little girl."

"Don't you call me a little girl!" she spat.

But his eyes left hers as if he didn't hear her; he was looking at a spot just over her shoulder. She turned to look, too.

Ridge was leaving the gravel walk that led from the Council House, crossing the boardwalk to his big black horse. Two men were trying to keep up with his long strides. He said something she couldn't hear and motioned them away.

He untied the horse and put his foot into the stirrup. Fiddlesticks! He was leaving right now, and here she was on foot; he wouldn't even see her, much less see her ride.

A narrow silver band on his saddle skirts drew the sun and flashed into her eyes, blazing against the black hide of the horse. A realization hit her brain at that same instant: Tom had been doing something to Ridge's saddle!

She whirled to demand that he tell her what he'd done, but she looked into the face of a complete stranger instead. Tom had gone.

Instantly she glanced both ways along the crowded street, but she couldn't pick him out.

Alarm drummed in the back of her mind. Tom

had been bending over beside Ridge's stirrup. He had to have been up to no good—last night his shouted threats against the man had echoed off the walls. He might have been putting a burr under the saddle or . . . he might have cut the cinch. And Ridge was in a terrible hurry.

Her eyes flew to him. He had mounted and was riding out into the middle of the street, the horse still at a walk. She had to stop him before he got out of town and urged the horse to go faster. If the saddle came loose at a canter, he could be killed!

She picked up her skirts and began to run, dodging the men sitting and standing, pushing her way through a knot of bystanders. Out of the corner of her eye she could see Ridge working his way through a group of new arrivals who were clogging the road. If she could reach the corner of the square before he did, she could head him off.

Her hat slipped and swung behind her on its chin straps, her hair began to come loose, but for once she didn't care. She ran straight ahead, trying to watch her path and keep track of Ridge's position at the same time. He was gaining on her; he'd be past the corner and gone unless she could go faster.

The knot at her throat came completely undone and she felt her hat drop away behind her. She didn't even glance back. Ridge got free of the congestion and broke the black horse into a trot just before she hit the street.

She rushed out into traffic without looking either way and dashed right in front of a mule-drawn wagon. The driver, yelling an obscenity, jerked back on the reins. The mules reared, squealing.

Going in the other direction was a fast-moving

buggy; she saw the horse pulling it as only a white blur. One big wheel caught at her skirt as the buggy passed.

She snatched back her skirt and ran out into the middle of the dusty street, facing Ridge, waving both arms frantically, screaming his name into the confusion. He was coming fast; he was almost on her now.

Didn't he see her? Great goodness, was he going to run her down?

His eyes met hers through the rising dust, incredulous surprise all over his face.

He pulled the big black down onto his haunches and they slid to a stop only inches from her feet. She stayed as still as stone, gasping for breath.

He stood in the stirrup and stepped off into the street. The saddle came with him.

One foot on the ground, one still in the stirrup, he glared first at the saddle, then at her. His eyes were so full of fury that she wanted to turn and run.

"What in the name of thunder are you doing standing out here in the middle of all the traffic in the Nation?" he yelled.

Well! So this was the thanks she got for almost getting run over! "Trying to tell you that your cinch has been cut!" she snapped.

He disentangled his foot. "And just how did you know that, miss?"

"I saw it being done."

"And you didn't have sense enough to find me or wait by my horse and tell me?"

A stronger fury swept through her. He was yelling at her—after she had risked her life to save his!

"I didn't know what I saw at first," she said loudly. "You might at least be grateful that I realized it when I did."

Dimly she was aware that a crowd had gathered around them, eyes and ears straining. Wonderful! Now Mama would be *sure* to hear the whole story!

"Well, thank you so much," he barked sarcastically. He heaved the saddle back into place with a disgusted shove, picked up the flapping end of the cinch strap, and glanced at it.

"Cut, all right," he muttered. He let go of the strap and glanced around impatiently.

The horse took a step sideways and his hind leg immediately buckled. He hobbled another step.

In a flash, Ridge went around and picked up the foot. He examined it for a moment, then set it down gently. He rounded the big black, his eyes searching for Lacey.

"Where's your papa?" he demanded. "Tell him to bring his horse. Mine has hurt his hock sliding around in the road to keep from running over you."

She stared at him coldly. "I came into town alone."

"Then bring me *your* horse. I'm late for a meeting."

He turned and pointed at a little boy standing in front of the crowd that had formed around them. "Hey, son, come here," he said, taking a coin from his pocket. "Walk this horse to the shade, slow. Water him and put some salve on his hock. Watch him 'til I get back to town around noon."

The boy, face beaming, came forward to take the reins.

Ridge glanced back at Lacey. "What are you doing? Get your horse!" he shouted. "I'm in a hurry, I tell you."

She whirled, picked up her habit to hold it out

of the dust, and ran for Lady, her eyes filling with sudden tears. Blast him! She'd risked her life and Mama's wrath to save his obnoxious hide and all he did was yell at her.

Lady's gleaming yellow haunch was just visible down the street. Lacey rushed toward her, blind to everyone in her path, Ridge's urgent words ringing in her ears. She'd reached the mare and untied her before she realized that he'd ordered her to do his bidding just as he had the little boy and that she'd complied just as quickly. They were both children in his eyes, children who should be glad to run a few errands for the grown-ups.

The tears grew and she swiped at them with the back of her gloved hand. She'd show him! She swung up into her saddle and turned Lady out into the street.

He came to meet her. "Thanks," he said briefly, taking Lady's head. He held out his hand to help Lacey dismount.

She stayed in the saddle. "I'll give you a ride," she said, holding her eyes firmly on his. "Swing up behind me."

His face clouded angrily. "I'll have to ride hard," he said. "She shouldn't have to carry double. Dismount and go visit one of your friends."

Lacey shook her head.

"Hurry," he urged.

He was so sure of being obeyed that she actually made a small move to comply, in spite of her determination. Then she shook her head again and took a deeper seat in the saddle. She was making her own decisions from now on.

"I won't dismount. You'll have to drag me off in front of all these people."

He threw a quick look over his shoulder then,

as if he'd forgotten there were other people in the world, much less in the same town. Lacey, too, glanced at the faces watching them. Their dark, waiting looks made the ominous feelings come back in full force.

Without another word Ridge let go of the mare's head, moved back, and vaulted up to sit behind Lacey.

"I guess I *had* better take you with me," he muttered, close to her ear, as he reached around her to take the reins. "No telling what other kind of trouble you'd get into left here by yourself."

The remark stung her anger into life again, and she tried to keep the reins away from him. His fingers brushed hers away as if they were totally strengthless.

"I'll rein," he said. "We have a long way to go and not much time."

Angry words boiled to her lips and awful resentment at being treated like a baby over and over again burned hotter in the pit of her stomach. But she couldn't say one thing.

Because his arms encircled her, bringing a rush of disturbing new sensations. His chest felt hard and solid as it brushed against her back whenever Lady's gait changed; his breath stirred her hair; his muscles pressed against her upper arms when they flexed. His hands were beautiful and strong, steady like rocks on the reins.

He seemed unaware that she was even there. He kept the mare moving fast and at the end of the street lifted her into a canter. Now his arms were even closer around Lacey. The tight feeling inside her, new last night, came back again, much stronger.

She took a deep, shaky breath of his scent. He smelled of leather, as he had last night, but today there was another fragrance . . . some kind of shaving soap or pomade. His clothes were crisply fresh, too: a different suit, although still a black one, and a stiff white shirt to replace the big-sleeved hunting shirt.

The dusty road flew by beneath Lacey's feet, the morning sun shone hot on their faces, and the blood pounded wild in Lacey's throat. Her eyes wouldn't leave Ridge's hands, which were all she could see of him. Red-brown as the soil itself against the white edges of his cuffs, they drew her like a magic stone. She wanted to rub them with her fingers and see what miracle would happen.

Other horses met them from time to time, trees and fences passed in a blur, then finally they were leaving the main road for a rocky trail that immediately began to climb. Thick branches grew out over one side; the other opened to a grassy slope that fell gently away down and down to a rolling green meadow far below. There the sunlight burned bright, but here the heavy shade shut out the sun and the world with it.

They climbed for a long time, Ridge leaning forward, and she with him to help Lady up the constantly rising trail. His closeness made her breath stop; she had only to raise her head and she could brush his chest with her cheek. How would that feel?

He never said a word to Lacey, only clicked and murmured to the mare to keep her from slowing too much.

They must have traveled two miles up the rocky path, but it seemed to Lacey they'd gone only a few yards when Ridge reined in beneath a huge hackberry tree. A wagon stood there, a nervous gray pony in its traces.

"Osiyo, Unisi," Ridge called. Lacey knew

enough Cherokee to understand, "Hello, Grandfather."

Startled, she looked around. Who was he talking to? The wagon was empty.

Ridge's hands covered hers. Sudden heat leapt with the speed of fire from one of her nerve endings to another until, within seconds, it had melted her to helplessness.

He put the reins into her hands and slid to the ground, leaving her as suddenly cold as if she'd just been tossed out of a warm room into a blizzard. Her breath caught in her throat and she couldn't get another one. She wanted to fall off the horse into his arms.

He looked up the trail; her eyes followed his. A narrow creek ran beside the trail, and between them stood a little grove of redbud trees. In their shade a tall, wizened man with skin the color of a hickory nut sat on a large rock. At his feet two squirrels, some birds, and a skunk nibbled at grains of corn scattered on the ground.

As she and Ridge watched, the man raised his head and looked at them with eyes that never blinked.

He was Drowning Bear, the medicine man. She had seen him once when he came to Pleasant Prospect with a potion Papa had asked him to make for Mama's chronic cough. Now, as then, he wore a turban and an old-fashioned hunting shirt of a soft, faded green as mottled as the leaves above his head. He sat still as the stone he sat on. He made no move to greet them.

"He feeds every creature," Ridge murmured. "He can't keep from it, ever since the starvation on the Trail of Tears."

He glanced up at her then, his eyes hardly seeing her. "Wait here," he said. "I'll talk to him."

"All right. But I want to give Lady a rest."

He reached to help her dismount, and her heart stopped. His hands came toward her waist and cradled it, then he lifted her as easily as if she were a doll. She looked up at him as he set her gently on the ground, but his eyes were hooded and far away.

She had to make him see her again. "What are you going to talk about with Drowning Bear?"

He glanced at her, but that was all. His gaze went back to the old man. "About coming back with us. He's the only one who can keep the peace on the square today. If they see Drowning Bear, every man there will remember that they are Cherokee first, and Union or Confederate sympathizers second."

"The Watie Indians won't," she said. "Drowning Bear is a friend of Papa and Chief Ross."

He looked at her again; this time he saw her. Did she see a flicker of respect? Had he expected her to know nothing about politics?

"Drowning Bear is friend to all the Cherokee, and they know it. But he likes to see them only one or two at a time. I have to persuade him to come into the crowds today."

She remembered Dorcas's grim predictions, and a sudden sharp fear flowed into her. "There won't be fighting, will there?"

He shrugged. "Who knows? The old Removal wounds have never healed, and now this white man's war has made them bleed again."

He stared down at her, looking directly into her eyes now. "You have no place at all there today, Lacey." His tone tightened with impatience. "Why in the world did you come, anyway?"

I wanted to see you. The words sprang to her lips, from somewhere deep in her subconscious, but she bit them back. "I wanted an adventure."

He shook his head, and the corners of his

mouth twisted ruefully. "Well, you'll very likely get it."

He glanced back at the old man, who was watching them through narrowed eyes. Hurriedly he said, "Your papa will be at the Council House when we get back. He can give you an escort home then."

He turned abruptly and strode beside the upward-slanting trail until he stood in front of the old man. He placed one foot on a tree root and leaned forward to speak to him, his arm resting on his leg in an attitude of appeal.

He looked relaxed, but even from here she could feel the vibrations of tension inside him. Unconsciously she sent up a little prayer. Oh, please make Drowning Bear come. And let him make peace. But if there *is* any shooting, please don't let Ridge get hurt.

The gray pony snorted and stamped one foot, rattling the rickety wagon on its wheels. Lady nickered in return.

Lacey looked at her in surprise. How could she have forgotten all about her beloved new horse?

The mare's sweaty sides still heaved from her run, and white foam showed here and there on her skin.

Lacey patted her neck. "I'm sorry you had to work so hard," she said, taking the reins to lead her. "Come and cool off, then we'll get you a drink."

She led the mare around in the grassy glade for a while, then took her to the creek. As Lady buried her nose in it and began to drink, the gray jerked restlessly again and whinnied. He lifted his head high and, ears pointed, gazed out into the brush.

Lacey followed his gaze, but could see nothing. Maybe he was thirsty, too.

Lady finished drinking and lifted her head, muzzle dripping. Lacey led her back toward the trail, pausing beside the two men. Should she ask Drowning Bear if she could water his horse?

The medicine man's opaque eyes went to hers and held them. He said something to Ridge.

Ridge turned to her. "He says there's corn in a sack behind the seat of the wagon. Get some and feed your horse."

"Thank him for me," she said. "And please ask him if I should water his horse."

The old man nodded once, a quick gesture of assent, and she realized that he could understand English. A smile touched her lips as she led Lady on toward the buggy. He could probably speak English, too, if the truth were known. And everybody thought he didn't know a word of any language but Cherokee.

She smiled because the old man had let her in on his secret. It would be fun to watch Drowning Bear around other people and see if any of them suspected, she thought, as she led Lady up to the side of the wagon. She'd do it on the square today—she wasn't letting Papa Melton send her home, no matter what Ridge told him to do.

Giving Lady one more pat, she dropped the reins and climbed over the wheel of the old wagon. She kneeled on the worn board seat and leaned over its back to look for the sack of corn.

She heard a loud thump, and the whole world exploded.

The gray pony reared, whinnying shrilly, and sent the wagon lurching backward. Lacey flew headfirst over the seat.

She landed hard on one shoulder. Pain stabbed through it and down her arm as she slid helplessly toward the tailgate, breathless with the shock of the fall. In the next second the gray gave a giant leap forward and was off at a gallop.

Dimly she heard Ridge's shout of surprise and then his bellowing yell, "Ho! Ho there!"

Her flailing hands could find nothing to grab; instinctively she pressed them hard against the rough planks and tried to brace her knees. But they were racing so fast over the rocky hillside that she tumbled head over heels and crashed against the ribbed side of the wagon box with terrible, bruising force. She gripped one of the supports with her fingertips and, pushing against the awful momentum, slowly braced her foot against another one.

Trees rushed by in an alarming smear of green and brown, then the next instant all she could see was the blue of the sky, far away and uncaring. The wheel directly beneath her hit a rock, jarring her loose.

Dear Lord above, she had to get hold of the lines. Any minute this wagon would jounce itself to pieces and she'd be thrown halfway down the mountain.

She rolled to the opposite side of the box and, somehow, through sheer force of will, clawed herself to her knees. She forced her stinging hands around the top railing and clung to it for her very life.

She had landed facing backward. She glimpsed Lady pounding toward her, Ridge leaning back in the saddle to balance her on her way down the slope, and then, a fleeting moment later, Lacey was shaken loose again.

This time the wagon bounced her violently forward, throwing her to a bruising stop beneath the springboard seat. She lay still, gulping for air. Finally she forced herself to raise her burning, aching arms and clasp the front edge of the seat. She dragged herself up and over in one long, frantic scramble.

The lines were knotted loosely around the unset brake handle. She reached out one hand to take them, clinging to the seat with the other. The gray pony swerved off the trail and ran closer to the trees. A low-hanging limb loomed huge in her face; she ducked it and lost her grip on the seat.

She landed on the floor again, so hard that the force jarred her teeth. Seconds later the near wheel hit a root and for the first time she squeezed her eyes shut. This was it. Here was the wreck.

But the crazy, rattling rush went on. She opened her eyes, fought her way back to her feet, and looked back.

Lady was closing on the wagon, her nose almost touching the tailgate. Ridge was leaning forward now.

Then she saw his intention and goose bumps broke out on her arms. He was getting ready to jump!

Oh, dear God, please let him make it. Don't let him get hurt. But let him save her!

The yellow mare, running at the very edge of the trail, pulled even with the side of the wagon. He dropped the reins to her neck, kicked his feet free of the stirrups, and, stretching his long arms out for the top of the box, made the leap. His hands caught it strongly and he threw one leg over the side.

He landed on both feet and held to the side, waiting for his balance. She knelt on the seat, her eyes glued only to him in this pitching, lurching, bouncing world. New strength surged through her, and she clung to the back of the springboard with a tighter grip.

Thank goodness! She wasn't going to fall down

the mountain because Ridge was here to save her. They weren't going to wreck, after all.

He got his balance and came toward her, his boots sliding on the planks of the floor.

The ride was even rougher now, if that was possible, and she felt herself begin to slip on the slick old board of the seat. She stiffened her hold.

Ridge was much closer now, moving faster. Another minute and he'd be at the front. He'd reach out and get hold of the lines, lift them from the brake handle, and that would be the end of it. He'd start the gray to slowing and then he'd sit down beside her . . .

The pony whipped in an instant to the opposite side of the trail. The wagon followed, lashing to the very edge of the sloping hillside. The momentum tore her loose and she felt herself hurled into nothingness.

"Ridge!" she screamed.

He threw himself at her, arms reaching. They found her the second she flew into the air.

He held her while they fell . . . down and down . . . forever.

He was beneath her when they hit the ground. They tumbled over, then over again; she gasped, winded by the crushing force of his weight.

Then somehow she got a breath before they started rolling faster and faster through the green-yellow grass of the hillside, its fresh, smashed smell following their flight. They were hitting the hard earth, but they were falling through the sky.

Loosened pebbles bit into her back, then tumbled downhill behind them, pelting them with sharp stings. The heavens flashed blue and white; she had one fleeting glimpse of the sun. Then Ridge's shoulder took a jolt and pressed hard into her face; she smelled the starch in his shirt and the sweat on his skin. Somehow those intimate scents made him familiar, a part of her, and the harrowing fear lifted. She gave herself up to the shelter of his arms.

They rolled into a shallow depression filled with blinding yellow black-eyed Susans and lay there, not moving, heaving for breath.

She drew air deep into her lungs . . . as far as the encircling pressure of his arms would let it go. He held her with a wonderful sureness, his muscles like iron ribbons against her back.

Her heart was pounding hard, a mighty rhythm that shook her body and leapt up into her throat. One slight movement sent fierce pain racking through her shoulder; it would have a cruel bruise. She felt the sharp sting of a splinter in her skin.

But the feel of Ridge against her was stronger than all the hurting. It was as newly dangerous as the race just finished and at the same time it was as familiarly safe as a part of herself. This was where she belonged. Forever.

She opened her eyes. He lay above her, his breathing quick and uneven beneath the shirt torn open across his bronze chest. He was looking straight at her, his face blazing with relief.

He smiled then, deep into her eyes, and all breath left her. He had a smile that changed the world—like the sun coming out on snow.

Then somehow he was too close to see and she could only feel: the wet of his sweat soaking into her blouse, the trembling of her breasts surging up against his chest. His face lowered to hers until her arms lifted to encircle his neck. He felt solid and strong; he was someone to depend on, someone to hang on to.

His breath smelled like clover honey. His lips

parted, sensuous and sweet; his mouth came down on hers in a delicious, languid fashion that melted her very bones.

His kiss shook the solid earth beneath her.

Chapter 4

Ridge's mouth gave more heat than the sunshine pouring down on them; it set off more lights in Lacey's head than a sky full of stars. Every color in the rainbow washed against her closed eyelids.

She floated, connected to nothing but the warm, melting sureness of his lips.

His fingers drove into her hair.

His mouth came down closer on hers, more insistent now, and a fresh, shocking pleasure cartwheeled through her.

His tongue? Had the tip of his tongue brushed against her own?

Instinctively, shamelessly, hers sought to return the caress.

As sudden as the crack of a whip, he broke the kiss. He pulled away. That left only the cold warmth of the sun on her lips.

She opened her eyes.

He was propped up on one elbow, staring at her with a look that pinned her to the ground.

His full, curving lips were still parted. His face looked as if it were chiseled from bronze, its other features as hard as his lips were soft. The cheekbones gleamed, their taut skin catching the light from the sun. Sweat stood out on his forehead.

But his eyes weren't hard. They gleamed velvet brown, full of feelings as wild and scattered as the ones inside her.

Had their kiss torn him loose from every other mooring as it had her?

They searched each other's faces while the sweet smell of crushed grass and the bitter scent of the black-eyed Susans grew stronger around them. A sweat-bee buzzed up from the bed of flowers and flew in a circle between them.

It threw itself at Ridge's cheek.

He brushed it away and dropped his head to wipe his face on his sleeve.

When he looked at her again, she couldn't read his eyes.

"We'd better get back to Drowning Bear," he said.

Come *back!* her heart cried. You're *mine!* Where have you gone? . . . Ridge!

He got to his feet and bent to help her up all in one fluid motion, and that same movement brought her heart into her throat and changed it into a stone.

He helped her to her feet with hard hands that could have belonged to anyone. She stood stock still.

"Are you hurt?" he asked. "We hit some pretty hard spots here and there."

"No."

He believed her, even though her lips trembled when she spoke. It was all he could do not to kiss them again. Silently he cursed himself for having no strength of will, no character at all. He ought to apologize for kissing her the first time.

He couldn't say the words, though. Because he wasn't sorry.

Yes, he was. He could kill himself for being such a fool.

He tightened his lips, trying to blot off the liquid honey of her mouth; he drew in a long breath and exhaled, trying to blow away the lilac scent of her hair and the hot, sweet smell of her skin.

But he knew it was too late. The memory of that shattering kiss had already driven deep into his bones.

Why? Why in the name of his own survival had he ever succumbed to the temptation to taste that soft red mouth? Had five years of suffering taught him nothing? Did he have to be hit on the head with a two-by-four twice in one lifetime to learn the simplest of lessons?

Loving a woman made a man vulnerable to the deepest hurt there was: the hurt of losing her. And he would lose a delicate white woman like this one.

Martha's flight had proved that. A white girl with a cultured background couldn't be happy on his plantation on the Canadian. Compared to Philadelphia or Washington City or Richmond, or even to Tahlequah, it lay far in the backwoods. He could give a woman every luxury there, but he couldn't give her the civilized society she would always crave.

"Drowning Bear is waiting for us. Let's go." The words scratched his throat. He tried, but he couldn't force any others to follow them.

He glanced up the hill, but for a moment he could still see her eyes, as dark blue as the sky in October.

He *must* not touch her. One kiss and he already wanted to keep her with him forever.

His feet felt like wooden stumps. He forced them to move. "Come," he said, without looking at her. "We have to get back to Tahlequah."

In a minute he would remember why that was true.

Obediently she turned to walk beside him. He led the way, determined to keep his eyes straight ahead. But he couldn't help glancing at her from the corner of his eye. She winced when she took the first step on the uneven ground.

His hand shot out to steady her. He would help her up the hill because she was shaken and in pain from the wreck. Then he would never touch her again.

Lacey fastened her eyes to the ground, blinking at the tears that threatened to come. Vaguely she knew that her shoulder hurt with every step and that one shin had a raw scrape that burned each time her skirt brushed against it. But those pains felt distant and impersonal compared to the hurt that gathered like a cold rock in the pit of her stomach.

How could this be? How could he kiss her like that . . . more puzzling yet, how could he *look* at her the way he had in that one, flying, unforgettable instant after his kiss and then immediately throw up this stone wall between them?

She forced her shaky legs to take another step. She would not lean against the strength of his helping hand.

He tightened his grip on her arm to guide her around a slippery rock half embedded in the grass. The gray of the rock and the bright green of the grass blurred together in front of her eyes.

The hill became steeper. Ridge put his hand on her back to steady her, but it was still the touch of a stranger. Her heart cried out its rebellion with every step she took. This couldn't be right.

Their kiss had spoken of something destined between them. It had been a promise—like the whippoorwill's call.

Ridge led her away from the trail of crushed grass and dislodged rocks and gravel that they had made in their fall to climb where the footing was better. They held on to the branches of wild plum bushes and made steps out of tree roots.

Halfway up, on a ledge of broken sandstone, they stopped to catch their breaths. Lacey looked up toward the road. They still had a long way to go.

She glanced back the way they'd just come. Had they really fallen all that way? How could they not have been killed?

She read the same thought in Ridge's eyes.

"We must have more lives than two cats," he muttered.

She didn't answer. She had no idea what to say to him, ever again.

But she knew how to touch him. His torn shirt lay open in a ragged edge of white against the dark, hard muscles of his chest. She had a sudden urge to lay the palm of her hand against his hot, smooth skin . . . there . . . just where the flimsy fabric came apart.

He dropped his arm and the shirt covered him again.

From somewhere above them came the jingling of a harness and the disturbing creak of the wagon's wheels. The sounds rasped over her skin; the memory of that terrible ride rushed through her body.

"I'm not getting back into that wagon." she blurted.

"You don't have a choice. Your mare will be winded."

He sounded as distant as the top of purple Sugar Loaf Mountain, far to the east across the valley. He took her arm and started climbing upward again.

She moved more and more quickly, her pains multiplying with every step. Still, they were nothing compared to the hurt to her feelings. If she could get back to Tahlequah, and away from Ridge, the torture would end.

He was climbing ahead of her now, finding the best way, reaching back to help her follow. She gave him her left hand; her right shoulder was beginning to pain her considerably. Mama would have an absolute fit when she saw what condition Lacey was in.

Mama! How would Lacey ever explain? She couldn't say that she'd gone to Tahlequah to find Ridge, forced him to bring her on his errand, been in a wreck in which he'd saved her life, and then let him kiss her!

She raised her free hand to her lips, in spite of the pain that shot into her shoulder. Did it show on her mouth? Could Mama tell that he'd kissed her?

She stopped in her tracks. One foot wedged between a rock and a tree root, the other dug into a toehold in the dirt that Ridge's boot had made. But it wasn't fear of Mama that paralyzed her.

It was the thought that she'd had her first kiss! She'd had her first kiss and she hadn't even realized it!

"Come on," Ridge said. "You won't fall. I've got you."

She barely heard him. For a moment her mind whirled with the old dreams, the old imaginings of the dashing young man who would dance her— dressed in clouds of baby-blue lawn, of course— out of the ballroom and down to the honeysuckle arch, where he would gently touch his lips to hers.

Instead, in real life, a brooding stranger had leaped off a wagon to catch her in his arms and had kissed her into oblivion while she lay in a bed of black-eyed Susans, dressed in a disheveled riding habit that looked as if it had been through a war.

She glanced down and brushed at the dirt on her skirt. The movement made her shoulder throb.

"For God's sake, this is no time to try to get cleaned up," Ridge said. "Come on. I'm about to lose my hold."

"Then let go of me! I can manage by myself!"

But she let him pull her to the next space flat enough to stand on. Now his head was even with the road.

The wagon was directly above him. Drowning Bear appeared at the edge of the drop-off.

She watched him and Ridge through the haze of her thoughts. She didn't know if they were speaking English or Cherokee and she didn't care, unless they could answer the question that pounded in her brain.

Was life always this way—completely different from what one imagined it to be? Was it impossible to plan or to predict?

She would never, ever be able to reconcile the beau of her dreams with the reality of this tempestuous man . . . a man she could never forget if she lived to be as old as her great-grandmother St. Clair, who would be ninety-seven in November.

That she could predict.

His hands closed around her waist. The breath left her body in surprise. And in a thrill of yearning.

"I'll lift you up to the road," he said. "Drowning Bear will help you over the top."

But the old man only held out one hand to steady her. Ridge lifted her so high that he set her feet on the hard dirt of the winding road.

She stood still, letting her eyes adjust to the

sudden shade. Ridge climbed up to stand beside her. He didn't even glance at her.

"What's the damage?" he asked Drowning Bear. "Will the wagon make it back to town?"

"Ayeh." The old man grunted. "Go many miles yet."

Ridge strode to the pony, murmuring to him in Cherokee, running his hands over his neck and then down his front legs, along his back and then down the rear legs.

"They're sound," he said. "Hard to believe."

He went to Lady next; Drowning Bear had caught her and tied her to the back of the wagon. Lacey followed, her feet taking her toward Ridge without any direction from her mind.

Concern for the mare nudged at her, but somehow, watching Ridge's square, strong hands examine the horse, she was much more aware of him than of her beloved new mount. He moved on the balls of his feet, graceful as a deer running.

He ran his hand down the mare's foreleg and lifted her foot. The muscles of his arm and his back rippled strong as a river current beneath the thin cambric of his shirt.

The new, unfamiliar aching deep within her came to life again, drawing all of her insides together into that same wild longing that had seized her the night before.

She couldn't bear it, she thought. She could not bear it if he never touched her again.

Ridge looked up and her heart leaped. But his eyes swept past her to Drowning Bear.

"Let's go," he said. "We can't push these horses."

Drowning Bear nodded and began clambering up over the wheel to the wagon seat. Ridge turned to Lacey then.

"I told you I'm not getting back into that wagon," she said, knowing even as the words came out of her mouth that she had no choice.

"It's ride in the wagon or walk," Ridge said. "Which will it be?"

Anger flashed through her. "Don't talk to me that way!"

"Then get into the wagon. If we aren't there by noon, all this effort will have been wasted."

Wasted? *Wasted?* The kiss, too?

He put his hands on her waist, set her in the wagon, and climbed in to sit beside her.

"Don't worry," he said. "I won't let you fall out again."

But his tone was distant, and he held himself very straight so that they wouldn't touch.

Lacey clutched the edge of the seat with both hands.

Drowning Bear picked up the lines and flapped them against the pony's back. The wheels creaked forward. The pony pulled them out into the road in a wide circle so they could head downhill.

Ridge's thigh touched hers in spite of his efforts to the contrary; the narrow wagon seat jammed her in between him and Drowning Bear. She pretended not to feel his hard saddle muscles through her riding habit.

"Did you get a glimpse of anyone?" he asked Drowning Bear across the top of her head.

"No," the old man said. "But I hear two or three voices and they sound like they'll tear down the trees, roots and all, they're in such a hurry to get away."

"Yellow-bellies," Ridge said. "I'd like to drag them out of the woods and into the open."

"Who? *What* are you all talking about?" Lacey asked.

"Somebody deliberately caused the runaway,"

Ridge said. "Drowning Bear heard them shouting and crashing through the brush while we were flying through the air."

He wished he could call back the words as soon as he said them; they made her face go chalky pale and her eyes indigo dark.

He needed to take her face in his hands and kiss away her fear.

He made himself look away, but he felt her hand against the back of his thigh again, gripping the edge of the seat with all her strength.

"Don't worry," he muttered. "Whoever it was is gone now."

He stared straight ahead at the narrow brown strip of road dropping in loops down the side of the ridge. He felt as if he had started rolling down it in a barrel with nothing at all at the bottom to catch him.

The wagon hit a bump and jostled her leg closer to his. Desire knifed through him.

I will not, he thought. I will not love her. I will never let all those feelings come back to life again. She is gently bred, just as Martha was. She is cultivated and civilized, and right now she is scared to death because there are barbarians in the woods who could have killed her.

Like that oaf at her party last night. Both of those incidents are proof: She isn't the kind who can survive in this wild country.

Which will be even wilder in war.

Tom Creekwater slowed his horse and pulled him to a stop in the middle of the overgrown deer trail. Enough was enough. If they tired the horses too fast they'd miss all the fun in town.

"Let 'em blow a minute," he called to the two riders pounding up behind him. "We've put plenty o' distance between us now."

Watty McCoy slid his horse to a stop beside Tom's and wrestled a dirty kerchief from his pocket. He wiped his round face, eternally gleaming with sweat.

Tom frowned at him. If Watty meant to keep on riding with him he was going to have to toughen up some, lose some of that lard.

"Distance don't hinder that medicine man," Watty said mournfully. "He can turn us into a lizard or a snake no matter how far and fast we ride."

Jake Taliferro rode up in time to hear the last sentence. "How come you so worried, Wat?" he drawled. "You're already the next thing to lizard now."

"Why, you . . ." Wat began.

"Shut up," Tom said. "Save your breath. We still got a long ways to ride and not much time to do it."

"Gonna be right in the middle of the square to lead the charge, huh, Creekwater?" Jake said. "Too bad yore lady friend cain't be there to see you. If'n you hadn't run her off the side of a hill, she coulda stood on the sidewalk and hollered for your side."

He shook his head and clucked in mock sympathy.

Tom said, "Shut up, I said. You're the one chunked that rock into the wagon without lookin' to see who was in it. If she's hurt, I'll kill you."

"Don't see why. Judge ain't never gonna let you court her."

"I'm courtin' her anyhow."

Both of the others laughed.

"You wait and see. Inside of a month I'll be her best beau."

"Yeah," Jake said, "and I'll be Principal Chief of the Cherokee Nation."

"Laugh if you want to."

"Who wouldn't laugh? She had her best beau right there with her—she come all the way out here with him with no chaperone. Now, what would any simpleton make of that?"

Tom didn't answer.

Jake cocked his head. "That Ridge Chekote's beatin' your time," he teased. "I wouldn't let him do that if I was you, Tom."

Watty stuffed his handkerchief back into his pocket and winked at Jake. He said, "Yeah, Tom, and he stole your gun and run you off from the social, too, remember?"

"Yeah, and I cut his cinch and dumped him in the dirt, didn't I? And give him a runaway wagon. I hope it run right over him and killed him."

They laughed in chorus. "No such luck," Jake said. "Last I seen him, he was chasing like the devil after *yore* girl."

"Yeah," Watty chimed in. "Why don't you just go on and hand her over to him, Tom?"

Hot, blinding fury shot through Tom. Damn them! They'd better learn some respect or he'd shoot them both and throw their bodies in the river.

"I'll whip both yore heads in for them remarks," he said coldly. "Just as quick as I raise that flag in Tahlequah."

He took up his reins and clicked to his horse. "You two giggling little girls gonna help me or not?"

Tom moved out at a fast trot without looking to see if they followed.

He tried to get his thoughts onto the coming set-to on the square, but in his mind's eye he kept on seeing that bastard Chekote. The picture made him so mad the whole world turned red and then yellow right in front of his eyes.

He'd kill him, he thought. One of these days.
Right after he took care of that high-and-mighty
judge and these two idiots behind him. They all
had to learn the same hard lesson: Nobody
shamed Tom Creekwater and got away with it.

Nobody.

The heavy air of waiting still lay over Tahlequah. More people had gathered, but that was
the only difference since Ridge and Lacey had ridden out three hours earlier. It seemed more like
three years since she'd run out into the middle of
the street and made a spectacle of herself.

Drowning Bear drove them slowly down the
wide main street toward the square. Ridge kept a
constant watch on both sides of the road, as he
had done since they started down off the mountain. Whoever had spooked the gray might try
again to keep the medicine man from reaching the
square.

Lacey shivered. Thank goodness, they were almost there.

The closer they got, the more self-conscious she
became. Everybody in the Tahlequah District
would be there to see her dirty, ragged clothing
and wild, unkempt hair.

They would see her with Ridge, too, and think
that there was some understanding between
them. Well, *that* idea would certainly be the mistake of all time!

She felt the heat of embarrassment rise in her
cheeks. What must *Ridge* think of her! She had let
him kiss her without protest and had even kissed
him back, when all the time she meant absolutely
nothing to him!

The red-brick Council House loomed tall and
stately inside its frame of trees. As they approached its west side Lacey could see the flag-

pole with the stars and stripes of the Federals still flying. At least they weren't too late.

Knots of people, most of them men, were scattered on the lawn and the sidewalk. Several women and girls were standing across the street on the porch of Martin's Mercantile.

A few horses stood tethered along the street. Only two vehicles were in sight. Drowning Bear drove the wagon up beside them and stopped the pony.

Lacey glanced at the shining black buggy beside her. Startled, she looked at it again.

Papa had brought their buggy! Thank goodness! She could climb into it and avoid being seen.

But a woman's skirt showed at its side, a fine navy blue bombazine skirt. Mama!

Now she was in for it! She could have sweet-talked Papa into overlooking her little adventure, but Mama was a whole different story. She'd probably not let Lacey ride alone again for the rest of the summer, the way she had done last year when Lacey had worn breeches to race her horse against the neighbor boys' horses.

Drowning Bear wrapped the lines and then sat, his hands in his lap.

Oh! If he would only climb out of the wagon on the off side so she could follow him before Mama saw her . . . while Ridge's solid bulk was still between them . . .

But Ridge saw Mama.

Lacey tried to shrink into invisibility.

"Mrs. Melton," Ridge said. And then, "Judge Melton. Good day. I was looking for you."

Lacey lifted her chin and made her back very straight. She'd just have to bluff her way through it . . . and pray for help.

Mama leaned out of the buggy and looked at Ridge.

She saw Lacey. "Dear goodness!" she said, then, louder, "Lacey!" She stared, her blue eyes wide. "Darling! What in the world?"

Mama stood up and motioned for the judge to help her out of the buggy. "What has happened to you? Why, you're an absolute mess! Where in this world have you been?"

The next few minutes flew by in a merciful blur. Mama fluttered and fanned and threatened to swoon. Ridge explained to Papa that it was all his fault for commandeering Lacey's horse, and he begged Mama (who was staring from Lacey's ripped riding habit to Ridge's torn shirt) not to fret about their lack of a chaperone since Drowning Bear had been with them.

At first, Lacey thought that he had successfully defused the situation. Then Mama pulled her off to one side.

Lacey decided to take the initiative. Sometimes that would distract Mama.

"I didn't expect to see you here, Mama."

"Chief Ross decided that Mrs. Ross and I should come with him and the judge. He said that we would be an influence for peace."

Oh, no! Lacey thought. The chief and Mrs. Ross were in the other buggy! They must have seen her, too!

"Lacey," Mama said. "The next time you beg me to give a social or let you go somewhere, I want you to think of this. Your performance today was one of a little girl who's still half tomboy and not that of a young lady. You will not leave the place without me for the rest of the summer."

Rebellious words sprang to Lacey's lips, but she never spoke them.

Because a wild yell echoed down the street.

Everyone froze, in spite of the dense July heat. Every person on the square . . . every person in

the town . . . the whole Nation . . . the whole
world waited. Only the tops of the trees moved.

Would it be Cherokee killing Cherokee right on
the square in front of the Council House? Which
flag would be flying when whatever would happen was finished?

The thunder of distant hoofbeats sounded, then
grew louder. For one long moment the hanging
silence became deeper, then answering yells
sprang up in different parts of the crowd.

So. Not everyone here had come to stop the
lowering of one flag and the raising of another.

The riders galloped into view. Clouds of dust
obscured their faces and their horses, but the
Confederate flag flying high above the leader left
no doubt about which faction they were. The man
a half-length behind the leader held a rifle above
his head in a stiff-armed gesture, as if to claim
victory already. Sunlight winked along the weapon's barrel.

They bore to the right, rode across the board
sidewalk, hooves clattering, and onto the square,
still shouting the bloodcurdling yells.

Somebody fired a shot. Mama screamed.

Another shot sounded. Riders came rushing
from behind the Council House to meet the pro-
Southern faction, forming a milling, yelling mob.
Two horses reared in the middle of the wild confusion. The Confederate flag on its long pole
dipped out of sight.

The two factions swirled away from each other
and faced off, men struggling to control their
horses. The stars and bars swept up again.

Lacey couldn't look away, but she felt the
movement of people along the side of the square,
some running toward the melee, some falling
back.

Shouts echoed from up the street. More horsemen came pounding. The sharp noise of a shot rang out again. The lead rider of the new arrivals clutched his shoulder and pulled his horse to a halt.

His followers parted around him and came on; one of them took aim as he rode.

Another shot cracked from the direction of the flagpole.

Mama clutched Lacey's arm and wailed into her ear, ''Oh! There's going to be a battle right here!''

From the corner of her eye Lacey caught a blurring movement, a horse and rider coming at a hard gallop from the nearest corner of the square. She turned to look.

A shot sounded; the rider ducked.

Lacey's blood stopped in her veins.

The horse, ears pinned, eyes rolling, cleared the hitching rail and the sidewalk in one huge leap. He hit the ground running hard, straight into the heart of the fray.

The rider was Ridge.

Chapter 5

The smell of dust hung suspended in the air.
Lacey pulled away from Mama and ran to a better vantage point by the water oak, where she caught a glimpse of Ridge's white shirt, squarely in the middle of the dangerous commotion.

Suddenly the crowd separated into two distinct groups.

Ridge held his rangy sorrel mount in the open no-man's-land between them. He thrust his right hand high into the air in a gesture of command.

His voice boomed into the falling quiet. "If you are loyal to your chief, you are loyal to the flag he flies."

One man on the pro-Southern side turned his horse sharply to face Ridge. He whipped his rifle across the pommel of his saddle; Lacey recognized him as the one who had carried his gun high in the air on the way into town.

She gasped. She recognized him, all right. It was Tom Creekwater.

Ridge carried no gun.

Surely Tom wouldn't dare shoot an unarmed man. Not in front of all these people.

The leader of the Confederate Cherokees rode through his men to stop beside Tom. He yelled back at Ridge, "If a chief is loyal to his people, he flies the flag that is best for them."

Angry murmurs rose from the crowd.

"The Federal flag flies by order of Cherokee law," Ridge retorted. "*That's* best for the people. While I live, no flag will fly over the Cherokee Nation by order of a bunch of renegades."

Tom raised the rifle and pointed it straight at Ridge's chest.

Ridge ignored him; he kept his eyes on the wiry leader with the flag. "If we split among ourselves for North and South in the white man's war, we're lost!" Ridge shouted.

The crowd's murmuring swelled.

Ridge's mount tossed its head and danced, resentful of its strange rider. Ridge held him still with an iron hand.

The armed horsemen shifted uneasily in their saddles. Finally the leader made a sharp gesture at Tom. After what seemed like an age, Tom lowered the gun back to its place across his pommel.

Lacey breathed again.

"We don't need no speeches," the Confederate leader cried. "What we need is a new chief!"

Shocked silence reigned all across the square, except for a few weak yells of support from the wiry man's followers.

From somewhere behind Lacey and to her left she heard a sharp click. Another rifle being cocked?

The yells came again, stronger this time, and echoed by a small group of mixed-bloods in the street. Lacey glanced around the square. There was still a great majority of stony-faced full-blood Cherokees, loyal to Chief Ross to the death.

The overall silence held.

"Drowning Bear will speak," Ridge shouted,

his commanding hand still raised high. "We will listen to our medicine man."

Drowning Bear climbed down from the wagon. The dappled shade from the oaks fell across his faded green clothing; he almost disappeared as he walked. He trudged toward the flagpole at a pace that plainly said he would not be hurried by the foolish quarreling of children. After an endless time he stood beside Ridge.

Ridge dropped his hand.

Drowning Bear spoke in Cherokee, in a dry, light voice that blended into the rustling leaves. Everyone strained to hear, but Lacey's eyes stayed on Ridge. His right hand lay confidently on his thigh; his left held the restless horse.

She looked at Tom, willing him to put the rifle into its sheath, to drop it, to throw it down, but it stayed as still as Ridge did.

It was too late now, though. Surely. The moment of crisis had passed.

Hadn't it?

Drowning Bear talked for a long time and then he stopped. No one moved, not even Tom or the men with him. Then, one by one, the people began to turn and leave the square.

The large knot of horsemen didn't move, though. The one holding the flag lifted the long stick and waved it once. He gathered his reins and for one horrible moment she thought he would charge at Ridge. But then he jerked the horse's head around and moved the other way. Slowly his men followed behind him.

All except Tom.

He sat glaring at Ridge, pure hatred in every line of his body. Then his voice rang out across the open square like a slashing blade. "I'll yet make you pay, Chekote," he yelled. "You'll rue the day you rode all the way up here to meddle into business that ain't none of yours."

Ridge's only answer was a long, contemptuous stare.

"Creekwater!" yelled the man with the flag. "Ride out!"

Tom hesitated for another endless moment, then he yanked his horse's head around and followed.

Weak to the marrow of her bones, Lacey slumped against the rough trunk of the tree. He was safe. Thank God, Ridge was safe.

Lacey thought about that moment hundreds of times in the disquieting weeks that followed. She decided that she must be trying to reconcile the reality of what happened in those next few minutes with what she had expected to happen. That was the only reason she could give herself. If she went over it enough times maybe she would understand.

For Ridge had not ridden straight over to her with that marvelous look in his eyes, that look that had made the two of them into one person after their kiss. In fact, he had felt no need to celebrate his survival with her at all.

He had dismounted and spoken with Drowning Bear, Chief Ross, and Papa. He had returned the snorting sorrel to its owner. He had gone off with the little boy whom he'd paid to watch his horse.

He had not told her good-bye. He had not so much as glanced in her direction.

Even now, on this crisp October morning, the memory stung.

She slapped her riding crop against her skirt in disgust as she climbed the steps of the veranda. And *why* had she expected anything different?

Because she was a witless dreamer.

Ridge had looked like King Arthur, riding out into battle to protect his flag. He was so brave he had made her heart stop.

She threw her crop and hat into one of the bent-willow rocking chairs on the veranda and herself into its mate. She hadn't seen Ridge Chekote since that day. Twelve endless weeks ago today.

And there had been no word. She had rushed to see the mail each time someone had brought it, but always it was only dull letters to Papa about the war and crisscrossed pages of scrawling script from relatives in Virginia. Never a note from the Canadian District with her name on it.

"Lacey?"

She jumped. "Yes?"

Papa Melton stood in the doorway. "I'm on my way to Riley's Chapel Crossing to meet a messenger from the southern districts. Your mother and I thought you might like to come with me and have a little visit with Felicity."

Her heart leapt into her throat. The southern districts! That included the Canadian. Could the messenger possibly have news of Ridge?

Her breath stopped. Could it possibly *be* Ridge?

Papa cleared his throat. "Well, Lacey? Do you want to go or not?"

They were settled on the buggy seat, ready to depart, in less than half an hour, even though Lacey had made Papa wait for her to change into her new, deep blue afternoon dress. She finished tying a matching ribbon in her hair while Mama fussed with the hampers of food and tried to tuck lap robes around their legs.

"Enough, my dear," Papa said. "We'll be dining with the Hawthornes. That is, if we haven't died of heat prostration and melted down into our woolen lap robes before we get that far."

"Hush, Mr. Melton, and do as I tell you," Mama said, smiling.

Lacey and Papa exchanged a conspiratorial glance and promised to stay all bundled up.

Then Mama frowned. "And do watch out for guerrillas and raiders. I do declare, the Cherokee are bent on destroying each other before the armies from the states even get here!"

They promised to be careful. Each of them kissed Mama good-bye.

Papa lifted the lines. "Giddy-up." He drove the gleaming matched bays at a fast trot down the lane.

Lacey relaxed and took a long breath. Today would be perfect. She would see Ridge . . . maybe. . . . For sure she would find out all the latest news from Fee.

She was going someplace at last! Mama hadn't let her leave the place all summer, and there had been little opportunity to do so since fall had come. Now she was being carried into a fairyland of colored sunshine. The oaks that lined the long driveway had turned to brilliant reds and golds. Their thick branches reached out to her from both sides of the lane.

They rolled out of the long drive and onto their branch of the Y on the Park Hill road.

Papa glanced at Lacey. "Now?"

"Now," she said. In unison, laughing, they took off their lap robes and threw them into the buggy's back seat.

At the main Park Hill road they had to wait for three overburdened wagons and their herds of livestock to go by, heading north. The man driving the first one gave Papa a hard stare. The man sitting beside him touched the brim of his hat and said, "Judge."

Nobody else greeted them, although all three

wagons held several people and Lacey recognized two girls who had attended the Female Seminary with her. She called to them, but not one of the northbound travelers spoke again while they passed in front of the Meltons' buggy.

Lacey and Papa watched them pass, silent except for the noises of wheels and hooves, and of the cattle, sheep, and hogs that they drove behind the wagons.

When they were gone, Lacey cried out, "Why wouldn't they speak to us?"

"They associate me with Chief Ross. When he signed the treaty with the Confederacy, these dyed-in-the-wool Union sympathizers decided to leave the Nation."

He clucked to the horses. "The chief had no choice," he said. "The Federal troops deserted us and the Confederates were pressing in. It was sign as allies or surrender as prisoners."

"I know," Lacey said.

"At least maybe now Stand Watie will be happy and the whole Nation can be unified."

Suddenly Lacey wanted to cry, not because the girls had ever been particularly close friends of hers but because there they were, going to some new home way up in Kansas where they had never expected to live.

How could they feel at home there when their real homes were here in the Nation? The whole world was falling apart.

Lacey looked back, hoping that at the last minute the girls would wave to her. Then things wouldn't be quite so strange. But all she saw was a small boy chasing a recalcitrant pig.

She sighed. "Well, I can imagine how they feel. A Cherokee treaty with the South surprised all of us. Especially after that day on the square when Ri——. . . I mean Mr. Chekote, risked his life to

stop Tom Creekwater and them from raising the
Confederate flag."

"I know. But it was also a way for Chief Ross
to take the leadership back from Stand Watie after
his Cherokees fought for the South at Wilson's
Creek and won."

"I wonder if Tom Creekwater was in that battle. He's such a coward, I doubt it."

"Well, don't say that where anyone can hear
you. We have a chance now to unify the Nation.
We want to be friendly toward all the factions of
the tribe, even Tom and his bunch."

"I guess I'll have to stay away from him instead."

The wonderful morning soon restored Lacey's
high spirits. It was still fairly early; a light frost
was fading from the big elms and oaks that lined
the road. Scarlet sumac waved in patches in the
fields and along the roadsides, the woods smelled
of pine and damp earth, and, far above her, the
October sky made a deep, deep well the exact
same color as her dress.

On a day like this, the messenger would be
Ridge.

They reached the Hawthornes' right at midday.
Lacey scanned the place for Ridge's big black
horse.

The rustic log inn sprawled parallel to the river,
a short way up the bank from the ferry that Felicity's family operated. Its barns and outbuildings
spread out behind. Several horses were tied to
the hitching rail in front of the inn, and two rigs
sat between it and the barn. Not one of the horses
was black.

Felicity ran out to meet them, shrieking her
welcome. "Oh, Lacey! I haven't seen you for
ages! Come in, come in."

She grabbed Lacey's hand the minute she was

down from the buggy and dragged her up the steps and across the plank-floored porch, ducking the drying gourds strung along its edge. Baskets of freshly picked apples sat in a row by the door.

The huge common room of the inn was gloomy after the crackling, brilliant outdoors. Since it still held the morning coolness, a fire burned in the big stone fireplace. The long trestle table down the center of the room was surrounded by hungry travelers; several other smaller tables were occupied as well.

Not one man in the room looked remotely like Ridge.

Mrs. Hawthorne bustled about, finding two more places at the big table. Felicity went back to her job of helping the serving girl with steaming bowls of food and filling plates and glasses. She hung around Lacey as much as possible so they could exchange bits of news and gossip.

The general conversation centered on the newly signed Cherokee/Confederate treaty.

"We had to get into the war on one side or the other," one man said.

Mr. Hawthorne, a large man who talked in a habitual mumble, agreed. "Neutrality was nothing but a dream."

He took a fresh platter of fried chicken from Fee and started it around the table.

"My brother, Eli, is one of Chief Ross's aides," Fee announced to the group at large. "He lives at Rose Cottage now with Chief and Mrs. Ross because there's so much work to do. He told me last week that we would sign with the South, so I knew it before anybody else."

Several people stopped eating and looked at her, obviously thinking of the implications of her remark.

84   GENELL DELLIN

Mr. Hawthorne spoke with uncharacteristic clarity. "Felicity," he said, "go to the kitchen."

Fee pouted. "But, Papa . . ."

"Now."

"Yes, Papa." She turned to Lacey. "Come out there as soon as you've finished eating, all right?"

Lacey was too excited to eat, anyway, and when the conversation turned to the many recent raids and killings perpetrated by the different Cherokee factions on each other, she excused herself and left the room. She wasn't going to let those awful happenings intrude on her flame-colored day.

She found Fee sitting in a swing on the porch, still pouting. "I only see a friend once in a blue moon," she said. "And then Papa sends me away."

"He thought you were telling tales out of school," Lacey said. "People might think Eli would betray Chief Ross's confidence."

"It isn't a confidence! The treaty's signed. Everybody knows it." Fee's lower lip stuck out even farther.

"Oh, well," Lacey teased, trying to comfort her. "Anyone who knows you knows that it wasn't Eli's fault. You probably wormed the secret out of him. You're famous for having to know every single thing that goes on in the entire Nation."

Felicity laughed. "I am. And I know a secret for you." She leaned close to Lacey. "Somebody's sweet on you."

Lacey's heart leaped and fluttered in her throat. Was she talking about Ridge? Had he come through here on the way home? Had he said something?

"Who?"

"Eli."

For a second the name didn't register. Finally Lacey repeated helplessly, "Eli?"

Felicity beamed. "Yes. That's something else he told me. Now that he has a job, he's going to come courting you."

She couldn't bear it, Lacey thought, not on top of everything else! If there was one thing she *didn't* want right now, it was to sit in the parlor and make boring conversation with Eli Hawthorne.

Fortunately, the sound of horses loping into the yard intruded, and she was spared having to think of a tactful reply. Both girls got up to see who had come.

Lacey's first thought was of the messenger. Could this be he? Could it, please God, be Ridge?

It wasn't. Instead of the big black, the lead horse was a scruffy roan. Instead of Ridge, its rider was Tom Creekwater.

Felicity saw him at the same time. Her hands flew to her face. "Tom!" she cried, clearly delighted.

Lacey threw her a disgusted look. "He's a renegade, Fee."

Felicity ignored her.

The half-dozen riders dismounted. Tom stood beside his horse and looked Lacey up and down.

How could he dare after cutting Ridge's cinch and holding a gun on Ridge in the square? He was probably the one who had caused the runaway, too.

"I see I'm in luck," he drawled. "What's the belle of the county doing way down here?"

Lacey and Felicity both stiffened.

"She lives here," Lacey said, putting a hand on Fee's arm. If Tom was the one Fee wanted, then she'd help her attract his attention.

But Tom barely glanced at Fee. "I meant you, Miss Lacey," he said. "And you know it."

He slapped the dust off his hat and started up the steps, his boots striking each board with deliberate intent. When he reached the top he stopped directly in front of Lacey. He brushed his hair off his forehead, then stood still, gazing down at her with his eyes full of malicious mischief.

"Long time no see," he said. "You're more beautiful than ever."

"As if you care," she said. "After you made me nearly break my neck."

"What?" Fee gasped. "What are you talking about?"

"*I* don't know, I'm sure," Tom said, still looking into Lacey's eyes. "But she's about to hurt my feelings."

"*Your* feelings!" Lacey said. "Why . . ."

He reached for her. She stepped back, but not before he'd caught hold of the blue ribbon tied in her hair. She tossed her head and the ribbon slipped from his grasp.

"Give me the ribbon," he said. "We ride with Watie soon and I want to carry it into battle."

Felicity cried out. "Battle? Oh, Tom . . ."

"What's this about a battle?" Papa Melton's voice boomed. Lacey turned to see him and Mr. Hawthorne coming out the door.

Tom whirled to face them. "We're on our way to join Stand Watie," he said. "No matter who tries to stop us." His eyes were full on Papa now, burning with defiance.

"Nobody'll try to stop you," Papa said. "We're all on the same side, now, remember?"

Tom gave him a look so hard it could cut glass. "The day *we're* on the same side of anything will be a long, cold day in hell. I mean, you being a high-and-mighty judge and a friend of the chief and all.''

"We have to be on the same side," Papa said calmly, "or the Cherokee Nation will disappear. Unity is our only hope.''

"Well, if we're so unified, how come your daughter won't give me her ribbon? All I'm askin' is a token to take into battle.''

Papa looked at Lacey.

"I won't give it!" she said.

"Please do," Papa said. "I know you want to support our troops, daughter.''

"But he . . .''

"He's going into battle. He would like to carry your ribbon.''

Lacey used the pleading look that usually melted Papa's heart, but this time he stood firm. His eyes told her to give Tom the ribbon. They never wavered.

Finally, her fingers trembling, she untied the scrap of silk.

"Thank you, daughter.''

"Thank *you*, Judge," Tom said. His tone was mock-grateful; his eyes were filled with contempt.

Papa didn't seem to notice. He and Mr. Hawthorne turned away as Tom's men began crowding up the steps and onto the porch.

"You men come inside," Mr. Hawthorne mumbled.

"Tell us your news," Papa said. "Maybe you've seen the messenger I'm waiting for.''

They all went back into the common room of the inn, but Tom lingered behind. As soon as the last man's back was turned, his hand shot out to take Lacey's hand. The ribbon tangled between their fingers.

"Think about me, Lacey. I'll be wearing your

ribbon around my arm." His fingers squeezed hers, hard. "And I'll think about you, just like you are now—so spitting mad that your eyes are shooting blue fire."

"That's exactly right . . ." she began.

But his lips covered hers as swift as thought. He kissed her.

She hit at his shoulder and struggled to get free. She pressed her lips tight together against his questing tongue.

All of a sudden he let her go. She staggered back against Fee.

He stood in front of them, legs spread wide apart, the ribbon dangling from his hand. He held it up, grinning in triumph.

"Thanks, Lacey," he said. "I'll be back soon for another one." His eyes went from the ribbon to her mouth. He turned on his heel then, and went into the inn.

Felicity gave Lacey a none-too-gentle shove. "Well, I hope you're happy, you greedy thing, you!"

Lacey stared at her. "Felicity! My stars, I didn't want him to . . ." Fury and astonishment destroyed her powers of speech. "I didn't offer . . . why, you saw . . ."

"I saw you kissing Tom Creekwater, that's what I saw! When you know that I want him to be my beau! You've betrayed our friendship, Lacey Longbaugh, and one of these days you'll wish you never had done such a thing."

Fee flung herself off the porch and ran around the side of the house. Lacey followed, but Felicity rushed in at the back door and up to her room in the loft.

Where she stayed.

So Lacey paced the garden until she thought she couldn't stand it another minute, glaring at the innocent flowers with a look that would have wilted them if the frost hadn't already done so. She wanted to run . . . to jump onto a horse and ride as fast as it could go . . . to do *something!*

She wanted to jump into the buggy, take the lines, and drive the team straight toward home at a gallop. Away from hateful, arrogant Tom Creekwater. Away from silly Fee and her unreasonable jealousy and . . .

Away from Ridge? She looked at the sun, starting its downward slide. Was there still a chance that he would come? Or that the messenger would have word of him?

Hooves clattered on the approach to the ferry. She ran toward the front of the inn. If only it could be Ridge! Then this whole miserable day would have been worth it.

Papa Melton was out on the porch when she reached it, looking toward the river. "Maybe this is our messenger, Lacey."

It turned out to be Josiah Williams from the next farm across the river, come to borrow an ax.

Papa tried to take her back inside, but she refused to enter the same room Tom Creekwater was in. She wanted to tell Papa about the stolen kiss, but she couldn't bear another scene with Tom. She just wanted him *gone* from there!

Also, if the whole countryside heard what had happened, Fee would hate her forever.

No, she could manage Tom all by herself. If he ever touched her again, she'd grab his famous gun and shoot him.

Soon, he and his men came outside, well fed and ready to ride. "Good-bye, Miss Lacey," he said, sketching her a little bow. "And I thank you again for the ribbon." Then he gave Papa that same contemptuous look. "I'll be seeing you, Judge."

Papa looked right back at him, his face impassive. "Good-bye, boys, and good luck."

They mounted, and with one grinning, backward glance from Tom, they were gone.

Papa waited until mid-afternoon, but no more riders came from the south. At last he declared it time to go—he didn't want to have Lacey out after dark when the countryside was full of raiders and marauders from all factions of the Nation.

Felicity appeared, at her mother's insistence, to bid Lacey a resentful farewell. Papa gave directions to Mr. Hawthorne in case the messenger should still arrive. Then the big bay horses pulled them out of the inn yard and down the graveled driveway.

Now it was certain that she wouldn't see Ridge today. Would she ever see him again?

The question went around in her head with every turn of the buggy's wheels.

In the course of the long drive home, Papa brought up a dozen different topics, trying, she knew, to revive her high spirits of the morning. She made an effort to respond, but now even the sunlight slanting into a blood-red stand of sumacs seemed painfully dreary.

Finally he said, "Daughter, I hope you aren't too resentful of me. I acted for the best of the Nation—it's hotheads like Creekwater that we have to tame." He smiled at her. "I'll buy you a boxful of ribbons."

He knew her very well, she thought. She *was* holding a slight grudge against him for making her give Tom the ribbon, even though she understood his reasoning. But his apology flooded her with instant forgiveness. After all, Papa didn't even know about the kiss.

She patted his arm. "Don't worry, Papa, I forgive you. And you don't have to buy me any more ribbons.''

For miles, then, they chatted comfortably, as was their habit. He was the best father she ever could have hoped for, she thought. She'd always been able to talk to him much more freely than she could to Mama.

They were driving up the Park Hill road when Lacey heard hoofbeats behind them. Mama's warnings came back into her head. Could it be marauders? Maybe some other Northern sympathizers who were angry with Chief Ross, and therefore with Papa, for signing the treaty with the Confederacy? She turned around to look.

The sun was setting, but there was still enough light to see by. The trees threw long shadows. In the low places out in the fields, especially over the ponds, fog was forming, but the road lay clear.

Papa looked back, too. ''I don't see a thing, my dear. Besides, I think it's too late for raiders to get us now. We're almost home.''

''But, Papa, it's two miles from the Y to home and we must still be almost a mile from the Y. Maybe I'd better keep watch.''

''Now you sound like your mother,'' Papa teased.

''Oh!'' she gasped. ''Speaking of Mother, we'd better not drive up to the house without putting on our lap robes.''

He laughed. ''You're right. Fetch them out and wrap us up or we're liable to be sent to bed without our suppers.''

Lacey leaned over the seat and picked up the woolen throws. She gave one more glance at the road behind them. It stretched empty. Above the long ridge to the east hung the shadow of the moon.

"Sundown's cooling us off, anyway," Papa said, as she sat down and faced front once more. "So the robes will feel good."

Lacey chose one and shook it out. She leaned over to put it across Papa's lap, the finely woven wool softly rough in her hands as he lifted the lines out of her way.

A sudden cracking noise made her lift her head. An instant later Papa slumped against her.

He jerked on the lines and the buggy swerved. Drops of liquid spattered onto her hands, and for one insane second she looked up at the sky. Could it be a sudden rain? Then she looked down at her hands and at Papa's, with the lines fast running through their square, brown fingers.

The popping sound came again. The horses sped faster. Papa pushed her almost off the seat, his shoulder in her lap.

Those noises! That snapping sound! That was a gun firing! Twice!

Those had been gunshots!

The incredible facts fell together through the shock in her brain.

Papa had been shot!

The raindrops, falling faster now, were not water at all but blood!

She screamed.

The buggy swerved, lurched to the other side of the road, and then back again.

Papa almost fell off onto the floor of the buggy.

Lacey clutched at him, still screaming, knowing that whoever had fired those shots was the only person near enough to hear.

Chapter 6

Lacey held on to Papa with all her strength. He had gone completely limp. The swaying jolts of the buggy threw them from one side to the other, striking her back against the struts that held the top, but she managed to keep them both on the seat, even when a third shot cracked through the dusk and the horses bolted for home.

Who was shooting at them? Would he never stop?

Wind rushed against her face. A heavy wetness soaked through her skirt and onto her skin.

More blood! Papa! Oh, dear God, was he dead?

What should she do? Should she halt the horses and try to stop the bleeding? How would she go about that?

Holding his slack body with one hand, she reached around him to try to grab the lines. One of them had caught on the footboard when he'd dropped them, but the other was flapping loose between the doubletree and the tongue, its end whipping at the horses' heels. She'd never be able to catch hold of that one. With only one line she could do nothing except turn them in a circle.

She could finally stop them that way, but it would be foolish when she needed to get Papa home to Dorcas.

That first rational thought steadied her. She clung to it while she wrapped the line much too tightly around her hand.

The only thing she had to do was to get Papa home to Dorcas. That was all. Dorcas could heal anyone. She knew as much as any doctor.

Lacey took a long breath of the air rushing into her face and lashed Nebo's back with the line. The team sped up; Papa lurched forward and Lacey had to use both hands to keep him from falling. Her movement pulled the line tight; the horses slowed.

With a sob of frustration, she cried out Nebo's name and then Moffett's. She lifted the line with an arm that was already aching and slapped Nebo on the back again.

The wetness spread on her skin.

Papa moaned.

Her heart leaped. He wasn't dead yet!

She braced both feet against the footboard and held him across her lap, his head heavy and limp in the crook of her arm.

Dorcas would save him. All she had to do was to get him to Dorcas. Dorcas would save him. She made those words a litany, chanting them over and over again.

The team was taking the Pleasant Prospect road before she realized they had reached the Y. Good. She didn't have to drive. All she had to do was to hold Papa. And get him to Dorcas.

The two miles home stretched longer than any twenty miles she'd ever traveled. Night fell before they had gone halfway; foggy darkness clutched at the buggy wheels. There was no sign of the moon.

She whipped up the horses.

Papa moaned again and gave a strangled cough. She held him until she thought her arms would break. The wetness seemed to have lessened. Was that a good sign, or did it mean he was dead?

"Giddy-up," she cried to the team. She pursed her dry lips and gave a commanding whistle. "Hurry!"

They sped up, but not as much as she'd hoped. Her blood chilled. Oh, God, please don't let them tire now.

She decided not to think about that nor about Papa's wound. Instead, she imagined what it would be like when they came safely home, surely just a few seconds from now. Dorcas and Mama would come rushing out of the house; Old Jasper and Linch would carry Papa inside, and Dorcas would stop the bleeding.

But the lonely darkness and Papa's helpless weight in her arms kept driving her fantasy away.

At the very moment when she thought she could not hold on for a second longer, the horses slowed and, of their own accord, turned in at the end of the lane.

Lacey opened her mouth to yell for help, but the wind pushed into it and carried the sound away.

When they passed beneath the huge black locust tree, she started hauling back on the line. The team would try to run all the way to the barn, no doubt, and she had to get Papa into the house.

The horses slowed. She pulled again. They came to a heaving stop at the foot of the front steps. Tears rushed to her eyes. Her arms trembled so that she was afraid she'd drop Papa.

Home! They'd made it home. Everything would be all right.

The windows showed light, but the door didn't open.

"Who be there?" Old Jasper's thin voice called. "Who drivin' in here so fast?"

Of course. How could she have forgotten? These days everybody in the country was suspicious of raiders.

Words wouldn't come through her cracked lips on the first try. Finally she called, "It's me." Her voice grew into a shout. "Help me, Jasper! Get Dorcas! Papa's been shot!"

She took a deep breath and screamed, "Dorcas!"

The door opened; light poured out. Hurrying feet sounded on the porch. Somebody called inside the house.

"Dorcas!" Lacey screamed again.

Then she bent over Papa, trying to see his wound, even while she went weak with dreading to see it. Oh, dear Lord, had she gotten him home alive? They had to get him into the house, stretch him out.

Even in the shadows she could tell that blood had soaked the front of his coat as well as the back. That made it impossible to find the bullet's point of entry.

But wherever the bullet had gone, Dorcas could get it out. Dorcas could save him.

Lacey lifted her head. Old Jasper, Linch, and Dorcas were running down the steps. Behind them loomed a taller shadow.

Her eyes wouldn't leave it. A second later, two strides nearer, and she knew. It was Ridge.

She went as still as glass. How could he be here? It was a miracle!

All of them surrounded her, hands reaching.

Ridge's eyes caught hers. "Are you hurt, too, Lacey?"

She shook her head. "No."

She wanted to fall off the buggy seat and into his arms. Thank God he was here. Ridge and Dorcas together could do anything.

Ridge turned to see about Papa. Dorcas and Jasper were already tugging at the limp form; Ridge brushed them aside. He gathered Papa into his arms and lifted him.

His stiff coat stuck on Lacey's dress, then came away with a little ripping sound where the blood had glued them together.

"Miss Lacey? Honey! You all right?" Dorcas reached for Lacey.

As much as Lacey needed the comfort, she pushed her maid away. "I'm all right. Go. See about Papa."

Ridge turned and started up the steps. Dorcas ran to catch up. Lacey, too numb to move, stared after them. Old Jasper pulled at her arm. She let him lift her down. He helped her all the way up the steps, her legs so stiff and cramped she could barely walk.

Linch came around to take her other arm. "You sees to them hosses, boy," Old Jasper told him. "And you does it now. They's plumb lathered."

Grumbling, Linch left them.

Once in the house, the sound of Dorcas's voice put the strength back into Lacey's legs. She followed it to the parlor, Old Jasper still clinging to her arm.

Ridge was stretching Papa out on the settee, taking the boots off his feet. Dorcas was bending over his chest, already cutting the blood-soaked clothes away.

Mama was standing in the middle of the room, not moving a muscle.

Lacey ran toward her, desperate to feel someone's arms around her, desperate for comfort after all she'd been through. Someone had to take care of *her* now that her awful responsibility was over.

Mama took one look at her, turned back to Papa, and fainted dead away.

Lacey cried, "Mama!"

Dorcas threw them one fast glance. "Her smellin' salts in her pocket," she said. "Use 'em fast. Then get me plenty rags from the bin in the pantry. My salves and potions be right above on the shelf. Jasper, put some water to boil."

Lacey fumbled for Mama's pocket, sobbing now.

"Shall I go to the quarters and fetch the other servants?" Ridge asked.

Dorcas stared at him.

"Miss Lacey can hardly help you," he said. "She's been through an ordeal . . . and Mrs. Melton . . ."

"Sir, ain't no other servants," Dorcas snapped. "Shiftless cowardly scums o' the earth done gone north when Chief Ross sign with the South. Only Timmy stay, and he simple. Him and us three."

"Then I'll help you."

She gave one sharp nod, her eyes never leaving Papa. "Put your finger here and press hard as you can."

Then, to Lacey's astonishment, Dorcas lifted her skirt. She took hold of her starched white petticoat and started tearing it into strips.

After that, time went by in a blur, everything that happened seeming equally as strange as Dorcas showing her underwear in front of a man. Mama finally came to, but she simply sat on the other settee, uncharacteristically silent. Old Jasper brought scarred, battered sawhorses from the shed and set them up on the beautiful Brussels carpet in the parlor. Ridge took the polished door off its hinges and laid it across them, then he picked Papa up again and laid him on the door.

Lacey got the rags and the salves, ran to the

barn to send Linch for the doctor, carried water to wash Papa, and got whiskey to soak Dorcas's tools in.

Then she worked side by side with Jasper, bringing tapers from the basement and putting them into candle stands, finding tables to hold the sconces, and arranging them all around one end of the door. Dorcas needed lots of light.

Dorcas and Ridge decided Papa was too weak for her to probe for the bullet. Or bullets. Maybe two of them had hit him.

Maybe two of them had killed him.

An awful, eerie feeling settled over Lacey. Time stopped running. The sweet, coppery smell of blood filled the parlor. Papa's breath rasped in and out, softly.

Lacey's bones turned to porcelain—she couldn't move fast or they would break.

Dorcas kept working over Papa, but she didn't give Lacey any more orders. She hardly spoke, and Mama didn't say one word. She did get up, though, and walk over to Papa. She stood very still, right by his head, and reached out one hand to hold his. The candles made a shield of yellow light around them.

Everything stayed that way for the longest time.

Then Papa's rasping breath stopped.

Just that quick.

Silence held them all helpless.

After an eon, Mama turned and walked out of the room. Her feet made a tiny, scuffing noise on each step of the stairs.

Dorcas began to cry. She closed Papa's eyes and crossed his hands below the awful wound. "You all leave this room," she said. "I's goin' to be the one to lay him out."

Lacey's mind rebelled. No! He *wasn't* dead.

There must be help somewhere. They ought to wait for the doctor. Where was Linch?

But she knew he couldn't have gotten any farther than Rose Cottage by now.

Suddenly Ridge stood in front of her. "Let me take you to your room," he said. "You need to lie down."

He took her hand and helped her up. She walked beside him through the door and across the foyer, up the stairs and down the hall.

The moonlight sifted through its wide end windows, pale as chalk. She stopped at her door. "I'll bring you some water for washing," he said.

She lifted her head and looked at him. "Not yet," she said.

He wrapped his arms around her and pulled her close. She leaned against him, soaking up his warmth. She wanted to cry, but she was too tired.

"Poor, dear Lacey," he murmured. "What a dreadful day you have had."

It felt so good to be comforted. For an endless age now, *she* had been the responsible one . . . ever since the first deadly crack of that rifle.

Her arms went around his waist and she hugged him. He tightened his hold. For a long moment they clung to each other. Then she felt his hand on her hair, one quick caress.

"You go in, now," he said. His hands gripped her shoulders, then slid down her arms to loosen her grip on him. "I'll leave some water just outside your door. Try to sleep. I'm here to sit up with your papa." He turned and left her.

She leaned against the doorjamb and listened to the sound of his boots going away. They struck the hard oak boards of the floor with a lonesome thud.

* * *

When she returned to the parlor she thought at first that Ridge was asleep. He sat beside Papa on a straight chair from the dining room, staring at the east window. The other dining chairs were arranged in a row on each side of the body, waiting for more mourners to come tomorrow. Only four candles burned now, two at Papa's head and two at his feet. He wore a different suit, and most of the smell of blood was gone.

Ridge wore different clothes, too, as did she. All the bloodstains were gone.

Oh, if only washing them away could have brought Papa back to life!

But there he lay, as still as midnight.

She walked in and took a chair.

"Lacey, you don't have to do this, you know."

"Yes, I do."

"How is your mother?"

"Silent. She won't say one word. She's lying in bed with her face to the wall."

"She'll probably be better tomorrow; she has to get used to the idea."

"I'll never get used to it. I don't see how *she* can."

"It takes a long time, but you do finally believe it at last."

He sounded as if he really knew. Of course. His wife and his baby had died.

"Ridge, thank you. I know this must be hard for you. What would I have done if you hadn't been here?"

"You'd have sat up by yourself."

"No, I mean it—God must have sent you. How *did* you come to be here today? Did you try to meet us at Riley's Chapel Crossing?"

"Yes, but I was too late. The last place I stopped to get a count I had to ride way out into the man's oat fields to talk to him."

"A count of what?"

"Cherokee volunteers for the Confederacy. We're forming a regiment and maybe a company or two. I'm bringing the numbers to Chief Ross."

"We waited as long as we could. Papa wanted to be home before dark." Her voice broke on the last word.

"I figured that, so I cut across country to see him here."

"It's all that man's fault," she said, a wild anger growing inside her with each word. "Every bit of it! Papa would be alive now if he had been at his house to meet you instead of in the fields! What is his name, anyway?"

Ridge shook his head. "It doesn't matter, honey. You're just looking for somebody to be mad at. *Somebody* to blame because it isn't fair for the judge to die."

She thought about that. Then, more quietly, she said, "I wanted to come home sooner. It was an awful day, even before the . . . shooting."

She started talking and she couldn't stop. The sound of her own voice soothed her somehow; maybe it made her feel she was actually *doing* something about this horror.

Or maybe she felt that if she examined every minute of the fateful day she could change its ending. She began with Papa's invitation to accompany him and relived the entire day.

Except for Tom's kissing her. She told Ridge all about the ribbon and how angry that had made her, but when she came to the kiss she paused, quiet for a minute.

Ridge waited.

The incredible anger rose in her again—this time directed at Tom. Maybe Ridge would swear to find Tom and kill him for taking her ribbon. Maybe he would be jealous and say that from now on Lacey should give ribbons only to him, to Ridge.

Instead, he said, "Do you think it could have been Tom who ambushed the judge?"

"No. He and his men had been gone for a long time, heading for Watie's camp."

"Then why did you stop in the middle of your story? What happened after Tom took your ribbon?"

She couldn't tell him. He might think she had encouraged Tom in some way. As Felicity had. She couldn't tell him about that, either—it would sound like tacky gossip from one silly girl about another.

So she said, "He and his men went into the inn to eat and I went walking in the garden."

She recounted the rest of the terrible day, not breaking down even when she told about the shooting and the awful drive home. She felt drained and dry and hollow inside. There were tears, somewhere, deep in the center of her, but she had no hope of getting them out.

Once she had finished they sat quiet for a long time. The candles flickered, throwing shadows where none had been before.

Ridge put his hand on her shoulder. "You'd best go and lie down now," he said, speaking so gently that it made her shiver. "Half the Nation will come to pay their respects during the next few days; you must be strong to help your mother receive the people."

"No. I don't want to be alone. Talk to me. Please."

His melodious voice took her out of that room to his plantation on the Canadian River. He talked about his crops and described the big white house sitting in a grove of old cottonwood trees. Its name was River's Bend.

He told her about his horses, most kin in some way to his tall black, and about the steamboat he'd bought to take his crops down the river to market.

That place was his life, she realized. When he talked about it he was more relaxed than she had ever seen him and there was love in his voice.

"I'll be a man favored by God if River's Bend comes through the war still standing," he said. "This whole country is liable to lie in ruins."

An awful feeling swept through her. It made her feel that the center of her being was a hollow hole with cold wind blowing through it.

For the first time, even though she had been hearing such talk for months and months, she actually knew that it was all true.

Life as they knew it was ending.

Even if the war from the states didn't reach them, the Cherokee factional fighting was already laying waste to the Nation. Nothing, not even the Confederate treaty, could stop it.

Papa was dead, almost all of the servants were gone, Mama was acting like a stranger—her world was crumbling down around her head.

Fear grew in the pit of her stomach and exploded all through her body. Goose bumps popped out on her arms. She hugged herself, shivering, although Jasper had kept the fire in the fireplace burning steadily.

She didn't dare look at Ridge. If she did, she would run into his arms, begging him to stay and protect her. She couldn't face this hard new world alone.

A wailing sounded outside. It floated in through the open window like a new presence in the house.

Lacey froze.

The crying came again, and then a rhythm

started. She could hear words, but she didn't understand them. After a moment she realized the words were in Cherokee.

"Drowning Bear," Ridge said. "To drive away the nightwalkers."

"But . . . how? How did he know that Papa was . . . dead?"

"He knew. Most of the Nation will know by morning."

Drowning Bear's words faded and then grew stronger again as he moved to each of the four corners of the house.

Ridge and Lacey sat listening, smelling the smoke of the medicine man's strong tobacco when he had worked his way around to the east side again.

They didn't talk anymore until the sun had risen.

The full-bloods who lived around Papa's old home arrived before good daylight. All the immediate neighbors to Pleasant Prospect had come by mid-morning. Chief and Mrs. Ross were the first, bringing servants to help Dorcas and a buggy load of food. Eli Hawthorne and two other young aides of the chief came with them.

Ridge stood beside Lacey while they filed by to pay their respects. From behind his glasses Eli's dark eyes kept flicking from Ridge to Lacey and back again. When all the others had spoken to her and moved on, he lingered.

"Step out onto the porch with me, Lacey," he said. "You need some fresh air."

She glanced around, somehow startled at the idea. She hadn't left this room for hours. She had forgotten that she could.

Several men had taken the straight chairs to sit with Papa for a while. Ridge was strolling out into the hallway with Chief Ross, deep in conversation. She could go outside.

She let Eli lead her to the side veranda. The day was breathtaking: golden trees embraced the house; birds chattered cheerfully in all their branches; the sky was so blue that it went on forever; the green-and-brown land lay content and fallow.

How could that be? The whole world should be mourning.

"I feel so sorry for you, Lacey," Eli said, taking her hand. "And I want you to know that I'll do anything to help you. I'm just a few miles away, you know. All you have to do is send word and I'll be here in no time."

Tears sprang to her eyes. He truly was a friend. He cared that she was hurting.

"Thank you, Eli."

He took her other hand and held them both. His hands felt soft and a bit sweaty. He swallowed hard. "Lacey," he said. "I've been thinking. I care about you a great deal."

She smiled at him, hardly listening to his words, clinging to his fingers curled around hers. He seemed truly concerned.

"I was planning to ask the judge if I could call on you," he said. "But now . . ."

"Yes, Eli?"

"I don't want to bother your mama on a day like this," he said, "but when I saw Mr. Chekote here again . . ."

He wasn't making a great deal of sense, but then, he was upset. Eli had admired Papa very much. This was a shock to him, too.

"Well, I just have to know right now," he blurted. "Lacey, may I come calling on you?"

She stared at him. Hadn't he just told her that

he was going to see about her and that he would
be at Rose Cottage if she needed him?

"Of course, Eli," she said. "I'll be depending
on you."

During the sad days that followed she did depend on him, and on many other friends from all
over the Nation. She could never have managed
everything without them. But it was Ridge she
needed most; she kept him beside her every minute that she could.

Without him, she felt too alone. Mama got up
only to come to the parlor for the funeral service
and to see Papa buried in the family graveyard on
the side of the hill. Then she went back to bed.

Ridge counseled patience. "She'll come out of
it," he said. "Grief is a terrible thing."

He said it again on the morning he was to leave.

Lacey stood in the door of the barn, racking her
brain for the words to make him stay.

"I don't think she will get over it, Ridge. She
told me yesterday that she has no desire to live."

"That'll change," he said, making one last
sweep with the brush down the black's long legs.
"Give her some time."

"I don't *have* any time. That letter came yester-
day wanting to know how much hay we'll sell
. . . Mr. Goingsnake asked about the oats. . . .
Ridge, I don't know what to do about any of it."

She tried to catch his eye, but he kept his back
to her. He threw the brush into his saddlebag and
picked up his saddle pad.

"Keep every bushel and every bale right here,"
he said. "It won't be long until two armies and
God knows how many different bands of renegades will be trying to take it all away from you."

"If that's true, how can you go away and leave

me?'' The words burst out, pushed by the welling tears in her throat.

He didn't even glance her way. "You have good neighbors and friends," he said.

She stepped closer to him, into the wide aisle where the tall black was tied. The rich barn smells of horses and hay, manure and leather, and long-aging secrets filled her nostrils.

But today they didn't comfort her as they usually did. There had been no comfort any place since Ridge had told her that he would leave for home on this day.

He arranged the pad on Blackjack and threw his saddle on top of it. Then he turned and looked at her.

"Take your mother and go back to Virginia, Lacey. Go while you still can."

Each unexpected word slashed at her. Not *I'll stay here and help you, Lacey.* Not *I'll see that you are protected.* No. Maybe he had stood by her in her grief, but in the end he wanted to be rid of her.

"You're trying to get rid of me," she blurted.

His eyes were very dark and very steady. "I can't take care of you, Lacey. You are not my responsibility."

Tears sprang to her eyes. Her lips grew stiff with the effort not to cry.

Well, then, damn him, let him go.

She whirled on her heel and stalked out into the early, slanting sunshine. But then she turned to watch him.

He bent beneath the horse's belly and caught the latigo strap. He ran it through the ring again and again. He made a circle of the leather strap, then pulled it through itself. He jerked it tight.

He was as graceful as a panther. And just as dangerous to her heart.

He slid the halter off, bridled the horse, and tied on his saddlebags. He led the horse out of the barn. Without a glance at Lacey, he stepped to the side of the black and mounted, but neither he nor the horse moved.

Finally he turned. "Come here."

She walked to the horse.

He leaned sideways from the saddle and cupped the back of her head. His hand was so strong that it pulled her to him like a river's current, so hot that it burned her skin through her hair. His chiseled cheekbones gleamed in the morning light as he bent to kiss her, his solemn eyes glittered with their mysterious, dark light. Then his mouth swept over hers like a fierce, wild fire that utterly consumed her, taking the soul right out of her body. She closed her eyes and gave it up to him.

Her surrender held him spellbound, a prisoner, for an endless moment. He drank in her shattering sweetness with his lips and tongue, unable to stop, powerless to part from her. Her tongue twined around his, her lips clung to his with a plea that threatened to break his heart. He had to leave her. Now. Or he would never be able to go.

He released her and kneed the horse into a fast lope.

She stood on that spot until he had disappeared beneath the swaying branches of the trees.

The two weeks after Ridge left were the most harrowing of Lacey's life. She worked from first light until long after dark getting the plantation ready for winter. Babe remained in her bed, except for rare trips across her room to sit by the window. Every decision, every choice—and she learned quickly that making the wrong choice could mean disaster for them all—fell on Lacey's head.

Neither of the armies from the war in the states had been seen in the district yet, but bands of guerrillas using the war as an excuse plagued the countryside. Bands of horsemen were striking at will and carrying off or destroying winter supplies from big and small farms alike.

The weather was still much too warm for killing hogs, but they gathered and stored every other kind of food (for animals as well as for people) that the plantation provided. Lacey worked harder than all the servants combined.

Then, in ironic contrast to Pleasant Prospect's wide reputation for openhanded hospitality, she had to think of hiding places for the food they had gathered.

She and Dorcas carried pumpkins and squash, onions and potatoes behind a false partition they built in the root cellar; Old Jasper and Linch made a covered shelter for bales and bales of hay deep in one of the stretches of woods by the river. All of them threw up a makeshift corral nearby, for if they had enough warning of marauders they would drive the animals in there.

Lacey let the unremitting work numb her emotions, especially her longing for Ridge. ·

Until one nerve-racking day when it seemed that no one spoke to her except to ask a question, Papa's Thoroughbred got out and cut his hock on a fence that needed mending, and Simple Timmy fell into the creek and almost drowned.

As soon as he was safe on the muddy bank, she sat down on a log and cried. She'd certainly never envisioned anything like *this* when she'd dreamed of making all the decisions. Being grown-up wasn't one bit as she'd thought it would be.

At that minute she would have traded all her independence gladly for somebody to make the decisions for her. For somebody to take care of her.

That evening with Mama was more troubling than usual. Just looking at her curled up in her cocoon of wrinkled bedclothes made Lacey want to scream. It had been too long now—far too long—for her to still be so silent, so apathetic.

She bent over and shouted at Babe as if she were deaf. "You've got to get up and help me, Mama! You've got to! It'll help you, too. Dorcas says you're liable to lose the use of your legs!"

Dorcas came in at that moment, but she didn't even glance at Babe. "Horsemen here, Miss Lacey. Already in the yard."

Lacey's hand went still on Babe's shoulder. "Who?"

"Don't know. I just now heered 'em."

"Drat that Linch!" Lacey said. "He's supposed to keep watch." She ran out of the room and started down the stairs. The front door opened and a man stepped through it into the early evening gloom.

She stopped in her tracks.

"Who are you? What do you think you're doing?"

He chuckled. The sound made her heart stop.

"Why, moving into my new headquarters, Lacey, my darlin'. Me and my men."

Tom Creekwater strode across the foyer and started up the stairs to meet her.

She tried to move, but not one muscle would obey her mind's commands. The sleek, oiled banister went cold under her hand.

"From now on, you don't need to fear one thing; we'll all be here to protect you and your sweet mama."

The light from the upstairs hallway slanted across his face, and she could see the smile that she used to find so charming. The sour smell of whiskey enveloped her.

He stopped on the stair below her and watched her for a moment. When he spoke again his voice was hardly louder than a whisper.

"Lacey, love, smile at me. I'm the answer to your prayers. Why, I'd be willing to bet good money that you've just been wishing for somebody to take care of you."

He reached up and ran his hand along her arm.

Chapter 7

R idge smelled the smoke before his steamboat docked at River's Bend. At first he didn't distinguish it from the fumes puffing out of the boat's smokestack; he was leaning on the rail, watching October leaves swirl past on the water, thinking of Lacey.

This homecoming was just like his last one in that way—he couldn't seem to banish her from his mind. He had thought it would be different, making a leisurely river voyage back to River's Bend from Webbers Falls instead of the hard ride straight home from Pleasant Prospect, but it was not so: He still longed to have her waiting for him. She was always with him in his spirit, tormenting him because she wasn't beside him in the flesh.

He pushed his hat onto the back of his head and turned away from the rail. The *Canadian Star* was almost home; he had his own plantation to take care of and other, older memories to exorcise. He had to forget her.

Captain Pettit crossed the deck, bellowing instructions to the deckhands as they prepared to dock at the plantation's private pier. The breeze brought another sweetly acrid, burning whiff to Ridge's nostrils.

He raised his head and looked toward the house, hidden in the cottonwoods atop the hill. A small black form was hurtling down the long slope to the river. It was Coody, the houseboy.

He came closer, wailing, then closer yet, until finally Ridge could hear the words.

"Raiders!" he cried. "Mistah Ridge! Raiders!"

Ridge swung over the rail and jumped to the dock, running as soon as his feet touched down. He met the boy halfway. Coody turned when Ridge reached him and they ran together toward the house.

The odor of burning doubled. Tripled. Were the raiders still here? Ridge pulled out his pistol.

"No need," Coody gasped. "They . . . gone since sunup."

Ridge replaced the weapon in its holster, his eyes searching his beloved place as he ran. When they reached the crest of the hill he could see that the white house, two-story and massive, still stood.

But the barns, hay, and livestock had disappeared, leaving masses of charred, smoking wood in their places and chaos spread out in every direction. The smokehouse and outhouse lay overturned at crazy angles, fences gaped open, broken windows and smashed doors dangled from the servants' quarters. Around the big house pieces of furniture littered the yard.

Ridge sucked in a great gulp of air.

"Was . . . Donner Beck," Coody said, still panting. "He say tell you this here's 'cause you rode to Tahlequah. He say yore life be next."

"Not if I see him first." The inadequacy of his words tore a bitter laugh from Ridge. They couldn't begin to express the rage surging in his gut. "Anybody killed?"

"No, just run off. Six of us left, plus Jenny."

"The horses?"

"All I could save wuz Blackjack."

"Good work!" Ridge gave the boy's shoulder a grateful squeeze.

"Hid him in the canebrake," Coody bragged. "Nearly jerk my arm off—he hate them caney smells."

Ridge started for the house, the boy sticking close to his side. Martha's yellow brocade chair lay on its side in the flower bed. The sight made the back of his head burn hot, then cold.

"By God, I'll kill Donner Beck for this," he said tightly, "and every low-down son of a bitch who rides with him."

"Yeah!" Coody said. "I he'p you, Mistah Ridge!"

Ridge bounded up the steps, across the porch, and into the house. What he saw inside made his jaw clench so hard he couldn't speak another word.

Martha's sewing basket lay overturned in the foyer, a muddy boot track glaring up from a piece of its white linen. Broken china and crystal winked from the dining room floor, sparkling in the noon sunshine.

He turned away and ran for the stairs. Maybe the most important things were still there.

That hope died at his bedroom door. The cedar chest stood at the foot of the bed—open and empty. Snatches of Martha's fine handwriting, blue against the white pieces of shredded stationery, glinted at him from all over the room. They blew gently about on the rug, rising and falling in rhythm with the swaying curtains.

He stepped into the room and his heart contracted. Edwin's tiny baby clothes! Torn to pieces!

His heart tightened into a leaden ball in his

chest. What about the baby's portrait? Only one had ever been painted. Had they found it, too?

They had. The tray of the cedar chest lay up-ended beside the bed. It held nothing but the baby's watercolor miniature—the heavy paper ripped in two from top to bottom.

Ridge snatched it up and held the pieces together. Edwin's solemn face looked back at him, now scarred forever between his baby eyes.

The pieces could barely stay together because his hands were shaking so. Here was more proof that he never should've married Martha and they never should have had a child: He hadn't been able to keep them from leaving River's Bend and getting killed. Now he couldn't even protect his only mementos of them.

He took one more long look at his son, then stacked the pieces of the picture together and wrapped them into his handkerchief. He placed the little package carefully in the inside breast pocket of his coat.

Where was Martha's portrait? Had they torn it up, too?

Ridge pawed through torn clothing and scraps of paper, picked up drawers dumped from the chiffonier, and searched under the bed. Gone. Not even the pieces were left.

He stood staring, unseeing, at the painful mess of the room. He couldn't remember what Martha looked like anymore, not even when he really tried. For weeks now, right before he went to sleep, the only face he could see had been Lacey's.

Guilt flooded through him.

But on its heels rushed a desire so strong his hands began to shake again—he wanted to take this sickening hurt to Lacey. This time it was *he* who needed to walk into the comfort of *her* arms and stand in the slanting moonlight at her door.

"Boss?"

Ridge jerked around to face the door.

"We gone ride after 'em, now?"

Coody wore a makeshift holster holding an ancient pistol half as long as his leg. His eyes, wide and trusting, held Ridge's.

Ridge stared at the boy. He was so young and so loyal.

So utterly innocent.

In a fight he'd be the first to go down as hundreds of innocents all over the Nation had already done.

Boys like Coody shouldn't die. And they should respect the law.

"We gon' kill them thievin' sons-a-bitches, Mistah Ridge?"

Ridge looked him in the eye. The blood pounded so hard in his temples he could hear it.

"No. I've decided to use the law, Coody. I'll ride to Tahlequah and take the Lighthorse with me."

"Naw!" the boy protested. "How come?"

"Because if I don't I'll be as bad as they are. There's law in the Nation and it has to stand." The words rolled bitterly off his tongue and he wished he could call them back. But he couldn't.

The Nation lay sickened already under so much killing. It would be destroyed before the war from the states ever reached it if every man kept taking the law into his own hands.

"Saddle Blackjack for me, please, Coody. Find me some camping tools and tell Jenny I need a flask of whiskey and as much food as I can pack. It may take us a week or two to find Beck."

Coody's shoulders drooped.

"Thanks for the offer to ride," Ridge said, "but

I'll need you here to help look after River's Bend.''

The boy went away, grumbling, his gun bumping against his leg.

Ridge took a deep breath and tried to force everything from his mind but the task at hand. He found several pieces of his clothing intact in the bottom of the armoire and packed them with his bedroll. He picked up the monogrammed, silver-handled comb, brush, and mirror that Martha had given him and wrapped them in soft cloths without letting himself consciously think of her.

He packed soap from the broken bowl on the dry sink, and his buckskin shirt and pants with the hunting knife that he always kept sharp. He planned the route he would take (he would go straight to Rose Cottage) and what he would say to Chief Ross.

All without ever once acknowledging the thought that was strongest of all in the back of his consciousness: After he stopped at Rose Cottage he would take this awful pain and go to Lacey.

Just the sight of her face would make it all better.

Lacey watched from the cover of the snowball bush until the last of Tom's men entered the summer kitchen. That should be all of the lookouts at breakfast now; the others were bedding down to sleep after their night ride.

She slipped out into the open, picked up her skirts, and started for the stables at a run. For a few minutes no one would be guarding the horses; she could saddle Lady and ride for help.

The thought made her blood pound with joy. If she had to spend one more day cowering in her mother's room to avoid Tom's advances, she would go crazy.

Early morning sunshine glinted off the frost on the grass. A sharp breeze from the southeast lifted her hair as she ran. On such a perfect day she couldn't fail.

Lacey ran around the corner, heading for the door that opened beneath the stable's overhang. It lay in shadow, and she had almost reached it before she realized that someone was there.

Tom stood in the wide opening with his feet braced wide, his arms folded across his chest. He was covered in dust; his eyes were bloodshot. They must have ridden a long way last night.

She skidded to a stop, so close to him that he could reach out and touch her.

He did.

He unfolded his arms and placed his hands on her shoulders with a flourish, as if accepting a gift.

She held her breath.

"Miss Lacey," he drawled. "I seen you hiding in the bushes and I thought you might be headed this way." He smiled lazily. "You know, to welcome me home after a hard night's work."

Her skin tried to crawl out of his grasp.

"I know you're tired, Tom," she said sweetly, forcing the words past the knot of fear in her throat. She tried to smile, too. "I won't keep you from your rest."

"I hate to rest alone."

She felt her cheeks flame.

"Want me to lay you down?"

"No!"

She tried to twist away. He laughed and tightened his grip until pain shot through her shoulders.

"Stop it, Tom! You're hurting me!"

"Too bad," he growled. "You're supposed to say yes."

She lifted her chin and looked him straight in the eye, trying for her haughtiest stare.

"Don't use that look on me," he said. "I'll have you, and I'll have you tonight. The only reason I don't take you right here and now is that I ain't the stable boy."

He dug his fingers deep into her flesh and pulled her face so close it almost touched his.

"I'm as good as any beau in this Nation that ever come courtin' you," he said, "and I'm sick of waitin' for you to treat me that way."

"No other beau in this Nation would treat me *this* way," she said coldly.

"I wanted you to be willing," he said, biting off every word in that sharp, cruel way he had. "I've told you that for nearly a week. Well, time's up. Tonight at sundown you be in that fancy parlor of your mama's waitin' for me to come callin' like you would for anybody in the cream of society." He shook her. "You hear me?"

She stared at him, stubbornly silent.

His lips thinned into a hard line. "I aim for us to set in the parlor, drinkin' tea and talkin'," he said. "And then, willing or not, I'm taking you to your own fancy bed."

"No other beau in the Nation would do *that*, either."

"Shut up!"

His mouth came down on hers. He kissed her forever and ever, setting her stomach churning, bruising her lips and cutting her tongue, sending the blood pounding to her brain with awful images of the evening to come.

She couldn't bear it. She absolutely could not bear it.

Ridge! If only Ridge would suddenly ride into the yard the way he had that first time! The way she dreamed that he did every single, sleepless night.

At last the kiss was over and she stood shaking, gasping for breath. But Tom's hands still gripped her shoulders.

She gathered all her strength. "That's the second time you've forced your attentions on me," she said scornfully. "Don't you ever do it again."

He slapped her, fast, a blow so hard that her head rang and her vision blurred.

"Tonight," he whispered, "willing or not."

He dragged her back to the house, walking so fast that she stumbled behind him, and ordered two of his men to watch the front and back doors.

"Sundown," he said softly, and pushed her, shaking, into her room. "Wear your prettiest dress."

Ridge dozed off in the saddle, then jerked awake when the black stumbled. He would have to stop somewhere; he'd ridden steadily for so many hours he'd lost count. It would be night again in an hour or two.

Thank God he'd had enough sense to stop at Tahlonteeskee and buy a second horse. If he hadn't, the black would've been ruined by now.

He reined Blackjack to a stop so he could take his bearings. The little bay mare he was leading trotted up beside him and stopped, too, throwing up her head to sniff the air. She whinnied.

Ridge caught the scent of water. So, he was nearing the river; he could stay the night at the Hawthornes' inn and still be at Rose Cottage by noon tomorrow.

And at Pleasant Prospect by the middle of the afternoon.

He gathered the reins and the lead rope and

smooched to the black. They headed in a slanting line across the wide, flat river bottom to find the ferry.

Lacey caught her mother's arm as she turned away and tried again to slip it into the sleeve of the coat; Babe jerked loose and put both hands on her hips. She glared at Lacey and opened her mouth, but still she didn't say a word.

This would all be worth it if it would make her talk again, Lacey thought. It actually would.

"Mama, we have to hurry," she murmured. "We must go just when it starts to get dark."

Babe shook her head and dropped into the armless sewing rocker by the window.

Lacey buttoned her own coat and glanced around frantically for a cover for Babe. That afternoon she'd used every last blanket to make a rope long enough to reach the ground.

She opened the small chest at the foot of the bed and snatched out a soft woolen shawl. It wasn't very heavy, but then Babe wouldn't need it for long; they'd be at Rose Cottage within an hour.

Lacey threw the shawl over her arm and ran to the window for the hundredth time. Careful not to move the lace curtains for fear one of Tom's men would notice, she peered out. Dusk was coming, but the sun wasn't quite gone yet.

Tom would look for her in the parlor at sundown—that was the moment she wanted to be going out the window with Mama. Any earlier and the lookouts would see them; any later and Tom would be coming up the stairs.

She glanced at her barricade: an oak chiffonier so heavy that she had barely been able to scoot it into place in front of the door. Surely that would keep Tom out until they could escape.

For the hundredth time, too, she tested the rope

of sheets and blankets. Following it back from its coil beneath the window, pulling every knot tight, she prayed that each one would hold.

She knelt to make sure that the last quilt was securely fastened beneath the fat, round poster of the bed. That alone had taken forever, slipping the cloth beneath the heavy post, inch by inch. Thank goodness, Dorcas had helped her with that.

Lacey gave the shining wood a last pat and ran back to her mother, who was rocking silently back and forth, back and forth.

"Come on, Mama," she whispered, trying to pull Babe to her feet. "Put on this shawl. We're leaving now."

The parlor was empty; the heavy furniture sat vacant, the candles stood dark in their sconces. Tom grabbed one of them and lit it. He walked into the room, anyway, even though he knew no one was there, and looked into every corner as if Lacey might be hiding somewhere.

She was hiding all right. Behind her mother's skirts again.

She wasn't going to sit in the parlor with him, not ever. She still thought she was too good for that.

He blew out the candle and threw it at a china figurine. It flew from the table and broke when it hit the floor.

Good. He'd do the same thing to Lacey if she didn't start treating him like quality.

He left the room and headed up the stairs, making his bootheels thunder against the planks of the floor. When he reached Mrs. Melton's room he grabbed the doorknob and turned it. When the door wouldn't open he crashed his fist against it.

"Come out of there, Miss High and Mighty,"

he shouted. "Don't make me wait another minute."

Lacey froze at the open window, one hand on her mother's arm, the other on the makeshift rope.

Tom knocked again, a horrible cracking noise that threatened to split the wood itself.

"I'm taking care of my mama," Lacey called, trying to keep her voice steady. "She's sick."

"I'll take care of you," he shouted. "I'll put the both of you flat on your backs. Then you can see if you can look down your noses at a Creekwater!"

Lacey squeezed Babe's arm so tightly that the woman whimpered. Tom hit the door again. "That might do old Babe some good. She's always thought she was made out of better mud than us Creekwaters; I'll show her she's just like any other woman in this country."

Lacey gasped and threw her arm around her mother. Tom's footsteps moved away from the door, and she let out a sigh.

But then, in a still louder shout, Tom yelled, "Watty! Bring me the ax!"

A little while before dark Ridge's black trotted into the yard of the inn.

The place was crowded with wagons and buggies, but Turley Hawthorne mumbled emphatically that there was plenty of room left. He sent the horses to be stabled and led Ridge to the supper table, which Felicity and the maids had just begun to clear.

Fee filled a warm plate for Ridge and brought it to the end of the table. She poured two glasses of tea and slipped into the chair at his right.

"I'll visit with you while you eat," she said.

Ridge nodded and cut a bite of the roast turkey.

He was in no mood for company, but a secret part of him was glad for Felicity's pushiness. She might have news of Lacey.

"You were so brave that night," she said. "I just can't forget how you did it."

He broke a stick of hot corn bread and buttered it. "Did what?"

"Took that gun away from me and Tom." She took a sip of her tea and heaved a deep sigh. "But I reckon it's not me and Tom anymore," she said. "Now it's *Lacey* and Tom."

Ridge choked on a mouthful of baked apple. The cinnamon and nutmeg burned his throat like vinegar. He grabbed the tea and drank off half the glass while he glared at Felicity for an explanation.

"That's right," she said sweetly, reaching for the tea pitcher. "Or maybe it's Lacey and that whole guerrilla band of Tom's."

"*What* are you talking about?"

"We got word this morning that Tom and his band are headquartering at Pleasant Prospect while they patrol around here."

He dropped his fork onto his plate. Lacey was at the mercy of a band of hoodlums?

"Hasn't anyone gone to see about this?" Ridge half rose from his seat, twisting around to look for Turley. "If the whole countryside knows that Pleasant Prospect has been invaded . . ."

Felicity gave his hand a soothing pat. "The whole countryside knows that Lacey Longbaugh has always had a soft spot for the men," she said. "Especially for Tom Creekwater. Why, when she gave him her ribbon to wear—you know, the day her papa got killed—she kissed Tom on the mouth in front of half the district! And she wasn't one bit ashamed!"

Staring at her, Ridge dropped back into his chair.

So *that* was the incident Lacey wouldn't tell him when she'd recited the story of that day.

"That Lacey," Felicity went on, leaning toward Ridge and speaking confidentially. "She always has been a rounder with the men."

She shook her head mournfully. "And now that her poor papa is dead and her mama's so sick, she's just going wild. There's nobody to control her, you see."

Ridge stood up so fast that his chair crashed to the floor. His blood roared in his ears, drowning out the rest of it. He turned and went outside, striding across the deserted porch and out onto the packed earth of the yard. Gossip. None of it could possibly be true.

Could it?

Maybe. The first time he'd seen Lacey, Tom had been ready to fight over her. Had there been something between them even then? And Fee's story of the kiss and the ribbon must be true. Lacey had obviously been holding something back when she told it.

He would kill Tom for kissing her.

His heart turned over. He could remember exactly the sweet, fiery taste of her mouth—her willing mouth. Had she been as willing for Tom?

She could be quite forward, too. She had been bold enough to walk into a room full of men and ask Ridge to dance.

But she was a captive now. Tom and no telling how many other men had moved into Pleasant Prospect, where there were only women, an old man, a simple young man, and a boy. Anything could happen to her.

He flung himself toward the stables. She was a

captive, by God, and not one yellow coward in the entire district was trying to rescue her.

But at the black horse's stall, he stopped, his hand on the latch.

What if she didn't want to be rescued?

She had asked Ridge to stay on at Pleasant Prospect; she hadn't seemed at all worried about how that would look to other people. Maybe when he had ridden away, she had sent for Tom.

Ridge leaned against the sliding door of the stall, sick to the heart.

The calm munching noises of the horses was no comfort; neither were the homey smells of the barn. Finally Ridge went in with the black and brushed the horse's sleek, warm hide while he ate the grain.

Ridge squatted to examine the hock that had been sprained the day Lacey ran out into the street in Tahlequah. He stared at the white stocking, but instead he saw Lacey's heart-shaped face, pale with worry about him, and her small womanly body risking flying hooves and rolling wagons to wave him down.

He stood up and hollered for the stable boy.

"Get Hawthorne for me," he said when the boy came running through the thickening dark. "I need a fresh horse and a packet of food—I'm riding out right now."

Footsteps thundered on the stairs. Tom going down or Watty coming up; Lacey had no idea. She tried not to hear them.

She looked below, but in the dusk she couldn't tell whether anyone was watching or not. She held the rope out the window and dropped it; if one of Tom's men was there, she'd face him on the ground.

Babe balked at climbing onto the windowsill.

She caught hold of the lace curtains and clung to them.

Lacey talked to her constantly, soothing, urging, ordering. Finally she moved her mother's limbs for her and somehow got her into the window with the rope in her hands.

"Go, Mama," she urged. "Hold on to the rope. You won't fall."

The fearful look on Babe's face made Lacey want to cry from pity, but she set her jaw and locked her mother's hands around the rope. Gritting her teeth, she pushed Babe off the ledge.

Tom pounded on the door again, as wild as a madman. "Open up!" he roared. "Lacey!" The words were slurred; no doubt he was drunk, as usual.

Lacey climbed out after her mother. Babe hung just below the window, clinging to the rope with both arms, whimpering softly.

"Lacey!" Tom shouted. She heard the ax strike the door.

She crept downward and got her arms around her mother, loosened Babe's grip, and started them sliding.

Babe resisted. They grappled, Babe fighting to go back up, Lacey fighting to go down.

Tears of frustration stung Lacey's eyes while the rough brick wall that used to seem so safe scraped and tore at her hands. Each time they bumped against it the knots slipped a little, too. How long could they hold her weight and Babe's, too?

After what seemed a lifetime of struggling, Lacey's breath was gone and her arms were weakening. Frantic, she pried Babe's hands loose from the rope, one terrifically strong finger at a time.

They slipped toward the ground, fast. With Babe in her arms, Lacey almost lost the rope from her hands; it twisted and banged her shoulder against a shutter with a loud thud. Tom's men would probably come running.

The ground beneath the dining room window caught them hard. They lay in a tangled heap, Babe whimpering, Lacey shushing her in panic.

Nobody appeared or called to them.

Lacey took one long breath, then scrambled to get them to their feet. Somehow Babe still had her shawl.

Lacey tucked the soft wool more tightly around her mother, put an arm about her, and started her moving toward the back of the house. They stopped at the corner, Babe staring into space while Lacey peeked into the wide backyard.

There, at the hitching post, a horse stood tied, saddled, bridled, and ready to go.

Lacey hesitated, holding Babe's arms.

The plan had been for Dorcas to saddle Maud and Lady and hide them in the pine grove. *If* she could get them past Tom. Had she succeeded?

Voices sounded from inside the house. Loud voices.

She would take this horse, Lacey decided in a rush of fear. If Tom caught them they wouldn't have a chance.

She pushed Babe into a run toward the strange gelding. He shied when they reached him, but Lacey calmed him with her voice.

He looked fresh. That was good for their long ride ahead, but bad if he tended to buck.

She untied him, put Babe's foot into the stirrup, and boosted her upward, appalled at how feather-light her mother had become.

The horse danced to one side. Lacey shoved her mother unceremoniously into the saddle; Babe would have to ride astride for the first time in her life.

Holding the reins in one hand, Lacey gathered

her skirts and petticoats, climbed up onto the hitching rail, and threw one leg over the horse's croup. She landed hard behind the saddle.

Immediately the horse was off in a wild, jolting, sideways trot. Lacey held on with her legs and wrapped her arms around Mama, a sudden sob of joy caught in her throat.

It was black dark in an instant, the way night came in the fall. The cold breeze cut at her face like the end of a whip, and the strange horse was trying mightily to get his head away from her. Her arms were trembling with fatigue, and Mama was trying to push her away.

But they were free! Tom could never get them now!

She lifted both legs and kicked the horse into a lope. In an hour or so they would be warm and safe at Rose Cottage.

Chapter 8

Tom hefted the ax and made a pass at the door, cutting a thin, crooked line he could barely discern in the lamplight.

"Hold that light up there!" he yelled at Watty.

Tom braced his legs wide apart, swung the ax back with both hands, and struck at the door again. The wood wavered—but it didn't split.

"Goddam rich planters! Gotta make everything out of oak!"

Over and over again he struck, working through the three-inch door a half inch at a time. At last it broke open with a satisfying crunch.

Tom smiled, cocking his head to listen.

They was too scared to scream. Both of 'em.

He turned the ax and used the back of its head to knock out the lock.

The knob turned, but the door still wouldn't open. Then he saw the barricading piece of furniture. He shoved at it, twice, then once more, and pushed past it into the room.

For a minute he stood rooted to the floor, dizzy from physical exertion and too much whiskey. But even dizzy, he could see that the room was empty.

Where the hell were they?

A lamp burned on the table by the open window. A cold breeze was springing up—it made the light flare bright for a minute.

The curtains flapped once, hard, outside, then blew back inside the window, parting to show the makeshift rope.

Goddammit to hell! He ran to the window and looked down. It was too dark to see much, but the sheets and blankets trailed all the way to the ground. He grabbed the top one and jerked, throwing them back into the room a little at a time, as if every greedy handful was bringing him closer to Lacey.

Dammit to hell and gone! Why had he waited so long? He should have known that she would never come to him willingly and treat him like a real beau. Oh, no; he was Creekwater trash and she was a Virginia lady.

Tom threw the last sheet back into the room with a mighty fling. The knot on the end of it knocked over the coal-oil lamp.

Flames leapt to life on the floor before he could breathe. The breeze gusted again and dragged the end of one curtain through the fire. The lace flashed into a blaze.

He bent down and picked up the lamp, pulled the wick holder out of it, and splashed kerosene onto the other curtain.

"That high-steppin' little bitch," he yelled, his jaw clenched against the rage roaring in his head. "That spoiled slut of a brat. Let's see how she likes this."

He doused the sheets and wet the wall, then threw the glass globe at the bed. It flew across the room in an arc, dripping a trail of oil for the fire to follow.

Tom stormed out of the room past an open-mouthed Watty. They both ran for the stairs.

"Get your horses, boys!" Tom yelled as he clattered down the steps. We're *all* gonna ride now!"

He ran through the hallway and out into the night without looking back to see if the men followed. He'd catch that high-toned little bitch and lay her if it was the last thing he ever did.

Ridge rode up on the ruins of Pleasant Prospect around midnight.

His hand froze on the reins; his pulse stopped. He literally could not believe his senses. The acrid burning smell must have come with him from River's Bend; the still-dancing flames must be from some forgotten nightmare of hell; the sounds of timbers cracking must be the wind rising in the woods.

But his borrowed horse, a feisty brown grulla Hawthorne had called Miss Tyree, snorted and danced to one side when a flying ember fell onto her neck. Another one landed on Ridge's hand. It hurt like sin.

The very air carried the taste of fire.

Lacey! Oh, God, where was she? Had she died in the flames?

He pushed the mare to circle what was left of the house. They moved at a walk, fighting each other for every step; the mare wanted to flee the fiery sights and smells. Ridge wanted to get closer to them so he could try to make them speak.

He strained his eyes to peer into the shrubbery and out toward the quarters. Was there a living soul left on the place?

Apparently not.

He stopped the mare and got down to light a torch from the wreckage; the strengthening wind whipped the fire at him, then away. He held the torch as far from the horse as he could with one hand and led her with the other, in circles. If Lacey had ridden away, he would find her.

But how could he know? Tracks cut into the ground everywhere.

He widened the circles, noticing each time he passed their hoofprints that two horses had angled off to the southeast, one following the other. Lacey and Tom?

Most of the others had milled around and scattered, obliterating any clear trail, but these two had headed straight out. Maybe Tom had attacked or threatened her and she had run from him. His blood pumped harder at the thought.

How much time would it take to catch up to them? How long had they been gone?

He squatted and ran his fingers over one hoofprint, crusting fast in the eddying wind, then swung back into the saddle and headed in that same direction, even though another voice inside him scoffed. Maybe they've had a lover's quarrel. Maybe you're making a fool of yourself.

Fool or no fool, he had to find her.

Lacey rested in the charmed circle of Ridge's embrace. His arms cradled her from behind just as they had done during the wild ride to find Drowning Bear; they felt solid as Sugar Loaf Mountain. Whatever it was that had been scaring her was gone now because Ridge would never let anything hurt her.

She took a deep, shaky breath of the smell of him—he smelled like the sweet earth baked in sunshine, like cedar, like honey, like rain in the distance. She turned slightly so that her cheek rubbed against his starched shirt. Beneath it his skin was warm.

His lips brushed her hair with a touch fleeting as a whisper, then his hand cupped her chin. He turned her face up to his and kissed her. His lips paralyzed her, yet they set every nerve in her body to dancing. . . .

Water pelted against her face.

Tears? What in the world? Was Ridge crying?

She opened her eyes to blackness. Cold drops of water peppered her again, harder this time.

Rain.

Her mother's thin hands squeezed Lacey's legs in fright.

Ridge wasn't there at all.

The rain became a downpour within seconds.

Babe gasped, whimpering out loud.

It had all been a dream! Ridge hadn't ever been there. Lacey had dozed off in the saddle.

Numb panic seized her. Her lips turned to wood; she couldn't even cry.

Wind whipped the end of Babe's shawl against the gelding's haunches, making him jump sideways, as if he'd never seen a piece of cloth before.

Lacey's legs automatically tightened; she threw one arm around Babe and fought the horse's head with the other. Oh, dear God in heaven! If only they could make it to Rose Cottage. Then somebody else would take care of Mama.

And of Lacey, too.

Babe leaned precariously to one side, sending a wrenching pain shooting through Lacey's arm. As light as Babe was, if she wouldn't help herself, Lacey couldn't keep her from falling.

"Mama!" she screamed into the wind. "Shift to the right. Straighten up!"

Babe slid farther to the left. It took all of Lacey's strength to hold her on the horse.

The roaring sound of a large body of water rushed at them beneath the noise of the wind. Blackbird Creek. It sounded more like the Arkansas River in flood.

Lacey braced herself and Mama. As scary as it was, they had to cross; this was the shortest way to Rose Cottage. The gelding trotted faster and faster toward the stream, as if he were dying of thirst.

Then the mettlesome horse balked on the bank.

Lacey's head snapped forward and hit Babe's with a painful smack.

She lifted both feet and kicked with all her might. He had to go in. Tom would be chasing them by now!

The kick made the gelding switch his hindquarters fast to one side, but he didn't move one inch forward.

Babe leaned harder against Lacey's arm.

Lacey took a deep, shuddering breath, shoved her mother deep into her seat, locked her own arms around Babe's waist, and shifted the reins into her left hand.

She picked up their ends in her right hand and whipped the horse, under and over with all her might.

He plunged straight down the rocky bank, and swam for a few yards, just enough to get them out into the strongest part of the current, and then he quit.

The water rose on Lacey's legs, up onto the saddle skirts, and began to pull at her. She could barely see it, shiny somehow in the dark, but she could certainly feel it. It was freezing her into an ice statue.

The wind swirled and keened like the crying in her head.

She gathered the reins again and lashed the stubborn animal front and back.

He reared. He reached for the dripping sky with his front feet and groped higher and higher as if he would climb the rain.

Lacey's pulse stopped. He'd fall backward and crush them both!

He threw them instead. Lacey struggled against the racing waters only to be sucked into a whirling, surging pool that propelled her, hard, onto the rocky edge of the creek.

She lay still for a few stunned seconds. Then she began scrambling for balance. Mama! Where was she?

Her boots slipped; her wet coat dragged her down. She fell to her knees. She struggled out of the coat, peering through the darkness, finally holding her hands over her eyes to keep out the rain. A glimmer of white, moving fast toward her, caught her attention.

It was the bald face of the horse—she could see one of his eyes, too. He passed her, swimming strongly for the opposite shore.

"You hateful beast!" she screamed, and lunged for the unseen reins that must be trailing behind him. Her hands closed on slick, mossy rocks that bruised her palms. The horse disappeared into the dark.

Lacey fought the night, wishing wish upon futile wish that she had some kind of lantern, some sort of light, even a candle. Straining her eyes, wiping the rain out of them, she whirled in a circle, trying to find the spot where Babe had fallen.

The sudden movement threw her off balance. She fell backward toward the middle of the stream and the current took her. Gasping for each desperate breath, she tumbled downstream, aware of only one thing: The world was made of water.

Rocks poked at her flesh, the creek flowed into her lungs, the blackness pressed her under the water with a giant, invisible hand. She threw back her head and gulped for air, struggling against the weight of her wet hair that was pulling her under again.

She bobbed up and opened her streaming eyes. Something white moved almost within her reach. Babe's white gown? Yes! Mama! Thank God!

The current swept Babe closer and closer, tantalizing Lacey. She stretched out both arms and strained to catch hold of her mother's gown.

She had it!

The water jerked it through her fingers.

Frantic, she tried to swim after Babe, but her wet skirts held her legs in a vise.

A new wall of water hit her from behind and tumbled her forward. She came to the surface again so near to the white blur that she could almost touch it.

She threw herself forward, straining mightily. Her hand closed on the sodden cloth, although she was almost too cold and numb to feel it.

Babe's weight pulled Lacey closer to the bank, out of the strongest current. She pulled her mother's head into the crook of her arm.

That victory sent fresh strength pumping through her veins; she made another effort to swim. She had to get Mama to shore.

Now, a hundred soaked skirts couldn't have kept her from moving her legs; using them and one arm, she took Babe into even shallower water. The creek still carried them downstream, but more slowly, and gradually Lacey got them away from it and into the shallows.

Gasping, she collapsed on the low, rocky bank, her arms locked around her mother. As soon as she could take one deep, trembling breath she rolled to her knees and stretched Babe out on her stomach.

Babe's head fell limply to one side and, even in

the dimness of the rainy night, Lacey saw water run out of her mouth.

Pure terror stole Lacey's breath. She picked up Mama's wrist and felt for her pulse.

Ridge leaned forward and patted the borrowed mare's neck. The rain had not only wiped out the trail he was following, it had made the ground slick enough that a less surefooted horse would have been slipping and sliding all over. This brown grulla hadn't lost a step, even at a trot.

He pulled her up and sat for a moment. Surefooted or not, she had to be nearing exhaustion. But he could hardly bear the idea of stopping—he might be close to Lacey by now.

Or he might be ten miles from her. Or more, if the tracks he'd been following were not hers.

He peered into the thin curtain of rain, knowing as he did so that it was a useless effort. He listened.

Nothing but the slow beat of raindrops hitting his hat.

At least Tom was having the same problems—unless he had found Lacey and they'd snuggled up together somewhere, warm and cozy.

That mental picture made Ridge kick the mare forward again. By God, he'd find out whether Felicity had told the truth about Lacey or not.

The grulla kept going until she stumbled. Ridge lunged forward; he had dozed off in the saddle.

He raised his head and let the cold rain wake him up, finally admitting the utter stupidity of his quest. He hadn't slept for thirty-six hours, and even this fresh horse was played out.

He reined her to the right, where the ground sloped upward. In a little while he reached an overhanging bluff; this would do.

He unsaddled and staked the mare, then rolled

up in his slicker beneath the meager shelter. He fell asleep in an instant, but not before Lacey's face floated, clear as a portrait, in front of his eyes.

Tom's head throbbed unmercifully. It took a wearisome effort to hold it still, and the torch as well, while he squinted at the dark ground.

No use. Lacey's trail was gone.

"Damn this infernal weather!"

Not only had the cold rain washed away all traces of the snooty bitch's horse, it had sobered him up.

He turned his horse and spurred him across the low valley. Over here someplace was that little homestead he'd noticed on his way back from the Cabin Creek raid. The falling-down barn he'd seen there would be a hell of a lot better than no shelter at all.

It took only a few minutes to find the place. He sneaked past the house in the noise of the rain and reached the barn without rousing anyone. Tomorrow morning he'd be gone before they woke; there was nothing worth stealing here.

Besides, he aimed to get out early and gather his men. With any luck, they could spread out and find the little jade before night came again.

The rain slowed, started up again fitfully, and then stopped. Lacey, kneeling beside her mother, glanced up at the sky in thanks. Now maybe Babe would have a chance.

She was alive, but barely; she wouldn't be for long if Lacey couldn't get her dry and warm. Oh, if only they had a horse—even the obnoxious one that had thrown them! Or a blanket; both Lacey's coat and Babe's shawl had been lost in the creek.

More than that, if only they had Dorcas!

Lacey's eyes filled with tears. This time she

couldn't take her burden to Dorcas. She would have to make all the decisions by herself.

The moon floated out from behind the clouds, its light seeming unnaturally bright after the rain-filled darkness. Lacey stood up, looking in every direction. She had to find some kind of shelter and dry wood to build a fire.

In front of her and to the left loomed an eerie shape. It looked like a wall, but there was no roof.

She bent over Babe and squeezed her hand. "I'll be back in a minute, Mama," she said. "I'll be right back."

The wet soles of her boots slipped on the rocks, but she ran without stopping. As she got closer she could see that the wall was one of three still standing; they were the ghostly shell of a burned-out house.

The yard of the little homeplace was surrounded by a low, solid fence made of stacked stones. The gate was gone; where it had been a space opened to the west. If she could carry Mama through there, they could shelter behind the walls.

Lacey turned and ran back to the creek, the keen wind chasing her all the way. Babe lay in exactly the same position as before.

"Mama? Can you hear me? Come on, we have to move now."

Babe's eyes fluttered halfway open, but not another muscle moved. She didn't speak, but Lacey was so accustomed to that she hardly noticed.

Lacey kept talking, murmuring constant soothing words as much for her own comfort as for Babe's. She tried twice to pick up her mother, but it was useless; they were too close to the same size for Lacey to manage it, no matter how little Babe weighed.

Finally Lacey got her to her feet and settled for an awkward grip around Babe's shoulders. She started half carrying, half dragging her mother across the rough ground.

By the time they reached the ruins the moon shone strong and pale through the space where the west wall had been. Lacey looked at its position. Thank God it wouldn't be too long until morning.

Shaking with fatigue, she laid her mother down inside the south wall, close to the corner. The wind would hardly touch her there.

She peered at the ground. Small bits of paper and trash were stuck to it near Babe's head. Cartridge papers?

Of course! A military patrol must have been here, hiding behind the wall, perhaps, to fire on their enemies.

Maybe they had left something she could use!

Lacey stood up and began to search through the rubble, her eyes darting to each shiny thing that the moon picked out of the shadows. She ignored her fears of scorpions and snakes and worked her way along the south wall, picking up a percussion cap, a broken knife, and then, over in the east corner, a gleaming button.

It was attached to some cloth—thick, dry wool. Her hand jerked back. A coat? Was someone in it?

No. There wasn't room for a person in this corner.

She took a handful of the fabric and pulled. The moon hit another button and then the coat came free.

Hugging it to her, she whirled and ran back to her mother. Babe lay limp; her skin felt as clammy as gooseflesh—like Papa's skin after he lost all that blood.

Lacey shivered. It couldn't be. It couldn't. She could not lose them both.

She stripped off Babe's sodden gown and rolled her into the coat. As an afterthought, she searched its pockets.

A neckerchief that the moon showed to be Federal and a powder flask came out of one. The other held only a small tin box.

Matches!

Lacey ran to the dry corner where she'd found the coat and began gathering pieces of wood that had escaped the rain. The air had turned quite cold; she would build a big fire, one hot enough to warm them both through and through.

If it burned so brightly that it brought Tom to her, then that was just too bad. After what she'd been through tonight she could kill him with her bare hands.

In a frenzy of hope, she dragged every piece of dry wood she could find to a spot near Babe. She heaped up some kindling and set it on fire; once she had a blaze she pulled her mother closer to its warmth and began rubbing her hands. She wrung water out of Babe's hair and used the Federal soldier's kerchief to tie up her head, talking all the while.

"Mama, this horrible night is going to cure you," she said. "The doctor said a shock could do it, and if this hasn't been a shock I don't know what would be. You'll wake up in the morning and be just the way you used to be, way back before Papa . . ."

Her voice broke. She grabbed Babe and cradled her in her arms, turning her head so the tears wouldn't wet her mother's face again.

Lacey stayed awake the rest of the night. If she fell asleep, the fire would go out and her mother would die. If she kept the fire going, in the morning her mother would wake up and talk to her.

She would be just like she used to be when Lacey was a little girl.

The night seemed to last forever. But Lacey never let the fire go out.

Then, all of a sudden, she realized that she could see the shoreline of the creek. It was becoming daylight.

She reached for her mother's hands—they felt much warmer now. Smiling, Lacey held on to them and let her eyes close at last.

Mama's voice roused her to full day. Lacey came awake with a start, happiness shooting through her before she remembered why.

Babe was talking!

"I've been living just to see you, Colin, darling," Babe said in her soft drawl. "Ever since Tullah brought your letter to me."

Colin? Daddy? Was she talking about Lacey's real daddy?

Babe flashed a smile, a grotesque imitation of her old coquettish one. "Why, sometimes when you're away for so long, I think I just can't live until I see you again!"

No. She wasn't talking about Daddy. She was talking *to* him!

"Mama," Lacey said hoarsely. "Mama, I'm not Colin. I'm Lacey."

"You haven't been off down there in Charleston flirting with those Sullivan girls, now, have you?"

Lacey began to sob, staring at her mother through the tears. She reached out and touched one of Babe's bright cheeks.

Her hand jerked back. Mama wasn't warm from the fire—she was burning up with fever!

Lacey threw her arms around her mother and cried harder, heedless now of where the tears might fall.

Babe wrenched away from her and fell back onto the ground where she'd lain all night, coughing her chronic cough, inhaling heavily between her cracked lips.

Lacey clutched at her mother's wrist. Her pulse was thin and thready. Her hand grew hotter and hotter.

Water. Enough water would cool her. Maybe it would even cure the fever. Maybe the fever was the only thing wrong with her now.

"Mama?" Lacey bent over Babe to catch even the slightest response. "I'm going to the creek, Mama. I'll bring some water."

She laid her mother's hand down very carefully and stood up, looking around. Surely the soldiers had left a canteen or the fire had spared an old bucket. Anything. Anything that she could use to carry water.

Lacey ran back to the east corner and sifted frantically through the rocks and debris. Nothing.

Then she saw it. On the crumbling hearth in the center of the north wall lay a wooden pail, the top of one side broken off by a falling stone. She ran to it.

It had no handle, but it would hold water. She snatched it up with both hands, turned, and ran for the creek.

The waters were already much calmer. Lacey looked up and down the creek for the horse while she held the bucket under to swell it watertight. If only she could find the contrary beast and get Mama to a doctor!

The wish went around and around in her head. It blotted out the smells of the rain-soaked woods and the sights of the early morning sunlight slanting against the water. She could only feel: the cold, wet mud pressing up around her knees like a portent.

Her mama was terribly sick. And there was no one but Lacey to help her.

What in the world should she do? Should she try to walk for help? But to where? She had no idea where they were. Just somewhere on Blackbird Creek.

She pulled the pail to the surface, as full of water as its broken side would allow. She set it down and got unsteadily to her feet.

She couldn't go anyplace even if she knew where to go. Mama could not be left in this condition.

Lifting the bucket carefully, she started back to the ruins. Mama would get better and then they'd both go.

But swabbing Babe's face and hands with the cold water made no difference. Forcing small amounts of it into her mouth only resulted in choking and more coughing. Lacey cried and begged, but her mother kept talking nonsense and moaning and coughing, refusing to even try to swallow one drop.

At last Lacey stopped trying to give it to her and began bathing every inch of Babe's frail body with cloth she'd torn from her damp petticoat. Babe's gown had long since been dried by the heat of her skin and she had thrown off the soldier's coat, only to snatch it back again when the shivering chills coursed through her.

The sun climbed higher, but nothing else changed. Lacey made endless trips to the creek and back again, performing the same chores over and over, finally making every movement without any thought in her head except a wordless prayer that her mother would live.

Early in the afternoon she came back to the ruins with another bucket of water. She set it down outside the broken south wall and took a better grip on the pail. Then she noticed the quiet.

The breeze was barely moving in the trees, a few birds were starting to chatter near the creek, but everything else was still.

Mama wasn't muttering and moaning anymore!

She dropped the bucket and ran.

Babe lay as she had left her, on her back, but her arms weren't flailing and picking constantly at her clothing. They lay peacefully on her chest.

Her ragged breathing had stopped.

Lacey dropped slowly to her knees, staring hard at Babe's still face. She felt her mother's wrist; already the terrible heat of the fever was fading.

There was no pulse.

A long, keening wail tore through the day. Lacey didn't recognize it as coming from her own throat.

She threw herself across her mama's body and began to cry.

She should have gone for a doctor, for help of any kind. She should have poured the cold water down her mother's throat. She should have stayed on that stupid horse no matter how much he bucked or how swift the waters ran in the creek. She should have been a less rebellious daughter.

She should never have wished for her freedom. Because now she had it and it was too scary for words.

Lacey cried until her sobs became dry heaves and her dizzy head made the earth tilt beneath her. Mama's body seemed about to float away from her; she gathered it into her arms, turned her head, and raised her wet face to the sky.

A sight met her eyes that stopped the tears on her cheeks. She stared at it, helpless.

It must be a vision. Yes, that was it. For comfort, God had sent her a vision.

It looked as if a man stood in the opening of the stone fence. He was tall and broad and beautiful, dressed in black and white. He wore a flat-crowned planter's hat.

He couldn't be real. She had grown up enough already to know that life did not immediately give a person whatever she expected or wanted.

So he couldn't be real.

Because this apparition was what she wanted most out of everything that existed on the face of the earth.

The mirage looked exactly like Ridge.

Chapter 9

The dream Ridge dropped the reins of his horse and started toward her. He moved with the same splendid strength that the real Ridge had, that magnificent sureness that a person could cling to.

He *looked* real. She could see the mixture of worry and relief in his face.

He called her name.

He *was* real!

Before she even knew that she could move, she was on her feet and running. Halfway across the open space she ran into his arms.

Sobbing again, she rubbed her face into the rough wool of his coat, trying to wipe away the past horrible hours. He cradled her head in his hand and pressed it tight against his chest. She started to shake all over.

Ridge widened his stance and pulled her nearer, fitting her body into the curve of his. He held her close and let her cry; he stroked her back and her hair.

She trembled beneath his hands like a wild bird caught in a trap. He wished he could spring it open and set her free; the wish cut him so sharply that it made tears spring to his own eyes.

But there was nothing he could do. They all

stood helpless against the pull of the Nightland, and that is where Mrs. Melton had gone. He'd known it the minute he'd spotted them there, just inside the jagged wall.

Lacey lifted her head. "I let her die, Ridge," she said, her lips so stiff in her tear-streaked face that he could hardly understand the words. "If I'd left her and gone for the doctor . . ."

"Hush. You couldn't have found the doctor, much less have brought him back here in time."

She looked at him, her eyes bleak as winter. "Are you sure?"

"I know it."

He stepped back and held her at arm's length until he could open his coat and wrap it around her, too. She came into it and they stood still for a long time, his chin on her head, rocking a little against the draw of the wind.

Finally he pulled away to look at her. "What about you, Lacey? Are you hurt?"

"No."

Her face and neck showed scratches, though, and her rolled-up sleeves revealed a terrible bruise on one arm.

"Did Tom do that?"

"No."

He waited, but she didn't say more. Was she protecting Tom? Was she afraid to complain about him? *Were* they lovers?

"Then what hurt you?"

"The rocks. The horse threw us in the middle of the creek." Her voice broke. "In the dark."

He took off his coat and put it on her, helping her slip her battered arms into the sleeves.

"You were both on one horse?"

"Yes. He ran away and stranded us." She fastened her eyes to his. "But now you've come with your horse, Ridge. At least we can take Mama home to be . . . buried.''

A picture of Pleasant Prospect, smoldering in ashes, rose behind his eyes. That sight would be too much of a shock for Lacey to bear.

Besides, with Mrs. Melton's body on their one horse, he and Lacey would be afoot. That was no condition in which to meet up with Tom, mounted and probably accompanied by several of his men.

"Lacey," Ridge said slowly, "come over here and let's talk." He led her to a low place in the broken south wall and brushed away some small chunks of debris so she could sit down.

He put one foot up beside her and leaned forward, his arm across his knee, to look into her eyes. Beneath the sorrow they were filled with a bone-deep fatigue.

"You're too tired to walk home," he said. "It's nearly fifty miles. We'll have to bury your mama here."

"No! She ought to be at home beside Papa."

"Her spirit is with his. That's more important."

She looked at him.

"That's what she wanted, you know."

"I know," she whispered. "Once he was gone, she didn't want to live."

She covered her face with her hands.

He waited.

At last she nodded. "We don't have a choice. I can see that."

She got to her feet. Her eyes met his; in that one long look she changed and grew older.

"Please find a pretty spot," she said, "while I lay her out."

Lacey walked the few feet to her mother's body, lying so incredibly still in the midst of the sunlit afternoon. She knelt and looked into Babe's face one last time.

Then she spread the soldier's coat out on the dried grass to make a shroud and moved the almost weightless form onto it.

Mama would be appalled if she knew. All her life she'd taken such pride in knowing that her costume set the style, no matter what the occasion. Now she was to be buried in a torn nightgown and the well-used coat of an unknown Union soldier.

If she did know, at least she would be glad that there was no one there to see except Lacey and Ridge.

Ridge. In every calamity he was there to save her.

Lacey fastened her mind to the thought of him while she smoothed her mother's hair, washed her as best she could, and wrapped her in the coat.

Ridge appeared at Lacey's shoulder. "Are you finished?" he asked.

"Yes."

"Then come over here and rest."

She nodded, but she knelt beside her mother for a little while longer. " 'Bye, Mama," she whispered. "I'll think about you every day of my life."

She touched Babe's face one last time, then covered it with the collar of the coat.

Ridge helped her to her feet and led her out through the gateway. They walked up a gentle slope to his horse, grazing beneath a huge white oak tree. He pulled off the saddle and untied his bedroll.

"Rest for a while," he said. "I'll come for you when it's time."

Lacey let him spread the quilt for her; she

dropped onto it, her face down. She couldn't bear to watch Ridge carry her mama away.

When she knew he had done it, she turned over to stare at the sky through the tangled branches of the tree. Her eyes wandered from one cluster to another of its red-and-brown leaves, thinner now because it was autumn, but still plentiful and talkative in the wind. They were trying to comfort her. She closed her eyes to listen.

The next thing she knew Ridge was kneeling beside her. "Come and say a prayer," he said.

She got up. He took her by the hand and smoothed her hair back from her face, first on one side, then the other.

He led her higher up the hillside, angling to the east until they were directly north of the remains of the house. They walked through a thin stand of pines into a clearing covered with pale yellow grass. The raw dirt of Mama's grave glared brown in the middle of it.

The tears started again, but Lacey ignored them. She walked around with Ridge to stand at the foot of the grave.

The sun shone on her face. The sky gleamed blue above and between the luxuriant green branches of the pines. Ridge's hand was a living rock to cling to.

She tightened her grip on it, lifted her head, and began to sing.

"All people that on earth do dwell . . ."

Ridge joined her on the second line, his voice booming like a great bass bell beneath her high soprano. Together they sang all four verses of the Old Hundred.

"That was Mama's favorite hymn," Lacey said. "May she rest in peace."

Then she let go of him, walked across the clearing to a shining sumac bush, and broke off a branch of its scarlet leaves. She came back and knelt to lay it across the gash of upturned ground.

"Good-bye, Mama," she said, for the last time.

She cried all the way back to the big white oak tree; Ridge walked with his arm around her, supporting her elbow. He helped her sit down on the quilt again.

"I'll get some water," he said.

Lacey barely nodded.

Ridge looked down at the top of her head. Poor child. She'd been through enough for a lifetime in these past few days.

He left her there and went into the ruins for the broken bucket, then he stepped over the low place in the south wall and strode toward the creek. They didn't have much time; the sun was starting its downward trek.

When he returned with the pail of cool water, Lacey was lying down, her head tilted back so that the mass of golden hair fell away from her face. Her eyes were closed, her lips barely parted. She was as pale as the winter sunlight.

Just the sight of her was enough to break a man's heart.

He set the bucket down and dropped to his haunches beside her. "Lacey," he said softly.

She moved one hand, but she didn't answer. She was asleep.

He watched her for a moment. It wouldn't hurt to let her rest a little. They needed to eat before they rode; she could sleep some more while he laid out the food.

He would get everything else ready to go, too, he decided, as he opened the saddlebags. Then he would wake Lacey; they would eat quickly and be off to find a safer camp before it got too dark.

Ridge took out the packet from Hawthornes', then rebuckled the bags. He caught the mare and

saddled her, putting the bags across the skirts before he tied his tools to the saddle strings. The
bedroll and blanket would fit on top of them.

He turned the grulla loose to graze again, reins
trailing, then he walked into the shade of the oak
and unfolded his single wool blanket near Lacey.
He filled two tin cups with the cool creek water,
sat down, and opened the cloth bundle of food.

He touched Lacey's shoulder. ''Little One,'' he
said. ''We'll have to ride soon. You need to eat
something now.''

Her long lashes fluttered, their deep gold color
startlingly dark against the white of her skin. The
low-slanting sunshine showed the trails made by
her tears.

Ridge took out his handkerchief and dipped it
into the water pail. He bathed her cheeks, washing away the sadness from her face, wishing he
could take it from her heart as easily. He washed
her hands.

She opened her eyes. ''I can do that,'' she said.
But she made no move to take the cloth from him.

''We have to ride soon,'' he said, dipping the
kerchief into the water again.

He touched it to her forehead. Slowly. ''Are
you hungry?''

''Yes.''

''Good,'' he said. ''We need to go ahead and
eat.''

''All right.''

His thumb traced the line of her fine eyebrow,
following it outward and into her hair; he let the
handkerchief fall away.

''We need to find a safer camp,'' he said, tucking one curl carefully behind her ear. ''It'll be dark
soon.''

''I know.''

He smoothed her hair away from her forehead.

She smiled at him.

The sunshine fell in strips of heat on her skin now, instead of on numb wood. She could hear: not only Ridge's rich voice, but the hollow, mournful call of a wild dove somewhere up on the mountain. She could see: Ridge's magnificent face framed by the crisscrossing brown branches of the oak with their clusters of red-and-brown leaves.

Ridge. His touch was bringing her to life again. The ice in her veins was starting to melt at the edges.

"You're hungry," he said. "So am I."

Lacey kept on looking at him.

In one quick, greedy movement he put his hands on her shoulders and sat her up to face him. For a heartstopping moment she thought it was so he could kiss her.

"I've laid out the food," he said.

She couldn't answer because his lips were only inches from hers. They tasted like hot honey; she remembered exactly.

Her eyes clung to them.

"Lacey?"

His voice sounded hoarse.

"I . . . I don't want to eat," she said.

His fingers tightened on her shoulders. They felt strong enough to pick her up and carry her away.

"You said . . ." He cleared his throat. "You said you were hungry."

They looked at each other for a long time.

Then he let her go.

He turned away to reach something behind him. Food. The aroma of biscuit and cured ham set her mouth watering in an instant.

"Try this," he said, and held the small sandwich to her lips.

She took a bite, then another. Nothing had ever tasted so delicious. Suddenly, she was starving, ravenous.

He fed her every last crumb, then took a cup of water and held it for her, too. She drank it all. He gave her a second biscuit and she nibbled at it while he ate. Her eyes never left his face.

"There's dessert," he said at last.

But he made no effort to get it. If he let his hands move from his cup they would go to Lacey, not to the food.

He must be losing his mind, and with it, all control. After all the child had just been through . . . with her mother . . .

Besides, he had to protect her. Tom was likely to come. They had no time.

Lacey reached past him to get the sweet; her breast brushed his arm. He dropped the cup and clenched his fists in his lap.

She broke the fried pie between them. They bit into the crisp crust slowly, their eyes still on each other, leaning closer and closer until their heads almost touched.

When they'd finished, he caught her unresisting hand and licked the dried peach filling from her fingers, one at a time. Her skin tasted infinitely sweeter than the pie.

At last he said, "We have to go now."

"Yes," she whispered.

She lifted her face to his. He tightened his fingers around her wrist and pressed her palm to his cheek. His hair felt like silk feathers.

"It'll be dark soon," he said.

"I . . . know."

"We should hurry," he whispered, against her lips.

A harsh voice tore across the side of the mountain. "Chekote! Give up the girl!"

Ridge threw himself on top of Lacey, forcing her back into the thick quilt.

The singing sound of a bullet echoed off some rocks.

"Tom!" she gasped.

"Yes, damn him!"

Ridge held her down with one hand and reached for his rifle with the other.

"He's out of range yet," he said. "You run for the ruins."

"Not without you!"

"I'll come."

"Then come now! With me!"

"No. We'll need this equipment. Besides, I want to cover you."

He rolled off her and got to his feet, pulling her up with him. "Run!" he said. "And take the mare. Hide her behind the wall."

"No! Ridge . . ."

"Now!" he roared. "Take the mare."

"Then I'll take the equipment, too," she said stubbornly. She swooped down, rolled the quilt and blanket into her arms, and grabbed the bucket, splashing water all over them.

"Lacey, my God, go! I'll bring it."

She threw both cups into the pail and ran with it bumping in front of her and the bedroll, Ridge's long coat sleeves sliding down over her hands. The mare stood still with her head up, looking in the direction of the shots.

"It may be after dark before I can move," Ridge called, taking a position behind the tree. "Find the safest corner and wait for me."

Another shot sounded against the rocks. Ridge fired back. Lacey grabbed the horse's reins and ran. Everything got quiet.

She had made it inside the walls, almost to the protected east corner, when Tom's voice called out again. He was closer now. "Lacey, honey, you runnin' the wrong way. Come back here and give me a hug."

She whirled and stared behind her. Nothing but the hillside in the early dusk.

Anyway, Ridge was there. He wouldn't let Tom get her.

"Lacey!" Tom yelled.

"Go away!" she screamed. "I'd rather die than have you touch me again!"

Again? Ridge listened to the word echo off the hills. How much of Tom's touch had she ever felt? *Were* they lovers quarreling?

If so, he was the biggest fool in the world.

"If I can't have you, I'll guarantee nobody else can!" Tom shouted back. "For sure not that interfering son of a bitch you're runnin' with right now!"

Ridge smiled tightly. At least he was getting under Tom's skin, no matter what else was true.

Tom shouted again. "Why don't you just send her on out to me, Chekote? You know *you* can't hold a woman. Your wife leavin' you and runnin' away shoulda learned you that much."

Lacey froze. Ridge's wife had run away? She had been *leaving* him when she was killed? How on earth could any woman ever leave Ridge?

A gun fired. It sounded like Tom's rifle to Lacey, but she couldn't be sure. It was much closer than the first shot.

She stood on tiptoes, squeezing the bedroll in her arms, straining with all her might to see Ridge. There was no sign of him; she could barely make out the white oak tree a hundred yards or so above the stacked stone fence. Soon it would be full dark.

Lacey turned and led the mare farther into the shelter, dropped her burdens, and began to or-

ganize them. She took off the bothersome coat
and rolled it and the blanket into the quilt with
the bucket inside, then stuffed the rattling cups
into the saddlebags. She tied the bedding to the
saddle strings on top of the tools and made sure
everything was tight and ready to go.

Then she crept along the north wall to look for
Ridge. Was he coming now? Or was he hurt? Had
that last shot hit him?

If he didn't show himself in one more minute
she would mount the mare and go back for him,
Tom or no Tom.

A sudden shot, then two more, sounded not
too far from the ruins. Lacey ducked back behind
the wall.

Someone caught her around the waist and
dragged her to the ground.

She gasped once, then a hard hand clamped
over her mouth. She couldn't have cried out, anyway—the shock was too swift.

In the next breath she knew it was Ridge. He
pulled her backward, into the lee of the wall, as
Tom fired again.

"Every Confederate Cherokee in the Nation's
after your hide, Chekote," he called. He was so
close now he didn't even need to yell.

Ridge dropped his hand from her mouth.
"Sorry, Little One," he murmured. "No need to
try to keep you quiet; he must've seen me come
in here."

Tom raised his voice again. "You never should've
warned Ross about that flag-raising," he said,
sounding more arrogant than ever, "much less in-
terfered with it yourself. Now, the girl's mine. Give
her to me and I'll see what I can do. Keep her and
you're a dead man."

Lacey gasped and twisted in Ridge's arms so she

could see his face. He smiled at her, his teeth flashing white in the growing dusk.

"Chekote?"

Ridge's mouth found hers with a rough, wild motion that stopped her heart. When he pulled away she felt he had marked her for himself with a burning brand.

He turned her loose and eased closer to the low place in the wall. "Mount the mare," he said, "and hold her over there in the corner."

"Are we going?"

"Yeah. It's likely he's stalling until his men get here. He doesn't have the guts to ride alone, not even after a girl."

"Chekote!" Tom yelled again. "Talk to me!"

Ridge rolled to his knees, placed the gun barrel on the top of the broken wall, and fired.

Tom shot back a volley. The bullets rattled against the rock wall as if the sky were spitting hailstones.

Bending low, Ridge turned and ran to Lacey and the mare. He shoved the rifle into the scabbard and mounted behind her. "Let me have the reins and the stirrups," he said. "Hold on."

He reached both arms around her and laid one of the reins against the mare's neck. They circled, already moving at a trot, and found the opening in the south wall.

Gunfire crashed close behind them.

"Shotgun," Ridge muttered.

He pushed Lacey flat onto the horse's neck until her face lay in its mane. He bent forward over her and swerved the grulla to the left as the next shot boomed.

He lifted the mare over the low, broken wall in a leap that took away what little breath Lacey had left and set them floating helpless in the air for a seemingly endless amount of time.

Lacey buried her cheek deeper into the coarse mane hairs and locked her legs against the mare's sides to keep from sliding onto the straining neck.

One of Ridge's arms pulled her tighter to his body; the other dropped the reins and gave the mare her head.

They landed with a staggering jolt.

Quick lights flashed, to the right and slightly ahead of them this time. For one mad second Lacey thought that lightning bugs were coming out into the early dark. Then they flared again, with that awful zinging sound, and she knew they were shots. Tom's men had caught up to him.

Tom yelled something Lacey couldn't understand. Ridge kicked the grulla into a long lope, angling to the right, heading for the water.

Tom shouted again. Was he right behind them?

The raucous sound of the shotgun, so close it set her teeth together like a vise, answered her question. A harsh, grunting noise followed, closer still.

The mare had taken another stride or two before Lacey realized that that last sound had come from Ridge.

He jerked straight up and pulled on her with a sudden lurch that almost yanked her out of the saddle, then he bent close, slumping against her shoulders. A slow, damp wetness warmed her.

Blood! Like Papa's!

Oh, dear God, Ridge was hit.

Chapter 10

The mare raced down the sloping bank, her hooves slipping in the soft ground, then cracking against the rocks. She plunged into the creek.

The cold water grabbed Lacey with merciless fingers. She hardly noticed; she was too scared about Ridge to feel anything except fear.

She tried to turn so she could see him. "Ridge, he hit you! How bad is it?"

He shook his head and shifted their weight to the right to help balance the swimming mare, his arm so taut around Lacey's waist that she couldn't get her breath.

"Ridge!"

"Nicked me." He grunted.

"No," she said. "There's too much blood."

Frantic, she twisted in his arms to see.

"Sit still. You'll have us both in the water and afoot if you don't."

"I don't care. The blood . . ."

"I'm not hurt bad," he said. "Believe it."

His tone was calm, but his breathing rasped hard in her ear.

"Are you sure? I can feel you bleeding on my back."

163

"Sorry," he joked. "I'll stop as soon as I can." The last word came out as a stifled groan.

"Ridge!"

"It's all right, Little One. I wouldn't lie to you."

She sat for a moment, stiff and still, as if using some inner sense to test his words for truth.

"It's true," he said, very low. "Now turn around and face front—we have to keep Miss Tyree here right side up in the water."

She obeyed and he almost wished she hadn't. Her face turned up to his had warmed him through and through, in spite of the cold creek water filling his boots; her agonized tone had sent a strange exhilaration into his veins.

She cared. It had been years—a lifetime—since anyone had worried about him so.

He pulled her body closer into his, resenting the cantle of the saddle rigid between them. Right now he didn't care what she had been to Tom.

A high, whining sound whistled past his ear; something splashed into the water a yard to his right. The mare pinned her ears and swerved away, but she never missed one swimming stroke. Lacey gave a little cry.

Ridge bent closer over her and urged the mare farther away from the bank. That was a shot from a Henry .44. Tom had traded his shotgun for a different rifle. Well, small good it would do him. He'd never get Lacey now.

Ridge kept the mare in the middle of the stream, where the current, still running strong as a river this many hours after the storm, carried them fast around a bend. The shouting and firing faded into silence behind them.

Lacey gripped the saddle horn with both hands and tried to believe what Ridge had told her. He couldn't be hurt very badly, he just couldn't.

She caught her breath and held it. That's what

she'd thought about Papa, though. And Mama. And both had left her anyway. Life seemed to always throw out just what you didn't expect.

Oh, dear Lord. She couldn't bear it if she lost Ridge, too.

They stayed in the twisting creek around two more curves, then Ridge nosed the mare toward the bank. She climbed in, water pouring off her in streams. At the top she stood, shaking, sucking in deep breaths of the night air.

"Ridge, let's dismount. I have to see . . ."

"Can't take the time," he said. "They'll try to follow us."

"But your wound . . ."

"When we camp," he said. "We'll take care of it then."

The creek rushed by them, some small animal made snuffling noises in the brush, the trees rustled here and there in the breeze, but there was no sound of pursuit.

"They're not coming yet. Just let me stop the blood."

"It's stopping."

"I don't believe you." Her voice trembled in panic.

He squeezed Lacey to him and clucked the grulla into a trot. "I'm not going to leave you, Lacey," he said, as if he'd been reading her thoughts. "Don't be so scared."

He touched the top of her head with his chin and wished he had kissed her for comfort when they were stopped.

No, he had been right not to. He still had the taste of her in his mouth from the kiss by the wall and, instead of satisfying, it had doubled his hunger for her. Never again would he be able to stop with only a kiss.

He kept the mare moving at a steady pace, talk-

ing in low tones to reassure her, and Lacey, too.
They made slow progress through the blackjack
timber until Ridge saw the pale ribbon of a deer
trail gleaming in the dark of the woods. He took
it and they started winding faster up into the hills.

The rising moon threw shadows into every
crevice, making man-shapes of each tree and rock.
He let his wounded arm hold the reins and put
the other hand on the butt of his gun. Would Tom
follow them, even this far?

He gazed down at Lacey's bright cloud of hair,
gleaming where the moonlight caught it, and answered his own question. Tom would follow if he
had any claim to Lacey at all.

Had Felicity been telling the truth? The thought
turned a thousandth jolting somersault in his gut.

No, it couldn't be. Lacey looked like an angel
from heaven.

But wasn't that the way life usually was—full
of irony and deception? Didn't devils usually look
like angels?

He flexed his left shoulder carefully. It stung
something awful, and he could feel that the blood
was still seeping, but he'd told Lacey the truth.
The shot pellets had scattered in the surface and
just beneath his flesh instead of penetrating deep,
the way a rifle bullet would have done. He was
lucky in Tom's choice of guns.

His jaw clamped. Tom was lucky, too. Lucky
that Ridge wasn't free to change from being the
hunted into the hunter.

Lacey sat quiet in her fear and he in his wari-
ness, so they climbed in silence except for the
thud of the mare's hooves against the beaten dirt
of the trail. It led over the top of the first foothill,
then down the other side; they crossed the shallow draw and started up the next, steeper hill.
The moon rode high and unreachable, making

dark shadows on the mountainsides and pale pools of light in the low places, where fog was starting to form.

The hills closed around them like the walls of a sanctuary, thick and black. On the highest ones the moonlight made paper silhouettes of the trees; they danced slowly to the jolting rhythm of the mare.

Lacey watched them until her eyes began to droop shut. Her legs had long since gone numb with the cold and no stirrups, her back refused to hold her up any longer. She dared not lean against Ridge because of his wound. She looked longingly at the hard ground, desperate for someplace to lay her head.

Finally her fatigue overcame her.

"Ridge, I have to get down and rest. I'm too tired to ride another step."

"We'll stop pretty soon," he said. "But we have to be where we can get our backs to the wall."

She nodded in vague agreement, then in exhaustion. Her fingers loosened on the saddle horn and she dozed, slumping back into the warm curve of Ridge's body.

He cradled her in his arms, shifting her head to his right shoulder to remove its weight from the wounded one. He settled her against him and relaxed into the rhythm of the horse's hoofbeats, luxuriating in Lacey's warm closeness. He refused to let himself think beyond that.

By the time the moon stood directly overhead they were far up into the hills of the Goingsnake district.

The grulla followed a moonbeam's path along the edge of a bluff and around the end of it. She stopped. Ridge let her stand.

Lacey stirred in his arms and then sat up

straight, rubbing her eyes open as if she were a very little girl.

In front of them lay a natural bowl-shaped valley hollowed out of the mountainside. Pale, frothy light reflected off the fog that filled it; it looked like a transparent copy of the solid moon.

"Oh, Ridge," Lacey whispered. "Let's stay here."

He nodded. "We've come far enough."

He kneed the mare into motion again, slower than before; the trail wound downward, holding close to the mountain. Ridge watched the sides of it while Lacey gazed into the magnificent moonlit ravine. After they'd gone only a few yards, he pulled the mare to a halt.

"Aren't we going down into the valley?" Lacey asked.

"Not tonight. The mare's tired, and the fog makes it harder for her to find footing, carrying double. Besides, I think we've found a cave."

"I'm not going into any cave! Ridge! Surely you don't mean to make camp in a cave!"

He laughed, shifting to one side to dismount. "Why not?"

"It could be full of snakes, or scorpions, or . . . a panther. Ridge, a panther could be living in there!"

"Don't forget bears," he said as his feet hit the ground. "There could be a big black bear in there making himself a home for the winter."

"Don't *say* that!" she wailed.

"Wait here," he said.

"But you might be in danger. . . . Here," she said, trying to draw the rifle out of the scabbard beneath her leg. "Take the gun with you."

He gave her a reassuring pat. "I have the pistol. Don't worry."

Ridge stepped away and in an instant the space

between them grew as wide as the surrounding hills. The air turned colder. Lacey shivered.

She twisted around to peer at the irregular dark spot on the side of the mountain.

"Be careful," she called.

She could still feel the print of his hand on her leg; it was the only warmth she had.

In a minute she saw a match flare; it showed the outline of his hat as he went deeper into the blackness. The tiny flame flickered, then went out. She didn't see another one, although she waited for a lifetime.

"Nobody here," Ridge said, so close to her that she jerked straight up in fright. "Not even a woolly bear to cuddle up to."

"You scared me!"

"I thought you heard me coming. You should have—I made plenty of noise."

"You did not!"

He chuckled. "Looks like you need a lesson in words lore, Miss Lacey. Now that you live in the woods, you'd better know how to survive."

"Oh?" she said archly. "And are you going to teach me?"

He pushed back his hat and smiled up at her in the moonlight, so richly handsome that she couldn't take her gaze away.

"You bet. Climb down now and I'll show you how to make a mountain camp."

He held up his arms to help her dismount. She wanted nothing more than to slide down into them and stay there for the rest of her life.

But the light caught his white shirt with its awful dark stain over his heart. Fear made her arms go weak.

"No," she said quickly, forcing one numb leg to find the stirrup and the other to swing over the saddle. "I can dismount. Don't make your wound any worse."

"It's all right. The bleeding's stopped."

"We'll tend to it first thing," she said, turning to face him the minute her feet reached earth. "*Please*, Ridge! It worries me sick."

He touched her cheek. "All right. But we'll have to have a fire to see by."

Dry wood and flat rocks were plentiful near the trail; soon Ridge had a fire going in front of the entrance to the cave. At his direction, Lacey unsaddled the mare and piled their supplies just inside the dark opening.

As she worked, she watched Ridge from the corner of her eye. He really was all right, she decided, with growing relief. The wound didn't restrict his movements much, and the stain on his shirt hadn't grown any larger. She took the first deep breath she'd had since he was hit.

Then she unrolled the bedding and took out the broken bucket.

"I'm going to turn Tyree loose and let her lead me to some water," she said. "I'll have to wash your wound."

He glanced at her, put another stick on the fire, and stood up. "I'll go with you," he said. "You might get lost in the fog."

"Well! The fog's not all that thick!"

"Yeah, but you're a city girl," he said. "You've already proved it once tonight."

"Am not!"

"Are too!"

Laughing like two children, they followed the mare down the sloping trail into the valley, weaving slightly because they hadn't walked for so long. Ty led them into the ball of yellow light, deeper and deeper into the heart of the hollow, straight to a running creek that pooled beneath some chinkapin trees.

They filled the bucket and headed up the gentle rise of the valley's floor, still staggering some as the feeling came prickling back into their legs. Lacey giggled.

"You look like you're drunk," she said. "Were you guzzling whiskey while I was asleep?"

"I was." Ridge lurched toward her, a mock leer on his face. "Lady, you're lost in the middle of nowhere with a drunken Indian."

She laughed. "Better that than a wooden one."

He laughed, too, far more than the jest deserved, and took her hand to swing her around. They twirled slowly through the yellow moonglow in an impromptu dance, reeling from silliness and fatigue, swinging with joy at having escaped most of the bullets, the river, the rolling rocks and ragged holes and dark shadows of the mountains, swaying closer and closer together until they came to a shaky stop.

His hands were sending fire through her veins.

"We'd better be careful," he said.

"Hmmm?"

"It'd be a shame to spill the water."

He was so close. His big, solid body and his warm, exhaustless strength and the scent of him— horse and cedar and sweat and his own masculine, musky smell—filled her senses until she truly was drunk with them.

She swayed toward him.

But he straightened her up and they made their way back to camp, floating free of the earth all the way, like the wisps of fog dancing onto, then off of, the trail they blazed through the wet grass.

Lacey came back to reality when she saw Ridge's wound in the firelight. She had to wet his shirt to loosen the big spider's web of dried blood, and when she slipped his arms out of his sleeves the sight of his shoulder made her gasp. His skin was pocked with more than a dozen small holes from the shot.

"Oh, Ridge," she said. "You've been hit in the front of this shoulder and again in the back. It's awful!"

He handed her his pocketknife.

"It could be a lot worse. Just wash the wounds with soap and water and then with the whiskey. Pick out as many of the pellets as you can."

She bit her lip and began.

"You don't have to get them all," he said. "I've still got one in my toe from a hunting accident a long time ago."

His breath went a little short on the last word; she could tell he was trying not to wince.

"Oh? And you're the one who's going to give me lessons in surviving in the woods?"

She exaggerated her mock indignation to try to keep his mind, and hers, off the pain.

"I didn't shoot myself. My cousin did it."

"Oh, sure. That's what all the great woodsmen say."

He chuckled. "I'll give you a shooting lesson as soon as you're done here."

"When I'm done here, I'll run screaming into that awful cave and hide my head," she said, between gritted teeth. "Don't talk to me anymore, Ridge. I have to concentrate; this is the worst thing I've ever had to do in my life."

She cleaned each small wound thoroughly before she dug into it with the point of his knife. Most of the pellets popped right out, but one or two she had to dig for, every stab of pain she caused him cutting at her own body, too.

Sweat formed on her face in spite of the cool autumn air. She got so tired that her hands started to tremble, but she held them steady through the sheer force of her will, squinting at his poor, hurt flesh in the firelight.

At last she was done. She bandaged him, front and back, with strips torn from one of his clean shirts.

She stayed on her knees beside him looking at her handiwork, then her gaze moved onto the copper skin of his chest gleaming in the firelight. His muscles rippled, hard and twisted as ropes. They made her palms itch to touch them; her arms went suddenly hot and heavy with the wanting.

It must show on her face, too. Thank goodness he wasn't looking; he was sitting quietly with his eyes closed.

"All finished," she said finally, her voice small from squeezing past the knot in her throat.

He opened his eyes. "Thanks, Lacey."

"You're welcome. I guess."

He grinned at her. "Was it so terrible? Are you going to run screaming into the cave now?"

"I'm too drained to scream," she said, standing up and pressing her shaky hands to her skirt. "But I am going into the cave and get the dried blood off of me, now that you're all fixed up."

"Use anything you need," he said. "Wear one of my shirts."

"Thanks." She turned away.

"If you're afraid to go into the cave," he said suddenly, "stay out here. I'll turn my head."

She looked back to see his face in the firelight. "Thanks," she said again. "I'd like that better."

He threw his legs over the log he was using for a seat and turned to face the valley. Lacey carried the rest of the water to the saddlebags at the mouth of the cave, stripped off her shirtwaist and chemise, and began to wash. The water was so cold on her skin that it made goose bumps, but she felt wonderful to be free of the sticky blood. It would be marvelous to be clean and dry all over.

On impulse she pulled off her boots and socks, unfastened her wet skirt and petticoat and let them fall to the ground. After cleansing herself fully, she picked up the wool blanket, draped it across one shoulder, and tied it around her. She would go and dry by the fire and then put on Ridge's shirt.

She sat down beside him to let her back warm first. Ridge looked at her. "Feel better?" he asked.

His eyes on her bare shoulder felt hotter than the heat from the fire.

"Much. Do you?"

The blanket made a slanting blue line across the rosy creaminess of her chest. He wanted to draw his finger along her skin, there, just at the edge of it.

"I'm not sure."

He smelled of soap, now, too.

"Maybe I'd better look at your wound again," she said. "The bandage may not have stopped the bleeding."

"Maybe not."

They turned together, in one motion, to face the fire. Its glow washed her one bare shoulder in gold as bright as her hair. It found the hollows along her collarbone and at the base of her throat and touched them with flame. It made her cheeks pink and her mouth warm and ready for his.

"There is one lesson I have to give you tonight," he said.

She looked up into his eyes, as dark as mystery. They were in shadow, but the bones in his face caught the light. Her hands ached to touch them, too, the same way they had needed to feel the muscles of his chest: as if she were blind and only touch could make him known to her.

"A lesson in what?"

Her lips stayed slightly parted, waiting for him. He couldn't think what he had intended to say.

"In . . . shooting," he said. "You might need to know. If Tom or one of his men does follow us this far."

She smiled. He glimpsed the tip of her tongue.

"And you're going to be the teacher? You, with the shotgun pellet in your toe?"

He smiled back. "I told you I didn't put it there."

He caressed her shoulder. He couldn't stop himself. It felt like warm silk. She leaned into his hand. All beneath the blanket she must feel like this.

"I need to take care of your wound more than I need a shooting lesson," she said.

"I'll make you a deal," he said. "Learn how to load and fire the guns and I'll let you do anything you want to my body."

The unexpected words took the breath from both of them.

Her cheeks flushed redder in the glow of the fire. A dry stick crackled as it began to burn.

Ridge brushed back a strand of hair from her face, silently cursing himself for not being able to keep his hands away from her. Nor his tongue under control.

But if he could just sleep in her arms tonight . . .

No. That would be foolish, as foolish as deliberately walking off the top of a cliff.

She dropped her eyes. "Really, Ridge," she whispered. "I'm serious."

"So am I."

How much did she know about what to do to a man's body? He wanted to know the answer to that question more than anything, but yet he didn't want to know.

So he took the pistol from his holster and brought it up between them. He broke the breech and showed her how to load the paper-covered cartridges, keeping his arm around her waist so they could both use two hands on the gun.

Her hair brushed the skin on his neck and set it aflame.

He spun the cylinder and shook the cartridges out onto her lap. They gleamed there, their yellow paper covers bright against the dark blue of the blanket.

"Pick them up and put them back in."

She did so, her fingers shaking.

He helped her straighten one, to slide it into its slot, and her trembling hand melted into deceptive stillness beneath his touch. Finally, somehow, she closed the rotating chamber.

"Right. Now pick up the gun with both hands and aim before you cock the hammer."

She lifted her head and shook her hair back from her face. The line of her throat in the firelight made him the one whose hands were shaking now.

"Look right along there to aim."

Her hands moved beneath his. They shouldn't be on the cold steel of the gun; they should be on his needy skin.

He leaned forward to sight with her and brought his hard cheek against hers. That made it beyond his power even to swallow.

"Lacey," he said, his voice raw.

"Yes?" she whispered.

"Lacey. You make me forget what I'm trying to do."

He let the gun drop back into her lap and

turned her to face him, his hands cradling her shoulders. Her eyes were enormous.

"And what *are* you trying to do?"

She could feel each one of his fingers separately on her skin. They marked her the same way as his kiss by the ruined wall.

"I'm trying to keep you safe." The words rasped softly on the foggy air. Slowly he brought one hand up to cup her face. "All I want is to keep you." After an age he added, "Safe."

Her heart stopped. Yellow moonlight wrapped around the two of them, the only living, breathing creatures in the magic valley. That cocoon of air-spun light was all that held them to the earth—attached as it was on one side to the solid dark of the mountain. The night lay sweet and still around them.

Like Lacey, it held its breath.

"Don't worry," she said, at last. "Tom likes his comfort too well to swim his horse for miles in a cold creek and climb all this way in the night."

His hands left her, swift as birds flying up.

"How do you know how Tom likes his comfort?" he cried. "Just how do you know? Have you been sleeping with that bastard?"

She sprang to her feet. The heavy gun bounced from her lap to hit the ground and fall away from her.

"How could you ask such a thing?" she cried in return. "How could you even think it?"

She jumped over the log and ran into the hateful cave, desperate for any wall to put between them. Inside, she slid to the ground and huddled with her arms around her knees like a child in pain.

Ridge didn't love her. He didn't care about her one bit or he would never have asked such a horrible, hurtful, insulting question of her.

She had no idea how long she had crouched there in the dark before she heard him just outside.

"Lacey," he called. "I've spread the quilt out here for you because I know you don't like the cave. I'll sleep on the other side of the fire if you'll give me the blanket."

She ripped the scratchy wool from her body and threw it at the mouth of the cave. Then she fumbled in the saddlebags for one of his shirts, hating the thought that she had nothing to wear except something of his.

Buttoning the shirt up to the neck, she crept out to find the quilt between the fire and the cave. She lay down and covered herself without ever once looking toward Ridge. Tomorrow she'd ride away. Alone. He could walk the whole way back to River's Bend for all she cared.

Ridge rolled up in the blanket and stretched out on the opposite side of the fire. He glanced out at the fog, gathering thicker now against the mountain's wall. It would protect them better than a dozen men on watch.

He closed his eyes and turned on his right side to shield his wounded left one from the bumpy ground. Lacey's scent permeated the blanket. How could she still smell like roses after camping in a ruin for two days?

He hated himself for having said what he said to her. What had it accomplished? He couldn't tell if she had been furious or insulted or guilty.

Whichever, she had been hurt to the core.

Dammit, he was sorry. What difference did it make if she had been with Tom?

A hell of a difference. He'd learned that tonight.

But why did he care? He wasn't falling in love with her.

He tossed and turned, his mind skittering from one picture of Lacey to another. No matter how much he moved around, his wound wouldn't stop hurting; no matter how close he got to the fire, he couldn't get warm.

So he was still lying there, wide awake, when Lacey began to scream.

Chapter 11

Ridge clawed the blanket away from his shoulders, untangling himself from it in the same motion that brought him to his feet. Pain shot through his wound.

He ignored it; Lacey's shrill cries were tearing the night apart. His eyes strained toward her, but he could see nothing except blackness on the other side of the fire.

"Lacey!"

She screamed again, the sound blotting out her name as if he'd never shouted it.

He crossed the short distance to her bedroll in three long strides and dropped to his knees to find her with his hands. She was sitting bolt upright, her body as stiff as stone.

"Lacey! What's the matter?"

The hair-raising screams continued.

"Did something bite you? A scorpion? A snake? My God, Lacey, tell me!"

The piercing shrieks came again and again, multiplying and echoing into the small cave, bouncing out again into the muffling fog.

He held onto her with one hand and grabbed a stick out of the fire with the other. His hand shook so hard he almost extinguished its flame, but at last the meager light shone on her face. It was a mask of fear and pain.

He moved the light, holding it just inches from her skin, searching for telltale red marks from a sting or a bite. He threw back the covers to examine her legs, lifted her hair to see the vulnerable nape of her neck. The bedding offered no clue, at least not before the stick began to crumble. He threw it back into the fire.

She hadn't moved. If something were stinging her, she'd be squirming away from it, even if she were still asleep.

Asleep! How could she be asleep and make that much noise? Could she be awake? Had the strain she'd just been through driven her crazy?

The thought slammed at his brain; he took Lacey by both arms. It could happen. Hadn't the dangers of this country driven Martha out of her mind?

"Lacey! Stop it."

But she wouldn't stop.

He shook her.

The screaming continued.

"Lacey, it's Ridge. Everything's all right."

She didn't hear him.

He shook her again. She was like a wooden doll in his hands, a doll that screamed. A few more minutes of this would tear her throat out, but she couldn't know that—she was far away, in some terrifying far country in her head. She couldn't come back by herself.

He slapped her.

All sound stopped. The fog gathered around them and muffled the last echoes of her voice; sudden silence filled the world. Ridge's heart quit beating.

Then Lacey's ragged breaths tore through the quiet and she fell forward, sobbing, into his arms.

"I'm sorry, Little One. I'm so sorry. I hated like poison to do that."

He tucked her head into his good shoulder and let her cry. She wept with a concentrated passion that scared him to death.

Was he the cause of this? Why had he ever yelled at her about Tom, anyway? She had been alone and helpless; he himself had ridden away and left her vulnerable to such scum after she'd begged him to stay.

"I'm sorry," he murmured into her hair. "Oh, Little One, I'm so sorry I said anything."

He held Lacey's cheek in place against his tear-soaked shirt, circled her with his other arm, and swung around to sit cross-legged on the bedroll. She burrowed into his lap, shivering as if she were lost in a snowstorm.

At last the flood of tears slowed to a trickle.

Lacey reached out her arms to get more of the life-giving warmth. The freezing water receded from around her legs and the shots stopped echoing in her ears. Tom disappeared, and then so did Mama and Papa.

Another racking sob shook her. It brought the words to release her pain.

"I couldn't stand it," she cried, clinging so hard to Ridge that her fingers dug into his flesh. "The harder I ran toward Tom the farther away he got."

The name sent cold needles of jealousy stabbing through Ridge's veins. Lacey had been screaming like a madwoman because she dreamed she couldn't get to Tom?

"Don't think about it now," he said. "Forget it. It was only a nightmare."

"But it seemed real as anything. Tom was shooting at Mama and Papa. . . . I was swimming and riding and walking and crawling through the cold water trying to take the gun away from him, but I couldn't get any closer, and . . .''

The icy thorns in his blood melted away.

"Don't worry, now," he said softly. "There's nobody here but us."

The uncontrollable shivering took her again. She pulled loose to scramble up onto her knees, wrapping herself around him as if she were trying to get into his skin with him. She buried her face in the hollow of his throat. Her hot, wet cheek burned his flesh. Her breasts flattened in soft torture against his chest.

His hands went motionless, suspended over her back and her cloud of hair.

She couldn't do this to him. He couldn't be only a comforting friend if she did this.

His hands dropped into the inviting softness of her hair.

"It's over," he murmured. "It's all over now."

"It was so terrible," she whispered. "I never was so scared."

"Shhh," he said. "Hush, now. There's nobody here but us, and nobody's shooting."

His fingers slid onto her lips; the taste of his callused skin dissolved the words on her tongue.

She tightened her arms around his neck, pressing her face deeper into its life-giving warmth. Her lips found the spot where the blood beat strong just beneath his skin. It slowed her pounding heart to match its perfect rhythm.

His hand caressed her hair. "You've had a rough time," he murmured. "Too rough for anybody."

Suddenly she remembered. Her body went stiff and she pulled away from him. "I forgot I'm mad at you," she said. "How could you ask if To—"

He stopped the name with two fingers across her lips.

"Little One, I'm sorry," he said. "I shouldn't have asked you that."

One last sob tore at her. He stroked her cheek. "Don't think about it now."

"I won't if you'll hold me."

"I'll hold you."

He folded her into his arms, and the hot ropes of his muscles made a barricade between her and all danger. The solid shape of his body fit hers so securely she would never be lonely again.

The growing pressure of his maleness cut loose the vague yearnings she'd felt since the moment they met and poured them into a deep-set course, as immutable as the bed of a river. They gathered and deepened, tumbled and rolled, surging mightier with every breath she drew.

Some instinct as old as time carried her with them. This was the pull of the life-force itself, and Lacey let it have her, knowing somehow that here was the way to negate all the death, dreamed and real, that haunted her.

She drew Ridge down with her to lie on the quilt.

He groaned. His hands cupped her shoulders, the back of her neck, then slid down the crevice of her back. They stopped.

"Lacey, no. Like this I can't only hold you."

"Yes, you can. Hold me 'til morning."

She rubbed her cheek along the line of his jaw and kissed his ear.

His hand flattened into the hollow at the base of her spine.

"I . . ." He cleared his throat, but when he spoke again the rawness was still there. "I'll have to do more than just hold you, Lacey."

"Then do more." She ran her fingers into his hair. "Do more, Ridge. I want you to."

"Do you know what you're talking about?"

"Yes," she lied.

She kissed the corner of his mouth. It tasted sweet. And salty. A thin covering of sweat had sprung out on his skin.

"Lacey," he whispered, "pretty Lacey. I wish we had a light so I could see you."

"I can see you," she whispered back.

"No, you can't."

"I can, too. I know exactly how you look. I've got you memorized."

He made a low sound deep in his throat. "After tonight you'll have me memorized," he growled. "Only me."

She rubbed her cheek against his. "Kiss me," she murmured. "I need to see if I've got your kisses memorized, too."

He caught her face in both hands and took her mouth with a sudden desperate passion that slammed through her body like a bolt of thunder. Her lips parted for him; her tongue rushed to find his with a lightning thrust to match his own.

Heat like a summer storm surged through her and opened every part of her to him. Ridge. He was the love she had been imagining forever.

Now he was real. His hands were everywhere on her body, but not soon enough. His kiss deepened.

She could not bear it. Both racking delights at the same time were too much.

She tore her mouth away from his and gave him the column of her throat to kiss instead. This way she would have no distraction from the new thrill of his searching, callused palms, which were waking every inch of her flesh from a long, long sleep and setting it alight with life. His hands held a wondrous magic stronger than a shaman's, a brushing touch lighter than a feather's.

They found her breasts and she went as motionless as the night. Such pleasure! She held very still so he wouldn't stop doing that.

But he did stop. He made a little sound deep in his throat and held himself up, away from her enough so he could press a string of openmouthed kisses down her throat and into the valley between her breasts.

Then he worked his way up the side of one.

She didn't dare to breathe.

He reached the peak. She gasped at the familiarity of such a thing, but she caught his head in both her hands and held it exactly where it was.

She would never, ever let him stop doing this.

His mouth wet the shirt at the same time it set fire to the skin underneath. She realized that the cloth was becoming an intolerable hindrance between them at the same time he began fumbling with its buttons.

She tried to help him with one hand, trying to hold his head still with the other. He reached for the hem of the shirt. His hand brushed her bare skin there and a new shocked thrill ran through her body.

Then the shirt was going up and his mouth left her breast so the cloth could go over her head. The sleeves slid over her hands and off, and the last impediment was gone. The cool, damp air moved over her skin.

Then Ridge's hands were back; they were her whole world again. Their heat grew stronger until they could have melted the deepest snow.

Her lips parted, wanting. Wanting Ridge. She closed her arms around his neck and their mouths fell onto each other like wild things.

The surging river in her veins changed from water to fire. She ran hungry hands up the sinews of his neck and into the silk of his hair, then down over the hard, muscled tops of his shoulders. She clung there, holding on, while she tried to comprehend what he would do, how he would save them both from these pulsing, driving flames that were such sweet torture.

A new, hard heat came against her, then into her, and she felt a sharp stab of pain.

She cried out.

Ridge hesitated, so lost in his passion that he couldn't think. Then he gave himself to it again, moving with all the force of desire that had been building in him since the first time he'd taken Lacey into his arms.

She cried out again, just as the barrier gave, and he realized what had happened. She was a virgin! She was just as innocent as she looked!

He tried to stop but it was too late. Joy and gratitude and guilt for even listening to Felicity flowed into him, but they were nothing compared to the overwhelming tenderness that claimed him. He had hurt her and he was sorry.

Hesitantly at first, then more surely, Lacey moved with him. The storm in her veins sent lightning to her loins; it soon made her blood roar and her pain fade into nothingness.

Here was her love, come to her at last. They were giving themselves, each to the other, in a way so wondrous that she never could have dreamed it, a way that meant they belonged to each other. Forever.

So they fed the fire sprung from the lightning strike and let it burn. They fueled the flames until they were roaring inside them, and at last they let it consume them in the conflagration.

Lacey cried, "Ridge!" and it threw them like sparks into the night, bursting into burning embers, flying off into infinity with nothing to hold on to but each other.

* * *

Before he opened his eyes Ridge knew it was nearly morning. And that Lacey lay in his arms.

He brushed his face across the curling cloud of her hair. After everything, she still smelled of roses. And of him a little bit, too.

She slept curled into the curve of his body, her head in the crook of his arm. She had been exactly next to him all night; even now, as he stretched his legs, she unconsciously moved hers to fit them. It made him smile. Then he sobered and buried his face in her hair.

If he lived to be a hundred he would remember this night and Lacey in his arms. Her voice calling his name had thrilled him like no other cry ever had; her soft, wild body merged with his had set his soul on fire. She had clung to him and kissed him senseless and healed every hurt he had ever felt.

He laid his hand on her belly, palm spread flat against her warmth, and pulled her closer to him. She had become part of his sinews and his bones.

The idle thought froze him where he lay.

No. He couldn't let his heart fall open like this. He could not.

What had he done?

She had been a virgin; he had taken her. She had lost her family; he was taking care of her.

He reached across her for the discarded shirt, a pale heap beside the dark quilts. He wadded it into a pillow for her and lifted her head from his arm. He had to get away from her soft breathing and her warm, smooth body so he could think.

But her soft curls clung to his fingers. His reaching arm brushed against her breast. She stirred and the scent of roses and warm skin and sex rushed into his nostrils.

He set his jaw, tucked the shirt under her head, and moved his arm. That took all the strength he had, so he hurried, slipping away from her as stealthily as if he were stalking a deer. He paused only to pull the cover up over her back.

His pants and his boots were still damp, but he thrust this feet into them anyway and began climbing up the hill through the half-light. The trees were black sticks, not moving, waiting to see where he would go. They stood as still as ghosts against the slanting earth, ready to stand judgment over him, but offering no answers to the questions churning in his brain.

He picked his way upward, his feet instinctively finding the soft, quiet places to step. The timber thinned out along the top of the ridge and he could see an overhang, a huge slab of sandstone, reaching out into the sky to the east. He walked onto it and kept going as if he would walk to the sun, not pausing until he came to the end.

Dawn was coming.

A fragile pink fingered the gray world, not strong enough yet to grasp and claim it. But soon the pale crimson would own the sky; it suffused the air with that promise. Surely in this time of day he loved, the time his Cherokee people called Morning Red, he could figure out what to do.

Ridge dropped to his haunches and touched the stone promontory. It still held a trace of warmth in spite of the night's chill; its grainy surface spoke to his hands. He sat for a brief time without thinking.

But then his mind rushed to Lacey, sleeping alone beneath the hill at his back.

He hadn't expected ever to make love with her, no matter how much he had been drawn to her. Because he had sensed from the moment he'd seen her—that heart-stopping moment when he'd thought she'd been shot—that if he ever loved again, it would be this girl with the honey-colored hair. And he had known that if he touched her, he would be lost.

He hadn't meant to touch her. He'd kissed her when they fell from the wagon and rolled down the hillside, yes, but that had been an expression of joy and relief. And he'd had to hold her and comfort her when the judge was killed. Only a man made of wood wouldn't have done that.

Just as it wouldn't have been human to ride away the day he left Pleasant Prospect and leave her standing so forlorn, so pale, beneath the dark green branches of the peach orchard without kissing her good-bye. Yesterday's kisses had been natural, too, mere expressions of relief at their safety after all they'd been through. She had needed that comfort.

But the lovemaking.

His mind wouldn't give him a logical reason for that, nor could he draw one from the reddening sky, although he stared at it until his eyes watered. The lovemaking had been because he'd wanted her. And needed her.

Because he had loved her.

She had taken him in and given herself back to him with a passion inconceivable in such a young girl. In a virgin.

He smiled, savoring the thought. She had given herself to him, Ridge Chekote, and never to Tom Creekwater or any other man. And so she had destroyed his own cynical idea that people are hardly ever what they seem.

But she couldn't change the nature of love. Not even her hot kisses and smooth, clinging limbs could do that. Love was too old and too powerful, too treacherous for even her young passion to change. Love, sooner or later, always brought pain too enduring to kill.

Rare experiences like that of last night lasted for

only a few fleeting minutes of an endless lifetime. Relationships always changed; outside forces always became more important than two people's hearts.

One day soon Lacey would see, as Martha had, that she belonged in Virginia or Boston or New York or Philadelphia—anywhere but here in this wild Cherokee Nation that seemed bent on destroying itself and everyone in it. Sooner or later, Lacey would leave him.

And when she did she would take his heart right out of his body.

He shook his head, squinting into the eastern sky, peering through the wisps of clouds for the first glimpse of Grandmother Sun. No. No, he would not love Lacey. He could not take such a chance again.

Ridge sat without moving, holding that thought, while Grandmother Sun poked her head over the horizon and strengthened her streaks of pink and vermilion. She made them so red and so radiant that day burst out like a song all over the sky.

She called to the birds and set them to chittering. She woke the animals and sent them rustling through the woods at Ridge's back, searching for food.

But she didn't tell Ridge that the decision he had made was the right one.

So he silently recited to her, the grandmother of his people, all the reasons why he must not fall in love with Lacey.

First, he needed to bring the raiders of River's Bend to justice. After that, he needed to stay in Tahlequah and take on his full responsibility as a member of the council as the government attempted to hold the Nation together. He might even be needed as an emissary to Washington

City to take the Cherokees' case to the Congress
and the president. After the war, he would be
busy rebuilding River's Bend.

A sharp vision flashed through him, a sudden
feeling as much as a sight, of Lacey at the foot of
the long, shining mahogany table in his dining
room, of Lacey in the summer kitchen directing
the cooks, of Lacey in a red velvet gown standing
in the Christmas-decorated entry hall of River's
Bend greeting their arriving guests.

Of Lacey in no gown at all in the middle of his
four-poster bed.

He snapped his mind shut on the picture.

Every one of the responsibilities he had named,
even that of rebuilding his home, would be better
done alone. He couldn't take on the happiness
and well-being of another person. He had all he
could do to take care of himself and the Nation.

Lacey stretched and yawned, letting the tiny
knots in the quilt's tacking run up and down her
arms. Every one of them made a separate little
thrill on her bare skin, just as every bird in the
woods was singing a separate call to wake her.
She opened her eyes.

The fog was gone. Sunshine filtered through
the trees into a day so clear that the top of the
mountain looked close enough to touch. The creek
chattered at her, its sound carrying sharply on the
autumn air.

Her body fit exactly the contours of the earth
beneath the quilt; she could feel each dip and rise
as she breathed. Never had she felt so amazingly
alive.

She was a woman now. She was with Ridge.

She turned her head to look for him.

He was squatting with his back to her, stirring
the fire. His shoulders looked as broad as the

mountain itself beneath the smooth white linen
of his shirt. It narrowed into a vee at the small of
his back and disappeared into his tight black
breeches.

There it wasn't smooth at all; he had stuffed
the shirttail carelessly under the thin black wool.
She needed to slip her hand into his waistband,
just at the base of his spine, and smooth out the
wrinkles.

Her cheeks went hot. She had become a hopeless wanton!

She couldn't do that, even if Ridge did belong
to her now. But she had to either touch him or
hear his voice, now, this very minute, or she
would go crazy.

"You dress like Old George Grape," she said
in a sleepy drawl. "The banker. I never realized
it before, but all your clothes are black and
white."

"What?" The word was a surprised grunt.

He swung around to look at her, a piece of kindling forgotten in his hands.

She lay propped on one elbow, her tousled hair
surrounding her face like a mist of sunshine. It
glowed deep gold in the shadows, dazzling pale
yellow where the light hit it. Her smiling lips
looked extra full and sweet, as if they'd just been
kissed.

In two steps he could reach her and make that
the truth.

He snapped the stick in half. How the hell could
he keep from loving her when she looked like that
and said such silly things?

"That's the first time anybody ever said good-
morning to me by insulting me," he said.

He cleared his throat. He hadn't meant for his
voice to sound so raw and harsh. But it hadn't
destroyed her teasing grin.

"You needn't sound so hurt. I wasn't criticizing *you*—you don't act like Old George Grape. You're a lot more generous."

"Well, I guess it could have been worse. Skunks dress in black and white, too, you know."

Then they were laughing, looking into each other's eyes. His weren't mysterious anymore; they mirrored all the same memories running through her own head.

He was hers now, this impossibly handsome man. Ridge belonged to her and she to him.

"I'm going to get you some colored waistcoats," she said. "Oh, and a brown velvet smoking jacket. A deep, deep brown the exact same shade of your eyes."

The words clanged a warning bell in his head. He mustn't let her start making plans; enough damage was already done.

"We're a long way from a store," he said. "Better just take care of what's in my pack, black and white or not. Every other garment I own is scattered on the floor at home, cut to pieces."

She sat up, clutching the quilt to her chest. "What? Ridge, what are you talking about?"

"Some Knights of the Golden Circle raided River's Bend when I took my cotton to Webbers Falls. They carried off everything that wasn't nailed down and tore up the rest."

"Oh, Ridge! They trashed your house? Because you stopped them from raising the flag that day?"

"Yes."

"I can't believe they even tore up your clothes! What about your people? Were they . . . killed?"

"No. Six of 'em stayed; the rest went north."

"And your horses! I wondered why you weren't riding Blackjack."

"My houseboy hid him in the canebrakes, but

he was worn out by the time I got to the Hawthornes' inn. The mare belongs to Turley.''

She leaned toward him to hear the whole story,
her eyes wide and dark blue, her fist clutching the
quilt so hard that her knuckles showed white. The
whole, hurtful story came pouring out of him.

When he finished he dropped the sticks and
buried his face in his hands.

The next thing he knew, Lacey was standing in
front of him, holding his face close against her.
She had put on the shirt again; its warm linen
held the scent of both of them.

''I'm so sorry, dear Ridge,'' she said.''So sorry.
I know how you love River's Bend.''

Desire swelled inside him, along with sudden
guilt. Here she was sympathizing with him, not
knowing that her own home lay in ashes.

His arms started to lift, to go around her, but
he clenched his fists to weigh them down. God!
How much could he take? He had managed not
to go to her and she had come to him.

He couldn't move, though, although he knew
he had to, and soon. Her sweet comfort was as
seductive as her sensual embrace.

He couldn't tell her about Pleasant Prospect, either, not yet. Her fragile body was shaking now
from all the bad news she already knew.

He put his hands at her waist and set her away
from him. ''We'd better feed you,'' he said.
''Your belly just rumbled in my ear.''

''Ridge!''

She moved away, her legs flashing beneath the
long tail of the shirt.

He picked up his blanket and tossed it to her.
''Here,'' he said abruptly. ''Wear this for a skirt
until yours dries.''

She shot him a puzzled look and then wrapped
the blanket around her waist. ''Can we have ham

and eggs and beaten biscuits?'' she teased. ''And red-eye gravy and blackberry preserves? And cold milk and hot coffee?''

''Not unless you can transform jerky and water,'' he said, responding to her mood in spite of himself. ''We need Drowning Bear here to cast a spell.''

She clapped her hand against her hollow stomach. ''That's all we have? Really?''

He opened the saddlebags. ''All but this sack of cornmeal I brought from home.''

''I'm too hungry to wait for it to cook.''

He held out the tin cups to her. ''Fill these up with water from the bucket, then,'' he said. ''I doubt you'll want to wait for coffee, either.''

She arranged their cups on a large flat rock a little way from the fire and he rolled the log up to it. He opened the package of jerky on the makeshift table. She ran to get one of his handkerchiefs to spread under it.

''I'll hunt this morning,'' he said, giving each of them a portion of the dried meat. ''And we can have a hot dinner.''

''Can I go, too?''

''No,'' he said gruffly.

She looked into his eyes, perplexed.

''You'll scare the game away,'' he said, forcing a lighter tone. ''You stay here and wash the blood out of our clothes and keep the fire going.''

She laughed. ''You sound like my husband. Really, Ridge, it's like we're making a little home here.''

The warning bell sounded in his head again, as loud as the one at River's Bend ringing out over the whole plantation.

''We'll only rest here for a day or two,'' he said quickly. ''I have to get to Tahlequah. I want the Lighthorse to ride with me after Beck.''

She stopped eating, the stick of dried meat just touching her lips. "Is that what you're doing up here, then? You didn't come looking for me?" Her eyes were huge and violet-dark.

He swallowed, hard. I mostly came looking for you, he wanted to cry. The Lighthorse was my excuse. But he couldn't say that. She was already jumping to conclusions about buying him clothes and making a home together.

"Yes," he said. "I mean no. I came north to find the law."

She stared at him in silence.

He broke off a piece of his meat, but he could not eat it. Her face was so forlorn it broke his heart.

He cleared his throat. "I followed your tracks, though," he admitted, "once I got to Pleasant Prospect and found . . . that you weren't there. Felicity told me . . . Tom had moved in, and I was worried about you."

Damn it! He didn't even know what he was saying.

"I knew you'd come," she said, the look in her eyes turning suddenly into the shine of stars. "Always, Ridge, ever since you left I knew you'd come back and save me. I prayed for that every night. But then when Mama and I ran so far and I didn't even know where we were, I didn't know how you could find me."

Her smile crashed against his heart like a stone rolling off a mountain. "It was a miracle, wasn't it, Ridge? It was a miracle from God that you found me."

He stared at her, wishing from his very bones that he had never met Martha and lost her. If that hadn't happened maybe he could have let himself love Lacey.

He put down his cup and stood up. "Finish your breakfast," he said.

"But . . . what about yours?"

"I need to get to the woods." He had to get away from her or he would bed her again. Right now. Here on the rock. Without waiting to get the bedroll.

His tone hit her like a dash of cold water. She sat without moving and watched him take the packs into the cave.

When he came out he looked like a primitive stranger. He wore buckskin all over—shirt, leggings, and moccasins; his belt held a large knife. A beaded headband, white and red against the copper color of his forehead, had replaced his black planter's hat.

But she didn't continue their joke about his clothing. His face held no expression at all and he moved with loose, careless, sure grace, like a bobcat in the woods.

He came straight to her, carrying his pistol. "You keep this, and if you go to the creek or anywhere, take it with you."

She took the gun with a frozen hand. "Do you think Tom will come?"

"If I thought that I wouldn't leave you. Tom couldn't track an army across a muddy barnlot or he would've been here by now."

He spoke so abruptly it made her fingers shake. He seemed in a terrible hurry, as if he wished he were already gone.

"Keep it with you, hear?"

Speechless, she nodded.

He turned away, then, and went to get his rifle. He walked out of camp without looking back.

She sat at the flat rock, the pistol in her hand, and watched until the trees swallowed him up. The sun and the shadows mingled on the red-

and-yellow leaves; they moved and threw mottled images against the brown trunks until she thought she saw Ridge coming back again.

All the woods got as quiet as death.

Lacey stared into them and tried not to cry, fighting the terrible, sinking feeling that she had lost him again.

Chapter 12

Ridge followed the deer trail out of the thick of the woods and into the sunlight's glare. He squinted upward. Grandmother Sun stood directly overhead. Good. He'd be back to Lacey long before dark.

He glanced at the blue mountain range to his right, its hills humped like bucking horses' backs against the paler sky. On his left, across the rocky ravine, he sighted the granite bluff he'd used for a landmark going in. Their camp lay directly west of him, over that next rise.

He started down the hillside, digging the heels of his moccasins into the soft earth to balance his weight and that of the wild turkey and the rabbit hanging from his waist. He would finish cleaning them in camp so Lacey could watch and learn how to do it.

And so he wouldn't lose any time returning to her.

He switched the rifle to his other hand and quickened his pace. It had been foolish to leave her alone, but they had to have food. And he'd had to get far enough away that he couldn't touch her.

The pounding in his head increased. He tried to ignore it, deliberately pushing himself faster through the deep, dried grass of the slope. The slight noise of his steps crackled in his ears loud as gunshots.

He had to stop and rest at the bottom. He dropped down onto a rock and laid the rifle at his feet, cursing the unaccountable tiredness that had plagued him all morning. He took several breaths, drawing air deep into his lungs, then exhaling into the tranquil day.

The earth and the sky would have to give him new strength. The dark green pines scattered like sentinels among the brown, shriveled post oaks whispered to him; a cool breeze talked in the grass at his feet. High overhead, a hawk circled, crying out a message to him from the heavens.

But Ridge couldn't understand what they were saying. They all blurred before his eyes as he watched them and the feelings boiling inside him roiled higher, swirling into and up and over each other until his arms went weak and he could hardly think.

Those draining, pounding emotions were the problem; they had been racing so out of control for days now that they were exhausting him, destroying his balance. All he had to do was get them in check.

And he could do so. After all, hadn't he kept iron control for all these years now, ever since Martha and the baby died? Where was the discipline he always had?

He bent over and picked up his rifle, then stood up and started walking. After he crossed the dry creekbed he broke into the ground-eating trot indigenous to his people. He could do it. He could get a grip on his feelings for Lacey and control them from now on instead of letting them control him.

He'd prove that just as soon as he saw her again.

* * *

Lacey's eyes went back at least a thousand times to the spot in the trees where Ridge had disappeared. Was that the tan of his buckskin shirt behind the red leaves of the sumac bushes? The glint of his black hair in the high sunlight?

The whole camp looked empty without him, from his cup on their makeshift table to his clothes dropped carelessly on top of the saddlebags. She crossed and picked up the shirt he'd discarded— it was still warm from his body. She held it against her cheek.

She wouldn't wash this one, she decided. He'd hardly worn it—just since she'd bandaged his wound—and she had to have something to hold on to until he came back.

When he came back would he be as strange and distant and hurried as when he had left? How could he be that way this morning after what they'd had together last night?

She buried her face in the shirt.

Lacey had her back turned when Ridge approached the camp. Her hair was tumbling in masses of curls to her waist, freshly washed and combed. She was dressed in his shirt, still, but she wore her skirt instead of the blanket. Their other clothes were scattered around on the bushes to dry.

She was bent over the flat rock they'd used for a breakfast table, completely intent on something. She moved her head, and he saw that she was arranging pussy willows and dried Johnson grass with pinecones and scarlet sumac leaves.

He shook his head. What a little girl! Decorating the camp while the fire went to nothing.

And to top it off, her vase was his small cooking pot—the only one he'd brought.

"Very pretty," he said, "if you plan to eat your dinner raw."

"Ridge!"

Her cry pealed through the valley, so full of joy it made his heart leap in spite of his resolve.

She ran to him, arms outstretched, her face alight. "Oh, Ridge, I'm so glad you're back!"

Her face blurred before his eyes, then he could see it clearly again. He caught her up and held her to him in spite of a vague voice in the back of his mind warning him not to.

"Ridge! You're so hot! You must've walked a long way!"

He hugged her hard, then he set her down. "Not too far. Have you been all right?"

"No! I'm starving," she said, holding on to his arm as he walked to the fire. She wanted to say, Starving for the sight of you . . . starving for your touch.

He showed her the rabbit and the turkey and built up the fire again. Then he led her a short way from their camp and finished cleaning the already gutted game while she watched.

"I'm so glad you're yourself again," she said. "Were you mad at me this morning?"

He lifted his head and shot her a glance that made his head go dizzy. He thought he might fall. "No," he said. "Of course not."

He couldn't think quite straight, but he knew that talk about feelings would be dangerous ground. Desperately he searched for a change of subject.

"Gather up the turkey feathers and some dried grapevine," he said, "and as soon as dinner's cooking I'll show you how to make a fan."

So she sorted the speckled feathers according to their shades of color while he made a cooking spit and put the turkey to roast over the fire.

He came to sit beside her at their rock table. She scooted close, but he didn't touch her. Her scent of sunshine and soap and roses filled his nostrils and made him dizzy again.

"Now this is what you do," he said, cutting six-inch lengths of the vine faster than she could count. "Wind the vine this way."

His fingers were so strong and sure, moving like magic, in between, up and over, the shafts of the feathers that she wanted to catch them and place them on her skin. Where they had been last night.

"Then, when you've got them all, wrap the vine around the whole bunch five or six times."

She slid closer to him, wanting to lean against his warm solidness.

He pulled the knot tight, then turned and looked down at her. "See? Can you do it?"

She looked up at him, trying to read his mood, trying to know him. His eyes were so dark they were almost black, but in their depths was a light like a flame.

"Lacey, do you know how to do it now?"

She watched his sensual lips form the words, but she couldn't think what he was talking about.

He raised the fan and whisked the feathers at the tip of her nose. "Lacey! Wake up!"

The feathers tickled, and she pushed them back at him, laughing. "Don't do that! I'm ticklish!"

"You are?"

Mischievously he brushed them beneath her ear, then against her neck. She squealed and jumped up, reaching around him to grab a handful of feathers for her own weapon.

"You'll be sorry, Ridge Chekote! When I find out *your* secret weakness I'll be merciless!"

"I don't have one."

He threw one long leg over the log and got up.

She ran.

"Yes, you do," she taunted over her shoulder. "Your weakness is your marksmanship."

He laughed, reaching for her. "I told you my cousin shot my foot. I'd never do such a thing."

"Ha! That's a likely story! Take off your moccasin and let me see if you mutilated any of your toes getting our supper today."

Laughing in his face, she ran around the table, holding the long feathers in front of her like a sword. "Take off your moccasin, I say! Do as I tell you or I'll tickle you within an inch of your life!"

"Impossible. I'm not ticklish."

"Not at all? Not even a little bit?"

"Not even the least bit."

He lunged and almost caught her; she whirled, shrieking with mock fear and laughter, and ducked under his arm to run past him toward the woods.

He caught the tail of her still-damp skirt as she flew by and held it, intending to pull her to him.

Instead, he leaned toward her.

Shocked at his lack of control over his body, he tried to straighten up. His head was suddenly too heavy to lift. He swayed.

The pain that had nagged him all day exploded inside him with the force of a powder charge.

He fastened his eyes on Lacey's astonished face. They clung to the pale heart shape of it until the world went black.

Ridge dropped to his knees so fast Lacey couldn't even try to catch him. He tugged her downward, too, his fingers locked in her skirttail. Then he was on the ground, crumpled sideways, his eyes closed tight.

"Ridge!"

Her scream shrilled against the mountainside and bounced back into her own ears. She went to her knees beside him in an instant and cradled his face in her hands.

He was burning up with fever.

She clapped her hands to her own face and screamed again, the heat from his cheeks transferred to hers.

"No!" she shouted to the rocks and the woods. "No! He will not die like Mama!" She bent over him. "Ridge!" she begged, "can't you hear me? Please, talk to me, Ridge."

His face stayed blank and helpless. She touched his lips, pleading for him to wake up and tell her what to do.

He was silent; he seemed half dead already.

He would die if she didn't do something to save him.

She dropped back to sit flat on the ground, forcing her numbed mind to work.

There was no chance that she could get him to a doctor. Even if she could somehow lift him up and across the saddle, there were no telling how many hilly, rocky miles between them and any town. Or any house or farm. She didn't even know which direction to go.

She was on her own. She had to figure out what was wrong and cure it or Ridge would die.

Had a snake bitten him out in the woods? Her heart lurched downward at the thought; she had no knowledge, no herbs, to treat snakebite.

Maybe it was his wound! Of course! It must be infected—she might be able to stop that with the whiskey.

She rolled him onto his back and unbuckled his belt. The buckskin shirt was stuck to him, but she pulled it up at last. She held it until she could untie the bandage.

Red streaks shot out from an angry yellow place in the center of his shoulder; around it small crusting spots were scattered over the muscled perfection of his skin. They showed where she had removed the pellets from Tom's gun.

Evidently she hadn't gotten them all.

And Ridge had been wrong. It did matter. Her fingers clutched at the bandage. She would have to try again.

She stood up and looked around through sudden new tears. Ridge lay near the edge of the woods, half in the shadows cast by the trees. She would need the full sunlight.

Her knees didn't want to hold her, but she ran anyway, first to get the blanket, then back to Ridge to roll him onto it. He was hard to move, and, at first, she was terrified of hurting him, but when he didn't make a motion or sound, even when she took the corners of the blanket and pulled him downhill, she walked more quickly. He was deeply unconscious.

If only he would stay that way while she dug for the shot!

Thank the Lord the sunlight was strongest there near the entrance to the cave, between it and the fire. That would be a protected place, and if it rained or a wild animal came during the night, she could drag Ridge inside.

She left him there and ran to the saddlebags. Her teeth bit her lip almost to bleeding while she opened them. She had nothing in the world to use but what was inside—Ridge's life depended on what she would find. Was there anything at all that she hadn't seen when she cleaned his wound last night?

The silver whiskey flask she set aside, then the one clean shirt that was left. There were no tools except for the small pocketknife.

She opened the other bag and tumbled out its contents quickly: The soap was there, which she put with the whiskey and the knife. Two small towels, some heavy socks and underwear, the handkerchiefs, and the silver-backed brush, comb, and mirror she left in the bag.

The cups still stood on the table; she ran to get them and saw the hunting knife beside the rabbit meat where he'd left it. She might need it, too.

She ran back to Ridge and poured water in one cup, whiskey into the other. She removed his bandages completely and washed both knives and his wound with the soap, dipped the blades in the whiskey, and poured a small amount of it over the wound.

She hesitated, then dribbled a little bit more. She wanted to use enough, but every drop was precious. If he came to while she was digging for the pellets he'd have to drink some for the pain.

She tied her hair back with one of his handkerchiefs to keep it from falling forward over her shoulders. Then she knelt beside him, facing the sun.

His shirt would have to come off. Bunched up like that, it might slide down into her way at a critical moment. Awkwardly she worked it off his good arm, then over his head, then off his injured side.

He didn't make a sound.

That set fresh fear to racing in her blood.

She tried to keep it from getting into her hands and starting them trembling. She would think about Dorcas, instead.

She would pretend that Dorcas was at her shoulder, telling her what to do. Then all of it would come back to her, everything she'd seen and heard while watching the competent black women at her doctoring.

The blade of the pocketknife slipped easily into the swelling; she prayed that it was clean enough.

She gritted her teeth and cut. Yellow infection oozed out, then some blood, then thinner yellow-red fluids. She narrowed her eyes on the silver blade, willing it to find the shot.

She moved it slightly to the left, then to the right. More blood came; it smelled. The odor carried her back to the horrid buggy ride with Papa in her arms.

Ridge. This was Ridge and he was still alive and she had to think about him.

She moved the tip of the knife slightly upward, but she couldn't feel it hit a thing. Surely the shot wasn't deeper than this!

What if she cut into his muscle? Or an artery or vein?

She clamped her jaw so hard her face twitched.

She moved to the right a few inches and eased the blade downward. It touched something hard.

Praying that it wasn't a bone, she tilted the knife and pushed. It moved, but not upward. Sweat broke out on her forehead. She wiped at it with one sleeve, holding the knife exactly in place with her other hand. She tried again. The same thing happened.

The shot was going in deeper.

Her mind began a constant prayer while her hands went to work on their own. She reached for the larger knife and widened the opening to let it in, too; she worked both blades around in the wound and got the pellet caught between them without ever giving her fingers a conscious direction.

When she knew she had the tiny ball between the knife blades, she stopped breathing altogether. She couldn't afford to lose it now.

The pellet came up out of Ridge's body on the

invisible thread of Lacey's will. She edged the
bigger blade under it and held the small one
against it as inexorably as if the bones of her wrists
were frozen into position. Once she thought she'd
dropped it, but she kept the knives constantly
inching upward and the next time she pulled, she
could feel it still there.

When it seemed that an entire lifetime had
passed and every drop of sweat had been wrung
out of her body, the pellet reached the surface of
the wound. She held it between the blades until
it was out and hovering over the blue-gray wool
of the blanket.

Then she dropped the knives, heedless now of
where the precious pellet fell, and slumped into
a heap beside Ridge, her arms shaking as if she
herself were racked with the fever.

She rested only a moment, though; the terror
tugging at the corners of her mind pulled her to
her feet. She poured another dollop of whiskey
into the wound, then made a new bandage from
the handkerchiefs.

She hurried, rolling him over to tie it in place
with more strips from her petticoats. He might
wake in terrible pain at any minute or, if the fever
continued to climb, he might not wake up at all.

Lacey fixed the folded shirt under his head,
slipped off his headband, and reached for the water bucket. Now she had to bring down the fever.

She sponged his whole upper body over and
over again, loving the feel of his perfect muscles
beneath her fingers, stopping from time to time
to touch his coppery skin. All day long she had
yearned to feel it under her palms again, but not
like this. Please God, never like this again.

She lost track of the times she went to the creek
for more water. Finally he felt distinctly cooler to
her touch.

He breathed differently, too; now he seemed more asleep than unconscious, so she left him long enough to put the meat on to cook. The rabbit would make a broth she could give him as soon as he woke; by tomorrow he would be well enough to eat some turkey.

After that she sat beside him, watching his face and the steady movement of his chest as he breathed. He would get well. He would.

The shadows fell from the west and lengthened; the breeze picked up. Lacey went to get the quilt to wrap around her shoulders. She brought the bedroll, too, and knelt beside Ridge. Should she cover him, or would that make him all hot again?

He groaned and stirred. His eyes came open.

She bent closer. "Ridge?"

He swallowed hard. "Thirsty," he said.

She leaped to her feet, kicking the quilt out of her way, and ran to fill his cup. Her hands shook so that she had to pour some back into the bucket so as not to spill. She rushed back to him.

"Here," she said, going down on one hip so she could support his head. "Here's water, Ridge."

She held the cup to his lips and tilted water into his mouth, words pouring off her tongue at the same time.

"I was so scared," she said. "Oh, Ridge, I'm so glad you're awake. You're going to be all right. You'll be fine. I got the last pellet out and now the infection will go away."

He nodded once, briefly, then pushed away the cup and closed his eyes again.

"No," she pleaded. Hugging his head in the crook of her arm. "Don't leave me. . . ."

Then she heard her own words and her cheeks

warmed with shame. How selfish could she be? He had to rest.

And he had to eat. That was the only way for him to get his strength.

She set down the water cup and lowered his head gently back onto the makeshift pillow, then she took the whiskey cup to the fire to dip into the broth. While the cup of broth cooled she held his hand and talked to him, trying to keep him from going really deep asleep until she'd gotten some of it down him.

He muttered unintelligibly once or twice and squeezed her hand, but he didn't open his eyes. The breezed sharpened; the sun dropped behind the mountain on the other side of the valley.

She cradled his head in her arm and brought the cup to his lips. He drank, rested, then drank again.

Tears sprang to her eyes. He was going to live. She just knew it.

But as the dusk deepened into full dark, she wasn't so sure. Ridge drank only once more, a sip or two of water, and the heat began to rise in his skin.

She went back to the creek for more water, feeling her way over the path she'd worn. The mare stopped grazing long enough to come snuffle at Lacey, and that was a comfort, but still she trembled inside from fear and it seemed hours before she could get back to Ridge.

His body gleamed in the firelight. It was hotter than ever.

She pressed both palms against his chest as if she could draw the heat out of him, then she wrung out the cloth and began to spread the cool water over his skin, willing him to come back to life.

His body seemed familiar now, yet strange and

wonderful, as if touching him was being able to touch the moon. She caressed the bulging muscles of his chest and shoulders, dipping into the sweet, secret hollows of his collarbone and his elbows, yearning for him to respond to her touch as he had done the night before.

"Ridge, I love you," she whispered.

Oh, why hadn't she told him last night, when he could hear her, that she loved him?

"I love you, Ridge."

That's what had been missing in their lovemaking and she hadn't known it until right now; the pact they had made with their bodies needed to be put into words.

She loosened the lacings of his buckskin breeches and bathed as far down as she could reach, trembling with the memories that assaulted her senses. He would say it, and so would she. She'd tell him again when he could hear her, right after he'd said "I love you" to her. He would say it as soon as he woke.

The breeze sharpened, blowing past the fire and through her clothing with all the bleakness of early November. Ridge shivered, then shook again, his whole body racking with the chill.

Lacey stood up and stepped across him to get the quilt; she spread it out and rolled him onto it, off the blanket he lay on, pulling up the top half of the bedroll as fast as she could. Then, sobbing with fear and frustration, she crawled in beside him and wrapped her arms and legs around him.

He shook with chill after chill, even after she reached for the blanket and his coat and covered him with them, too. She curved her body into the shape of his and tried with all her strength to hold him still.

Finally he was tranquil and she slept.

His voice woke her. She came awake with a

terrifying suddenness sometime in the wee hours of the night, every nerve trembling until she realized who was in her arms.

At last her heart slowed its pounding and her breathing came back to normal. His voice rang against the rocks again. ''Martha!'' he called. ''Martha!''

Lacey's arms went limp around his middle.

He grasped them with iron fingers and flung them away. ''No, Martha,'' he cried. ''No!''

Lacey's blood turned to icy water.

Didn't he know that she was Lacey? Was Martha still the only one in his heart?

Chapter 13

In the gray light before sunup Lacey saw that Ridge was deathly ill. His skin had lost its color and he lay hardly moving at all, as if he were using the last of his strength simply to breathe. The one good thing was that his fever seemed to be gone, or nearly so.

She watched him constantly as she replenished the fire and the water and tried to freshen her dress and hair. He came to for a few precious minutes; she used them to urge some water and a little of the broth past his lips. He looked straight at her, but he didn't speak before he dropped back into the same lifeless sleep.

Lacey hovered over him, leaving only to go get water and to check whether the mare was still in sight. Her life became nothing but watching for a change in him and waiting: waiting for him to know her, to call her name.

She dropped down to sit flat beside him on the ground, still cool in the early morning, and damp to her legs even through her skirt and petticoat. She stared at Ridge's handsome features, drawn now to even more sharply chiseled perfection by the pain, as if she could force them to divulge the answer to the question that had become her torment.

How deeply was he tied to the past?

How important to him were those whirling, spellbound moments when he and Lacey had made love in the night? Had he been holding Martha in his heart all the time he held Lacey in his arms?

Had Felicity been right all those ages ago when she said that Ridge would never love again?

Lacey watched the shifting sunlight play on his face, so vulnerable now that it broke her heart. She would snatch him away from Martha's memory, she decided. She would make him love her. Only her.

She threw herself into tidying the camp, crushing sandstone for sand to clean the cups and spoons, folding the clean clothing and putting the supplies in good order. Ridge's coat lay in a pile by the bedroll; he'd thrown it and the top quilt off when the sun's rays shone on him directly.

Lacey picked up the coat and shook it, wishing she had a clothes brush to lift the fine nap of the wool. She rubbed it with her hand; then, on impulse, she slipped her arms into the sleeves and put it on.

It felt as if Ridge had his arms around her. She hugged herself and smoothed out the wrinkles in the coat, slipping her hands into and out of the pockets to see if there was something she could use as there had been in the Union soldier's coat.

The inside breast pocket rustled every time she moved. She shouldn't look into it, though; obviously it held only a paper of some kind. And that pocket was somehow more private than the outside ones.

But her fingertips crept inside the coat, anyway, and touched the heavy paper wrapped in cloth. She drew the little package out and unwrapped it.

The top piece showed part of a face with dark hair and a large dark eye. A portrait!

She carried it to the stronger sunlight at the rock table, her heart suddenly pounding in a painful, ragged way.

Whose portrait? Martha's? Did he still carry Martha's picture? Probably, if he still loved her so much that hers was the name he cried out in the night.

Lacey didn't realize that her hands were trembling until the pieces fluttered against the rough rock. She made a motion as if to put them back into the coat she still wore, but her arm wouldn't complete the action. She took a deep breath and spread them out, arranging them into a face before she breathed again.

A baby! Ridge was carrying a miniature of his baby. It must have been the raiders who tore it in half.

She would have recognized the child anywhere. The eyes were Ridge's: big and dark as the center of a black-eyed Susan, yet burning in their depths. They even held that same sense of knowing that Ridge's had sometimes—the look that said he possessed some rare piece of wisdom about the ways of the world.

The shape of the face was the same, although Ridge's prominent cheekbones and strong jaw were hidden beneath a childish roundness. Only the curling dark brown hair was different.

The baby blurred before her eyes. He had died too young, this tiny Ridge; he had barely lived. The cruel tear across his face looked like a fresh cut from a knife—she could feel it in her heart.

She turned the paper over. "Edwin Ridge Chekote, 1856" was written on the back in finely scripted black ink. Now it was 1861 and Edwin Ridge Chekote was gone.

And he had been so beautiful! She could understand why Ridge hadn't gotten over his loss.

But he had to get over losing Edwin's mother! He just had to.

She feathered the edges of the paper against her fingers and tried to think. Tom had said Martha had been leaving Ridge when she and the baby were killed. Maybe that had made Ridge feel that she didn't love him, had never loved him.

Absently Lacey put the portrait pieces back into their wrapping. If that were true, maybe now Ridge thought that he couldn't trust any woman to love him always.

Did that make sense? Was that the way a man's mind might work? If only she had Mama or Dorcas, or even Fee, to ask! She puzzled over that as she put the handkerchief back where she had found it.

Ridge groaned.

She jumped up and ran to him, feeling like a sneak thief. But as she bathed his head again and urged some water past his lips, she began to smile. If her theory was right, she knew exactly what to do: As soon as he woke up she would tell him that she loved him, and then she would prove it to him over and over again.

For two more days he floated in a nebulous world of half consciousness, taking water and broth, but not opening his eyes more than a slit and not talking at all. Lacey couldn't tell whether he knew her or not.

At least he didn't call Martha's name again. She took comfort from that.

She continued to sleep beside him, sometimes putting her arms around him in the night, but he never responded. By the third morning she thought the awful loneliness would crush her.

For a while after she woke up she lay still, her

thigh touching Ridge's. She kept her eyes closed and pretended that he was well, that when he awoke he'd turn and take her into his arms.

He would remember all the things they had done and they would do them again. He would call her Lacey. And Little One.

He would say that he loved her even before she said it to him.

She lay there for a long time, pretending, knowing that she ought to get up and see about the fire and go fill the water bucket. The day was going to be a hot one for November.

Finally Ridge stirred and muttered, "Water." He wasn't really awake; he moved his legs restlessly beneath the quilt and picked at its top with his fingers, but his eyes hardly opened. She got up and poured him the last of the water in the broken bucket.

Then she went to the creek for more, looked to see that the mare was still grazing nearby, and struggled with the fire to heat the broth. When she had it ready, though, Ridge wouldn't rouse enough to drink any.

She dropped down beside him, glad to rest with the sun on her back. The weather was so wonderful and warm for November—it must be November by now.

But what if it should turn? In the Nation a storm could drop the temperature forty degrees or more in ten minutes. Summer could turn to winter overnight.

What would she do if it should snow?

What would she do about food, even if the weather stayed good?

What would she do about Ridge if he didn't wake soon?

Suddenly it all seemed brutally overwhelming.

Hot tears dropped onto her hands and into the broth before she even knew that she was crying.

She set the cup down, careful not to spill, wrapped her arms around her knees, and sobbed into her skirts until she fell asleep.

When she woke, the wind had died completely and the sun shone as hot as early June. It already had a mid-afternoon slant; she must have slept for a long time.

Two bobwhites called to each other, one in the woods above the cave, the other halfway down the hill into the valley. Ridge had kicked out of his bedclothes; he lay still, but breathing, his face half in the sun.

Lacey stretched, then straightened out her cramping muscles and got up, holding her skirts so they wouldn't knock over the cup of broth. She must offer it to Ridge again right away. It had been hours since he'd had any nourishment.

She turned to carry the precious liquid to the cooking pot, to warm it. Something looked different. She stopped and rubbed her hand over her still-sleepy eyes, then looked again.

The fire had gone out.

Lacey stared at the gray coals as if her look could ignite them and set them burning again.

They had to have a fire. Ridge would never drink the broth cold.

Without a fire tonight he would get chills again, maybe pneumonia, and wild animals might come too close. Even if they didn't attack, they might steal what little food was left.

Lacey set down the cup and smoothed her hair back from her face with shaky hands. She kept staring at the dead fire, her hands clutching her skirts.

There was no strength left in her to deal with

this. She was tired and trembly from sleeping all hunched over in the daytime, she was exhausted from being lonely and worried, she was sore in every muscle from carrying water and wood all day and all night.

She couldn't go on anymore. She simply could not.

She whirled to look to Ridge, staring at him the way she'd been staring at the fire, as if the power of her will could bring him to life. He sighed and threw one arm up, pushing his hair off his forehead with the back of his wrist. His lips curved a bit, almost as if he might smile.

He was as defenseless as a child; he couldn't save her this time, no matter how much she wished for it. This time she had to save him.

Wasn't there a custom in some cultures that if one saved another's life then that life belonged to him?

Lacey smiled. Perfect. She and Ridge belonged to each other.

She bent and picked up the broth, took it to the pot and poured it in. Then she picked up a stick and poked in the embers. There was a bit of fire left; maybe she could save it.

Lacey ran to the firewood she had piled at the edge of the woods and hurried back with sticks of all sizes. She arranged them over the coals, trying to remember how Dorcas and Old Jasper had made the fires at home. She formed a nest of small kindling in the middle, stirred the embers again, blew on them.

They wouldn't catch.

Matches! She rushed to get the tin out of Ridge's coat. But when she brought it out and opened it she paused for a minute. There were so few! Not more than ten, at most. She would have to be very stingy with them. Clutching the tin to her, she ran back to start the fire.

The first match went out as soon as she struck it. The second one burned. It kept burning, but the twigs didn't catch.

They had to catch! She went down on her knees and blew on the tiny flame. It went out.

She leaned closer and rearranged the kindling, then struck a third match.

It couldn't set the wood on fire, either. She held it to the kindling until its flame licked her fingers with a shocking pain.

Lacey dropped it into the pile of sticks and stood up, ready to run screaming off the mountain. She had to have help. Somebody had to help her.

The breeze lifted again; it dipped into the wash of dry leaves that had blown against the woodpile and swirled them into a tiny whirlwind of red and yellow. Two of them spun free and cartwheeled toward her, chased by the wind.

Lacey stared at them, too numb with despair to move her eyes away. Then the answer dropped into her mind like a gift from heaven.

She scrambled to her feet and ran to gather leaves into her skirt, adding dry pine needles, too, when she noticed them under the trees. In minutes she had a new fire blazing.

Triumphant, she was standing over it stirring the broth when Ridge said her name.

"Lacey," he called. "What are you doing?"

She dropped the stick and ran to him. His eyes showed pain, but they were clear; he was rational for the first time in days.

"I'm warming your supper," she said, her voice breaking. "And making turkey feather fans. I intend to find out whether you really are ticklish or not."

He gave a weak chuckle.

Then she remembered her plan. She dropped to her knees and looked straight into the dark depths of his eyes. "Ridge," she said, "I want you to know that I love you."

He gazed back at her for one long minute, then just before he closed his eyes again he gave her a smile that lit up her heart.

By morning Ridge felt well enough to sit up after Lacey had changed his bandage. She folded a shirt and slipped it between his hurt shoulder and the rough trunk of the big sycamore, then she stayed there on her knees, frowning at him.

"I'm worried," she said. "Should I leave you sitting up while I go for water? Do you think you'll get too tired?"

"I have to get tough," he said. "So I can hunt. We'll need more meat soon."

She adjusted the makeshift pillow and smoothed his hair away from his forehead. "When the turkey's all gone I'll go hunting," she said. "I can do it if you'll tell me how."

"Oh, no," he gasped, giving her an unsteady grin. "We'll die of starvation. What a shame after all we've been through!"

"Now, you listen here, Ridge Chekote!" Lacey put her hands on her hips and tried her best to frown. "I can hit any piece of game that runs, jumps, or flies!"

He laughed out loud, wincing from the pain it caused. "So you're making your brag, are you? Well, one day soon, Little Miss Sureshot, you can go out and see if you can make it good."

"You're in no shape to issue any challenges, sir," she retorted. "At least I can say that I've never shot myself in the foot!"

His eyes narrowed in mock anger. "And how

many times do I have to tell you that neither have I?''

His hand flew out and caught her at the nape of the neck; he pulled her lips close to his and kissed her.

Her mouth clung to his. Her hand clutched his good shoulder to steady her whirling heart.

''And just why are you smiling like that?'' he demanded after he broke the kiss. His hand was still on the back of her neck; she didn't move so he would keep it there.

''Because you kissed me. Because you're awake. Because you're alive.''

Because I love you, she wanted to say, but she held the words back. She had told him once. Now, please God, let him say it to her.

''I've been smiling ever since you came to,'' she said. ''I smiled all night long, without stopping for a single minute.''

''So did I,'' he whispered. ''Oh, Little One, so did I.''

The nestlike valley and its mountain cave became their own newborn world. They ruled it together; Ridge knew its secrets and Lacey had the strength to carry out his directions. He praised her mightily when she trapped two squirrels and gathered her skirts full of persimmons and acorns and hickory nuts.

Ridge grew stronger with each day that passed, but with each gain he made they saw how far he had yet to go. It took five days after he came back to consciousness before he could sit up for more than a couple of hours at a time, and Lacey held his cup and helped feed him for another day or two after that.

The day after he'd fed himself for the first time he got up early and cleaned both guns. When she came back to camp with fresh water he was wearing his fast-lengthening hair tied back and was strapping on his holster.

Lacey set the bucket down so fast that water splashed all over her feet. "Where are you going? You can't be planning to hunt!"

"I won't go far," he said. "I heard a deer crashing toward the creek while you were gone. I'll just wait by the trail for him to come back."

"You aren't able . . ." she began, but he turned away, picked up the rifle and walked across the camp, heading for the edge of the trees.

She ran after him. "Ridge, you can't do this."

"I have to do this."

His stiff back was so unyielding that it scared her senseless. If he went into the woods she would lose him for sure this time; he was weak as a newborn foal, weaker by far than she was.

"Ridge, if you pass out again I can't carry you back to camp."

Over his shoulder he snapped at her, "You don't have to carry me anywhere."

He started walking even faster, and before she could reach him he staggered and fell.

"Damn it!" he burst out as she helped him up. "Just damn this eternal weakness to hell, anyhow!"

She tried to put his arm over her shoulders for support; he jerked it away. But then when he took a step, he stumbled. Lacey took hold of his elbow and turned him back toward camp.

"You are pride-foolish," she said, in her best imitation of an indignant Dorcas. "You know you aren't able to hunt yet."

He shot her a furious glance. "I've got to try sometime! If I don't I'll be nothing but a lump on a log for the rest of my days."

"That's the silliest thing I ever heard," she scolded, walking him back toward the fire.

"That's easy for you to say," he said fiercely. "You don't know how it galls me to be so helpless. . . ."

"Ridge Chekote, if I can learn to build fires and cook game and dig out bullets and tend the sick, you can surely learn to be patient and let your body heal."

His astonished eyes met hers.

"I mean it," she said steadily as she helped him sit at the trunk of the sycamore again. "I'm not going to let you ruin all my good handiwork."

He slumped against the tree trunk, trembling all over from his exertions. But he forced enough breath to talk. "Ah," he said. "So that's it. You aren't concerned about me, you just don't want your work wasted."

"That's right. How can I become a doctor unless I have my very first patient all healthy and strong to display?"

A faint sheen of sweat, from weakness, covered his face. She knelt and began wiping it away with his handkerchief.

"So you're going to be a doctor," he mused. "I didn't know that. Are we going on the lecture circuit?"

"I think we may," she said, feeling a smile of relief beginning to tug at her lips. Thank God, Ridge was going to let her tease him out of his bitterness.

"Or maybe we should go into the circus, instead," she said, sitting back on her heels so she could see his reaction. "Yes. Now that I think about it, the circus would be much better for us."

"How so?"

"We wouldn't have to work at all; we could

just be famous for our heads. You could be the
Wooden-Headed Man, Hardest Head in the
World, Bar None, and I could be the Bald-Headed
Woman.''

He put one shaking hand into the profusion of
her hair.

"And how could you ever qualify for that?''

"Because if you keep this up I'll have pulled all
my hair out over you.''

He laughed and reached for her. She came into
his arms and pressed her face to his. Then his full
lips were hot against her cheek, and she was dis-
solving.

She felt the tantalizing brushing of the tip of
his tongue, felt it all the way into her loins, and
then his mouth was looking for hers. Lacey turned
her head slowly, ready to give it to him, but not
willing to let his lips leave her skin.

Then his lips found hers and their mouths
melted together, their tongues meeting in an im-
portunate embrace that sent fierce, throbbing
pulses all through her. They kissed until they
couldn't breathe, kissed with a sure, headlong
passion that made the kiss a promise—a pact that
had nothing to do with joining the circus.

All through the next, warm Indian summer
days they kept that pact, living every moment for
itself, staying together all the time that Lacey
didn't have to be away from camp. They talked
and laughed and teased each other, making up
for all the days and nights he was shut away alone
in his pain and she was coping in a scary world
with only loneliness for a companion.

He taught her woods lore and how to use the
guns. He related stories he'd heard as a boy,
the legend of the terrapin and the deer and of the
yellow mockingbird who desired to see ice; he
told her tale after tale of the Little People, small

magic beings, sometimes invisible, who lived in the woods.

She listened and she sang to him, the old songs of her childhood in Virginia and new ones like "Aura Lee."

But they never talked about the past.

Or of the future.

Ridge didn't mention Martha or baby Edwin. And he didn't tell Lacey that he loved her.

He didn't make love to her, either. She told herself it was because he wasn't strong enough yet.

One morning they woke very early in the shivery dark and stoked the fire to cook some corn-meal cakes. Ridge sat wrapped in the blanket, watching as she worked.

She loved him.

The words had been living in his heart ever since she'd said them, one minute warming him with surging joy, the next minute chilling him with fearful sadness. She loved him now. But for how long would that be true?

Far off in the eastern valley a mourning dove called; a whippoorwill answered from the west. Squirrels chattered in the woods behind them.

He wanted her so badly it made his hands shake. He had crawled out of the bedroll before dawn because he couldn't bear sleeping beside her like a brother any longer.

But he couldn't be her lover again. One more time and she would hold his heart helpless in her hands.

"I ought to go set some traps," Lacey said, as she served the meager meal. "We're running out of meat."

He nodded and bit into the warm scone she'd given him. "I'm not going to regain any real strength without it. I hate to let you out of my sight, Little One, but you're going to have to try for a deer, or at least some big rabbits.''

She smiled at him across the fire. ''Don't worry. I'll go this morning and bring in three deer and a bear.''

He laughed. ''That ought to do it. I'll eat the heart of the deer and by tomorrow I'll be running off this mountain and across the valley like a two-year-old buck.''

''No,'' she said, losing her smile. ''If that's what will happen I'll keep you on cornmeal and acorns.''

She got up and came to lay her cheek against his. ''Let's stay here forever, Ridge.'' Her voice broke on his name and she had to swallow hard. ''Let's not ever leave this place.''

Her words pierced him like a knife in the gut. Lacey was thinking that, if they left, she would go home to Pleasant Prospect. Poor child. He ought to tell her that she had no place other than this mountain, that her childhood home was only a pile of ashes.

But he couldn't do it. Not now. His hand slipped beneath her hair to stroke the side of her neck. He looked at the scarlet strips appearing in the sky, blazoning the news that dawn was coming, and said the first words that sprang to his tongue.

''All right, Little One. It's agreed. We'll never leave this valley.''

The sun hit the trees to the east with a blinding light. Lacey squinted into it and crouched lower behind the screen of sumac bushes. The noise came again—a loud rustling in the dry branches of the willow thicket.

She raised the rifle and sighted along its barrel. It must be a rabbit in there, maybe even two of them. The scrabbling noises were coming from the ground, not from the tree branches, so it probably wasn't squirrels.

It was about time she found something. She'd been hunting most of the morning. Ridge would be frantic if she didn't come back soon.

She fixed her finger on the trigger and waited while the noise grew louder. The tall grasses parted, and a big rabbit, then another, burst into view.

Lacey gasped. Perfect!

She steadied the gun, following the first rabbit with the muzzle as Ridge had taught her. Then she settled her finger onto the very middle of the trigger and squeezed.

The rifle shot cracked. The first rabbit raced away. The second one ran after it, both of them bounding faster at the sound of the gun.

Lacey, still sighting along the barrel, stomped her foot and swung to follow them with the muzzle of the gun. She fired again. Something else moved in the edge of her vision.

A deer! He leaped on the very heels of the rabbits, huge and brown, his hide gleaming in the sunlight like brushed fur. The rack of antlers on his head looked like a forest of miniature trees flying through the air.

Lacey gaped, fascinated. He was beautiful!

The buck took one more long stride, dropped his head, and faltered. He shook from side to side, slowly, the spreading antlers swaying as if a sluggish breeze had sprung up to blow them around. He fell in his tracks.

Lacey stood transfixed. Her eyes glued themselves to the animal; she watched for a long time, until the birds set up their chattering again, but the deer didn't move.

She stepped out from behind her cover. Not a

twitch of a muscle. Reloading the gun mostly by
feel, she kept her eyes on the deer. Hadn't Papa
told stories of wounded deer charging at hunters?

She walked to the deer, a step at a time, holding her breath. Long before she reached it, she
knew it was dead.

But it had been so gorgeous! And she, Lacey
Longbaugh, had killed it!

Tears stung her eyes and for a minute she had
an awful, empty feeling in the pit of her stomach.

Then she thought about Ridge. He needed meat
and she had gotten it for him. Now he would
regain his strength!

She laid the rifle down and took hold of the
deer's hind legs. She tugged and pulled, and finally got them propped onto a windfall of dead
branches. She wished she could hang it the way
Ridge had said, but it was far too heavy. She
turned her head away and cut its throat, hoping
that it would bleed clean.

Then she straightened and just stood there.
She'd have to have help, but not from Ridge. He
mustn't even try. It must be a mile and a half,
maybe more, back to camp.

The mare! Tyree could haul the deer for her!

She picked up the gun and started following
her own trail back toward the creek and the
mare's grazing grounds.

Lacey and the grulla worked the rest of the
morning and half the afternoon moving the venison. Muscadine vines and thick pine branches
made a crude travois, and Lacey thanked her
lucky stars that the horse had been trained to pull
a buggy in harness.

She was fortunate, too, that the trail was fairly
open once they got through a narrow section of
woods and that much of it was covered with thin,
dying grass that made for good sledding. Even

so, by the time they reached the valley floor, her
arms were trembling with the exertion of carrying
the rifle and guiding the mare.

On the way up the sloping hillside to the cave
she tried to imagine Ridge's face. Now he'd have
to admit that she could shoot.

She chuckled and the mare turned to look at
her. "You want me to let you in on the joke, don't
you, Ty?"

Lacey stroked the strong, sweaty neck. "We're
going to let Ridge think I shot the deer on purpose, that's what. Don't ever tell him any different."

Ridge came to meet them, smiling like mad
when he saw the expression on Lacey's face.

"Look what I brought you!" she called. "Didn't
I tell you that I could shoot anything that runs,
jumps, or flies?"

He laughed. "So. You just had to make good
on your brag, did you?"

"Of course. And I'm challenging you to a
shooting contest when you get well."

He was close enough now that she could see
the light that burned deep in his eyes. It set her
heart to dancing.

"And what'll be the prize?" he asked.

The answer burst from her on a wave of gladness. "A kiss," she said, and ran into his arms.

They spent the rest of the day taking care of the
meat. Ridge had slept for many hours, so he had
enough energy, with Ty's and Lacey's help, to
hang the carcass from a tree limb and to start the
skinning and butchering. When he had to rest, he
directed Lacey in cutting the venison into strips
for salting and drying.

"I hate to see him dead," Lacey said, averting

her glance from the buck's brown eyes. "He was so beautiful leaping through the woods."

"I'm surprised you could bring yourself to draw down on him," Ridge said. "Knowing how you are about animals."

She shot him a glance. Did he suspect the shooting was accidental? "Mmmn," she said noncommittally, and kept on working.

"You must be an absolute natural shot," he said. "It takes some kind of skill to hit a running deer."

"I guess I am," she said, looking at him with wide-eyed innocence. "And I truly did hate to aim at him, but it was more important that you have meat to eat. I've learned that a hunter does what she has to do."

Ridge raised his eyebrows in surprise and then he roared with laughter.

He took several of the first strips she cut and put them to boil over the fire and then began to make wooden racks for the smoking. Lacey fussed and worried that he was doing too much, and she made him stop for more cornmeal cakes and some coffee.

They laughed and talked over the scanty dinner, as excited as if supplies for the winter had just dropped out of the heavens. Lacey's heart thrilled to see that Ridge's hands didn't tremble and that his voice stayed steady even after all the exertion he'd had.

They worked until long after dark, but at last the cooking venison was done and the rest of it was smoking over a fragrant hickory fire. Lacey brought water so they both could wash.

Neither had the energy to eat any of the hot meat; she spread out the bedroll in the moonlight and they crawled into it without even thinking of taking off their clothes. Lacey had never been so exhausted. She was too tired to sleep; too tired to live.

"Hold me," she whispered. "Ridge, hold me."

He folded her into his arms and drew her close, locking her body into the haven of his with his chin resting gently on top of her head. She inhaled deeply, drawing in a long breath that brought with it the essence of him.

She lay for a long time without moving, her face against his chest, unable to do more than simply lie close. A tremor ran through the muscles of his chest; he was as exhausted, more so, than she.

But now he had meat to make him strong; they had enough food to keep them safe in their own little world for days and days. Soon Ridge would be well and he would make love to her again.

Then he would tell her that he loved her, too. When he was sure of her love.

She was almost asleep at last, but she did have the strength to whisper. "I love you, Ridge," she said. "Sweet man, I love you."

Chapter 14

Ridge woke with her words still in his ears. The sun lay across him, as warm as wool, but Lacey was gone. He opened his eyes, a sudden desperate need to know her whereabouts making the blood pound fast in his veins.

She stood on the edge of the clearing, at the head of the trail she had made going back and forth to the creek, face-to-face with the big grulla mare. They seemed to be visiting. Lacey was talking—he could hear the lilt of her voice—but she was too far away from him to make out what she was saying.

As he watched, she took a persimmon from behind her skirts and held it out to Tyree, who gobbled it down without even stopping to smell what it was. Lacey laughed and threw her arms around the mare's neck.

She was so full of love it scared the life out of him.

He pushed back the covers and leaned on one elbow to watch her, spirit-piercing joy rising in him again. She loved him. She had said so twice.

The mare dropped her head and began to graze; Lacey gave her a last pat and turned toward the camp. She went to the fire and stirred the food in the pot, then to the meat racks to turn the venison

strips smoking over the hickory fire. With her hair
hanging in a braid down her back she looked like
a little girl, but she moved like a woman at home
in her own kitchen.

He had to hear her voice.

"Lacey."

"Ridge!" She whirled and ran to him, dropping to her knees beside him on the pallet as she
had done a thousand times during his illness.

He looked stronger; his eyes were bright and
full of energy, even after the exertions of the day
before. Maybe because he was happy that she'd
said she loved him. Could that be?

"I've been worried that you slept so late," she
said.

"You shouldn't have been. I'm just a sleepy-
head."

He was smiling that rare, melting smile that always changed the world for her. Would he say it
now? Would he tell her that he loved her, too?

He had heard her, last night, because his arms
had tightened around her, just for a second or
two, in answer. But she needed a spoken answer.
She searched his face, not talking so he could
speak.

A covey of quail rose out of the tall grass near
Tyree, their fast-moving wings making a deafening whirring sound. The slow breeze rustled the
sycamore limbs over their heads; several yellow
leaves, as big as a man's hand, fluttered down.
One of them caught in Lacey's hair.

"Lacey, I . . ."

She held her breath.

He reached to take the leaf and brushed her
cheek with his hand.

"I've never seen your hair plaited before."

He'd started to say, "Lacey, I love you." He
wanted to say that more than he'd ever wanted

anything—more, even, than he wanted to hold her. The words gathered like quicksilver in his mouth.

But there they stayed, clinging and burning as if he'd stuck his tongue to a tin dipper coated with hoarfrost.

Finally, hating himself for a coward, he said, "How'd the venison stew turn out?"

"It's good. I added some persimmons like you said your Aunt Dovey always did." Her eyes were as purple as woods violets. "Want me to bring you a cupful?"

He threw off the covers and got up. "No, thanks, Lace. I'll wash up and come to the table."

He took the half-filled water bucket and walked into the woods that grew closest to the camp, every step a battle between running away and running back to her. She loved him.

And he loved her, he knew that now. But he wasn't going to tell her so. He was not. The words would only bind them into a wondrous web of pain.

The day turned out to be the most fabulous of the whole Indian summer. Lacey gloried in the warmth of the sunlight and of Ridge's voice; he talked more than she had ever heard him, joking and teasing her while they did the morning chores and turned the smoking strips of venison. But he never said the words she was waiting to hear.

When they had finished their noon dinner and were sitting on the log, sated and barefooted, just talking, she said, "I have a surprise. Close your eyes and hold out your hands."

While he obeyed, she ran to get the bundle of precious fruit she'd hidden from him. She put it in his open hands.

"Guess!" she said. "You can't open it until you've guessed what it is."

"Pawpaws!"

"Ridge!" she shrieked. "No fair! How could you get it on the first guess?"

"The smell," he said, opening his eyes and the package at the same time. "One whiff made my mouth start to water."

They ate the long, narrow fruits as fast as Ridge could slit the skins with his knife, scooping out the soft goodness inside each one with their tongues.

"Umm," Lacey moaned, getting the very last drop of sweetness out of her third one. "These *are* ambrosia, just as you said. They taste exactly like custard."

She watched him smile, his lips shiny with the juice. They were curving and soft and sensual; they had the most delectable shape. They would taste even more delicious than they looked.

"I'm glad you knew what these were when you saw them in the woods," he said.

"Well!" she said, pretending to pout. "You needn't sound so surprised. I can survive anywhere now; I've had woods lore lessons from a full-blood Cherokee."

He laughed and turned to face her, throwing one leg over the log to straddle it. His eyes gleamed. "So you're an expert now, huh?"

"Certainly," she said, picking up his knife and another piece of fruit.

But her wrists were so weak she couldn't cut into it. His eyes held her still, even her breathing stopped.

"Don't peel it," he said.

She held the long, narrow fruit to his lips.

He bit into it and sweet nectar spurted out onto both of them, once, then again. It filled her palm and ran down her arm to gleam on the skin of his chest in dancing copper lights.

He grasped her wrist and held it while he ate the pawpaw, then he licked the juice from her fingers as he had done beneath the white oak tree all those ages ago. On the day he had first made love to her.

Each stroke of his tongue sent ripples of pleasure shooting up her arm and darting down into the very center of her.

''Oh, Ridge!''

Her pulse beat like thunder beneath his thumb. Her wet, sweet mouth tormented his. Because it was too far away. Surely one kiss could do no harm. It wouldn't commit him to anything; it wouldn't be the same as telling her he loved her. . . .

Yes, a kiss would be as right and natural on a day like this as the mountain breeze caressing their faces. It was as inevitable as the sunshine making yellow fire of her hair.

He leaned forward and wiped out the distance between them. She sank like a stone into the bottomless well of his kiss. He tasted of custard, he felt hotter than the highest sun.

He sipped the sweet juice of the pawpaws from her mouth then gave it back to her. Its magic nectar sealed them together and she abandoned her tongue to his stroking as if she were starving. Then they parted, her lips bruised by the power of his kiss, her heart hammering in a ragged rhythm with his.

''Ridge,'' she said, his name floating out on her first breath. ''I . . .''

''No,'' he said. ''Don't.''

His eyes burned hers; they fixed her lips apart, the words silent on her tongue.

"No," he said again. He turned her loose and got up.

"This is all over me," he said, glancing down at his bare, sticky chest. "I'm going down to the pond."

She stared after him as he went to the cave. He came out with the towels and the soap, his clean black trousers over his arm. He took a few steps, staring straight ahead, then he stopped and looked at her across the sun-dappled space.

"Can you go that far by yourself?" she asked.

"Yes," he said.

But he made no move.

She got up and walked to him.

He let her take his arm as she had done during his weakest days, and they started down the hill together.

The breeze from the south caught Lacey's skirt and make it flare, whipping it lightly against her legs and his. It wrapped the two of them together and drew them down the sloping trail.

The pond lay like a secret in its circle of trees, surrounded by chinkapin oaks, whispering and talking, holding on to some of their leaves and letting some float on the water like red-and-yellow treasures. Other fallen leaves crackled beneath Ridge's and Lacey's feet. That was the only sound.

The two of them walked down to the water's edge, where sunlight shone on the shimmering water like a celebration. At their feet they could see the gray-brown gravel on the pond's bottom.

"If you want to bathe, too, this is the best place," he said. "I'll go around there behind the red cedar bushes."

Disappointment hit her like a blow. He wasn't going to bathe with her, for he was thinking the same thing as she. If he did, they would be sure to make love again.

He didn't want her with the same tearing longing that she had for him. He didn't need her body the way she needed his. He didn't love her after all.

Ridge turned to look at her and read every one of those thoughts in her eyes.

Their expression almost killed him, but maybe that was for the best. He knew it was. Just one time with her had made him yearn so for more, had made him so obsessed with the memory that he could never forget it, ever. Another such memory would only mean another torture.

He was right. They shouldn't do it again.

She read his thoughts, too.

"You must be tired," she managed to say. "I'll go."

But the same sunshine that soaked into her back played on the muscles of his arms. It made dancing copper lights in the hollows of his neck and on his high cheekbones.

On the left side of his chest the myriad of little scars showed pink and shiny, some of them already turning white. So near his heart.

How could she have borne it if they had hit him there?

As well as she could bear this separation today.

"We'll have to share the soap," she said.

He took the long bar between his hands and broke it, the powerful muscles in his arms barely tensing.

The pounding need for him grew inside her like a rose blooming. How could she turn and walk away?

She held out her hand for her half of the soap. He opened his fingers. It lay in his palm. She glanced up. He was staring at her, his eyes heavy-lidded and suffocatingly fierce.

"We can't," he said, his voice rasping in the quiet. "Not again."

She didn't answer.

He let the soap fall and put his hand on her shoulder, sliding it up the back of her neck; her hair lay against his knuckles, heavy as gold.

She came to his kiss like a lost child to its daddy.

Ridge moved backward one step at a time; Lacey clung to his mouth and went with him. Her bare feet sank into wet sand.

He pulled them out again. He kissed her with such slow, voluptuous yearning that she arched on tiptoe, then off the ground completely, holding fast to his shoulders, following him wantonly deep into the hot afternoon. The water swirled like another warm and lazy mouth up onto her bare legs.

She began to kiss him back, heedless of anything that had gone before or anything that would come, exploring his mouth with the same desperate desire that he had brought to hers.

Ridge stepped into deep water and they went under. The kiss didn't break.

Then they were rising again, into the warmth and the air of the sun-dazzled day. He pulled away and looked at her, cupping her head in his hand, wiping the water out of her eyes with his work-callused thumb.

She brushed the wet black feathers of his hair to one side of his forehead. The rest of it clung to his head and his neck; he looked like a carved statue, the head of a god, the eagle god.

"I thought you were going to bathe alone," she said.

"I am," he said. He found the end of her braid

and brought it over her shoulder. He began to untie its ribbon. "Later."

She sculpted his face with her hands, forming it between them as if she were blind, while he loosened her hair and set it free. When it was trailing behind her on the water, his hands cradled her waist.

"You're the one who was going to the red cedar cove," he said.

He lifted her higher until her breasts, straining at the buttons of her wet-plastered shirtwaist, were even with his mouth.

"I am," she said. She pulled his head to her. "Later."

His lips and his tongue set off the wildfire in her body, flames not dampened one whit by the fact that she was soaking wet. She put her hands on his shoulders and let him melt her completely, glorying in the feel of his mouth on her body, reveling in the sight of it. She was limp, clinging, helpless, when he let her go.

His eyes were glazed. He was as much captive to her as she was to him, she thought. Maybe he did love her, after all.

His eyes fastened, burning, to her throat, to the sweet hollow at its base where the top button was undone. All the others stood closed, locking him out.

He began to tear them open, ravenously, the primitive need to have her building and building inside him like a hawk circling.

"This time I want to see you," he said, in a voice so hoarse it sounded like a stranger's. "I have to see you, Lacey."

She lifted her hand and smoothed the shiny black wing of his hair. "All right," she whispered. "You shall."

He picked her up in his arms, then, and walked

to shore, to the red cedar cove, where the dried grass stood tall and yellow. He laid her down and knelt beside her.

He ran the heels of his hands down the valley between her breasts and pushed the shirtwaist open, thrusting it off her shoulders and away. He captured her breasts with his palms all in the same ruthless motion.

"Lacey," he said.

The light in his hooded eyes held her mesmerized.

The magic in his hands held her captive.

Then he moved to the ties at her waist, undoing them in an instant, setting her legs free, flinging her soaking skirts away, down, down, to vanish from the tips of her toes. His breeches followed.

Her lips parted to speak his name, but his mouth made them silent and his tongue found hers. She forgot what she had meant to say, forgot what she had wanted him to say.

He was taking her into a whole new world of hot delights where words did not exist.

With a trembling moan his mouth left hers and was immediately everywhere: bringing her breasts to bursting with pleasure, blazing a trail up and down the vulnerable column of her throat, tracing the way from her mouth to the tender skin of her waist.

He knelt between her legs in the slanting sunlight and kissed her flat belly. It took her breath away for one shining moment. Then she reached up and pulled him to her.

She pressed her open mouth to his flesh; his skin tasted of sweet sweat and woodsy pond water. He smelled of honey.

He came into her secret center and she lost the need for anything else. He moved in her, then moved again; she caught his mighty, pulsating rhythm, the throbbing force that sent comets of joy shooting through every vein in her body until she was melded to Ridge forever, until he was her world. He was the source, the earth, the shining, endless sky.

At last the exquisite pleasure burst like a shower of stars and he shouted her name in a wild war cry. They collapsed, tangled together, to lie languid, naked in the burnished afternoon.

Then they slept wrapped together, as still as the woods that surrounded them, until the squirrels came back to the chinkapins and two deer trotted down to the pond for a drink. Lacey and Ridge watched them drowsily through half-closed lids.

"Looks like we're part of the scenery now," he whispered.

"Aren't they beautiful?" she whispered back. "I couldn't believe I killed one, even by accident—"

She clapped her hand over her mouth.

"What?" His deep laugh went booming out across the pond; the startled deer dashed away, scrabbling for the safety of the trees.

"I knew it!" he chortled. "I had a feeling that was an accident!"

She beat on his chest with her fists, laughing and whimpering with frustration. "It was not completely accidental. I meant to shoot. I had my gun all ready and aimed."

"At what?"

"At two rabbits."

He hugged her hard, whooping with helpless laughter. "*Two* rabbits! No wonder you didn't hit either one of them."

"Well, at least I hit something besides my own toe!"

"You think that entitles you to be Warrior

Woman, do you?'' He dropped a kiss on the end of her nose. ''Well, we'll see. Remember that shooting contest you proposed? Now I know that I'm going to win.''

She kissed him back, right where his wet hair curved under his ear. ''And what will be the prize?'' she asked.

His hand went to her breast and his mouth came to hers. ''I'll show you,'' he murmured against her lips.

Just before she was lost in the mindless pleasure, Lacey had one last thought. She needn't worry anymore. Ridge had already told her that he loved her.

And now he was going to tell her again.

They didn't leave the pond until late in the day. Lacey held on to Ridge's hand all the way back to camp, loving the closeness that bound them, inside and out.

She stopped halfway up the slope, holding one of Ridge's hands in both of hers, and looked back across the sweep of the valley. It lay sparkling in the sunlight, purple in the shadowed places and red-gold on the high ones.

The ragged, dark lines of trees kept it safe on three sides; on the fourth their camp and their cave stood sentinel.

She shivered.

Ridge put his arms around her and pulled her back against his warm belly. ''Cold?''

''No. It's just that . . . this day was so perfect.''

He nodded, his chin resting lightly on the top of her head. ''It was,'' he said. ''The first perfect day I can remember.''

They walked the rest of the way in silence. At the edge of camp, Ridge stopped still.

Lacey froze in the crook of his arm. "What is it?"

He didn't answer; his eyes were darting over every inch of the camp.

"Ridge! What's wrong?"

He made a sharp gesture with one hand. "The fire."

She looked. Flames were curling around pieces of new wood, throwing yellow lights onto the black mouth of the cave.

Her bare toes dug into the hard-packed earth. "Somebody's been here!" she whispered.

"And probably still is."

She clutched his hand harder, her palm slick with sudden sweat. "Tom? Do you think it's Tom?"

"I don't know."

They looked into the cave first, using a pine stick grabbed out of the fire. The low, damp walls reflected the light of their torch; the shallow space the walls enclosed lay empty except for their guns and packs.

"Nothing missing," Ridge said.

She clung to Ridge, staying as close to his side as she could. "In the trees up there," she whispered, pointing to the north as they came out of the cave. "I thought I saw something move."

She scrambled up the rocky embankment at his heels, heedless of the painful gravel digging into the soles of her bare feet. The thin grove of black-jack oaks held some squirrels, nothing more.

They turned back to walk above the cave's entrance and into the scattered pines on the south. There was no sign of anyone there.

Ridge looked down at the campsite and went still again. "Over there," he whispered. "In the sumacs by our table."

Lacey could see nothing but the red sumacs and the green pines behind them.

They climbed down, and Ridge left her just inside the cave with the rifle. He took the pistol.

It seemed to Lacey that two lifetimes passed, then Ridge called to tell her to come out. She did so, still holding the rifle in both hands.

Ridge was coming toward the other side of the fire with a short, slight man who seemed, at first glance, to be composed entirely of constantly moving arms and legs.

And mouth. He talked very loudly, as if he were hard of hearing, a steady stream of Cherokee, spoken so quickly that Lacey couldn't catch a single word.

She watched him, her stomach turning as cold as the rifle in her hands. This little character had ruined the perfect day.

Then he glanced up and saw her. "Ha! Just now! Wait a minute," he called out in English. His windmilling arms flew straight up in the air and stayed there. "Don't shoot, pretty lady, don't shoot."

He screeched with laughter, then bent double and began slapping his thighs, apparently overcome by his own joke.

"You'd better not laugh, Horse Fly," Ridge told him. "This pretty lady killed the venison you'll be eating for your supper. She can hit a horsefly at a hundred yards."

That small witticism set off a new paroxysm of laughter and more flapping of the man's wiry arms.

When it had subsided, Ridge introduced him to Lacey. "Horse Fly is a traveler," he said. "He goes from one end of the Nation to the other."

Horse Fly's wrinkled face sobered. "The entire Nation is my home," he said in a dignified tone, drawing himself up straight to his full height, which was about the same as Lacey's. "I am a wandering Cherokee, but I am always at home."

Lacey greeted him. The traditions of hospitality ingrained in her very soul were all that kept her from telling him how much he had frightened her and to go away.

Ridge and Horse Fly sat at the fire and talked, mostly in English, as Lacey prepared the simple meal. Horse Fly had been traveling south along a higher mountain trail when he noticed their fire, he said, and then Tyree grazing in the meadow. Lacey blushed to think that he might have come upon her and Ridge by the pond.

He came down into their camp to investigate, he said, to see if someone were lost and needed his help.

Ridge laughed. "Why don't you tell the truth, Horse Fly? You know you just came in to cadge your supper, as usual."

Horse Fly laughed mightily and didn't deny it, and, as he refilled his plate again and again, Lacey silently agreed with Ridge.

His eating hardly slowed his talk, however, especially his attentions to Lacey. He mopped up venison stew with scraps of cornmeal cakes, beamed at her, and talked to Ridge, all without missing a single bite.

"Ridge Chekote, you are a lucky man. What other woman goes out to hunt, brings in the game, and cooks it, too?" He grinned at Lacey and reached for another of the flat, fried cakes.

She forced herself to smile back at him across the fire, picked up her spoon and lifted a bite to her mouth. Then she let the stew drop back into the bowl, untasted. She couldn't eat. Food didn't even smell good to her.

She shouldn't be so upset; Horse Fly was

charming company. Thank God he wasn't Tom Creekwater and he wasn't dangerous.

But he sat between her and Ridge. He had intruded in their own secret world and somehow everything had changed.

Chapter 15

Early the next morning Lacey woke to find the world full of fog. It seeped through the thick quilt of the bedroll to find her skin; it floated in fat clouds in the valley. It made her shiver.

She hugged herself and tried to curl into a ball in the warm spot where she'd slept. If Ridge would put his arms around her, then she wouldn't be cold.

Ridge! He had slept in the blanket instead of sharing the bedroll—sometime in the night she'd known that. He and Horse Fly had sat up talking long after she had crawled, exhausted, into the quilt.

She flopped over onto her stomach, tugging at the cover to keep it over her. It was all Ridge's fault that she hadn't rested well and that now she was trying to sleep cold.

He had been trying to avoid gossip, no doubt. He didn't want Horse Fly telling the Nation that Ridge and Lacey were sleeping together before they were married.

Before they were married. After they were married. When they were married. . . .

All of those phrases sounded marvelous.

She smiled and closed her eyes tighter so she

could concentrate. What a wonderful new dream to plan!

This would replace all the others, especially the one about the well-mannered young man. Ridge was different from him, very different from what she had expected for her husband, but he was the one. She'd known that for ages; she'd known it for sure ever since they'd made love together that very first time.

Then, after yesterday at the pond, there could be no doubt. Even though he hadn't said in words that he loved her, or talked about marriage, his body and hers had made a betrothal that couldn't be broken. He had to know that as well as she did.

So. They would have a big wedding at Pleasant Prospect.

Oh! But Mama and Papa wouldn't be there! She was always forgetting that because sometimes she pretended they were at home and everything was the same as ever.

But she wouldn't think about that now; if she did she would start to cry and she didn't want to wake Ridge and Horse Fly. The little old man would probably stand over her, flapping his arms and demanding at the top of his lungs to know what was wrong.

So she would think about the wedding, instead—she'd plan it down to the most minute detail, just as she always did her dreams for the future. She would wear her mother's wedding gown, the white one she'd worn to marry Daddy. . . . It would be a small wedding, but it would be at Pleasant Prospect, for she had to be married from home.

They would decorate the front parlor with . . . oh, they just had to wait for the Harison's Yellow roses to bloom! Perfect! A summer wedding would be perfect.

That would give Ridge time to get to know his feelings and put them into words, she thought sleepily. He could talk over the past with her and get it out of his system and they could make all their plans. They would stay here in their perfect world and do just that—if Horse Fly would go away and leave them alone.

Lacey spun out her daydream until the dozens of details lulled her back to sleep. When she woke again, the sun was trying to break through the fog.

She had slept in her clothes because Horse Fly was there, so she just threw off the quilt and got up. Her stomach churned.

Clutching it with both hands, she stood perfectly still for a minute. Of course! She hadn't eaten a bite of supper—what did she expect?

Hurrying into the cave to use Ridge's comb, she thought about breakfast. She'd fry some of the venison, she decided. Better fry a lot since Horse Fly ate so heartily. With red haw berries and corn-meal cakes that would be enough.

On her way out to the meat-smoking racks she picked up the skillet and glanced at Ridge, rolled up in the blue blanket. Horse Fly had dropped his gear on the opposite side of the fire in the fog. What a pair of sleepyheads! But, no wonder. They had talked way into the night.

Well, at least Ridge had enjoyed their first houseguest in their first home. Lacey was still smiling at that when she got to the racks over the hickory fire. She held the skillet flat and was actually reaching for the meat to put in it when she realized that the racks were empty!

Her brain couldn't comprehend what her eyes were seeing. This couldn't be!

Then there, on the ground at her feet, she saw a small cloth sack and a . . . piece of a stick?

She knelt and looked more closely. That was Horse Fly's sack of salt—he'd taken it out of his grubby pack last night when she'd mentioned that she and Ridge had used most of theirs to cure the deer. And the stick was the turkey call he had demonstrated so proudly!

What in the world were these things doing here? Without thinking she scooped them into the skillet to take back to camp.

But *where* was the meat?

She turned and ran back to the other fire. The fog was thinning fast, and when she actually looked for Horse Fly's bedding she could see that it was gone.

How could he be gone? Would he leave without telling them good-bye? Surely not, the way he loved to talk.

"Horse Fly is gone!" she called to Ridge, still peacefully sleeping. "And so is our meat, but his turkey call and salt . . ."

As the words came out of her mouth in order, all the unbelievable facts fell together and made sense.

"He took our meat!" she screamed. She stomped her foot and threw the skillet and the peace offerings it held at the hard-packed ground. "He took it, didn't he?"

Ridge stood up, his blanket hanging crazily from one shoulder. The turkey call bounced to a stop at his feet.

"Didn't he?" Lacey demanded.

"How should I know?"

"How should you know? You sat up half the night talking to him, didn't you?"

She snatched up a rock and threw it at the sack of salt. It hit with a furious thump.

"Well, yes, but he never told me he was planning to take our meat and sneak off in the dark," he drawled, tucking his shirttail into his pants.

Lacey stared at him, her eyes narrowed in fury. Was he grinning? He was. Grinning!

She started toward him, kicking a stick of wood out of the way with a swirl of her skirts. "He took every single scrap of it!" she shouted. "Every piece of food that I cut off that poor, pitiful animal that I killed!"

She shook her finger at Ridge's laughing face. "Now we don't have any food after I killed that beautiful deer, and I skinned him and cut him up, hating every second of it, using that dangerous sharp knife that I could have killed myself with!"

"Or me," he said. "If you'd had blood in your eye then the way you do now."

"Don't you dare make fun of me, Ridge Chekote! I broke my back dragging that carcass in here and bending over that drying rack! And now that silly little laughing hyena has stolen it all!"

"Surely not."

"Surely so," she yelled, still advancing on him.

"Didn't he leave you anything in return?"

"A sack of salt and that stupid turkey call."

Ridge laughed. "Well, then. Horse Fly didn't steal your meat. He traded you for it."

"Traded! Some trade!"

She was close enough now to see the twinkle in his eyes. Her fists clenched.

"He gave you the salt so you could cure another deer," Ridge said calmly. "After all, Lacey, the woods are full of deer."

"Yes," she screamed. "All uncooked and still wearing their skins!"

He burst into helpless laughter. She ran the rest of the way to him and began pounding on his chest with her fists.

"Stop that!" she yelled, "Just stop that laughing. There isn't one funny thing about this."

He grabbed her wrists and held them. "Yes, there is," he said. "You. Don't you think it's funny that you're trying to kill me because Horse Fly stole your deer?"

"No! You ought to suffer for that! You're the one who let him stay here. You're the one who knew him. You're the one who left me alone all night so you could listen to his rantings and ravings!"

She began to cry, struggling to free herself.

"Ah, come on, Lacey! I had to offer hospitality. You know that."

He loosened his grip and her hands fell to her sides. "And you know that was *our* deer," she said, "and not just mine like you said. Ridge, that was our winter food supply."

He stared down into her eyes, wide and blue as the sky in summer, wet with tears. "Honey," he said softly, "we couldn't stay here all winter if we had *three* whole deer smoked and dried."

"Yes, we could. You know which berries to eat and which plants and nuts. And there're squirrels and rabbits. And we can sleep in the cave when it snows."

He shook his head. Suddenly his eyes were sad. "We'd freeze, Little One." He pulled out his shirttail again and wiped her cheeks.

"Not if we stayed together and held each other really tight."

He put his arms around her. She slipped hers around his waist and laid her head on his chest.

"Like this?"

"Yes. Like this."

They rocked back and forth for a minute, their hearts pressed together and beating like drums, then she lifted her wet face up to his.

He gave her a look that broke her heart.

His kiss was long and slow and gentle, as if he would never let her go in this lifetime.

Finally, gradually, with one last sweet brush of his lips on the end of her nose, he pulled away.

"We've known all the time that we'd have to go in sometime," he said. "I'll be strong enough to travel in three or four days."

She tore herself free and stared up at him. Then, with an inarticulate, heartsick cry, she turned and ran blindly toward the creek.

"Lacey!" Ridge called. "Little One, let's talk about it."

"Leave me alone!"

"But, Lacey, you know . . ."

She closed her ears and ran faster.

Tyree came trotting to meet her. Lacey threw her arms around the big grulla's neck, then took a handful of the thick mane and hurled her body up onto her back, not caring that she had no bridle and no halter to guide her.

She leaned over the mare's neck and squeezed with her legs, urging her into an immediate canter. Ty's powerful muscles moved warm and strong beneath the skin of Lacey's thighs; she ran faster and faster against the push of the wind.

She was in a steady, perilous gallop when they jumped the creek and headed straight for the faraway blue of the mountains.

Halfway across the far side of the valley Ty began to tire. She slowed, gathered herself, then stumbled, throwing Lacey so far up onto her neck that her head bumped the mare's poll.

She slid back down again in an instant, then went half off the side. She clutched all the mane she could catch and hung there while Ty limped to a stop.

Lacey dropped to the ground and stood, trem-

258 GENELL DELLIN

bling, clinging to the horse's sweaty neck. Then she pulled away and began to circle her. Before she had taken two steps she saw it.

The off hind hock hung useless. Blood dripped from it, as red as rubies on the pale brown grass.

"Hold her!" Ridge said, as Tyree jerked her foot away from him for the third time.

"I am!" Lacey tightened her grip on the bridle and stroked the mare's nose. "If you wouldn't sound so angry, she'd be still."

His answer was a sarcastic grunt. He squatted down and tried again; this time the mare let him spread the salve he'd made on her wound, although she still winced each time he touched her.

"I hate for her to be in pain," Lacey said. "It's all my fault."

"Yes, it is."

"That's a mean thing to say!"

He laughed, but it was a bitter sound. "I'm only agreeing with you."

"I meant to say that I'm sorry. I shouldn't have galloped her so soon and so fast."

"Exactly. I'd think even a pampered little Virginia belle would know better than that. This mare is our only transportation back to civilization."

Lacey took a deep breath. "Actually," she snapped, "even though you might not expect such a sentiment of a 'pampered Virginia belle,' I would call what we've had here for the past few weeks civilization."

He didn't answer. He slapped on another layer of the poultice and straightened up. "Where's that handkerchief?"

She handed it to him and he folded it catty-cornered against his thigh.

"This had better stay on," he muttered. "If that cut gets proud flesh, we could have to walk out."

"Well, if you're so anxious to go, why don't you start tonight? I'll pack your dinner."

He squatted to tie on the bandage. "I'm still too weak to walk that far on cornpone and berries."

"I could give you some strengthening venison if your little laughing maniac of a friend hadn't stolen it all."

He crossed the ends of the handkerchief and tied them again. "Now, now," he said, "a southern lady ought to have a little mercy. Poor Horse Fly's old and his shooting eye's not so good anymore."

"Stop calling me a lady! And a Virginia belle! I haven't lived in Virginia since I was ten years old and I can survive in the woods as long as any of you Cherokees can!"

He snorted. "Not if you keep on crippling your horse and trading off your meat, you can't."

"You let your friend 'trade' for our meat," she said, biting off each word with bitter precision. "So don't blame me for that."

He tied the last knot and gave the bandage a pat. "I'll take her over to that patch of high grass and hobble her," he said, "while you fix our dinner."

"You know where it is," Lacey shot back. "I'm not hungry."

Ridge did fix the simple meal when he came back from tending to Ty, and he brought Lacey a bowl of red haw berries and a corncake. She sat on the ground with her head on her knees as she had done ever since she had quit holding the horse. She refused to look up or to take the food.

"Lacey," he said gently, setting the bowl down beside her. "You need to eat. You haven't eaten for the last two or three meals now."

"I can't," she said, the words muffled in her skirt.

"Why? Are you sick?"

"No."

"Well, then. Eat this now and I'll get us a squirrel for supper."

"I can't eat it and I won't try."

"That's stupid," he snapped. "If I don't have
the strength to walk out myself, I certainly can't
carry you, too."

She jumped to her feet, upsetting the bowl of
berries. They scattered and rolled toward the fire.

"Will you stop talking about getting out of
here!" she shouted. "Or else go on and do it!
Don't worry about carrying me out—I can take
care of myself!"

She wheeled and ran into the woods.

"Lacey!"

"Don't talk to me!" she yelled over her shoulder. "I don't want you!"

Lacey ran, sobbing, pushing tree branches and
bushes out of her way as she went, until she was
so far from camp that she couldn't hear or see
Ridge. In a grove of pines she found a bed of dry
needles and fell onto it, sobbing.

She did want him, though. That was the problem. And she wanted him to want to stay with
her in their own romantic world.

Oh, dear God, why didn't he want to?

During the next few days Lacey almost got used
to Ridge's not sharing the bed. A terrible fatigue
held her in its grip and she felt so drained, so
incredibly tired all of the time, that she napped
every day and fell asleep quickly at night.

But she could not get accustomed to his never
touching her at all. He went out of his way to
keep distance between them, with his words and
his silences as well as with his achingly familiar
body.

When they peeled and pounded the sassafras bark for Ty's medicine, when they gathered berries or cleaned rabbits and squirrels for cooking, when they carried water from the creek or gathered dry wood for the fire, Ridge carefully, meticulously, painstakingly made sure that he never touched Lacey or she him. He behaved as circumspectly as if he were a visiting preacher and she the head deacon's wife.

Lacey marveled at how incessantly she could pine for his caress. The memory of his hands and his mouth, of his long body over hers, stayed constantly at the front of her consciousness like a dream does when it comes right before morning. Every time, then, when Ridge stubbornly made sure that the dream wouldn't become reality again, she thought her heart would surely break.

And every time she tried to talk about it, he cut her off short.

Ty's hock healed steadily under the poultices of sassafras and cornmeal. They had to spend more and more time each day bringing in wood; the weather grew steadily colder, like Ridge's traitorous heart.

But then she would catch a look in his eyes when he didn't know she was watching or he would suddenly start to talk to her in his old, familiar way, and she would forget that he had betrayed their silent betrothal. He looked so sad and sounded so sweet that she would puzzle for hours why he had thrown up this wall between them.

Was it Martha? Had he suddenly realized that there'd never be room in his heart for anyone but her?

Or had he suddenly realized that he would simply never love Lacey enough to spend his life with her?

Had his body told her a lie?

She tried again to talk to him, around the confusion and hurt that clogged her throat, but he deflected every mention of feelings, hers or his, with a look or a word or with a stubborn silence.

On the fourth or fifth day after Ty was hurt—Lacey was so lethargic she hadn't really tried to keep count—Ridge removed the bandage and washed off the dried medicine.

"Should be only a day or two," he said. "Then it won't hurt her to carry both of us."

The words echoed in Lacey's head all day. Another day or two. One or two more days.

Then, if she could believe Ridge's current behavior, he would take her home and leave her. She'd never see him again.

That night, despite her fatigue, which was greater than ever, she spent hours trying to fall asleep. Ridge had moved the bedding into the cave when the weather turned and he had brought piles of pine and cedar boughs to add warmth. But he had not crawled into her quilt with her to keep out the cold.

He acted as if he hadn't even thought of it.

She lay awake, listening to his even breathing, smelling the pine and the light, sweet scent of cedar. Ridge certainly wasn't losing any sleep over her.

How could he have changed so quickly, so completely?

Why?

When that question had worn a hole in her brain, Lacey fell asleep.

Before dawn she woke with a sudden, trembling start, her heart beating like a wild thing in her throat. Her skin rasped raw every place the soft quilt brushed against it; her ears plucked every sound out of the night; her eyes strained into the blackness.

But the thing she needed to see was inside her mind. Some dream had awakened her.

She clutched the padded cotton between her fingers and willed the hot, tight net of nerves that covered her scalp to loosen. She had to think.

But she never could when she was so on edge. Like when she had her monthlies.

Her monthlies.

For one long moment she thought that that was what had waked her; that she could feel the warm, heavy blood on the insides of her thighs. Without even looking, though, she knew it wasn't so.

But that was what had waked her. Somewhere deep inside she had realized something was wrong. How long had it been?

She tried to think, to count, but so many days had passed so haphazardly, so much had happened, that she didn't know. All she knew was that she had been wildly sick with her courses the week before Tom had invaded the house. If he had arrived then she probably would have killed him the minute he stepped across the threshold.

That had been a long time ago. Plenty long enough.

She sat up and pushed her hair back from her face with both hands. Her stomach lurched with now-familiar nausea. She fought it down. She had to think.

Lacey pressed her fingers to her temples, digging them into her flesh until it hurt, but her mind refused to cooperate. It flowed in circles, flashing images and pictures; all the while a tiny seed of truth hardened in its center.

She couldn't see it at first; the kaleidoscope whirling in her head obscured it. But gradually all the pictures and the memories, all the half-forgotten feelings and the burning colors, wheeled to a stop around that infinitely small kernel, and she knew.

She was going to have a baby!

That explained the tiredness and the eternal nausea and her lack of appetite. It explained everything.

A sudden fierce gladness shook her, and she crossed her arms around her belly and rocked, as if she were already holding the child in her arms. A baby! A baby of her own to hold and love!

Would it look like her? A girl? Was it a girl? Or would it look like Ridge? Was it a solemn baby boy with huge, wise eyes?

Ridge!

She opened her mouth to call to him, to yell, to shout out her news at the top of her lungs. Now they would have to make some plans!

But she jammed her fist between her lips and bit down on her straining knuckles. She couldn't tell him. She would not tell him.

Not until he had told her that he loved her.

Chapter 16

Lacey dropped her face into her hands and slid down, going back under the covers as if she were crawling under a rock to hide.

Ridge would never tell her that he loved her, not if he kept acting the way he had these past few days.

The quilt shut out the sound of his breathing and every other sound in the world. Lacey huddled there for a long time, alone in the universe except for the tiny spark of new life inside her.

Two days. Ridge said they had two more days.

Finally she straightened out her legs and turned over onto her stomach, careful not to jostle the baby. She had two days to try to change Ridge back to the way he used to be.

Some time after dawn they both got up and began doing the necessary chores. Ridge was as gloomy as the lowering clouds that hovered over the tops of the mountains, and he seemed as far away.

He oiled the saddle and bags and bridle in silence; when he began to talk it was only of the coming journey. He told Lacey to cook the rest of the cornmeal into pones and brought her another batch of haw berries for the trip. Around noon he took the rifle and left the camp.

The day closed around Lacey like a smothering pillow. The clouds, mottled and bluish, began to build in the north as if they were an army about to attack, and the birds gathered in flocks, chittering constant warnings as they picked and picked at the ground.

Lacey sat at the rock table wrapped in Ridge's coat and wished that he loved her. How could she have his baby without him at her side?

He would be there if she could make him love her again. But how could she do that when she didn't know what had made him stop loving her in the first place?

Or had he ever loved her?

He came back late in the afternoon with three squirrels. "Fry these," he said. "If you make stew we can't take it with us."

Take it with us, take it with us, echoed over and over in her head while she prepared the meal. Tomorrow would be the day. She had to do something before tomorrow.

As she turned the meat for the last time, big flakes of snow began to fall into the skillet. Snow! It was like an answer from heaven, a reprieve from God Himself. Oh, maybe they wouldn't be able to travel for a week!

Ridge dragged some of the cedar boughs to the mouth of the cave and they sat on them, just out of the weather, to eat the crisp, hot meat. The snow fell between them and the valley, its great, wet drops slowly covering the darkening earth with white as if determined that this time night would not win.

"It looks like it could snow five feet," Lacey said. "It could be on the ground for a week."

Ridge looked at her. "Or it could be gone by noon tomorrow; this time of year you never know. I remember one twelve-inch snow that didn't last a day.''

He finished his meat and reached for a handful of haw berries. His thigh brushed Lacey's. She sat perfectly still.

"I remember that, too," she said. "But it was in the spring.''

He shrugged and ate another berry. "Spring, fall, first or last snow, neither one lasts long.''

She shivered. "Well, it's cold while it does last.''

He put one arm around her shoulders. "Want me to get the blanket?"

"No.''

She was afraid to move, even to shake her head. Ridge was touching her at last!

"We may have to build a fire in the cave," he said, "and endure the smoke. The snow could put this one out.''

His heavy arm felt so wonderfully good on her back.

"It might." She swallowed. "It's snowing pretty hard.''

This was her chance. It might be her only one.

"We ought to drag some wood in here before it all gets wet," he said.

He didn't think he could do it, though; he couldn't leave Lacey for that long. He didn't think he could ever turn her loose again.

"No," she said. "I don't care if we have no fire.''

Her low tones made him shiver. Her voice sounded the way he remembered her skin felt: like hot silk. He had to hear it again. "You aren't afraid we'll freeze?"

"No." She turned and looked into his face. "I can keep you warm.''

Her eyes were enormous, blue-dark as the fading light.

He had to love her one more time.

Their mouths came together as slowly and silently as the snow came to the ground.

The sudden burn of tears took her sight. He smelled like cedar and smoke and the wind. She slipped her arms out of the coat and put them around him so her breasts could look for the solid muscles of his chest. They pressed through her thin cotton shirt and found them, tensing beneath the supple buckskin of his shirt.

He closed his arms around her and fell back onto the bed of cedar boughs; the haven of the woodsy-smelling cave enclosed them. Lacey caught the scent of pines coming from someplace far off where the snow was born.

Lips still clinging lightly, almost hesitantly, they caressed each other with soft, questioning touches that asked, Are you still the same? Do you love me? Do you believe I love you? Where have you been for so long? What happened to us?

Lacey ran her hands lightly up the corded muscles on each side of Ridge's backbone; he measured the fine-drawn shape of her waist.

Her fingers interrogated his face and then loved it, tracing the high, fine cheekbones, losing themselves in the sleek softness of his hair. She followed the fascinating whorls of his ear.

His lips came to hot, full life against hers, and she dissolved into him with the vehement passion of a true seeker. She explored every inch of his mouth looking for the words she needed so desperately to hear, coming back time after time to his teasing tongue, entangling it in hers, trying to compel it to say them that instant.

He found her every secret place, too, and when she tried to take her mouth away, to tell him that she loved him, to ask if he loved her, he crushed her lips again and made them utterly useless for telling and for asking.

Useless for everything except kissing him in the purple silence of the snowfall.

They rolled over and over in their fragrant cedar bed; he fumbling with her buttons and her ties, she groping for the laces of his buckskin breeches. Through it all, until the moment his shirt had to come over his head, they held their kiss.

When at last they were free of restraining garments, they threw themselves back into each other's arms and found each other's ravenous mouths again, demanding, and giving, and taking, hopelessly drunk with the sweet sliding of skin upon skin.

His hot, hard tongue darted everywhere, making her wild; her soft hands drove him off the cliff of desire into a valley of exquisite torment. His rising hardness brushed her thighs, pushed against her belly, then he entered her like a dream coming true, bringing her sure warmth and safe passage and a hot delight such as she had never known.

Locked together, they moved in the ancient rhythm born into their bones, fitting into each other like a soul into its destiny, growing closer and closer each time they pulled away, birthing wonderful delights that grew and grew until they had created a pleasure as perfect as the pristine snow-covered mountains outside.

The sun was already eating away at the snow when Lacey emerged from the cave. She stood just outside its mouth, blinking into the sudden brightness.

The sight of Ridge blinded her again.

He was enough to melt a mountain of ice all by himself. He stood hip-shot and loose, with the new sun catching the blue-black lights in his hair. He had on the tight black pants; one of the white shirts lay open down his chiseled chest, its tail half in and half out.

He smiled when he saw her. "Who's the sleepy-head this time?" he said.

She started toward him, but he turned and stirred something over the fire. "I used the first bucket of water to boil some of the berries," he said. "I'll go back for coffee water in a minute."

He dipped her a cupful of the warm red-purple berries and she took it; his fingers brushed hers and caused a tingling ache that almost made her drop it.

"The snow's melting, isn't it?" she said, sitting down on the log. He took his and sat on a rock across the fire from her.

"Yes. We'll be able to travel tomorrow."

She clutched the cup with both hands. "Tomorrow's too soon," she said. "Remember once we promised to stay here forever?"

"Don't set your mind that way," he said abruptly. "Nothing lasts forever."

"Oh?" Her voice rose even though she tried to control it. "Nothing does? Is that what you told Martha when you married her?"

The words were out before she could prevent them, rushing up from the raw, hurt place in her heart that had burst open without warning.

"A gentleman planter ought to be a little more gallant, I think," she went on sarcastically. "But if you did tell her that, then she knew how you felt. After all, it is customary for a gentleman to declare his intentions."

His face went livid. But he pretended to misunderstand. "If you're still angry that I called you a pampered belle, I'm sorry. I was wrong—you can hold your own with the best of them. Not many women could dig out shot pellets and nurse me day and night and kill and dress a deer.''

The words of praise softened her anger.

"Could Martha have done it?"

"Martha couldn't bring herself to eat venison or any other kind of game, much less prepare it," he said. "She was too delicate to clean up her own child's vomit, much less perform surgery."

He placed both elbows on his spread knees and leaned toward her. "Martha hated it out here. She wanted symphonies and stores to shop in and big parties by the dozens. My bringing Martha to the Nation was a terrible mistake. My marrying Martha was a terrible mistake. There was no good in it."

Lacey gasped. "But your baby! You can't say that! Your marriage gave you your beautiful baby. I saw his picture. I didn't mean to pry, Ridge, but I ran across it while you were sick."

He shrugged, as if to say it didn't matter.

She persisted. "How can you say your marriage was a complete mistake when you had such a wonderful son?"

"Edwin was a mistake, too."

"Ridge! How can you possibly say that? How can you think that?"

"Because the world's too hurtful. Life is too full of pain to ever bring a baby into it."

The cup shook in her hands; some of the juice sloshed out onto her skirt.

"Well, it's a little late for you to be saying that!" she cried. "Soon you'll be responsible for another mistake because I'm pregnant with your baby!"

He froze where he sat, leaning toward her with his elbows on his knees. His face went perfectly blank while the sound of her words died away against the rocks. Finally he jerked to his feet, moving stiffly, as if he were a toy made out of wood.

"I'll get the coffee water," he said, in a voice so raw she didn't recognize it.

He turned on his heel and strode toward the creek.

Lacey stared after him until her tears blotted him out, then she threw her cup at his unforgiving back. She turned and ran into the cave, reaching in the dark for the comfort of the cedar boughs where Ridge had loved her such a short time ago.

Ridge half fell, half stumbled down the last muddy yards to the creek, his heels plowing furrows in the melting snow. He made no effort to watch his footing; Lacey's stunned face filled his vision.

Dear God, what had he done?

She was so young. And therefore so vulnerable. He was the one old enough to know what misery love could bring—he should be horsewhipped for not having had more sense.

Why had he ever let himself touch her?

He had reached the edge of the swollen branch and squatted on his haunches beside it before he noticed that he hadn't even brought the bucket. He couldn't draw water.

In the next second he knew it didn't matter.

He got a quick sensation that someone was rushing at his back, then a blow cracked his head and pain ran down his neck into his shoulders.

Pure determination made him whirl and strike out one time and then they were all over him, three of them at least. His head slapped backward into the cold mud; its wetness soaked through the seat of his breeches.

Talking and laughing, they dragged him to his feet and bound his hands in front of him. He shook his head to try and clear his vision, but his only reward was more sharp, spreading pain. The ground was a blur of brown and white; he couldn't distinguish the toe of his boot.

Then somehow a bunch of horses, including Tyree, was there, and they were lifting him onto her back. His thighs grasped her wide, warm sides through sheer instinct; the rest of his body slumped limp as a sack of seed.

"Git his hat," one of them said.

Ridge blinked away the haze and looked at the man. He was a stranger. He was obviously Cherokee, though, and so was one of the others. The third one might be, or might not.

That one took Ridge's hat from the mud, mounted, rode over, and jammed the hat onto Ridge's head. The sweatband circled his forehead like a frigid halo; icy silt dribbled down his ear in a crooked line.

"There," the man said. "Don't want you going without your hat. I'd hate to tell ol' Horse Fly that we let you catch cold."

"Horse Fly?" Ridge croaked.

The leader answered. "Yep. Good ol' Horse Fly. Come flittin' in and offered news of your whereabouts for five dollars and a mule to help carry his venison. Reckon he's headin' somewhere to hole up for the winter."

Ridge nodded. It didn't hurt quite as much now to move his head. "Good ol' Horse Fly," he said.

The man who'd brought Ridge's hat thrust a rope into his hands. They'd rigged a hackamore on Ty; they were ready to ride.

But Lacey!

The thought of her cleared Ridge's mind in an instant, loosing a surge of fear through his veins that kicked every nerve into life. He had to get free and get back to her.

He flexed the muscles in his arms; his wrists swelled against the rope. It was rawhide, wet, and knotted as tough as the bark on a basswood tree. He tried it again.

"No use to even think about it, Chekote," the leader drawled. "We said we'd have your hide for what you done at Tahlequah last summer, and we wasn't lying. You jest git comfortable now and git ready to meet General Watie. He'll find you a mighty nice surprise."

"Thanks, but the general and I have already met."

As he spoke, Ridge forced himself to look at the man instead of glancing up toward the cave. Evidently Horse Fly hadn't mentioned Lacey when he sold Ridge out.

What should he do? Would she be better off with him, even as a captive, than alone in the wilderness? Could she survive alone as she had claimed?

Probably. He had taught her a great deal about the woods in the past few weeks, and she had more grit than any woman he'd ever met.

And if she came with them he couldn't protect her. What if these men were drawn, as he was, to put their hands on her honey hair and her porcelain skin? What man wouldn't be?

They could do as they pleased with her while he sat with his wrists bound in rawhide and watched. The thought made his guts twist in pain.

No. She was better off free, even in the wilderness. He would break loose and come back to her—maybe when they made camp tonight.

So he kept his eyes on his captor's and smiled. "Well," he said. "Shall we ride? We surely don't want to keep the general waiting."

They surrounded him, and the white man struck Tyree across the croup; the horses took out down the creek at a long lope. Ridge kept his face blank and his eyes straight ahead.

Hooves sucking mud, men talking low, saddles creaking: all those noises barely registered in his brain. The only sound he could hear was his heart, crying inside.

Lacey was alone in the woods, carrying his child. What would she think? That he was dead? That he had deliberately left her?

He would give anything—River's Bend . . . life itself—if he could tell her now that he loved her.

Lacey cried until she couldn't. Then she turned onto her back and lay for the longest time, one arm flung over her eyes, smelling the cedar, waiting for Ridge.

How could he ever say that sweet, solemn Edwin was a mistake? He was so beautiful in his portrait—he must have been a wonder to look at in the flesh.

And now her baby. Their baby. It would be just as marvelous. More so.

Panic began to gather in her bones. Would Ridge not love their baby? How could he not?

She squeezed the arm that crossed her face until the skin inside her elbow hurt. Did Ridge not love her?

He had to. The man was not a liar, and his body had told her in a thousand ways that he cherished her. . . .

Before his honest face had told her how horrified he was at the idea of her having his baby.

She dropped her arm and stared out of the mouth of the cave. He had been gone for a long time. She got up and went outside, holding one hand over her eyes against the sun. Nothing moved near the creek—maybe he had gone for a walk in the woods to get used to the whole idea of a baby. After all, it was still a shock to her and she had had much longer to think about it.

The pot of red haw berries was simmering over the fire. Her stomach growled.

Her cup lay on its side on the ground; she went to Ridge's, sitting full and untouched beside the rock. She dumped those berries back into the pot, stirred them with the cup, and dipped out some warm ones. They tasted like heaven; suddenly she was so hungry she felt as if she could eat anything, everything, in the camp.

She finished two cups of the berries, went to the head of the trail, and stared down at the creek again. Finally she sat down at the rock table and waited.

Ridge didn't come.

Lacey got up, took the water bucket, and started down the familiar trail. This way, Ridge wouldn't think she was looking for him.

The only solid snow left was on the tops of the hills. She watched the farthest mountain's cap while her feet slipped and slid on the muddy path. Maybe if she didn't look at the creek again until the very last minute Ridge would be standing beside it.

He wasn't.

Loneliness seized her heart with two icy hands and shook it, hard.

She began to run, calling and whistling for Tyree, letting the bucket bump heedlessly against her leg.

The mare didn't come.

Lacey dropped the bucket and picked up her skirts. She ran upstream toward the pool, her throat too full now to make one sound. She caught glimpses of the brown grulla color everywhere she looked, but every time it was a tree branch, or a pile of leaves, or a hillock in the shade.

Finally, gasping for air, she stopped. She drew in enough breath to call one last time.

Nothing. The horse was gone.

Lacey's knees let go. She sank to the ground, her head nodding loosely like a doll's. She let it fall forward against the soft earth, her forehead pressed into the wet grass like a prayer.

Ridge had left her.

She lay in a desolate heap, utterly unable to move. Her body felt like a hollow shell, a fragile framework with an enormous hole in the middle where an empty wind came streaming through, crannying into every corner of her bones.

Finally a flock of killdeer, chattering and picking for food, came so close that Lacey lifted her face. The sudden movement startled most of them into flight. But one of the females stayed on the ground, fanning out a miraculously fast wing to drag behind her while she swept along uphill, keening the mournful cry of distress meant to draw danger away from her nest.

The bird watched Lacey with one tiny brown eye, never taking it off her for an instant.

She would fly at my head and peck out my eyes, Lacey thought, if she had to. If I got any closer to her babies. I'll feel the same way about mine.

My baby.

She still had the baby.

The thought fell into the hole inside her and exploded, filling her as rapidly as if the baby were growing to term in one moment instead of nine months. She still had the baby, and she'd better take care of it.

Lacey closed her hands around the grass in her fingers and ripped it loose from its roots. This baby's daddy had left it because to him it was nothing but a terrible mistake; however it still had a mama. And she would fly into the face of danger for its precious life.

Lacey got up and went back to find the bucket. The wind discovered every wet spot, even infiltrating her muddy skirts. It made her shiver.

She picked up the bucket and squatted beside the creek to fill it. She dipped it into the water and glanced downstream, her eyes following the muddy bank. There was a mass of blurred hoofprints there.

Forgetting the pain of the freezing water on her fingers, she tried to read the sign.

Ridge must have ridden Ty up and down here several times. Why? Had he been trying to decide whether to leave or not? Had he been looking up toward the cave while she lay inside it waiting for him to come back?

The hoofprints smeared even more while she watched: The rising waters in the creek ate at some of them while the sun melted the edges of others. They faced both ways, she couldn't even tell which way he had finally gone.

She forced her eyes back to the full bucket and pulled it out of the water. It didn't matter which way Ridge had gone. He had gone and left her alone in the wilderness, so he couldn't ever have loved her at all.

She started back up the trail to the cave, putting one foot firmly in front of the other although what she really wanted to do was collapse again and weep until the earth opened and swallowed her up. But she couldn't do that. She had a baby to take care of.

She would have to turn off her feelings. When she was safe at home, in her bed, covered up with the quilt that Grandma Lacey had made her and drinking hot tea with lots of sugar that Dorcas had made her . . . then, and only then, would she take out her feelings about Ridge and look at them. Now, if she and this baby were going to survive, she had to stop feeling and think.

When she got to camp she drank a cupful of the cold water and stared at the sun. It was nearly noon, the ground was muddy, and she had to decide what to take with her and bundle it into a pack she could carry. She would wait until morning to leave.

Lacey built up the fire beneath the berries and warmed up some of the squirrel. She would force herself to eat today and in the morning, too, and all the time she traveled. For the baby's sake.

If she ran out of food, she'd have to make good her brag that she could live off the land. Now her silly jest sounded like a challenge that would be insurmountably difficult.

She hoped it would be, so that she'd have not one shred of strength nor one second of time left in which to think of Ridge.

The afternoon and night passed somehow. Lacey actually slept for a few hours, then she woke before dawn with the vision of Ridge's incredulous face before her.

She rolled over and clutched both arms around her middle. He had looked so horrified when he heard the word "baby." Absolutely appalled.

He hadn't cared a fig for her. He was a liar and a faker, and she was better off without him. Everything about him had been false—even his southern planter courtesy. He hadn't even had the gallantry to leave her the horse.

But he had left the tack. She stared at the saddle and bridle. Ridge hadn't come back to get them because he didn't want to face her.

She got up, shaking in the sharp, night air, and

carried her pack out to go through it by the light of the fire. The knives were in it, and the pistol. She would carry the rifle in her hand.

He'd been in such a hurry to get away from her that he had even left his guns. Well, good. She couldn't always hit what she shot at, but she felt safer with them.

She had his clothes in the saddlebags in case she fell in a creek or got caught in the rain. The wool of his pants felt warm to her hands.

Suddenly she stood up and started stripping off her still-damp skirts, shaking violently in the cold. She pulled on the pants and put another of his shirts on top of the one she'd worn for a coat in the night. She abandoned her muddy skirts. They were too bulky to fit into the bags.

Dorcas would be scandalized when she saw her, but Lacey didn't care. She wished she'd thought of it earlier.

She handled each of the other items she had chosen, too, carefully, as if willing them to see her through to safety: the matches, the silver flask with the rest of the whiskey, the silver-backed brush and comb. She held them for a moment. Those she ought to leave—they were too heavy for their value on a trek as long as she'd have to make.

But when she lay them on her discarded skirts, she reached to pick them up again. They were silver. She might need them to trade. She squelched the little voice that said she needed them as reminders of Ridge.

Lacey went through the pack twice and ate the last of the berries before the sun was up. When finally it was light enough to see, she stood for a long time looking to the northwest, back up the trail she and Ridge had come.

That day seemed a lifetime ago.

Finally she spread out the blanket and picked up the hunting knife. She cut a slit down the middle of the finely woven wool big enough for her head, put the knife back into the pack, and pulled the blanket over her shoulders. She took a long drink of the water and threw the rest of it onto the fire.

Then she picked up her pack and started walking in what she thought was the direction of home.

Chapter 17

Lacey walked all day, stopping to drink twice, once from a spring and once from what must have been a curving loop of the same creek that had supplied their water for so long. At dusk she huddled beside a huge fallen tree, using its trunk for a table while she cracked several black walnuts with a rock.

Picking out bits of their sweet meat with the point of the knife exhausted her, though, and she ate only two of them. Then she stuffed the others back into the pockets of Ridge's pants, wrapped her blanket-coat more tightly around her, and stretched out beside the log. She slept until the sun was well up the next morning.

She got up and started walking.

After that she lost complete track of the days. Her scant food supply soon ran out, and the few edible berries and nuts she found weren't enough to keep her from feeling light-headed; the days and nights all ran together, and the rocky hills and grassy valleys all began to look the same. The only surety in her mind was that she had to walk and keep on walking.

She walked until her boots were in tatters. The smallest pebble on the trail felt like a boulder because of the holes in her soles. Her toes poked through the thin leather of the tops. Soon she would be barefoot.

So when she sighted a horse grazing in a narrow hollow and then, behind it, a ramshackle cabin with a smoking chimney, she headed for it. She stumbled into the packed-earth dooryard, populated by three scratching chickens and an emaciated dog. They cackled and barked to announce Lacey's presence.

"Hallo, this house," she called, as she had heard Papa do. If a horde of dangerous men poured out of the door, she couldn't help it. She had to have transportation and she had to have something to eat.

A stick-thin old woman stepped onto the porch. Her bird-eyes went from Lacey's hair—one long braid hanging over her shoulder—to the man's trousers showing under the blanket she wore.

"Well," the woman said, and clapped her hands to quiet the barking of the dog. "I 'uz wonderin' if my company was man or woman. Now I see you and I still ain't sure."

"I'm a woman," Lacey said. Her voice scratched her throat because she hadn't used it for so long.

"Come in."

After spending such a long time outdoors, the cabin seemed as dark and confining as the cave, but it was filled with the smells of beans and corn bread. The food tasted like heaven.

The woman didn't tell Lacey her name, but said that her husband was gone to the war and that she had no kin nearby and no help on her place. "Whyn't you winter here?" she asked. "We'uns could play checkers all day."

"I have to get home," Lacey said, reluctantly laying her spoon on her tin plate. It made an empty, clicking sound, but the woman didn't offer her any more beans; the pot was almost empty. "Am I going the right way to get to Park Hill?"

"Park Hill?" the woman said, her eyes bright with curiosity. "Ten mile or so that way." She gestured in the direction Lacey had been traveling. "Whereabouts you live at Park Hill?"

"Ten more miles!" Lacey said. With the bruises on her feet it sounded like a hundred. "Could I buy or borrow your horse?"

The tiny black eyes gleamed brighter. "What you got to buy 'im with?"

Lacey reached for her pack. Not the comb and brush with Ridge's initials. She'd use the flask instead.

The woman was delighted with both the flask and its skimpy contents and went immediately to catch the horse. "I'll throw in this here bridle," she said, "since you're throwin' in the whiskey."

Up close it was obvious that the gelding was old and spavined and far too thin. But he could walk and carry Lacey, and at that moment she was ecstatically happy to settle for that.

She threw the saddlebags over his withers and the woman gave her a leg up. "Good luck to ye," she said. "And keep his head up."

"I will," Lacey said, knowing that the horse didn't have strength enough to buck. "And thank you for my dinner."

She gathered the reins into her hand and turned the gelding's head to the north, toward home.

Ridge and his captors were traveling fast, straight south through the mountains. Their leader, Buck Rabbit, knew the deer trails and the lay of the country so well that they hardly deviated from the direction at all.

He also knew Ridge's reputation, and he and

his men watched him like hungry hawks would
watch a chicken. That first night he hadn't had a
prayer of escaping; one man had guarded him
while the other two slept. Four days later the pattern hadn't changed.

The only thing that had changed was his regret
about Lacey. It had grown until it consumed him.

Her forsaken face haunted him; he saw it
painted on the trees and the trail in the daytime
and on the backs of his eyelids at night. He
dreamed over and over again that he hadn't stood
up and walked away when she told him about the
baby; that, instead, he had said to her the unspo-
ken words that were choking the breath out of
him now: I love you, Lacey. I love you.

He would shout them into the sky if it would
do any good.

Late in the afternoon Lacey came onto Pleasant
Prospect from the back, without realizing exactly
where she was. One minute she was riding
through the woods, the next they had given way
abruptly into a wide meadow. She let the poor
gelding stop, as he had been trying to do for
hours.

The lay of the land looked familiar, even
through the gathering dusk. The woods behind
her curved in a crescent down off the mountain;
the pasture rolled and dipped toward a rise
straight ahead. Of course! This was the south hay
meadow! She was home!

She kicked the horse into life again. "I'm sorry,
old boy," she muttered, "but we're nearly to the
house. You can have some grain and I can sleep
in my own bed tonight!"

She forgot that Tom and his men had ever been
there; for a minute she imagined again that Mama

and Papa would come running out onto the veranda to greet her.

The horse broke into a long trot as if he understood that his travels were nearing an end.

They topped the rise and Lacey stared toward the house. She blinked. There, it would be. There, in its own grove of oaks.

She strained to see. The trees were nothing but bare branches now—the house should loom huge and white among them.

It did. She could see the chimneys. The light must have been playing tricks on her; that always happened in the time right between daylight and dark.

She squeezed the horse and clung to his mane as he lurched along even faster. In just a few more minutes she would be home.

She rode up through the oak grove at the fastest pace she had gotten out of the gelding yet. He swished through the fallen leaves and clattered across the graveled drive. He ran straight up to the well house and stopped.

The foundation of the big house stood startlingly clear in the fading light, its top jagged and charred a blackish gray above the meticulously set golden brown stones on the bottom. Its huge rectangle held three feet of ashes and twisted timbers, sparkles of broken glass, and drifts of feathery cinders.

At each end, Pleasant Prospect's great rock fireplaces stood intact, their chimneys rising into the air like giant sentinels guarding the mournful residue.

The coarse hairs of the horse's mane slipped through Lacey's fingers. She let them go and leaned sideways, toward the ground that was reaching up to meet her.

* * *

She came to because something cold—some cruel, freezing-cold liquid—splashed into her face. She turned her head and tried to get away from it, but it sprayed her again.

''You wake up now, little Lacey girl, you heah?''

Lacey moaned. Who was that talking?

''You home now, baby. Only the Good Lord know how, but you got yo' sweet self home to Dorcas.''

Lacey let out a long sigh and held out her arms. She didn't have the strength to do more, not even to open her eyes.

She was lifted up, off the cold ground, and then she was moving. When she opened her eyes, it was to flickering lantern light in the summer kitchen.

Now hot liquid was mixing with the drops of cold on her cheeks: Dorcas was crying her eyes out. She carried Lacey to one corner and laid her down on a pallet of quilts.

''Jest look at you, honey!'' Dorcas sobbed, running her affectionate hands over Lacey's face and down her arms. ''You mus' surely be half dead. You doesn't weigh no more 'n' a little bitty baby!''

''I'm alive, Dorcas,'' Lacey croaked. She cleared her throat and struggled to sit up. ''But the house is gone! It's burned to the ground!''

Dorcas pushed her shoulders back down onto the pallet. ''I knows it, honey. This 'ere summer kitchen's the only thing left standin'.''

''What started the fire?''

''I cain't say, not now,'' the big black woman said, ''not 'til I hears where is my sweet Miss Babe.''

She sank heavily to her knees beside the quilt and then sat flat on the floor, each movement solemn and ponderous, as if she already knew the answer that Lacey would give.

Lacey let her bones collapse against the quilts and then into the hard flatness of the floor beneath them. In the pale yellow light Dorcas's face looked worn and as old as the earth.

How could she tell her? Dorcas had come with them all the way from Virginia. She had been with Babe ever since she was born.

Lacey drew a long, shaky breath. The summer kitchen smelled like coal oil and wood smoke, fried fatback and dried apples. It smelled just like it always had. It smelled like home.

But it wasn't. Home was gone. Forever.

"Oh, Dorcas," she whispered, her lips so stiff they would hardly form the words. "Mother's dead. She's gone and left us, just like Papa did."

Dorcas shook her head. "No," she whispered back.

Then she fixed her eyes on a spot way off in the corner and stared at it, at last nodding, "Yes," and "Yes," and "Yes."

"She couldn't see past it," she said. "That Babe jest couldn't see past losin' the judge."

Lacey closed her eyes. "No, she couldn't." Finally she said, "Dorcas, what happened here?"

"Tom Creekwater, he set the big house afire over his own head, he was so wroth you slipped out'n his mean hands."

"Did he get burned?"

"Naw, honey, he not that drunk. Him and his men chase outta here like a gaggle o' geese." Dorcas sighed. "Was them raiders that come later what burned the barns and all. Scoured this place like the locusts in Egypt. Found and took ever' scrap we done hid—people food and animal food—greedy scoundrels done took it all."

Lacey sat straight up. "The food? From the root cellar? Did they find the hay we hid by the river?"

"We'uns don't need no hay. Not one head o' stock left on all of Pleasant Prospect."

Lacey grabbed her arm. "The potatoes and onions that we hid behind the false wall?"

"Them, too. I tells you, them boys was outlaws, but they wasn't no fools."

"But the baby!" Lacey wailed. "I have to have something good to feed my baby!"

Dorcas fixed Lacey with fierce, unswerving eyes. "What you talkin'—yore baby?"

Lacey threw her arms around Dorcas's neck and buried her face in her ample bosom. Dorcas's arms tightened around her. "Did he get to you and I didn't know it?" she growled. "That Tom. Did he?"

Lacey lifted her face. She smiled. "No, Dorcas. That's the one thing we can be thankful for. This baby's daddy is Ridge Chekote."

She told Dorcas the whole story, stopping only to drink some weak tea and eat some cold corn bread. When she'd finished, Dorcas nodded.

"We'll feed this baby, don't you fret," she said. "We'll go to Judge Melton's sister's for the winter. I done sent Old Jasper and Simple Timmy over there whilst I was waitin' here for you all."

"No! No, Dorcas!"

A picture flashed through Lacey's head: Ridge, riding up Pleasant Prospect's long, graveled drive to find her. Suddenly the summer kitchen was home, after all.

"I can't leave again, now," she said. "And think of the look on Aunt Maizie's face when the baby starts to show!"

Ridge would never think of looking for her at Aunt Maizie's. Not in a million years.

Dorcas frowned.

"I'll go to Tahlequah tomorrow," Lacey burbled. "I'll ride the horse and trade him for food! Then we won't have to worry about feeding him! That's it, Dorcas! That way we can stay at home and it won't matter that we lost our hay and grain."

"All right, lovey," Dorcas said. She soothed Lacey's trembling limbs back into a prone position on the pallet. "We see about it all tomorrow. You get some rest. All you has to do now is sleep."

But Lacey didn't sleep for a long, long time. She watched Dorcas lumber to the lamp and blow it out, then she stared into the dark for the longest ever, trying to see the vision again—the one where Ridge might come.

But this time she saw his back walking away from her. Why in the world would he come to find her here when he'd cared little enough to leave her alone and lost in the wilderness? When he'd told her straight out that he didn't want their baby?

Tahlequah wasn't nearly as busy as it used to be. Too many of the Union-sympathizing Cherokees had moved north and too many of the ones who had stayed, neutral and Confederate-leaning alike, were keeping close to home to protect their possessions. So Mr. Greenberry Pigeon was the only one there when Lacey opened the door, jangling the bell of Pigeon's Trading Post.

He leaned on his countertop and stared at her while she crossed the big room. Just before she reached him, she saw recognition glint in his eyes.

"Miss Lacey," he said, just as if she'd been in the day before. Just as if she were wearing her blue wool riding habit instead of Ridge's trousers and Dorcas's coat. "What can I do for you?"

"You can trade me some groceries and supplies, Mr. Pigeon," she said, forcing confidence into her voice. "And the fee to have them delivered to Pleasant Prospect."

She clenched her hands into fists inside the coat sleeves. Mr. Pigeon was a notoriously sharp trader. He smiled. "And what do you offer me in return, Miss Lacey?"

She could hardly say the words; there was too much—everything—at stake for her and Dorcas. "That horse I've just tied to your hitching rail, sir."

"My pleasure," he said, with a little bow. He went outside to look at the poor gelding.

Lacey stood very still, looking around. The wealth and variety of Mr. Pigeon's goods overwhelmed her senses after so long away from such things. But, even so, she knew they weren't nearly so plentiful as usual—some of the shelves were completely bare.

She and Dorcas needed coal oil and matches besides food. And maybe he'd give her enough to get a blanket or two. And shoes. She had to have shoes.

Tears stung her eyes. It was hopeless. Mr. Pigeon would never give her all that for one skinny gelding who might be on his last legs.

The doorbell chimed again. Lacey stepped behind the cracker barrel; she hated for anyone else to see her in these clothes.

"Lacey!"

Oh, no! Whose voice was that?

"Lacey Longbaugh, can that possibly be you?"

Eli Hawthorne!

A few long strides brought him to her, his footsteps ringing on the wooden floor.

He grabbed both her hands in his. "I knew I couldn't mistake that hair!" he said. "Oh, Lacey, where have you been? We scoured the country for you after Dorcas sent word you'd escaped the fire.''

She murmured some tale of running from Tom and of her mother's dying and of an old woman in a cabin feeding her and giving her a horse. If Eli got the impression that she'd sheltered with the old woman all these weeks, fine; she could not get Ridge's name past her lips. That was none of Eli's business, anyway.

In fact, she was none of Eli's business, but he immediately went outside and set about haggling with Mr. Pigeon over the horse for her. He got much more than she expected.

"She'll take it in cash," he said, as Mr. Pigeon returned to his counter.

"No! In trade!" Lacey cried. "Dorcas and I need food."

"You and Dorcas are coming to Rose Cottage," Eli said. "Chief and Mrs. Ross would never forgive me if I didn't bring you there to stay."

"No! Eli . . .''

She took him by the arm and pulled him aside while Mr. Pigeon watched avidly.

"Eli," she whispered. "I have to stay at home. We're living in the summer kitchen. We'll be absolutely fine."

They argued at length, and finally he gave in. "Just so you can get accustomed to being home again," he said. "And until the weather gets too cold."

So he helped her gather a great pile of supplies, thinking of necessities she would have forgotten, and had them all loaded into Chief Ross's wagon. He drove her home himself, his eyes hardly leaving her.

"Lacey, honey, forgive me," he said, "but

you've got to have some dresses. I was so startled
to see you wearing those . . . trousers."

She laughed. "Why, Eli, don't you like my
breeches? Even Dorcas said they showed I had
sense enough to keep warm, and I'd expected her
to throw a fit about how unladylike I was!"

"You couldn't be unladylike if you tried for the
rest of your life," he said, his voice oozing with
admiration. "But I can't wait to see you all pret-
tied up again. Felicity is in town for a visit—I'll
send her to you this afternoon with some dresses
and things."

"Oh, Eli . . ."

"No arguments, now." He clucked to the
horses, then reached out and took her hand.
"And I'll come back tomorrow evening. I'll bring
you some of Molly's peanut candy."

"Eli, you're far too kind."

"No, no," he said. "Tomorrow evening I'm
coming calling."

She turned her head and stared at him. The sun
winked back at her off the round lenses of his
wire-rimmed spectacles.

"I intend to court you, Miss Lacey Longbaugh.
Remember, you gave me your permission a long
time ago."

Ridge tried to escape when they crossed the Arkansas River. It washed up his legs and over the
mare's withers, wetting him with brown water to
his waist, a bath so cold that his teeth chattered
in his mouth. But he pushed the grulla with his
numb legs, urging her to float downstream with
the current.

Dusk was falling. The men were excited because they had almost reached their destination.
Maybe, just for a few crucial minutes, nobody
would notice him.

When the mare splashed out onto the sandy southern bank he took a good handful of her mane and turned her due east.

Before they'd gone a hundred yards Buck Rabbit caught Ty's head in the loop of his braided rope.

"Too late now, Chekote," he said cheerfully. "We're within spittin' distance of camp. You're headed straight for the stockade."

The stockade was a fence and two huts made of small, unpeeled logs. It sat on a sandbar that jutted out into the river, in the middle of a grove of cottonwood trees.

Rabbit led Tyree straight to it through a scattered camp that looked to hold twenty or thirty men. Two more men lounged inside the walls of the jail drinking coffee beside a tiny fire.

The white man came up to offer a handshake once Ridge's hands were untied. "Eliot Marshton," he said, "Bridgeport, Connecticut."

The other man was Cherokee, and he waited until Ridge joined them at the fire. "Johnny Grass," he drawled, and held out a cup of hot coffee. Ridge took it with a curt nod of thanks and a long look at the man's face. Johnny Grass was the most notorious outlaw in the Cherokee Nation.

They ate the beans and bacon that the guard brought, then, and the two asked Ridge why he was there. Neither seemed to feel that Johnny needed to comment on his presence in jail, but Eliot Marshton explained that he had been caught spying for the Union.

"They ain't hanged 'im yet, though," Johnny Grass remarked in his leisurely way. "Nor me. We heered they're talkin' exchange—the Pins have got some close kin of Watie's."

Ridge relaxed for the first time in days. In a prisoner exchange he would obviously be first choice.

Felicity drove up to Pleasant Prospect in the middle of that afternoon, just as Eli had promised. She brought dresses and petticoats, underthings, a riding habit, and a heavy cape a foot too long for Lacey.

"These are from everybody," she said, after the two girls had hugged and kissed and cried. "Mrs. Ross sent you her best habit, Lacey, the one she had tailored in London."

Lacey fingered the fine wool. "Look at this," she said, wanting to laugh and cry at the same time. "And I don't even have a horse to ride."

"I'll get Papa to lend you one," Fee said. "Now look at this beautiful cape. It's from Sarah Anna McIntosh. She said it'll be too long—go ahead and cut it off."

That made Lacey cry again. "I'll come over soon and thank them all," she promised.

"Oh, do! Come before I go back home. It's so much fun at Rose Cottage—it's like Council Day— the house full of guests and lots of full-bloods camped by the cabins."

The day was too raw to stand outside for long. They went into the summer kitchen, and Dorcas served them tea and muffins made from the supplies Eli and Lacey had brought.

"So, Lacey," Felicity said, as she let Dorcas fill her cup for the third time. "What really happened with Tom? I've heard only rumors—I know you'll tell me the truth."

Dorcas grunted angrily. "What I tol' wadn't no rumors, miss."

Fee ignored her, her narrow eyes on Lacey's face.

Lacey set her teacup into its saucer. "The truth, Fee, is that Tom tried to . . . take advantage of me. Just like all our mothers always warned us."

"I don't believe it!"

"It's true. He even threatened Mama, too."

"Lacey, no!"

"He meant it. Dorcas saw him break down her door with a chopping ax, and he's the one who burned down the house."

"Maybe it was an accident," Felicity said. "Maybe he knocked over a lamp. . . ."

"On purpose, Felicity. Dorcas saw him and heard him."

She set the cup and saucer onto the dry sink beside her chair and leaned forward to take Felicity's hand. "Stay away from Tom Creekwater, Fee. He's mean as a snake. I'm warning you, now."

Fee tossed her head. "I just hardly can believe that, Lacey. You always did exaggerate every little thing Tom did wrong and so did everybody else in the Nation. But in spite of that, you know you always flirted—"

Lacey squeezed her fingers so hard that Fee squealed. "Listen to me, Felicity Hawthorne. You mess with Tom Creekwater and you'll live to regret it. If you're lucky."

"Well, you don't need to be so tacky about it," Fee said, and jerked her hand away. "I don't have a chance to mess with him. Nobody's seen Tom and his men anywhere in the district for weeks and weeks—somebody said they're way off up in Missouri."

"Doing what?"

"I don't know," Fee said sulkily.

"I can tell you," Lacey said. "Anybody can tell you: looting and killing, that's what. It's general knowledge all over the Nation. Tom and his men are not soldiers and they're not guerrillas. They're nothing but outlaws using the war as an excuse to pillage and steal and burn!''

Felicity stared at her, hard. Her eyes were blazing and she was white around the mouth, she was so angry. For an instant Lacey thought Fee might throw tea in her face. Or send her cup and saucer flying into the stone fireplace.

''It's obvious that we cannot discuss this subject any longer, Lacey, and remain friends,'' she said. ''I think we ought to talk about something else.''

Lacey picked up her cup again with a shaking hand. ''You're right, Fee,'' she said. ''But one day you may need to believe what I said.''

Dorcas offered more muffins, and after an age Felicity took one.

''How is Sarah Anna?'' Lacey asked.

''She's all right,'' Felicity muttered, biting into the muffin. ''But if she knew what people were saying about her sister, she couldn't hold her head up in company.''

''Her sister? Which one? What are they saying?''

''Mary Louise,'' Felicity said, her voice coming back to normal to tell the interesting gossip. ''They say she's being way too friendly with her new beau, Autoe Brown.''

''Oh, pooh,'' Lacey said. ''How do 'they' know?''

''It's true!'' Felicity insisted. ''Maggie Crawford seen them. In Crawford's pasture, down by the creek. And in the middle of the afternoon, too!''

''Saw them? Saw them what?''

Fee looked horrified. ''Lacey! You know what! And he'll never marry her; everybody knows that. Autoe's not the marrying kind.''

Felicity chattered on; gossip always cheered her. But Lacey hardly heard a word she said.

In only a few short months her baby would be rounding out her skirts and she'd be big as a mother cow and the whole world would know that she had been "way too friendly," too. And neither was her beau the marrying kind.

She could just hear Felicity now.

That night Dorcas used the new blankets to make Lacey a bed by the stove. Lacey was crawling into it, wearing a nightgown for the first time in over a month, when she realized that Ridge's blue-gray blanket was gone.

Dorcas had put it on her own bed.

Lacey ripped her top cover off and took it to Dorcas to trade.

"But, honey," the woman protested, "this old thing good 'nuff for me. You needs the thick ones, the clean ones."

"No, Dorcas," Lacey said, "I need this one. I can't sleep without it."

But she couldn't sleep with it, either. Wrapped in the familiar scratchy-warm folds that still held a trace of Ridge's scent, she remembered every time and every way he had ever touched her.

She began to cry, stuffing her fist into her mouth to silence her sobs. How could he have lied to her so . . . with his body, if not with his words?

When she cried herself to sleep at last, he lied to her some more. He came into her dreams and lay with her, loving her again and again, until the red dawn came.

Eli was true to his word. He arrived at Pleasant Prospect right after supper the next day, dressed in his Sunday suit and carrying a split-elm basket full of peanut candy.

Lacey had thought about him gratefully while she and Dorcas organized their supplies, but as they went through the rest of the day, cooking and cleaning and stuffing rags around the windows of the summer kitchen against the winds constantly turning to come out of the north, her heart and her mind had been filled only with Ridge. Sometimes it had seemed as if he were right there with her.

She had put on a clean dress when they'd finished, though, and after they'd eaten the evening meal, she'd made a fresh pot of tea. She knew Eli would come.

He drank two cups of tea before Dorcas passed around the candy. He ate three pieces of it and never stopped talking the whole time. It seemed to Lacey that he could do nothing but brag.

"Chief Ross depends on me to make peace between the Knights and the Pins," he said. "And recently I've had an idea that really impressed him. I'm completely in charge of it—want to know what it is?"

He waited, his eyes gleaming at her through his glasses. Lacey had to drag her thoughts away from comparing Eli's dreary, tenor monotone to the melody of Ridge's deep voice. She nibbled at a piece of candy to gain time. What was it he had just said? Ah, yes! The idea for factional peace.

"Yes. What is it?"

"A prisoner exchange," he said. "It's bound to create goodwill on both sides."

"That depends on who the prisoners are," she said, laughing. "And whether or not their people want them back."

A hurt look settled over his serious features. He frowned. "Lacey, I wouldn't expect you to make fun of this. Your own troubles all stem from the factional strife among the Cherokee.''

''Oh, Eli, I'm sorry. I wasn't making fun.''

She hastened to pour him some more tea. What kind of ungrateful wretch was she, anyway, to hurt his feelings after all he'd done for her?

''Forgive me,'' she said. ''I think it's absolutely wonderful, Eli, that you thought of such a thing.''

After that she hung on his every word out of a sense of obligation, but when he was ready to leave and she walked out to his gig with him, she could barely stand to let him take her hands in his.

He squeezed them hard in his sweaty ones and leaned close to whisper that he was so happy to have found her again. Then he drove away down the winding graveled road.

Before the crunching of his wheels died Lacey had forgotten all about him. Compared to the memories of Ridge living like lights in her heart, Eli was nothing but a worrisome shadow.

Chapter 18

Eli's help was very real, though, during the two weeks that followed. He brought meat from the Rosses' smokehouse and canned vegetables from their cellar, cut wood for the fireplace and the cookstove, and escorted Lacey to Rose Cottage and back to Pigeon's store, where he bought more coal oil and some sewing supplies for her with his own money.

Lacey began saying to Dorcas, "What would we do without Eli?"

One time Dorcas would say, "We'd be in the canebrakes, a-tryin' to catch wild hogs to eat, that's where we'd be." Another time she'd reply, "We'd be living on charity, at your Aunt Maizie's mercy, that's where we'd be."

Lacey knew either or both answers could be true. She had Eli to thank that they were not.

At night, though, she still dreamed of Ridge.

Eli came to call as often as his work would allow, and he never stopped insisting that Lacey should accept the Rosses' offered hospitality and come to stay at Rose Cottage. She resisted his pleas, although deep down she knew that he was right when he said that she couldn't possibly live in the summer kitchen through the cold of January and February.

Going to Rose Cottage would be much more pleasant than going to Aunt Maizie's, but it had the same drawback: Ridge might not come to look for her there.

Eli surprised her one gray day by riding up to Pleasant Prospect just after noon. She went out to greet him, shivering beneath Sarah Anna's cape; the air held a hovering chill.

He swung down from his horse and surprised her even more by saying, "Lacey, I need to talk to you. Let's go for a walk."

"Don't you think it's too cold?"

"We won't be long. Tell Dorcas you'll be back in a minute."

As she turned and opened the door to obey, he added, "And get that blue shawl Fee brought you—the one that matches your eyes."

Lacey hesitated long enough to throw him a questioning look. He made a shooing motion as if to hurry her.

She threw the shawl over her head as they walked down the driveway and into the orchard far enough that none of the ruined outbuildings was easily in sight. For an instant Lacey remembered standing on the other side of these same peach trees the day Ridge bent from his saddle to kiss her so hard on the mouth, but she sent the thought away.

Ridge had left her that day and he had left her again. She had to stop thinking of him. She had to think about the baby instead. Maybe Eli was here to beg her again to move to Rose Cottage.

Maybe she should do it. The last weeks of December could bring sleet and snow that would blow through the cracks and form ice on the inside of the plank walls. Then, even with the new blankets and extra clothes and plenty of wood for the fireplace, they wouldn't be able to stay warm. Would that harm the baby?

Eli stopped beneath a tree in the middle of the grove and brushed the shawl off Lacey's hair down onto her shoulders. He smiled.

"I want to see your hair," he said. "It truly is your crowning glory, my dear."

Lacey had to hold herself still. She smiled back, but all the time she was praying that he wouldn't try to kiss her. She didn't even like to feel his soft hands on hers.

"I have to go away soon," he said. "Ten days or so from now."

"Where?"

"South of the Arkansas, to conduct the prisoner exchange. Lacey, I can't leave you here like this when I'm so far away. I want you to come and stay at Rose Cottage while I'm gone. . . ." He peered down at her through the round wire rims of his spectacles and waited for her complete attention.

When he had it, he finished with dramatic precision, ". . . as my intended."

She stared at him. What was he trying to say?

"I . . . I don't understand."

"I'm asking you to marry me, Lacey. I know this has been what's called a whirlwind courtship, but these are times of war. Before I go away I want you to say that you'll be my wife."

Lacey's numb brain scrambled for words. Any words. Except, Yes, I will.

"Why, Eli!"

"I admire you," he said. "And I love you. I have always loved you. And I'm going to be an important man in the Nation someday; as my wife you'll have an established place."

"Oh!" she said, clasping the cape closer around her. "No, Eli, I'm afraid . . . I couldn't.

I'm sorry . . . I'm very grateful for all you've done for me . . . but I must refuse.''

The words tumbled out willy-nilly, only vaguely connected to the thoughts roiling inside her head. The uppermost one was: Her first proposal of marriage wasn't at all what she had expected it to be.

Why, it wasn't even coming from a man she loved!

And the man she loved would never ask her to marry him.

The irony of that thought set a bitter taste on her tongue. She turned away from Eli's eager face and pulled the shawl back up over her head. Nothing else had been the way she expected it to be, not one thing since her seventeenth birthday. Probably nothing in her life ever would be.

Her head whirled so that she thought she might faint. She ought to say yes to Eli. This was her one chance to provide a father and a home for her baby. It, and she, could have respectability instead of being the subject of gossip.

Lacey turned quickly, looked into his eyes, and opened her mouth to speak. But no words came out.

She took a death grip on the ends of her shawl. If she turned loose of it, if she made one sound at this moment, she would shake her fists at the sky and scream and rail against heaven.

''I understand, my darling Lacey,'' Eli said. ''You're a lady, a very young lady, and I've shocked you by speaking so boldly. But please think about what I have said.''

He brushed his fingers against her cheek. ''I'll ask you again very soon.''

Felicity Hawthorne was on the front porch of the Hawthornes' inn, shaking the crumbs out of the supper tablecloth, when somebody grabbed her from behind. She dropped the cloth and opened her mouth to scream.

The somebody (from the feel of him it was a strong man, medium tall) clapped his hand over her mouth and tightened his other arm around her waist.

"Don't holler," he said, his breath warm against her ear. "It's me, Tom."

She knew his voice. She could pick it out of a hundred others. Tom! He had come to see her!

He stepped down off the porch, carrying her easily into the shelter of a freight wagon parked in the side yard.

She twisted in his grasp to throw her arms around him. He hugged her close. "Don't say a word to nobody, hear me, Fee? I don't want my whereabouts known."

He smelled so good, even if he was all sweaty and dusty from riding. She lifted her face to try to see him in the dark. "I won't tell," she murmured. "Oh, Tom, you're really here! I'm so thrilled!"

"So am I," he said. He ran one finger in a shivery trail down the side of her neck. "You're the very one I've been needing to see."

"Why?"

"You've been on my mind every minute, that's why," he drawled. "Especially these last few days."

He walked her around to the deep darkness at the end of the wagon, picked her up and set her on the tailgate.

"I think about you all the time, too, Tom," she whispered.

He leaned forward and kissed her, full on the mouth. When he broke the kiss, he took her hand in both of his, as if he couldn't bear not to be touching her.

"I've been gone a long time," he said. "How's everybody doing?"

For one hot, jealous instant she thought he meant Lacey.

But then he said, "Eli. How's your brother doing? Still working for the chief, ain't he?"

"Yes," she said, laughing with relief. "He's Chief Ross's right-hand man."

"Reckon he'd know where to find my friend, Johnny Grass? I heard he's been caught, but not who holds him nor where."

"Eli knows everything. Of course he could tell you."

He tickled her neck again and she trembled with pleasure.

"How about you find out for me and you can tell me next time I come calling on you?"

She nodded her agreement, reaching up to touch his cheek. "Of course I'll find out for you, Tom. You say his name is Johnny Grass?"

"Umhm." He bent closer. "And ask him where Ridge Chekote is, too, while you're at it."

"Why . . ." she began, but he stopped her words with another kiss. He kissed her until she lost her breath.

When she finally got it back, she leaned her head weakly on his shoulder. He nearly made her forget what she wanted to know. What was it? Oh, yes. "Why do you want to know about Ridge Chekote, Tom?"

"I don't want Ridge in the same place with Johnny when I go to break Johnny out," he said. "If I see that arrogant s.o.b. again I'll kill him."

He dropped a light kiss on her hair. "And I'll tell you, Felicity, I can't afford no big trouble like that right now."

He touched her breast. She gasped and caught his hand, but she didn't move it away.

"No, sir," he said. "I don't want no more big trouble, ever again."

"What do you mean?"

"Now that we're together. Now that I know you been wishing for me like I been wishing for you."

She froze, holding her breath there in the dark. It was unbelievable! A dream come true!

"We do love each other, don't we, Felicity?"

She threw her arms around his neck. "Oh, yes, Tom! Yes! We've always loved each other!"

He closed his hand around her breast and took her mouth again with his. She tightened her hold on him, surer than ever of one thing.

Everybody had lied about Tom.

"I'm going to marry him, Dorcas."

Lacey made the announcement when she first got up on the morning after Eli's proposal.

Dorcas flashed her a glance, then continued to stir the grits she was cooking. "I allus figured you'd marry for love," she said.

Lacey threw down the boot she'd just picked up. The boot Eli had bought for her. "I always figured that, too, but I've learned that life has a way of not working out the way we plan."

"Hmpf," Dorcas said.

Lacey picked up the boot again and jammed her foot into it. She put on the other boot and stomped over to the cookstove. She peered into the round, black face. It told her nothing.

"Dorcas, what are you talking about? I thought you wanted me to marry Eli! You're always telling me what trouble we'd be in without him!"

The big woman peered into the pot of grits and

kept stirring. "As we would," she said calmly. "We would be in one sad shape 'thout Mr. Eli."

"But you don't think I should marry him?"

"I never said that."

"You did, too."

"You has to decide for yo'self," Dorcas said. "Who to marry is somethin' nobody can tell you."

Lacey made a sound of pure exasperation and stomped back across the room to find her petticoats. "I can't marry for love!" she cried. "The man I love doesn't love me! At least not enough to love my baby, too."

She pulled the full-circle skirt over her head and tried to tie it at her waist with fingers that trembled too much to do the job.

"You tell Mr. Eli 'bout this here babe?"

"Not yet," Lacey said. "But I will. I can't possibly trick him—he's done so much for me."

"Tell him," Dorcas said, and began dipping the grits into two small wooden bowls. "You might not have to marry him after all."

Lacey forced the two strings of cotton into a messy knot and jerked them tight. "That's a comforting thought," she said sarcastically. "Since my only other choice is to try and eke out a living here, alone and disgraced."

Lacey worried about Dorcas's words all day. What if Eli did take back his offer when he knew the truth? What would she do then?

Eli wasn't about to take back his offer. He watched Lacey's face and the changing colors of her eyes in the lamplight, and even as she made her shocking confession he was thinking what an asset she would be to a man of his ambitions.

But the news of the baby did shake him deeply.

The way she spoke its father's name shook him even more.

When she told him softly that he might not want her to be his wife since she was carrying a child, his pulse quickened and his hands closed around the arms of his chair. When she explained how it had happened that Ridge Chekote was the father of her baby, he had gripped the splintery wood with both his hands as if he could strangle the worn-out rocker.

Her face glowed lustrous with love when she spoke Ridge's name, and her eyes darkened until they were the color of a purple sunset.

He leaned forward and reached for her hands. "Lacey, forget Ridge Chekote. He left you, so it's obvious that he doesn't love you." He squeezed her fingers, then let go of one hand to tilt her face up to his. "I will consider your child to be my own," he said, choking the words past the bile of jealousy rising in his throat. "From this moment on, that baby is my baby."

He searched his mind for an even stronger statement, for whatever words it would take to put that look in her eyes when she gazed at him. "I'll do everything in my power to wipe Ridge Chekote from your memory."

And from the face of the earth if he was still alive.

But Lacey's memories of Ridge grew stronger with each of Eli's efforts to destroy them. His insistent, clumsy kisses brought back Ridge's sure, wild ones; his eager attempts to draw her out reminded her of the natural way she and Ridge had talked.

Most of all, his moving her to Rose Cottage set her every instinct to longing for home and Ridge riding up to find her there. When Eli pressed her to set a wedding date and they agreed on Christmas Day, since he would be back from the prisoner exchange by then, she insisted that the ceremony be held in the summer kitchen at Pleasant Prospect.

"At least I'll be married from home," she said, and turned a deaf ear to his pleading that the parlor at Rose Cottage would be much more in keeping with the occasion.

So Lacey and Dorcas, and Mrs. Ross and her other houseguests, including her visiting nieces, began to make the wedding plans. They scoured the district for scraps of fine white fabrics and laces and sent to Tahlequah and beyond for black walnuts and dried apples to make the wedding stack cakes.

They would roast a goose and three turkeys, and make hominy soup and beaten biscuits for the wedding dinner, to be held at Rose Cottage at noon before the two o'clock wedding. They would bring in cedar and spruce branches, and holly berries for color, to decorate the poor summer kitchen.

Lacey could hardly believe it was happening. Ridge was more of a reality in her mind than Eli was in the flesh. She slept very little and ate only for the sake of the baby. She fell into the habit of staying in someone's company every minute of the day except for very early in the mornings, when she roamed the rolling grounds of Rose Cottage alone.

One morning, shortly after sunrise, she saw a tall figure coming up the hill from the direction of the river. The man moved at a tranquil, somehow familiar pace, each deliberate step keeping him silhouetted against the winter sunrise.

Drowning Bear!

Lacey picked up her skirts and ran to the old shaman as if only he could save her.

He greeted her with a slow smile.

She reached out and took the handle of the bucket he carried, letting her glove touch his hand on the narrow bail as she shared his burden. It was only a bit of grain, though, rattling around on the metal bottom; he had been feeding the wild creatures again and the food was almost gone. From his other hand swung a worn leather pouch.

As usual, Drowning Bear was silent. Lacey walked along beside him with hundreds of words, hundreds of questions, crowding madly into her throat. Had the medicine man, by any chance, seen Ridge or heard of his whereabouts?

They knew each other well or Ridge wouldn't have been able to talk him into coming to the square in Tahlequah that day.

Besides, Drowning Bear knew everything.

But he told very little. And in English he told nothing.

She racked her brain for her few words of Cherokee. "Unali i Chekote?" she asked. "Friend Chekote? Hadlv? Where?"

His bright brown eyes flashed to hers, quick as a squirrel's. "Gadohv?" he answered.

She recognized that as the word "why?"

"Because I love him," she blurted in English, knowing that he understood. "And because I'm promised to wed Eli Hawthorne on Christmas Day."

"Gadohv?"

"Because Ridge left me. Because he doesn't want our child."

The brown eyes waited patiently for more. They didn't blink.

"He went off and left me stranded in the mountains," she said, trying to justify getting be-

trothed to Eli—to herself as well as to Drowning
Bear. "We only had one horse and he took her!"

The words jumped out of her mouth on puffs
of her breath that looked like smoke rings in the
frosty air. They hung there between them.

Drowning Bear stopped walking and stood very
still. He looked at her. Steadily.

The accusing words echoed in her mind,
searching its farthest corners, calling up the
knowledge that had been hovering there since
that awful moment days and days ago when she'd
found both Ridge and Tyree gone from the valley.

Ridge would not have taken the mare and left
Lacey afoot. Drowning Bear's face confirmed it.

Her subconscious had been trying to tell her
that every time she'd complained about it, but her
anger and hurt had blocked the message.

Or maybe her fear had blocked it—her fear of
what had happened to Ridge if he hadn't simply
ridden away.

Oh, dear God in heaven! Had a wild animal
killed both Ridge and the mare?

"Is . . . is he dead?" she stammered into the
old medicine man's calmness. "Chekote . . ." She
couldn't think of the Cherokee word for dead, if
she had ever known it.

The acorn-brown face didn't change. Not one
iota. At last Drowning Bear spoke. "The call of
the whippoorwill is longer than the cry of the
owl," he said.

He had taken the cold pail from her hand and
walked away before she realized that he had spoken to her in English.

Chapter 19

❧

The next day Lacey slept until noon. She had lain awake until dawn puzzling over Drowning Bear's words and had fallen into a fitful sleep only after Dorcas had brought hot milk and had wrapped her legs and feet in flannel warmed at the fire.

Before she could get out of bed, her door flew open and Felicity popped in. "Fee! What are you doing here?"

Felicity practically danced across the room to sit on the side of Lacey's bed. "Oh, I just came to see my dear brother," she said. "And his bride-to-be, of course!"

Lacey shook her head, then abruptly held it still, fighting down the nausea that still plagued her early in the mornings. She didn't want Felicity, of all people, to know of her condition.

"Come on, Fee, tell," she said. "Seeing Eli and me wouldn't cause you to be grinning like a cat that just found a nest of birds on the ground."

Felicity giggled. "Well, I do have a secret," she said. "But I can't tell it to you now."

"You'd better! After you've come bouncing in here waking me up."

"You were already awake. But I'll give you a hint." Fee leaned forward and whispered to Lacey so low that Dorcas couldn't hear. ''Yours and Eli's may not be the only wedding in our family this year.''

''Fee! Are you getting married? Who? Who is he?''

Felicity grinned and shook her head. ''I'm not saying another word.''

Annoyed, Lacey threw back the covers onto Felicity's lap and got out of bed. The minute she stood up she knew she'd made a big mistake.

Gagging, she bent over and dizzily reached for the basin just underneath the side of the bed. Dorcas ran to her and held it and her forehead while she threw up.

When she had finished and Dorcas had set her down beside Felicity and crossed the room to pour cold water from the china pitcher, Fee reached to take Lacey's hand.

''I think you're the one with the secret,'' she said, her black eyes snapping with excitement.

Lacey shrugged. She still didn't dare open her mouth.

''I can't believe this!'' Fee squealed. ''Miss Perfection isn't so perfect after all!''

Lacey glared at her. ''Felicity, if you say one word . . . if you tell one single, solitary person . . .''

Felicity sat up very straight, the picture of injured dignity. ''Do you think I'd do that to my own mother?'' she said. ''Not to mention Papa, who embarrasses quicker than a maiden aunt. Of course I won't tell a soul.''

Lacey stared at her. What in the name of Heaven was she talking about?

Felicity leaned close again and whispered, ''This'll surprise all the boys who call Eli a sissy.'' Her smile was so broad Lacey thought her face would split. ''It surprises me, too. I had no idea he could be so bold.''

Lacey dropped over backward into the feather bed in relief. Fee thought the baby was Eli's! If she, with her nose for gossip, had made that assumption, then so would everybody else.

She closed her eyes and breathed a little prayer of thanks. But then, as quick as thought, she followed it with a solemn, silent vow. When this baby was old enough to understand, she would tell him who his real father was. She swore it on her mother's memory.

But after Felicity had gone, while Lacey put on her clothes and let Dorcas dress her hair, her mind flew back to another vow, the promise she'd made to herself during the night. She would find out what had happened to Ridge no matter how painful the answers to her questions might be. She could never rest until she knew.

How, though? She would have to have help—she had been right there when he had disappeared and had seen and heard nothing. How could she find out after so many weeks had passed?

Eli? He was the natural one to turn to, and his position did bring him news from all over the Nation. But he had sworn to wipe Ridge from her memory, and he needed to believe that he had succeeded. Besides, he was jealous of Ridge, she knew, and he might hide things from her.

Chief Ross? He was kind and he would help, but he was oh, so busy! And how would she explain her interest in Ridge to the chief? Besides, Eli would be sure to find out—he was privy to all John Ross's business.

Lacey took some hairpins from the top of the dresser and held them up for Dorcas to use, giving her an absent smile in the mirror.

Drowning Bear! He would be the one. He had the second sight and his full-blood friends were aware of everything that happened in the woods. He already knew that she was looking for Ridge and why, and he would never tell anyone else.

Hurriedly Lacey stuck the last of the pins into her hair herself and, giving Dorcas an apologetic hug, flung herself out the door. She would find the old medicine man and beg him to help her. And she would keep after him until he had explained every single one of his riddles!

Felicity spent almost all of her time outdoors when she went home from Rose Cottage. Her mother and all the hired help commented on her behavior—never before had she willingly fed the chickens or carried water to the kitchen. Each day she ignored them and stayed outside wandering in the garden even after all the chores were done.

On the third day she got her reward. Just after dusk, when all the guests were eating supper, Tom rode in and dismounted beside the long stone watering trough at the barn.

Felicity ran out of the shadows and into his arms. He kissed her, then held her at arm's length.

"Well?" he said. "Did you talk to your brother?"

"Yes, and guess what! He's going to get married!"

"Oh, yeah? Who's the girl?"

She edged sideways so the light from the lantern at the barn door would fall onto his face. "Lacey Longbaugh."

Nothing changed: His muscles didn't tense, his face didn't fall, his eyes didn't waver. Her rising happiness bubbled over into delighted giggles.

How wonderful! He wasn't crazy about Lacey anymore.

"Good luck to your brother," he growled. "That little stuck-up bitch'll lead him a dog's life."

"Tom!"

"Sorry. Now, what did Eli say about the prisoners?"

She pouted. "I thought you'd want to talk about weddings first." She ran one finger down the front of his coat. "After what you said about us the last time I saw you."

He gave her a brief peck on the lips. "I do," he said, "but later. After business is outta the way."

"They're getting married Christmas Day," she said, sighing blissfully. "Isn't that romantic? You know, Tom, we could make it a double wedding."

"Hmmn."

Miffed, Fee whirled away from him, flouncing her skirts. "Well! You sure are singing a different tune!"

Tom took a quick stride toward her and caught her hand. "Come 'ere, you little minx."

He jerked her to him and smothered her gasp of surprise by bringing his mouth down hard on hers. He kissed her until she went limp in his arms. Then he touched her breast.

"A Christmas wedding might not be such a bad idea," he murmured. "If I'm back from freeing ol' Johnny by then."

"You can be," she murmured back, and kissed him on the cheek. "They've got him at Crane's Bend, on the south side of the Arkansas."

He nuzzled into her hair. "He the only prisoner?"

"No. There's Ridge Chekote and somebody else. Eli's going to exchange—"

"Chekote, huh?"

Tom let go of her as he spoke the name and turned toward his horse, drinking noisily from the long stone trough.

"Hey!" Felicity caught his arm. "Tom! Where are you going?"

He shook her off. "I'll see you later," he said.

"No! You haven't even seen me now!"

He kept moving toward the horse.

"Tom Creekwater, you just stop right there! You can't treat me like this!"

He stopped beside his horse, one hand on his stirrup. "We'll talk later, Fee. I'm on my way to the Arkansas. I'll kill that bastard Chekote the same way I killed the almighty Judge Melton."

"Wh—— . . . what?"

Felicity ran up to him and grabbed his arm again. She could not possibly have heard him right.

"Ain't nobody treats Tom Creekwater like a no account and gets away with it," he said.

The beat of her own heart sounded louder than a cannon firing. But not louder than Tom's soft-spoken words.

He jerked his arm free of her grasp. "I won't never forget the night of that party. If you hadn't had my gun, I'd've shot Melton and Chekote the very minute they opened their goddam mouths."

The words hit Fee's brain like white-hot brands; they burned a swath through her body that freed her from all bounds. She pushed at Tom in a frenzy.

"You trash!" she screamed. "You are scum! You used me! You never meant one word you said about us."

She backed up and rushed at him, hitting out

with both hands, shoving at him, barreling into him with a furious force that sent him reeling backward. He scrambled for purchase with his heels, but they slipped on the packed earth and he fell. Hard.

His head hit one of the stones that bulged from the corner of the watering trough. It made a sickening thud, like a watermelon bursting, that stopped the blood in her veins.

Before Felicity touched him she knew he was dead.

The stockade glittered in the dawn like a magic land; it reminded Ridge of his and Lacey's enchanted valley. The morning red gave way in an instant to the blinding brightness of day, and the frost coating the crude logs transformed them from the dull brown barrier they had been when Ridge had gone to sleep, into glistening, silver spikes. He barely glanced at them—they had lost their power, they could no longer hold him. Today was the day of the prisoner exchange. He was on his way to Lacey.

He could see nothing but her face as he dressed and walked toward the gate. A man stood guard, but he smiled and pushed the creaking contraption in the middle; it swung open on hinges completely covered with icy dew. Ridge had no coat, but he didn't feel the cold. The thought of Lacey, freedom and Lacey, had set a warm river running in his blood.

Chief Ross and two aides were waiting, standing near Buck Rabbit's tent with some officers in gray uniforms.

"Chekote!" the chief called, hurrying toward Ridge.

His aides followed, leading four horses, all saddled and fresh.

"The exchange is complete," Chief Ross said, shaking Ridge's hand. "If we start now, we can sleep in our beds at Rose Cottage tomorrow night."

"Lacey," Ridge croaked, his throat nearly too full for talking. "Is she there?"

The diminutive man paused in the act of mounting his horse and said, "Judge Melton's step-daughter? Yes, Mrs. Ross is enjoying her company."

They rode out, Ridge's heart singing. Lacey was safe. Soon he would see her and tell her that he had never meant to hurt her.

He let the fast roan they'd given him set the pace, and the miles flowed away behind them. Finally the others wanted to stop and rest, but Ridge wouldn't, couldn't, not with Lacey waiting at the end of the road. He went on alone, the miles falling like wind-driven leaves beneath his horse's hooves. Never had the winter world looked so beautiful, never had the sun been so strong in December, never had the killdeer and the whippoorwill calls been so clear. He was free to go to Lacey and he knew where to find her.

When he arrived, Rose Cottage was suspended in that time between day and dusk, when every creature on the place felt the urge for heat, and light, and supper. Inside, the servants were laying the table and carrying warm dishes from the kitchen to the house; outside, the men drifted about, getting ready to feed the animals. Each person's face was indistinct in the coming dark; no one gave Ridge more than a fleeting glance when he rode into the yard.

He let himself into the dim, front hallway of the house, calling out softly to make himself known. The place answered with silence except for the cozy sounds of dishes clinking together, and soft voices and laughter somewhere far in the back.

Ridge turned and started up the stairs, pulled toward Lacey by a thread of instinct as invisible and as real as those chattering servants in the dining room. He could find Lacey's room in the dark, in a maze, in a blizzard if he had to. It, and she, would be full of golden warmth and the smell of roses.

He never paused at the top of the stairs, just paced down the hall toward the one broad door that glowed in the last rays of the sun. As soon as he fastened his eyes on it, the door opened.

Lacey came through it, her deep blue skirts floating out into the golden beam of light, and she turned to face him as if she'd known all along he was there.

In two long strides he reached her and caught her up in his arms.

"Ridge!"

He couldn't answer. His heart was too full for the words he'd sworn to say the instant he saw her again. Instead, he lifted her and held her so close he could feel the pulse in her throat beating against his neck like a winged creature gone wild. Her hair was a pillow of soft silk for his cheek, full of her fresh, clean scent.

Lacey! At last!

Silent joy surged through his veins like water from a bursting dam.

They whirled around and around like mad people, clinging to each other, cheeks pressed together and glued there by tears. At last he stopped and planted his feet on the outside of hers, letting her go just far enough away so he could feast his eyes along with the rest of his senses. The late, low-slanting light spun her hair into a gold cloud.

He let his fingers sink into it, deeper and deeper until he cradled her beautiful head in his hands.

"Lacey, I've been so worried about you," he finally managed to say. "I didn't leave you on purpose."

She went as still as their tree-shaded pond in early morning. Her eyes were huge in the gathering dusk, dark purple as a night on their mountain.

"I thought you did," she whispered. "Oh, Ridge, I thought you left me because of the baby."

He lowered his head to seek forgiveness in her parted lips. She tasted like warm sorghum on his tongue, like ripe pawpaws, like sweet, wild honey.

She gasped and slid her arms upward, over his shoulders, until they rested in a slender circle around his neck. He deepened the kiss, exploring her hot mouth, demanding pardon.

His lips tried to tell her all that he had longed to say for all the agonizing days and nights they had been apart. He drew her closer into the shelter of his arms and legs; her sweet shape, the soft curve of her breast, made tears spring to his eyes.

He wanted to lie with her. But he couldn't, not yet. Not with the burden of regret still crushing his heart like a boulder.

He tore his mouth away from hers. "Forgive me, Lacey," he said, squeezing her so hard he could feel her ribs against the insides of his arms. "I didn't mean to be cruel about the baby. I was shocked, that's all."

It was too dark to see into her eyes. Her voice trembled as she said, "Oh, Ridge, I thought you didn't want our baby."

"The very word 'baby' made me feel guilty as hell," he said. "You're hardly more than a child yourself, and I'm old enough to know better than to get you into such trouble.''

''But it isn't trouble anymore,'' she whispered, her breath like gossamer against his face. ''Is it? Not if you . . . if you . . .''

She inhaled in a long, ragged gasp that went all the way to the bottom of her lungs, as if she'd just run a long, long was as fast as she could.

''I put you through so much,'' he cried. ''Oh, Lace, honey, I'm sorry. I'm sorry, my darling.''

Without a word she turned and led him by the hand through the open door and into her room, glowing with lamplight, smelling, indeed, of roses.

''I want to see your face,'' she said, ''while you tell me.''

She was going toward the two chairs at the lamp table, but he dropped onto the side of the bed as they passed it and drew her down into his lap. He needed her close, as close as his heart.

''I love you, Lacey,'' he said, his voice breaking under the weight of his feelings, pent up for so long. ''And I love our baby. I want you both. Always.''

''Oh, Ridge!'' she cried. ''Somehow I always knew that you did. My heart knew it all the time.''

His lips sought hers, but she held him back, murmuring against his mouth. ''I love you, too, my darling Ridge. Don't blame yourself anymore.''

Then, without warning, she was kissing him back with more passion than he could believe, throwing her arms around his neck so ardently that he fell onto the bed, Lacey on top. He was spinning into space, into heaven. Lacey understood, she forgave him, she loved him!

She deepened the kiss, finding the back of his tongue with the tip of hers; she twined the two together, then broke away to tease him with such hot, rapid thrusts that he groaned and took her breasts into his hands.

Lacey hovered over him like an avenging angel, her hair a golden halo in the light from the fire of the lamp.

"I'm going to make you pay, though," she teased, laughing. "You have to pay for scaring me so."

He laughed, too, and rolled over so that she was on her back, her perfectly heart-shaped face glowing in the circle of creamy light.

"I'll pay," he said with fierce hoarseness. "I'll pay anything for your love."

The blaze of joy on her face lit an answering fire in his blood. He locked his gaze on hers, and lowered himself into the featherbed, reaching for the row of tiny buttons running down the back of her bodice. He undid the first one.

But not the second.

It rolled around in his fingers and refused to slip through the silky loop. It suddenly was not attached to anything at all. He tried again to grasp it, but it tumbled out of reach.

A rough claw caught his shoulder and shook him, hard.

"Lacey?" Ridge cried.

His fingers scrabbled again; they dug up bits of dirt.

"I ain't Lacey," a gruff voice said. "And you ain't the gen'rl in charge o' this outfit, so don't try to lay around and sleep all day."

Ridge clenched his eyes shut and closed his arms around his straw mattress in one last, futile try, but he knew already that the guard was reality and Lacey only a dream.

Only a dream!

A dream so powerful that it had torn him to

shreds inside. A dream so wonderful that its passing filled him with acrid bitterness that spread poison over his tongue and set his heart to pounding so hard it threatened to leap right out of his body.

He opened his eyes and summoned all his will to push the memory of his dream away, down into the very cellar of his soul. He slammed the door to keep it away from him, hating it, loathing it as if it were a living person who had purposely betrayed him.

His burden of guilt still tortured him. Lacey was still in pain, in her mind, even if she were safe in body. She didn't know yet that he loved her and their child.

Where were they? Were they both all right?

He forced himself to his feet. The morning was cold, gray as a sparrow's wing and damp, to boot. Nothing at all like the morning in his dream.

Except in one way. The one way that enabled him to put his left foot in front of his right and walk to the fire for some coffee. It really was the day for the prisoner exchange. He really would be leaving this abominable stockade today, and he would find Lacey wherever she was. He would not think of his treacherous dream until he really held her in his arms.

Ridge came out of the stockade between Marshton and Grass and looked for the grulla mare. When he rode out of here today he wanted to be mounted on her; she was one staying horse. Besides, he had to return her to Hawthorne.

He glanced at the grove of bare cottonwoods and then at the sky. Thank God in just a few more minutes he'd be free!

There was a knot of men in front of the captain's tent, deep in conversation. They'd be the ones who had come in for the exchange.

While he watched, they turned and walked toward him. Something about the tall one in the middle looked familiar.

Eli Hawthorne! What a piece of luck!

Even if the Southern sympathizers were only giving up one man for Watie's kin instead of two or three as they had heard, Ridge was sure to be chosen. Hawthorne had met him, he knew that Ridge was a prominent, law-abiding citizen and a member of the council.

The guards led the prisoners forward. When they were within a few yards of each other, Ridge looked Eli in the eye and spoke to him.

Eli stared straight at him. The sun flashed off his wire-rimmed glasses; that was the only greeting he offered in return.

Buck Rabbit walked up on one side. He was leading two saddled horses. Neither of them was the grulla mare.

"Marshton and Grass," said the captain. "Mount up!"

"What?" Ridge shouted. "What about me? Where's my mare?"

Eli smiled. "You won't be going with us, Chekote. Two for one seems amply fair to me."

Ridge rushed at him. "And you chose an outlaw and a spy over an innocent man? You're crazy, Hawthorne."

The two guards closed in on Ridge and caught his arms. Eli took one step toward him and smiled into his face. "Better luck another time," he said. Then, with an arrogant sweep of his head, he turned away.

"I meant to offer my congratulations on your Christmas wedding, Mr. Hawthorne," the captain said. His voice carried back to Ridge and the guards.

One of them asked, "Who's that four-eyed gelding gonna marry?"

The one clutching Ridge's right forearm answered, "Judge Melton's stepdaughter. Can you fathom that?"

Ridge stared at Eli's back until he couldn't see. Judge Melton's stepdaughter. Lacey.

She'd decided that he was dead. His darling Lacey. That's why she'd agreed to marry that snake. To have a father for Ridge's baby.

The baby he had said was a big mistake.

And that's the reason Eli wouldn't exchange him. He wanted Lacey to think Ridge was dead.

Ridge was as docile as a lamb while the guards took him back inside the stockade; his heart was pounding so hard, his thoughts were springing off so in every direction, that he had no energy to resist. At least Lacey had survived.

He smiled. He had been right. She had managed to get herself and the baby across the mountains and back to Park Hill.

He waited until the guards were out of sight, then he began to search every nook and cranny of the stockade for items he could use.

"We'll see, Hawthorne," he muttered as he picked up a piece of an old case knife and slipped it into his pocket. "Next time, I'll be the one to find you, and then we'll see who's alive and who's dead."

Early the next morning Lacey was still as wide awake as she'd been at midnight, when Dorcas left her. She'd lain down only because Dorcas had nagged until she couldn't bear it. She'd known there was no hope that she could sleep.

Every time she stretched out and closed her eyes—every time she sat up and opened her eyes—her thoughts flew to Ridge and his fate. If a wild animal had attacked him and Tyree—he had mentioned once that bears might be lurking somewhere on the mountain—then he had not left her on purpose.

But there had been no bear tracks, no tracks of anything except the mare, on the creek bank that day. And in all their hunting on that mountain they had never seen any sign of a bear.

One could have come into that country, though, or a bobcat could have caught them in the woods. Maybe he had gone in to rescue Tyree and the wild thing had turned on him and killed him.

If he were dead, he still loved her. He hadn't deserted her at all.

But, oh, if he were dead . . .

She could not stand to think it.

What had Drowning Bear meant? The cry of the owl meant death, everybody knew that. Did the call of the whippoorwill mean love?

Love and death? Was Ridge alive only if she loved him?

She had to see Drowning Bear again. She would make him tell her.

She threw back the covers and swung her feet out onto the cold floor. Maybe she could see him at sunrise again today.

A scratching noise stopped her as she reached for her clothes. At first she thought it was a mouse. Mrs. Ross would be scandalized if there were mice in Rose Cottage!

Then she realized it was coming from the window. It became a rattling sound, then an actual knock. Someone was there!

She almost swallowed her tongue. Ridge? Oh, dear God in heaven, could it be Ridge?

She ran on numb legs to open the curtains. But why would Ridge climb onto the roof of the porch? Why would he . . .

A small, pale face with terrified eyes stared at her through the glass. The fear in them was so contagious that Lacey sucked in her breath and clapped her hands to her chest. Who was it? What . . .

Fee? In only a low-cut summer dress and a shawl!

"Lacey, for the love of God, let me in!"

Lacey pushed up the sash. "Fee . . . !"

But after pleading to come in, Fee wouldn't budge. She clung to the window frame, squatting on the shingles of the roof in a dismal heap, saying, "Come out here and help me, Lacey. Come on. We've got to bury him before sunup."

For the longest moment Lacey's voice wouldn't work; then she blurted, "Bury who? Whom?"

"Not so loud!" Fee hissed, flapping one hand in a shushing motion so hard that she almost lost her balance. "Bury Tom. God help me, Lacey, I've killed him!"

Lacey coaxed her inside and dressed hurriedly while Fee poured out the whole story. At first Lacey advised Fee to plead attempted rape and self-defense, assuring her that anyone who had ever known Tom would believe that.

But Fee wept until she hiccuped uncontrollably, saying her family would never understand how she'd gotten into such a situation in the first place. It would ruin her. It would ruin them all.

Lacey relented.

She went to the armoire and got a coat of Mrs. Ross's for Fee and Sarah Anna's cape for herself. If it hadn't been for Tom she'd be wearing her own fine things and actually sleeping in her own beautiful room in her own home. She thought of her mother's death and of Tom's burning Pleasant Prospect and of the horrible surgery she had had to do on Ridge to dig Tom's bullet out of him.

"Come on," she said. "He deserves no better."

"He killed your papa, too, Lacey. He told me so."

Lacey stopped in her tracks, her hand on the window sash. "Then he's lucky he's already dead," she said.

Ridge got over the wall of the stockade without anyone's seeing him and broke into the tack shed with a strength born of pure desperation. He found several bridles hanging on a nail and picked up the top one. He wouldn't burden himself with a saddle.

But when he crept through the wet grass toward the herd of horses, the guard heard him. "Who goes there?"

Ridge turned around to run into the cottonwoods. A second guard stood directly in his path. The man reached for his holstered pistol; Ridge swung the bridle and hit him in the temple with the bit. Then he threw himself at the guard's arm.

He took a hard blow in the face from the man's other fist, then they were grappling, falling, rolling on the ground. The first man shouted again.

Ridge drew back his arm and struck out blindly, then groped for the gun, knowing as he did so that he didn't have a chance of getting it. His fist hit solid flesh again and the man's hold on him loosened for a fraction of a second.

Ridge jerked away and scrambled to his feet, slipping in the dewy grass.

"Halt! Hold it there, damn you!"

Ridge ran for the river. He dropped the bridle over his head to hang aslant across his chest and took the bit in his hand to stop it from clinking. He'd steal a horse someplace else—if there was a horse left in this country.

The moon gave light enough for him to see the edge of the curving sandbar—and for his pursuers to see him, running along its edge.

He picked the spot where the crossing looked best, took a long, deep breath, and plunged into the icy water.

Lacey and Fee sneaked past the scattered camps of the Cherokee who had come to see the chief. "That one's Drowning Bear's," Lacey whispered, gesturing toward a shelter made of saplings.

"I never did ask him to help me with Tom," Felicity said, peering into the dark. "I wonder if things would've been any different if I had."

She turned to Lacey, shivering even under the coat, and handed her the shaded lantern. Fee took the spade and shovel they'd taken from Chief Ross's toolshed.

"There's enough moonlight to work by," she said. "We've got to be done by sunup."

"We will be," Lacey soothed. "Don't worry, Fee, we will be."

They found a leaf-covered spot in an oak grove where the ground looked soft and took turns digging by what moonlight filtered in between the trees' branches.

The two girls worked until the sweat poured off them. They shed their coats, and Fee tied her shawl across her back, as Lacey did her petticoat, for a thin covering against the bite of the wind.

At last, their limbs trembling with fatigue, they agreed that the hole was deep enough. Felicity led Tom's horse with his body tied across the saddle up to the grave. Both of them struggled to lift the stiffening form off the horse.

Once it was on the ground they tried to lift and carry it, Lacey at Tom's head, Fee at his feet. They tried not to look at him.

"He's too heavy," Lacey gasped. "Fee, how on earth did you ever get him onto the horse by yourself?"

"Sheer panic," Fee said panting.

They ended up rolling Tom's body into his grave.

Lacey collapsed onto the pile of fresh earth, wiping her forehead with the tail of her skirt. "I wish we could rest now."

"We can't," Fee said, her voice cracking with fear. "We have to cover him before the sun comes up."

At last it was done. Fee stood like a stone carving, staring down at the mound of dirt while Lacey scattered the last of the leaves and small rocks over it.

Then Lacey, too, stood still. "God forgive him," she said finally. "And help us to do the same."

Fee turned and began to strip Tom's horse of its saddle and bridle. When they lay in a heap at her feet, she slapped the animal on the rump. It crashed away through the trees, branches crackling in its wake.

Felicity stared down at the saddle. "We should've buried that, too," she said wearily. "Now it's too late. I can't dig anymore."

"Never mind," Lacey said. "I'll come back later today and carry all this to the barn. So many people's tack is in there, this won't even be noticed."

Fee walked wearily to her own horse and mounted. She gathered the reins and looked down at Lacey with tears in her eyes.

"Thank you, Lacey," she said. "Now we're sisters already, even before you're married to Eli."

She turned the sorrel mare away as Lacey lifted her hand in farewell.

It was good that she hadn't told Lacey about Ridge being a prisoner, Fee thought. Even if Eli was the one Lacey loved now, there had been a time when she had been as crazy about Ridge as Fee had been about Tom. And if a woman had ever loved a man that much, bad news of him was bound to hurt, no matter what.

She kicked the sorrel into a lope and, tears pouring in a river down her face, headed for home.

Ridge climbed the north bank of the Arkansas, water cascading off him in icy sheets, and set out for Park Hill at a steady pace. The bit felt frozen to the skin of his palm; the air flowed frigid as frost into his face. He took a deep lungful of it and began to trot.

He figured that he had covered five miles when he slowed to take a bite of the corn bread he had saved from his supper.

A sound floated to him in the still, cold night. He listened.

It came again—a high, wild howling that ripped through the curtain of the dark. Chills ran up his spine.

Wolves.

Chapter 20

December 23 dawned clear and bitterly cold. Lacey lit the lamp and looked at the calendar five or six times, unable to believe that Christmas Day was coming so close, so fast.

Maybe Eli would be delayed. Maybe Eli would decide that Stand Watie had a good chance of becoming Principal Chief and would stay to work for him. Maybe Eli would get lost, wander into Texas, and meet the governor's daughter. Then he could really have a career in politics.

She threw on some clothes, paying no attention to which ones they were. There was only one garment in the room that she could see, and she was trying not to look at it: the ghostly wedding dress hanging on the door of the armoire. She managed not to touch it as she reached inside for the cape.

Lacey climbed out the window just as she had with Felicity, loath to meet anyone who might be an early riser. Once off the porch roof, down the corner post, and into the yard, she began to run. Her only hope was a miracle from heaven. She had to find Drowning Bear.

The red, eastern sky was fading; soon all the pink would be gone and the cold sun would paint the whole world white. She had to hurry.

The shaman stood on the bank of the creek, in

the middle of the woods, exactly where she had seen him on other mornings. The serenity of his stance stopped her headlong rush.

He faced the east, pale sunlight falling across his face, his arms extended. He began to speak, delivering a long incantation in a resonant voice that sounded nothing like the dry, light tones of his normal conversation. The only word she understood was *gahlgwogi* or seven, which she knew was a sacred number.

When the recitation was finished, Drowning Bear bent his arms and brought his hands to his body in a gesture of gathering in. Then he slowly turned to the north, extended his arms, and began the recitation at the beginning again.

Lacey walked slowly toward him, setting each foot onto the forest floor with care so as to make no sound at all. She stood, quiet, at the edge of the trees while he repeated the ritual twice more, facing west and then south.

After that she approached him. The quiet surety in his face kept her from crying out the questions that seared her brain: Did you find out for me? Did you send word to ask whether Ridge is alive or dead? Did you set your people to scouring the woods and the mountains as I begged you to? What have you learned? *Where is Ridge?*

Something about the old shaman, something in the very air around him, said that he would tell her only when he was ready.

Finally, she spoke calmly. "I must have help, Grandfather," she said. "For myself and my babe, and for Ridge Chekote if he lives."

The dark eyes were completely opaque this morning, and their look was faraway. But they stayed on hers for one long, intent moment.

At last Drowning Bear nodded and made a vehement gesture, meaning that Lacey should leave him. She obeyed.

The wolves trailed Ridge for miles. At least they made him move faster, he thought sardonically. Maybe he was, even now, right on Eli's heels.

Small chance. Eli had been mounted on a long-legged gray and would be hurrying to get back to Lacey.

Lacey. The hope of kissing her beautiful face, not the longing to bash in Eli's smug one, was what kept Ridge putting one foot in front of the other. Sometimes it even made him forget about the wolves.

Finally, a little while after daybreak, a great crashing sounded in the woods and a snuffling, squealing herd of wild pigs ran across his path. The wolves veered off to the west to follow them.

Ridge found a hiding place and slept.

Eli rode in while Lacey was at breakfast on Christmas Eve. She listened to him and his companions stomp up the steps and across the porch, but she kept her attention on her plate and pretended not to hear the servants speak his name in the entry hall.

He strode into the dining room calling for her, however, so she had no choice but to look at him. His long face was ruddy from the cold and shining with satisfaction.

"Lacey, my dearest, I'm back!"

He came straight to her; she could do nothing but stand up and accept his embrace. He folded her into long, thin arms that closed around her like a trap.

"I can't wait until tomorrow," he whispered, too low for the others to hear. "Then you'll belong to me."

A clamorous urge to run roared in her head and chased down her shaking legs. She belonged to Ridge and the arms around her should be his, only his.

But Eli meant safety for her baby. There was no other way.

Lacey and Dorcas and Felicity spent that afternoon at Pleasant Prospect, cutting holly branches and pine and cedar boughs to decorate the summer kitchen. Lacey worked like a madwoman, trimming the mantel with an exquisite precision that took every scrap of concentration she could muster. It blanked her mind.

But it never touched the pool of sickness in her heart. How could she possibly be married, and not to Ridge?

Ridge woke in mid-afternoon. He came to his feet with an instinctual urge for self-preservation driving him on. If he didn't get to Lacey he wouldn't live.

He stretched and started north again at a jog trot, his thoughts keeping time with his feet. Eli would not get them. Lacey and the baby belonged to him. Lacey and the baby belonged to him.

Damn his own hide for letting this happen, and for acting like such a cold-blooded bastard over the baby that he had broken Lacey's heart. He deserved to have to crawl every step of the way to Park Hill on his hands and knees.

Ridge broke off a twig of slippery elm and chewed on it as he ran. His stomach knotted in pain; he needed to eat pretty soon, and he needed to rest. But he wouldn't sleep again until he reached Lacey and took her into his arms.

Somewhere just south of White Oak Mountain the trail branched off near a cabin. Two horses stood tied to the porch, saddled and bridled. They would never be mistaken for first-rate Thorough-breds, but they looked healthy enough.

Ridge dropped the bridle he'd carried for so many miles and began to creep through the trees. He bent low and ran across the clearing to the side of the rickety house.

Rough voices and the smell of frying meat floated out to him through the window. Saliva formed in his mouth, and for one wild instant he considered rushing in through the door and grabbing the food from the pan.

Instead, he clamped his teeth together and inched closer to the horses, murmuring to them in Cherokee. He untied the knots in their reins, and, crouching between them, led them at a soft walk away from the house.

At the edge of the yard he wrapped the reins of one around his wrist and mounted the other.

"Hey! Whaddya think you're doing!"

Another voice yelled, "Baker, get the gun. That son of a bitch is stealin' our horses!"

The sound of shots rang out just before Ridge hit cover. He bent low over the saddle horn and galloped the horses into the brush.

Christmas Day broke as brilliant as diamonds. Lacey stood by her window and watched the eye-aching brightness grow. She didn't turn around when she heard her door open.

"Mrs. Rose, she say is you coming down for the Christmas presents," Dorcas said.

"No."

Some streaks of light pink hovering over a Kentucky coffee tree in the side yard burst into wreaths of lavender smoke.

"Mr. Eli, he waiting for you, too."

"Tell him it's bad luck for him to see me before the wedding dinner."

Dorcas waited. "Child. Turn around and look at me."

Lacey didn't move at all. "Dorcas. Would you run out to that coffee tree and bring me some luckbeans?"

Dorcas said, "Look at me, Lacey."

When Lacey still didn't move, she spoke more sharply. "Miss!"

Slowly Lacey turned. Dorcas's broad face was shining with compassion. "You don't has to do nothin' that hurts this bad," she said. "We two can go back home."

Lacey looked at her for a long time. "No," she said. "I do have to do this, no matter how bad it hurts." A sob sprang full-blown into her throat; it tore its way free as she cried, "It's we three, Dorcas. I could stand the disgrace for myself, but I won't let this baby be born already shamed."

She ran across the room and threw herself into Dorcas's open arms.

Just at sunrise, Ridge's mount went lame. He got off, stripped it, turned it loose, and climbed onto the spotted gelding he'd been leading. The horse responded to his heels and loped northward.

The main Tahlequah road wasn't too far away, Ridge calculated. He should reach it by noon.

He also calculated the days. He remembered every night and every sunrise since he'd broken out of the stockade. If the guard had told him the truth that day when Eli rode away, today was Christmas Day.

The wedding dinner was a bleak torture for Lacey. She had to speak, and smile, and nod, and handle her silverware, and eat (or at least pretend to), in spite of the fact that her five senses had been destroyed.

The other guests' lips moved and they smiled at her, but she couldn't hear what they said. She could barely see well enough to recognize them.

Her fingers were numb; she couldn't feel the heavy silver or the fine damask tablecloth. She couldn't taste the food. She felt that her chair, out of all fourteen of them at the table, was sitting under water, at the bottom of a faraway river.

Once in a while Eli's voice penetrated the roaring in her head, ringing clear like a warning bell. "That won't matter after today," he said to someone across the top of Lacey's head.

How strange. What was he talking about? Lacey turned to him. "Eli, what won't matter after today?"

He jumped. "Nothing, dear one. Nothing at all." He patted her hand that lay limp on the table. "I see you're coming out of your nervous state a bit. I'm so glad. Now take a bit of the turkey; it's delicious."

As he served her, Felicity began chattering from across the table, and the moment passed. It stuck in Lacey's consciousness, however, biting as deep as a thorn. Not only was she about to be married to a man she didn't love; he was also a man she didn't know.

She forced herself to sit up very straight and took a biscuit from the basket in front of her. Eli loved her and he wanted her child, which was more than she could say for Ridge.

Eli would take care of them both, and that was all that mattered at the moment. She would learn to love him in return. How could she not love him? Eli was a good man, a wonderful man. There weren't many like him who would so generously take on another man's child.

When Lacey walked outside on Eli's arm, the world was so bright it hurt her eyes; she shaded them with her hand. The cold wind whipped her wedding veil around her face.

Eli handed her up into the carriage and she settled into the back seat beside Mrs. Ross. Fee and Sarah Anna arranged her skirts so that they wouldn't wrinkle; Eli lost his balance trying not to step on them as he climbed in after her and fell into the facing seat beside Chief Ross. Everybody laughed, and several called teasing remarks as they ran to get into their own vehicles for the drive to Pleasant Prospect.

The driver clucked to the horses and the carriage began to move. Lacey took a deep breath and practiced her smile. Today was her wedding day and it was Christmas. Everything was bound to be all right.

She had wanted so badly to grow up; now she had done it. This was real life—she'd already learned it was never what she had imagined in her childish dream fantasies.

They rolled down the road behind the trotting horses, the carriage swaying. It seemed to Lacey that they must be galloping; within only seconds they reached the Y in the Park Hill road.

The driver slowed the horses almost to a stop to make the sharp turn up the road to Pleasant Prospect. Lacey glanced out the window, then she looked again. There in the fork of the Y sat Drowning Bear in his wagon. His pony dozed in the traces, its harness winking at her in the mocking, windy sunlight.

She turned away. Not even Drowning Bear could save her now.

* * *

When Ridge hit the Park Hill road, a surge of
energy rushed into his veins. Just a few more
miles.

If only the horse could hold out!

Lacey wouldn't be at Pleasant Prospect, since
the place was nothing but a pile of ashes. The
wedding would be held at Rose Cottage; Eli had
been staying there for a long time, and Chief Ross
and his wife would be the logical ones to act as
guardians for Lacey.

Yes, he definitely should head for Rose Cottage.

Please God, the wedding was a late afternoon
affair. This horse was all but played out.

"Come on, boy," Ridge muttered, squeezing
the horse with his legs and patting his neck.
"Step out, there. You can't quit on me now."

The carriages and buggies rolled up to Pleasant
Prospect's summer kitchen in a festive flurry. Eli
and the chief got out and helped the ladies step
down, Lacey coming last to a chorus of shouts.
The familiar yard was already a confusion of
voices and faces.

Eli offered her his arm and she took it. The
preacher came out of the kitchen to greet them,
and others crowded around them on the stoop.

Lacey stepped out of the group and into the
doorway. The summer kitchen was warm and
bright; winter sunlight streamed through the
western windows, pouring onto the windowsills
and touching the mantel of the massive old stone
fireplace. It lit the waxy green holly branches and
the deep red clusters of berries flashing here and
there bright as redbirds.

A long, white-clothed table sat at the back of
the room. It was loaded with the wedding stack

cake and muffins and tea cakes, plates and cups and hot drinks. Dorcas was there.

A homey fire danced in the hearth. The pungent scents of the decorative pine and cedar boughs reached out for Lacey and took her in. She thought of that same fragrance filling the cave on the mountain, and of Ridge in her arms.

For one wild, desperate moment she thought she would run inside alone and bar the door behind her.

Ridge squeezed the horse again, trying to transmit some of his new energy. The animal was all but staggering now; he'd gone about as far as he could go.

A few yards later, the horse began to slow even more.

Ridge pushed him. "I'm sorry, old buddy," he muttered, "but you can't go down on me now."

He kept him moving until he got to the Y in the road. Drowning Bear's wagon sat there, behind the gray pony, looking exactly as it had the day he and Lacey had found it on the mountain.

A terrible hurt slashed through him. He had had her in his arms then, that day a hundred years ago, but he had not been smart enough to keep her there.

Drowning Bear moved into sight from the off side of the pony. He was unhitching him.

Ridge's horse stopped dead, head down, sides heaving.

The old man went ahead with his work without so much as a glance at Ridge. He walked to the pony's head and led him out from between the shafts of the wagon. Then he looked up at Ridge. He made a silent gesture that Ridge should come to him.

Ridge made his exhausted muscles obey;
Drowning Bear handed him the pony's lines.
Ridge crossed them over the withers, took a
handful of mane, and vaulted up onto the animal's bare back. He thanked Drowning Bear with
a nod, then turned the pony's head to the Rose
Cottage road.

The shaman caught the bit and swung them
around to go toward Pleasant Prospect.

Ridge flashed him a look, then raised one hand
in a gesture of thanks.

Pastor McLaughlin arranged himself in front of
the fire, turning twice to make sure he stood pre-
cisely underneath the pinecone wreath that Lacey
had hung in the center of the chimney. He
clapped his hands.

"If the bridal couple will approach and stand
before me," he intoned, "the ceremony will begin."

The din of excited voices dropped to a murmur.
Lacey wrapped both her hands around her teacup; Dorcas caught the saucer before it fell to the
floor.

Eli turned and, with a flourish, took Lacey's elbow. She let him give her cup to Dorcas and lead
her to the preacher.

The Reverend smiled at them, gazing into Eli's
face, then into hers. His eyes looked kind and
happy. How could he do such a horrible thing as
to marry her to Eli?

"My children," he said. "And friends." He
opened the small, worn book in his hands.

Behind him, the homey fire snapped and crackled. Lacey fixed her eyes on it. She would not cry.
She absolutely would not disgrace herself that
way.

* * *

Ridge kicked the pony into a lope. The little animal moved faster, his feet four-beating in a resentful gallop. Ridge kicked him again.

The preacher gave a homily about Adam and Eve and man and woman. He talked about Eve's being made from Adam's rib and about helpmates and obedience and the responsibilities of loving and cleaving to each other.

Lacey closed her ears and stared into the fire.

Then he began reading the ceremony. The first question was whether anyone knew of a reason that this marriage shouldn't take place.

Lacey looked up and met his eyes. Yes, she tried to tell him without words. This marriage should not take place because I love another man.

But the pastor only smiled at her and then glanced around the room. Please, Lacey prayed, let somebody object. But nobody did.

"Then do you, Eli Coleman Hawthorne, take this woman, Lacey St. Clair Longbaugh, to be your wedded wife?"

She felt Eli turn toward her, but she wouldn't look at him.

"I do," he said. Never had his voice sounded so deeply confident.

"Then repeat after me: I, Eli Coleman Hawthorne . . ."

Eli repeated the entire vow, a phrase at a time, all in that strange new voice.

Pastor McLaughlin turned to Lacey. "And do you, Lacey St. Clair Longbaugh, take this man, Eli Coleman Hawthorne, to be your wedded husband?"

Lacey stared into his eyes, helpless, as if he had mesmerized her.

He smiled reassuringly. "My dear, answer 'I do,' " he whispered.

Lacey's lips parted. "I . . ." she said. The other word wouldn't come out. It was stuck behind the enormous lump forming in her throat.

The preacher glanced at Eli and muttered something. She caught the word "nerves" and then "understandable."

There was a long silence.

"Let's try it again," the pastor muttered.

"Do you, Lacey St. Clair Longbaugh, take . . ."

Lacey didn't even hear the rest of it. The only words she could string together in her mind were those of Drowning Bear's proverb. *The call of the whippoorwill is longer than the cry of the owl.*

It was true. Even if Ridge were dead, she still loved him. Even if he had run off and left her, she still loved him. She couldn't help it.

But she owed Eli so much! He would take care of her baby.

The preacher's voice stopped. Everybody waited.

She had to marry Eli; it was her only choice.

Lacey opened her mouth to take her vows. But she couldn't speak.

Behind her, a buzz of horrified whispers began.

Eli took her arm and walked her into the corner beside the fireplace, keeping his body between her and the rest of the room. He bent over and hissed into her ear. "Lacey! What's the matter with you? You promised to marry me. Why won't you take your vows?"

She wouldn't look at him. Eli grabbed both her hands. "Listen to me, Lacey Longbaugh. In a few months you're going to be having a baby who needs a father and a home . . ."

She threw back her head and looked him straight in the eye. But I need a husband whom I love, she wanted to scream. And one who loves me. But those words wouldn't come out, either.

"I love you, Lacey," Eli said, as if he'd read her mind. "And I will love your baby. I promise."

The preacher appeared at Eli's elbow. He looked at Lacey with his kind eyes. "Young lady, your groom and your friends and I are all waiting for a wedding," he said, smiling. "Let me assure you that a bit of apprehension is only normal and that it will go away, probably as soon as you take your vows."

"I'm sorry, Reverend McLaughlin."

He waited. Eli squeezed her hands.

They were right. The baby was coming and it couldn't live here in the summer kitchen next winter with no papa and a mama who had no means of support.

She nodded. "I'm sorry," she said again.

"Fine," the preacher said. "Now, let's go back to our places and complete this lovely ceremony."

Ridge rode up the graveled driveway, ducking the lowest of the overhanging tree branches. They rattled bare in the wind, clacking together like a flock of cackling hens.

Beyond the burned-out ruins of the house stood the summer kitchen, a dozen or more buggies and carriages gathered in its yard. His heart turned over.

No groups of men were standing around outside, smoking and talking; no women were bustling in and out of the door. The ceremony had already begun.

This time the Reverend didn't take time to arrange himself in the center of the hearth. As soon as Lacey and Eli stood before him again, he rattled off Lacey's vow at record speed. "Do you, Lacey St. Clair Longbaugh . . ."

Lacey was determined to repeat it this time. She listened to every word, thinking of her helpless baby to give herself strength.

When the Reverend's voice stopped she said, "I, Lacey St. Clair Longbaugh . . ." She hesitated. No one in the entire room took a breath.

Then she whirled to face Eli, her holly bouquet flying out of her hands and sliding across the plank floor.

"I can't do it, Eli!" she cried. "I'm sorry, but I simply can't!"

Reverend McLaughlin snapped his book shut and, with a loud sound of exasperation, pushed past them toward the door. Everyone else stayed quiet, all their eyes on Lacey and Eli.

He grabbed her by the shoulders and shouted, "What do you mean, you can't, you ungrateful little jade? After I've done everything for you! Why, I've even put my future in jeopardy—and maybe my life as well!" His eyes glittered wild behind his glasses. "Chekote could kill me if he survives prison!"

Ridge's name on Eli's lips roared into her ears and drowned out all the other words he was saying. She tried frantically to understand.

What? What was he telling her about Ridge?

Ridge kicked the pony into a faster lope just as the Reverend McLaughlin came out onto the stoop. His heart died within him at the sight. He was too late. The ceremony was over.

He was too late. The rhythm of the pony's slow lope repeated the phrase. Too late. Too late. Too late.

Lacey was married to Eli now.

His heart was dead and would never beat again.

* * *

"What do you mean?"

Lacey grabbed the lapels of Eli's black coat in spite of his painful grip on her shoulders and tugged at him.

"What do you mean about Ridge? What prison? Is he in prison?"

Eli ripped her hands loose and held them down stiff at her sides.

"Yes," he shouted. "But that shouldn't matter to you. You promised to marry me. *Me!*"

Ridge's mind kept telling him to turn the pony around and ride away. He had no right to another man's wife.

But the same force that had made him break out of prison, that had kept him moving over the endless, weary miles long after he should have dropped in his tracks, kept him traveling straight toward Lacey.

By God Above, the Great Protector, Lacey was his woman and her baby was his.

He would have them, no matter who had just said what meaningless words.

Lacey tried to jerk free. Eli held her fast.

"I'd never have promised such a thing if I'd known how you could deceive me!" she cried above the buzzing voices of their friends. "So that's what you meant when you said it won't matter after today! You knew this all along! Where is Ridge? Where is he?"

Ridge jerked the pony to a stop when he reached the parked buggies. He vaulted to the ground and ran past the departing Reverend without even a glance in his direction.

He took the flat steps of the flagstone stoop in one long stride, shoving the door back with both hands, ramming through the opening at the same breakneck pace. He was halfway across the room before he could check himself.

There. In the middle of the crowd, turning toward the blast of cold air from the door. Not even the white wedding veil could dim the golden flame of her hair.

And Eli loomed over her, far too close.

"Hawthorne!" Ridge roared. "Get away from her!"

People stepped aside and Lacey's face appeared, a white cameo in the frame of Eli's black sleeve.

"Ridge!" His name was a cry of pure jubilation.

She was struggling to get free of Eli's grip, the white dress swirling around her.

Eli threw Ridge one quick glance, his face frozen with shock, then his eyes went back to Lacey.

Ridge drove toward him, fists clenched. "Step back, man!" he bellowed. "Turn her loose!"

She had one wrist free, her whole body straining to run to Ridge when he reached them, but Eli had a death grip on her other arm and the set of his thin lips said he would never let go.

Ridge drew back and hit him.

He was only dimly aware of Eli's howl of pain because by then Lacey was in his arms.

She smelled of roses.

He caught her up and held her face against his, tucking it tight with his shoulder, pressing her body to his as hard as he could while he struggled to get his breath.

"I love you, Lacey," he said as soon as he could speak. "I love you and I always have. I love the baby. I want the baby."

She clutched him tighter. "Say it again."

"I love you, Little One," he said, and plunged

his fingers into her hair, pressing his palm to her cheek and holding her warm softness to his cheek until all the cold of his terrible journey had burned away.

Then he let her slide down the front of him until they could look into each other's faces. But he kept her pressed to him, hard, at the waist.

"I didn't leave you, Lace," he said. "I was fool enough to get captured at the creek."

She touched his face. Her eyes were like stars. "I know," she said. "Now I know."

"But I was a bigger fool when you told me about the baby. I want that baby, Lacey. I've fought my way out of a stockade and over a hundred and fifty miles of rough country to tell you that I want that baby and I want you."

She let those magical words fall into her heart, one by one. "I'll have to hear that again," she breathed. "Soon."

He ran his thumb across her lips. "You will. As many times as you want."

Her bones melted against him.

"You are thunder in my blood," he rasped. "You have been since the night we met . . . when the whippoorwills called . . . but I—"

She stopped his words with a smiling shake of her head and a finger on his lips. "I've loved you that long, too, Ridge. I only thought I had to marry Eli for the baby's sake."

"You're mine!" he said hoarsely. "I don't care what vows you took with Eli—you belong to me!"

He touched her cheek, his hand shaking from fatigue and from hunger. A hunger for her that blotted out his hunger for food.

"But I didn't marry Eli!" she exclaimed, her eyes sparkling. "I surprised myself. I expected to, but I just couldn't do it."

She laughed up at him, at the realization dawning in his eyes. "You didn't?"

"No! You know, Ridge, since I've grown up I've found that life is hardly ever the way one expects it to be."

His laugh came rumbling up from deep inside him, that wonderful laugh she'd thought she would never hear again, and he caught her up fast to swing her around.

"You're such a wise, old woman," he boomed, squeezing her even closer to him. "And I always thought you were too young for me."

He kissed the tip of her nose. "Reckon you're old enough and wise enough to marry me, here and now?"

"Yes!" she cried. "Oh, yes, I truly am!"

"Somebody go bring back the preacher!" he shouted out over her head. "We're going to have a Christmas wedding here after all!"

Some boy let out a resounding "Waa-hoo!" that echoed through the excited buzz of voices springing up around them and bootheels rang against the floor. Then came the quick slam of the door.

Ridge tightened his hold on Lacey, smiling down into her eyes. "Now that that's taken care of," he said. "I'm going to kiss the bride."

Epilogue

L acey held up the last of the new dresses she was folding into the leather trunk placed on two chairs beside the bed. The gown was beautiful: a deep blue bombazine with lace collars and cuffs. But she frowned at it.

"I just hope this is big enough for me and the baby, too," she said, fitting it to the front of her like a paper doll's dress. "And warm enough. Mrs. Jumper couldn't get much wool because of the war."

Ridge didn't glance up from the letter he was writing to the overseer he'd hired for River's Bend. "Mmhm," he said.

"Ridge, please listen to me. Do you think it'll be very cold in Washington City?"

He raised his head and gazed at her. She looked like a Rembrandt there in the slanting light of the January sun, her face a perfect heart above the jewel-colored dress. "What did you say, Lace?"

"I said, 'Do you think it'll be very cold in Washington City?'"

He dropped the pen and pushed his chair back from the secretary-desk. He got up. "You're worried about the cold?"

He looked even more like a bronze god of the forest here than he did outdoors. Her borrowed bedroom at Rose Cottage used to seem like a large room; now Ridge dwarfed it with his presence.

"Yes. I can't recall very much about the winters in Virginia; were they colder than here in the Nation?"

He came toward her, his glittering eyes on hers. "I don't know," he said. "I've never spent a winter in Virginia."

He moved like a panther about to pounce on her heart.

"I . . . have," she said slowly. Suddenly it was hard for her to breathe. "But I can't . . . remember."

He finished crossing the bare planks of the floor and stepped onto the rug where she stood, rooted fast by the look of desire on his face.

"I remember what you told me on the mountain when I was worried about the winter," he said.

She dropped the dress onto the bed.

He came very close, placed his feet on each side of hers, and closed her into his arms.

"What did I say?" she murmured, tilting her head to look up at him.

He smiled at her, that marvelous sudden dawn of a smile that she'd seen the first time he ever kissed her. "You said, 'I can keep you warm.' "

She wrapped herself tighter around him.

He grinned. "Trust me, Little One. You won't need one single, solitary dress in Washington City."

"Ridge!" she gasped. "Remember our hotel suite will be right next door to Chief and Mrs. Ross!"

He raised one black eyebrow. "So?"

"Ridge! You must promise . . ."

He pulled her even closer.

Quick footsteps sounded on the stairs, then a knock at the door.

"Damn!" Ridge muttered against Lacey's lips.

"Lacey! It's Felicity!" a shrill voice called.

Ridge's arms tightened around Lacey. "Don't answer," he whispered.

She pushed against him, laughing. "We have to let her in," she whispered back. "She knows we're here, Ridge, and it's the middle of the day!"

"I don't care." He scowled at the door.

"She'll probably only stay a minute."

He grumbled, "I doubt that, as much as she likes to talk."

Reluctantly, he let Lacey go. She tried to straighten her clothes and hair as she rushed to the door.

"Fee!" she said. "Come in!"

The girls hugged each other and then Felicity bustled into the room, taking off her gloves and hood. Her sallow cheeks were pink from the January wind.

"I'll only stay a minute," Felicity said, and Lacey shot Ridge an I-told-you-so grin.

He made a face at her behind Felicity's back that said he didn't believe it.

"I know you're busy packing," Fee went on, "but I wanted to say good-bye and good luck in Washington City." She turned to Ridge. "I do hope that you two and the Rosses can convince that silly Congress that the Cherokee Nation isn't Union or Confederate and that we shouldn't have to choose."

"Why, Fee, I didn't know you were interested in politics," Lacey said.

"I am," Fee said. "I'm interested in everything."

"Even if it isn't gossip?" Lacey teased.

"I'm talking to Ridge," Fee said. "Hush, Lacey. I also came to apologize for lying to you that night at the inn," she said, looking Ridge straight in the eye.

"When?" Lacey asked. "What night at the inn?"

Felicity's narrow eyes opened wider. "You didn't tell her?"

"No," Ridge said.

"Oh, then, would you please not?" she asked, looking from one of them to the other. "I was just feeling mean and jealous and I knew Eli loved you, Lacey, and I was hoping you'd love him, too, and be my sister."

If the secret had anything to do with Eli, then Lacey didn't want to hear it.

"You're forgiven," Ridge said quietly. "Forget it. I have."

Felicity smiled at him, then turned to Lacey. "And I should've told you Ridge was in prison," she said. "I'm sorry for that, too. But by that time I thought you loved Eli at last."

"You had no way of knowing how I really felt," Lacey said. "I was pretending."

Felicity gave her another big smile. She couldn't seem to stop smiling. "Well, I can tell you aren't pretending this happiness with Ridge," she said. She went to Lacey and took her hand. "I'm so happy for you. And you know you're still my sister, even if you didn't marry Eli."

Lacey squeezed her fingers. "I know."

Ridge said, "By the way, Fee, what has Eli decided to do?"

"He's gone to California," Fee said. "He started talking about it as soon as he lost his job with Chief Ross."

A silence fell. Lacey looked at Felicity, who was

still smiling broadly in spite of the somber turn the conversation had taken.

"I don't think you've yet told us the real reason you came, Fee," Lacey said. "I have a feeling you have something else up your sleeve."

Felicity started giggling. "Not up my sleeve— out in the wagon," she said, pulling Lacey across to the room's north window. "Look," she said breathlessly. "Peek at him. Don't let him see us, now!"

She pushed the curtain aside.

Directly below, in Rose Cottage's circle drive, sat the Hawthornes' large freight wagon, loaded with supplies. On the driver's seat was a big, burly boy with a shock of blazing red hair.

"Lacey, I'm smitten with him." Fee sighed. "I just walked into the stable . . . you see, I didn't know Papa had hired him, I never had seen him before, and . . ."

"And what, Fee?"

"And it was almost like love at first sight!" Felicity burst out. "But it can't be. He's nowhere near as handsome as Tom, and he's not the kind I usually fall for."

She dragged her eyes away from the boy and looked at Lacey. "Lacey, how can this be? I can't be in love with him!"

Lacey began to smile, a smile that felt as big as Felicity's. She glanced at her beloved husband and then back to her friend.

"Now why are you smiling?" Felicity demanded. "What's that wise, all-knowing grin all about?"

"Nothing, Fee, except that it's so much fun to know something before you do, for once."

Felicity's passionate curiosity burst into full bloom. "What? What do you know, Lacey?"

Lacey laughed and gave her friend another hug. "What I know, Fee, is that a woman often finds love where she least expects it."

Author's Note

In spite of the intense lobbying done in Washington City by prominent Cherokees, the Civil War brought calamitous ruin to the Nation. It became a desolate wasteland, ravaged alternately by the Union and Confederate forces as well as by its own people caught up in the vindictiveness of their factional disagreements. Schoolhouses, churches, and other public buildings were burned, as were homes, barns, fences, and outbuildings by the thousands. The Principal People came out of the war 7,000 fewer in number and with the entire country in ashes.

The years immediately following demanded from them a strength and determination like that exacted by the Removal. Survivors worked side by side to put their lives back together again. They rebuilt their plantations, their farms, and their businesses; finally they prospered again. Publication of the *Cherokee Advocate*, their national newspaper, resumed, and the presses printed schoolbooks in the Cherokee language. High schools and over one hundred primary schools were built. The railroad came to them.

The land lay green once again, but it would pass from the hands of the Cherokee Nation. Pressure

from white settlers caused it to be incorporated
into Indian Territory, and finally, in 1907, into the
state of Oklahoma.